THE PROTECTOR

Silent Phoenix MC Series: Book Two

SHANNON MYERS

SHANNON
MYERS
stories that stick with you

CONTENTS

Cover Model: Josh Mario John

Photographer: Wander Aguiar

First Printing: 2019

ISBN- 978-1-7332748-1-4

Created with Vellum

ALSO BY SHANNON MYERS

From This Day Forward Duet

(David & Elizabeth's Story)

From This Day Forward

Forsaking All Others

Standalone Novels

(Travis & Katya's Story)

You Save Me

Operation Series

(Dakota & Zane's Story)

Operation Fit-ish

(Kate and Nate's Story)

Operation Annulment

Silent Phoenix MC Series

(Grey & Celia's Story)

The Deserter (Book One)

The Protector (Book Two)

The Renegade (Book Three)

The Traitor (Book Four)

The Savior (Book Five)

The Mercenary (Book Six) *Coming 2022*

Fairest Series

(Charm & Neve's Story)

Through The Woods

(Killian & Ariana's Story)

Wait For It

Fictioned Series

(Hayden & Jake's Story)

Protagonized

For the women who survived the unthinkable; the protectors. The ones who were incinerated by the world around them, yet rose from the ashes stronger than before.

TERMINOLOGY

1%er (One-Percenter)- *If 99% of motorcycle riders are law-abiding members of society, the rest is the 1%. Advertised through a patch or tattoo, usually on a diamond shaped back field.*

13 - *Patch worn by a biker, usually a 1%er. May stand for the letter "M" (13th letter of alphabet), and indicate the wearer smokes pot, or uses "crank" (meth-amphetamine). Can also mean "The Mother Club", or original chapter of a motorcycle club.*

1916- *The nineteenth letter of the alphabet (S) and the sixteenth (P). Stands for Silent Phoenix.*

3-Piece Patch- *Configuration of back patches, consisting of: a top rocker (club's name), a center patch (club's emblem), and a bottom rocker (geographical territory).*

69 - *Patch indicating someone who has performed cunnilingus with witnesses present.*

Air Condition- *Riddle with bullets*

ATF- *Bureau of Alcohol, Tobacco, Firearms and Explosives.*

Broad- *A female whose sole purpose is being used as a sexual object; similar to a one-night stand.*

Cage- *Non-biker's car/truck.*

Church- *Club meeting.*

Club Whore- *Also known as a Mama. Sexual equivalent of a public well. Anyone can dip into her, at any time, as often as he wants. These are woman who belong to the club at large. They belong to every member and are expected to consent to the sexual desires of anyone at anytime. They perform menial tasks around the clubhouse, however do not attend club meetings.*

Colors- *Patches, logo, or uniform associated with a motorcycle club.*

Fly Colors - *To ride on a motorcycle wearing club's kutte.*

Gathering: *A scheduled social event or meeting. This is not Church.*

Grocery-getter- *A biker's car/truck.*

Hang Around- *a person that hangs around a motorcycle club and may be interested in joining.*

Jacket- *Arrest record*

Kill-Light- *A flashlight used as a weapon.*

Kutte- *A jacket which has had the sleeves cut off. All club patches are sown onto kuttes, which are worn as the outer-most layer of clothing. Most, if not all, outlaw clubs have kuttes as their basic uniform.*

Mother- *Founding/original chapter of the club.*

Nomad- *1) "Nomad" on a bottom rocker patch means that motorcycle club member travels between geographical chapters. Kind of like working in a secretarial pool, a Nomad goes where he's needed. 2) "Nomad" on a top rocker patch or car plaque means "Nomad" is the name of that club.*

Ol' Lady- *Wife or long-time girlfriend of club member. She is considered property of the member and is off-limits to other club members.*

Property Of- *displayed on a shirt, patch or tattoo to show who the woman "belongs to." Example: Monica wore a "Property of Torch" vest in Renegade. That meant that she associated herself with Torch and would do anything he needed/wanted.*

STRUCTURE WITHIN CLUB

National President- *Many times the founder of the club. He will usually be located at or near the national headquarters. He will be surrounded by bodyguards and organizational enforcers.*

Territorial or Regional Representatives- *In some cases called the National Vice President in charge of a specific region or state.*

National Secretary / Treasurer- *He is responsible for the club's money and collecting dues from local chapters. He also records any by-law changes and records any minutes.*

National Enforcer- *This person answers directly to the National President. He acts as a body guard and gives out punishment for club violations. He has also been known to locate former members and retrieve colors or remove the club's tattoo from them.*

Chapter President- *This person has either claimed the position or has been voted in. He has final authority over all chapter business and members.*

Chapter Vice President- *This person is second in command. He presides over club affairs in the absence of the president. Normally, he is hand picked by the Chapter President.*

Chapter Secretary / Treasurer- T*his is usually the member with the best writing skills and probably the most education. He will maintain the chapter roster and maintain a crude accounting system. He is also responsible for collecting dues, keeping minutes and paying for any bills the chapter accumulates.*

Chapter Sergeant (SGT) at Arms- *This person is in charge of maintaining order at club meetings. Because of the violent nature of outlaw gangs this person is normally the strongest member physically and is loyal to the Chapter President. He may administer beatings to fellow members for violations of club rules. He is the club enforcer.*

Road Captain- *This person fulfills the role of a logistician and security chief for club sponsored runs or outings. The Road Captain maps out routes to be taken during runs, arranges the refueling, food and maintenance stops. He will carry the club's money and use it for bail if necessary.*

Members- *The rank and file, fully accepted and dues paying members of the gang. They are the individuals who carry out the President's orders and have sworn to live by the club's by-laws.*

Prospect- *These are the club's hopefuls who spend from one month to one year in a probationary status. They must prove during that time if they are worthy of becoming members. Some clubs have the prospect commit a felony with fellow members observing in an effort to weed out the weak and stop infiltration by law enforcement. Must be nominated by a regular member and receive a unanimous vote for acceptance. They are known to carry weapons for other club members and stand guard at club functions. The prospect wears no colors and has no voting rights.*

Associates or Honorary Members- *An individual who has proven his* *value or usefulness to the gang. These individuals may be professional people who have in some manner helped the club. Some of the more noted are attorneys, bail bondsmen, and auto wrecking yard owners. These people are allowed to party with the gang, either in town or on their runs; however, they do not have a voting status or wear colors.*

AUTHOR'S NOTE

Please be aware that The Protector is not recommended for readers under the age of eighteen, as it contains strong language, sexual situations, drug use, and graphic violence.

If you, or someone you care about has been a victim of sexual assault, RAINN is available to provide confidential support.

RAINN Hotline: 1 (800) 656-4673

PROTECTOR

prə-ˈtek-tər/

noun

1. One who covers or shields someone or something from exposure, injury, damage, or destruction.

See also: guardian; defender.

PROLOGUE

Celia: 1983 (Age: 11)

"What are we celebrating today, Yiayia?" I asked, trying not to trip over the long skirt on the satin drop-waist dress as I sat down in the dining room chair.

She'd let me borrow it just for the occasion, but had yet to tell me what exactly that was. The lace cape tickled along my shoulders while the crepe slip crinkled loudly with every movement. My hair had been drawn into a loose chignon and wrapped in ribbons, making me feel like the Greek goddesses we loved so much.

Yiayia added blueberry scones to the three-tiered caddy on the dining room table with a sly grin. "Lady Celia, you must know how honored I am to have you for afternoon tea."

Her own hair was piled on top of her head in a bun, and she wore a dress and cape similar to mine. I imagined the looks we would get if we ventured out of the house together, and it brought a smile to my face.

"Is it Zeus and Hera's anniversary?"

She paused to consider it. "Good heavens, could you imagine the fiasco that would be? No, today we're celebrating... the summer solstice!"

I frowned. "By taking afternoon tea?"

"Well, why not?" she asked with a wink. "In ancient China, the summer solstice was yin, or feminine energy; while the winter was yang or masculine energy. So, my dear, today we are celebrating our sacred femininity by eating sweets and drinking tea."

My mother once told me Yiayia's mother had filled her head with crazy ideas. Apparently, my great-grandmother had been known for her lavish parties as much as she was for her wild political views. Yiayia often claimed my mother took life too seriously—something her son, my father, had never done.

"So, what do you say, Lady Celia? Tea, and then a little dance around the maypole?"

I placed the linen napkin across my lap with a giggle. "Sure. Can we build a bonfire again like last year?"

She passed me the tray of cucumber sandwiches with a shake of her head. "The fire department strongly recommended that we not. You burn down one fence, and everyone loses their minds."

It wasn't just the one fence. The neighbor's prized Bradford Pear tree had gotten caught up in the blaze as well. It had been both exhilarating and terrifying to watch.

"Makes sense." I piled my plate high, ignoring the pulling sensation in my belly. I had been feeling off since I woke up, but wasn't about to let it stop me from celebrating with my grandmother.

We spread fresh strawberry jam and clotted cream on the scones and stuffed ourselves on the cucumber sandwiches, but the ache didn't go away. If anything, it seemed to be intensifying.

I finally excused myself to the guest bathroom and began the nearly impossible task of freeing myself from the many layers of lace and satin. After a brief struggle with the zipper, I got the slip down, only to find a bright red stain.

I'd gotten careless with the jam.

I stared down at it in horror, knowing I was going to be in a lot of trouble. The heaviness in my lower belly reminded me of my reason for being in the bathroom, and I reluctantly placed the slip on the side of the tub.

What was I going to say?

Maybe if I ran it under cold water, the stain wouldn't set. With a groan, I began tugging my panties down and then froze, hovering over the toilet in shock.

It hadn't been jam.

Blood.

I knew what it meant. My mother had been warning me for a year now that it was coming. The other girls in fifth grade had begun wearing training bras, but when I asked if we could go shopping for one, she had been horrified.

Who are you trying to impress, Celia?

"Celia?" There was a soft knock at the door. "Everything okay?"

"Yeah." I buried my face in my hands to stifle the sound of my sobs. I would just sit tight until the bleeding stopped and then ask Yiayia to take me home.

Everything was going to change—hadn't my mother said that?

The crystal door knob squeaked as it turned, and I looked up in embarrassment.

"What seems to be the trouble, Lady Celia?" Her eyes landed on the slip, and I held my breath, waiting for her anger. "Oh."

"I'm sorry," I cried. "I'm trying to stop it."

"Trying to stop it?" Yiayia's brow furrowed. "My darling girl, this is a cause for celebration."

I studied the tile pattern on the wall and shook my head. "I know what it means. I can't talk to the boys at school anymore or wear dresses—"

"Why not?" Yiayia demanded.

"Because," I gestured down. "I might make them feel... sexual. My mother told me that as women we have a responsibility to not make men lust after—"

"Oh, for Pete's sake. I knew she was behind this. Celia, look at me."

I reluctantly brought my eyes up to meet hers.

"You do not have to change one thing about yourself. Every woman has a period—it isn't something that makes you sinful or unclean or—or any of the other garbage you've been told."

I protested, "But my mother said that it changes everything. I can't sit on the furniture during my time of the month because I might leave a stain behind, and I can't touch a boy's arm because he might think I want to do... things."

Yiayia opened the cabinet by the sink and retrieved a washcloth. She ran it under the faucet with a shake of her head. "I swear, I will never understand why a woman's cycle is made into a shameful event. Every month, our bodies shed the old and rebuild. A new start, every twenty-eight days. What's wrong with that?"

"But it hurts."

She nodded as she picked up the slip and placed it under the running water before coming back over to me. "It does. In order to change, we have to endure the pain. It's your body's way of telling you to let go."

She handed me the warm washcloth. "And you are so much braver than you give yourself credit for. Women like us, Celia? We're like that bonfire we built last summer. Beautiful to look at, but we can't be contained or controlled. Once you realize that, my dear, you'll see how powerful you truly are."

More tears fell onto my cheeks. "I don't want to feel like this."

She knelt in front of me and wiped them away with her fingers. "You won't feel like this forever. The pain will lessen, but you won't forget it. You'll take that hurt and use it to become stronger, and heaven help anyone who gets in your way."

CHAPTER ONE

Grey: November 2000 (Age: 36)

"No, no." I held my hand up. "No more tequila."

Slim grinned and took a swig from the bottle. "You turnin' into a lightweight now? C'mon, Grey, it's your last night as Pres. Drink up."

I looked down at my wrist, trying to decide which of the three watches I was seeing was the real one. I closed my left eye and brought my arm up toward my face. "Night? Fuck, it's just past six, Slim. I'd say it's time to shut this shit down and get some sleep."

We'd been so deep in drinking and reminiscing about the early days that I'd lost track of time; along with any hope of getting home by dinner.

Bear stumbled over and collapsed onto the bar stool next to mine. "Shit." He pinched the bridge of his nose and cursed again.

"Yes, Bear? Somethin' you need to share with the class?" Slim asked with a smirk.

"Fuckin' prospect just called me Pres—"

"As opposed to... what? Dickhead?"

"Fuck you, Slim. It took me by surprise; I actually looked around for Grey when he said it. Never thought I'd live to see the day that I wasn't ridin' by his side, you know?"

I blinked slowly and lifted my head. "You know I ain't dead, right? I'm right here, and as far as I'm concerned, I'm the motherfuckin' boss for..." I squinted down at my watch again. "Six more hours."

He sighed and rested his arm against the bar top. "Thank fuck for that. I'm gonna need to sober up before I'm expected to make decisions and shit."

"Bein' sober ain't gonna make a damn bit of difference," I grumbled. "You'll still second guess every call you make; wondering if it was the right one."

"You're really goin' all out to sell me on this, aren't ya? Fuck, Grey, at least give me some positives to work with here."

I looked up at him. "What do you want me to say? That your life is goin' to be filled with sunshine and every mornin' when you wake up, you'll shit rainbows? That ain't this life, and you know it. It pays better than anything else out there, but this?"

I gestured around the New Mexico chapter's clubhouse. "This don't come for free. You gotta fight for it... every fuckin' day."

"Jesus," Slim noted from across the bar. "Is that the motivational speech Wolverine gave you when he stepped down?"

"Nah." I grinned, remembering the night I'd earned my road name. "Fucker had me convinced I'd been born into the role—said I'd shown some real impressive skills and wanted me to wipe out any motherfucker who didn't respect Silent Phoenix."

Bear grabbed one of the many empty shot glasses littering the bar and pried the tequila from Slim's hand. He carefully poured out a shot and looked it over before tipping the entire bottle back into his open mouth.

"Well, that's one way of dealing with a promotion." Slim glared at me. "Any other words of wisdom you care to impart? Now, think carefully, because Bear's liable to end up with alcohol poisoning before it's all said and done."

"What do you want me to say? He's been ridin' longer than I have. If he don't know how this shit works by now, then I made the wrong fuckin' decision."

The empty bottle landed against the scarred wood with a thud and Bear ran the back of his hand across his mouth. "What are you gonna do, Grey? Where are you gonna go that people don't immediately know who the fuck you are? You stick out like a goddamn Viking!"

He was right.

We had thirty-three chapters worldwide. The odds of me disappearing forever were slim, at best. Hell, it had been damn near impossible to stay off the feds' radar over the past three years.

"Who said I was runnin' away? In fact, I found a nice little mini mansion out by the golf course. Maybe that's where I'll be spending my days. Golfing with the other rich fucks."

Slim hunched over the bar, wheezing with laughter. "Shit, I can guarantee that you'll be the only one on that course. Can you imagine the looks you'd get? Feds would be all over your ass within an hour."

"You could leave the country," Bear said, suddenly serious. "We've got the connections. A couple of phone calls to our guys, and you and your family are gone forever."

I'd looked into it, but with the war over, there was no sense in hiding.

"I think I'm good. We'll let the girls finish school and then maybe rent a camper..." My voice trailed off, and I let myself get caught up in the life we were going to create outside the club.

"A camper?" Slim asked, his lip twitching as it curved up into a smirk. "You're tellin' me you're going to willingly put yourself in a small space with your Ol' Lady and two daughters for an undetermined amount of time? Shit, Grey, you're takin' more risks now than you ever did as Pres."

Bear cracked a smile. "What I'm about to do is a cakewalk compared to that shit. Thanks for the pep talk, Grey. I needed it."

I climbed off the stool, stumbling slightly as I straightened. "Yeah? Well, fuck you two. I'm gonna sleep this off and get on the road—"

"Who the fuck is this?" Wolverine snapped, bolting up on the couch across the room, cell phone pressed firmly to the side of his face.

"Fuck me. I thought he left hours ago." Bear propped his arm under his head, watching the old man with amusement. "Didn't he say that he was out?"

I shook my head with a sigh and leaned against the bar for support. "You know him. Never—"

"Where are they right now?" Wolverine growled before looking around the clubhouse. When his eyes landed on me, an icy chill ran the length of my spine.

Something was wrong.

Shit had gone south for someone within the club, meaning I would not be getting home as quickly as planned.

"You listen to me—take them to breakfast and—no, dammit, you can't fuckin' stay there. Do you want them seein' that?"

"Looks like someone didn't get the memo that Wolverine ain't a mornin' person."

When Slim made no move to hand over the bottle clutched in his fist, Bear hopped off his stool and walked around the back of the bar, whistling loudly.

I opened my mouth just as Slim piped up. "Shut the fuck up, Bear."

I glanced back and saw that the smile was gone from his face. "You heard from Comedian?"

He nodded. "About two hours ago. That ain't him."

"How much blood?" Wolverine pinched the bridge of his nose and leaned over. "Fuck!"

"Somethin' happen with his boys?" I quietly asked.

Slim shook his head, watching Wolverine intently. "Kids are home for Thanksgiving break. Lucy's had them on a tight leash with family activities. Besides, he would've recognized the number. Bear, you checked in with Molly?"

"Yeah, talked to her right before she fell asleep." He paused before screwing the lid back onto the bottle of whiskey and replacing it on the shelf. "The fuck's goin' on?"

"Who would be callin' this early that he didn't have a number for?" Slim left the question dangling in the air.

The liquor soured in my gut when Wolverine jumped up and began pacing, never once taking his eyes off of mine. "You get them as far away from this as possible, you hear me—I know what it fuckin' looks like!"

In just a few short hours, I was turning over the entire club to Bear.

By all rights, none of it was my problem anymore. I knew better than to involve myself, but that didn't stop me from pushing off the bar and stalking over to him.

Wolverine lowered the phone and ran a hand over his face. "Jesus, fuck—"

"Give it to me."

"Jamie..." He mashed his lips together and swallowed. "You need to get home."

"I ain't leavin' you to ride on your own. I'll stay for whatever the fuck you need me to do—"

The phone fell from his hand and I saw something I'd never seen before in his eyes—dread.

Wolverine had faced other clubs and done time with little to no emotion. Whatever had happened was worse than anything we'd ever encountered.

I was sure of it.

The blood drained from my own face and I swayed on my feet as my mind raced with worst-case scenarios. Slim put a hand on my shoulder to steady me before asking, "What happened?"

Wolverine's nostrils flared. "That was Richard. Celia called him this morning, just before six. Asked him to take the girls to school—said she wasn't feeling well."

I exhaled. "Shit, old man, you damn near gave me a heart attack. So, she's sick—"

"There's blood, Jamie. A lot. He thinks she's locked in the bathroom but can't get her to respond. I told him to take the girls and get them the fuck away from there."

Ma.

There it was—as if twenty-six years hadn't passed. I dragged a hand through my hair before clenching it into a fist. My heart thrummed against my ribs, fighting to break free from its cage.

Same as me.

"You did what? We don't know whether my Ol' Lady is dead or alive and you told him to leave her there? Alone?" My voice rose until I was shouting. The vein in my neck pulsed with each word.

Slim tightened his grip on my shoulder, but I pulled away, moving toward Wolverine.

"Jamie, if you'd just give me a goddamn second. We're not leavin' her alone. Comedian is in town—"

"So, you're gonna hand her over to the butcher? Jesus fuckin' Christ!" I raised my fist, but Slim easily brought it back down.

"Jamie, look at me," he hissed. "Wolverine's tryin' to help. Comedian ain't gonna do shit to her—"

I lifted my hand and pinched my lower lip between my thumb and forefinger; a nervous habit I'd never been able to kick. As I did it, I realized what I'd been missing. "Where's Hawk? How the fuck did this happen? He was watching her... the girls. Are they okay? They're not hurt, are they?"

Wolverine shook his head. "Girls are fine. They didn't know anything was wrong. Look, would you feel better if Angel went over with Comedian?"

"Angel?" I repeated, no longer remembering the question. Hawk should've been there. It didn't matter what the fuck was going on; it was his job to keep her safe and let me know if there was a problem.

He'd pay for that.

"Send Angel. Send Comedian—fuck, send everybody within a hundred-mile radius," Bear spoke up from the bar. "Slim, you and I are gonna get him home. Wolverine, you're gonna round up everyone here and have them ride in. We don't know what we're dealin' with. Until we hear otherwise, prepare for war."

I turned to him in surprise. "Who the fuck do you think you are?"

"I'm the fuckin' Pres and I'm gettin' you home to your Ol' Lady."

CHAPTER TWO

Celia: November 2000 (Age: 28)

The sky was still dark when I woke up. I was in the same position as before, slumped against the bathroom wall next to the shower. My right eye opened to only a slit, but it was enough for me to see that the window was sitting wide open.

The curtains flapped against the cold breeze—their rustling enough to have roused me from my stupor. I stared into the dark, waiting for my tormenters to reappear.

How had I ever believed we were safe?

I tried to straighten, and my tongue connected with the back of my front teeth, sending a jolt of pain throughout my body. The vise around my belly tightened, and I bore down with a guttural groan before blacking out.

The next time I opened my eyes, the sky was tinged with red and pink, just like the pool of blood surrounding me.

The outer edge had begun to congeal into something resembling gelatin, and I gently touched it with my big toe.

The sticky mess spread along the grout lines in the tile, looking like outstretched fingers, reaching toward the door for help.

Help that would never come.

My lips were sealed together with a combination of dried blood and vomit, and I tried shifting my jaw from side to side to loosen them, but it was no use.

Panic bubbled up in my chest, along with another round of nausea. My stomach muscles cramped up, and I retched onto the tile. The force reopened the wounds around my mouth, prying my lips apart and sending fresh streams of blood and vomit down my chin.

The bitter taste of bile lingered in my mouth, and I stared longingly at the faucet above the claw-foot tub before sinking back down to the floor in exhaustion.

I just needed a drink. Then I could rest again. With a grunt, I pushed myself up onto my forearms and began inching forward.

My body was a mess of tender flesh and broken bones—even the smallest movements left me clinging to consciousness with all the strength I had left.

The girls.

I dragged myself away from the tub, and toward the door before remembering my father's pleading.

Celia, baby, open the door!

They were safe now.

My back ached, and my head throbbed to where I was seeing double, but that didn't stop me from reaching up to pull a towel down from the bar on the wall. I wadded it up between my legs and closed my eyes again.

Endure the pain.

Low voices carried through the open window before moving inside the house.

They were back.

"No." With a moan, I rolled onto my side and searched for a weapon. They'd taken my gun. I was sure of it. I took comfort knowing that the girls were safe and would never see their mother like this.

I wouldn't live through another assault, but wasn't going down without a fight. Not this time. I lightly bit down on my tongue to keep from crying out while pulling myself across the tile, leaving more blood in my wake.

The mirror above the sink had shattered when Cobra threw my head into it, littering the floor with bits of glass. The smaller shards embedded in my skin as I moved over them. I snagged a larger, jagged piece to tuck away in my hand.

The heavy tread of boots stopped just outside the door. I panted through the agonizing pain that seemed to radiate from my head down into my toes, fighting to stay quiet.

"Celia?" A gruff voice called out, and I curled in on myself, squeezing the glass until the sides sliced into my palm.

I needed the pain to stay awake.

The door handle shifted—first to the left, and then to the right, but the lock held. I breathed a sigh of relief just as there was a sound right outside the bathroom window.

"Jesus—fuck," another voice cursed.

I gulped down a shaky breath before reluctantly bringing my head up. The first rays of sunshine had broken free from the horizon, obscuring the man's face.

I closed my eyes against the blinding brightness and croaked, "No. Please."

"I got you, sweetheart."

You're doin' great, sweetheart. Absolutely fuckin' perfect.

The carousel in my head spun faster as he climbed through the window, making it appear as if there was more than one of him coming for me. I fought against the dizziness and dragged myself under the small vanity area with a soft whimper.

The man let out another rough curse as he squeezed through, dropping into the tub with a grunt. I shrank back, ignoring the sharp stab of pain in my chest as I made myself as small as possible.

I tightened my grip on the piece of mirror, watching warily as the blurry figure moved away from me and toward the bathroom door.

The second man kicked in the bathroom door, only to stumble back into the wall with a startled cry upon seeing me. "Jesus Christ! Mary!"

"Celia," the first man moved closer. "Do you know where you are?"

I was in hell.

I blinked and narrowed my good eye, straining to see my attackers. It wasn't until the man knelt beside me that I gasped in recognition. "Comedian?"

He gave a curt nod. "It's me. Let's get you checked over, yeah?"

His fingers trailed over my cheek, the contact sending a shiver through my body. I turned away and pulled the bloody towel up from between my thighs until it was under my chin, trying to maintain some sense of modesty.

"Angel, I'm gonna need your help."

Angel slumped against the wall, fist pressed against his mouth, shaking.

She lost the baby...

Angel came, but it was too late.

"Get him out of here," I whispered. "Please don't let him see me like this."

"I'm fine, doll." Angel took a deep breath and stood tall. "Comedian, I need the first aid kit from my saddlebag and more towels. What else? Bleach, and um, fuck—just bring all the cleaning supplies."

His jaw settled into a hard line, and he ran a hand through his hair before quietly repeating to himself, "I'm fine."

I reached up and gripped the edge of Comedian's vest with a moan as my body contracted painfully. Sweat, or blood, ran from my hairline and I bit down on my lower lip to keep from screaming.

Comedian looked down, his mouth falling open in shock. "Fuck." The skin bunched around his eyes as he backed away from me, the muscles jumping in his neck.

I saw the question in them but couldn't answer as the bathroom disappeared into darkness again.

Movement brought me back to reality with a cry. Angel managed to stay on his feet as he pulled me out from under the vanity, but his skin still had a greenish hue to it. Comedian was nowhere to be found, and I briefly wondered if the sight of my blood had shaken the tough biker.

"How did you know to come?" I asked, my voice sounding like the rusted gate at the cemetery. It was fitting, really, as I was rapidly coming to the conclusion that I was dying.

He covered me with a clean towel and flipped on the faucet at the sink, letting the water heat up before running a washcloth under it. "Your old man called Wolverine, and he called in me and Comedian. We were closest."

His jaw tightened, and he paused before adding, "I had no idea you were still in town. Just assumed that when the club pulled out, you went with 'em. If I would've known—make no mistake, every last one of the motherfuckers'll be meeting the Reaper."

"My dad took the girls away, right? Did they seem—were they okay? Not like this?" My voice cracked as I gestured toward my face.

He knelt on the tile, seemingly oblivious to the fact that my blood was now soaking through his jeans. "Your girls are safe, darlin'. Now, let's get you cleaned up."

"It's not fair to make you do this."

"If I don't, who will?" He gently dabbed at the blood on my chin with the damp cloth, but I jerked back.

So fuckin' good.

"Don't touch me," I hissed suddenly, batting away his hand. I wanted to claw at my skin until I couldn't feel their touch anymore.

Angel rocked back on his heels, shifting gears. "Where's Hawk? He do this to you?"

I stared at the crescent-shaped markings on my thighs and traced the red indentions with the pad of my thumb, letting his words sink in.

Had he?

"I did this to myself." I squeezed my eyes shut as more tears fell. Jamie had worked so hard to make the other clubs think he was dead, and I'd blown it.

Why hadn't I just told him the money was missing?

I thought I was so bright—entering games and making my own money. The truth had been staring me right in the face over the past three years, yet I'd never once suspected that Hawk could steal from us.

"Celia, did you hear me? Jamie's on his way."

I studied the wounds on my legs again. "He can't come here."

That was exactly what they wanted.

Angel brought his hand down to rest against a rug burn on my knee. "You're shakin'. Look at me—it would take a damn army to stop Jamie from getting to you."

And it would take an army to save me once he discovered the truth.

CHAPTER THREE

Celia: November 2000 (Age: 28)

I mashed my lips together and shook my head again. "You can't let him, Angel. He can't—" My voice cut off in a sob and he tried to pull me into his arms.

With a whimper, I tugged the towel up again and fought to free myself from his grasp. I didn't know why I was concerned with keeping myself covered. It didn't matter. There wasn't a single part of my body that hadn't been marked.

We had some good times together, didn't we?

I sat up and squeezed Angel's arm to the point of leaving bruises, roaring, as another small gush of blood spread from between my thighs.

He grabbed the small trashcan by the toilet and held it under my face when I began retching.

It shouldn't have been him.

"I'm sorry," I moaned through the pain. "I'm so sorry."

"Shh... don't you apologize. You're gonna be okay." He rubbed small circles across my back.

I expected him to run away to join Comedian, but he stayed at my back with his legs on either side of mine.

When my strength fled, I let my head fall back to his chest and confessed, "It's my fault, Angel. They know he's alive because of me. I led them here."

There was a soft knock at the door, and then six Comedians walked into the bathroom.

It was like the start of a bad joke.

I promptly began giggling while Comedian eyed me warily. "I, uh, I got the shit."

Something tore loose in my chest, and my laughter turned to tears again. I knew how crazy I must have looked when Comedian kept his eyes trained toward the ceiling, seemingly doing everything in his power to avoid looking at me.

Angel shifted me in his arms and reached for the kit while Comedian hung back with the towels, looking like he wanted to be anywhere but where he was.

"Let's get you in the bathtub—" Angel began.

"No." I just wanted to be left alone to die in peace.

My girls were safe. Angel would tell Jamie that the clubs knew he was alive so he could prepare. The rest was out of my hands.

"Okay," he nodded. "Comedian, look in the closet and see if you can find a robe or something for her to put on."

"No," I moaned. "Leave me alone."

Angel shifted me over before standing up. The two bikers had a silent conversation with their eyes before Comedian disappeared again.

I lay back and let my neck rest against the side of the tub, the coolness of the cast-iron welcome against my sweltering skin. My body relaxed, and unconsciousness pulled me away again. I'd had fever dreams as a kid, but they were nothing like this.

This one was some cross between a nightmare and a hallucination—vivid and terrifying. It was only when I fought for consciousness that I realized it wasn't real.

"You're safe, Celia," Angel said softly when I jerked awake with a muffled cry. "Can you give me a name?"

"I told you, I did this to myself."

Comedian hovered nearby with a bottle of water but waited to approach until Angel nodded to him. "I got you some water."

"Comedian," I croaked. "You can't tell Jamie. Neither of you. He can't know that this happened."

He knelt beside me and held the bottle to my lips. I obediently took a small sip before begging, "But, Jamie—"

"Drink, Celia," Comedian commanded. "You need the fluids."

I drank half of it before pulling away to try again. "Comedian, you can't let him know—"

"It's, uh, it's Michael. Like the archangel. Do you remember what he does?" His voice was soft and steady, as if he was speaking to a small child. "He's a protector and a warrior. Me and Grey? We're gonna handle this shit, so don't you be scared."

A tear fell, and then another. I couldn't stop them if I tried. My body twisted and tightened as the war raged within. Angel passed the trashcan over to Michael, but through sheer will, I kept the water down.

"I'm not scared," I whispered. "It's because of Mary."

Angel froze at the sink with a washcloth in his hands before slowly turning to face me.

"What happened to his mother nearly killed him, Angel. You and I both know that." A shudder passed through my body, and my teeth began to chatter. "If he knew about this—"

I let my words trail off, but both men knew what I was asking of them. If Jamie knew what we had lost because of my actions, it would destroy him.

"Fuckin' Christ," Michael whispered. "He's already on the road—he's gonna see this."

"We'll clean it up and say they beat me, but nothing more."

Angel shook his head. "Celia..."

"I'll give you the names of the men who did this, but only if you agree. Swear he'll never know what happened."

Michael pushed the water bottle to my lips again. "Drink the rest of this, and I'll do it. Angel?"

I greedily gulped the rest down, ignoring the sting of the cuts inside my mouth. Meanwhile, Angel watched warily from across the bathroom.

"This is what you want?" he finally asked.

I nodded, even as the pain rose like a wave, battering me just as I came up for air.

"Okay. We'll do it, but there's gonna be a day where you have to tell him the truth. Strong or not—he deserves to know."

It was better if no one knew.

This would be the sin that I carried to my grave, along with the things they'd done to my body. The shameful secrets that I buried deep.

"Give us the names, Celia," Michael urged.

I took a deep breath. "Hawk was working against the club with a man called Cobra. Said he was a Serpent. The third man..." I fought through the haze settling over me to recall Lip Ring's actual name. "Cobra called him Manny—said he was Los Dicta—the gangbangers that hurt Molly."

Michael's eyes widened. "It ain't possible. We killed all of 'em—"

I recalled Cobra's words, my tongue heavy in my mouth. "You can drive out a nest of snakes, but if you don't kill every last one of them, they come right back. Only this time," I panted. "They're mad as hell."

The body that had been wrecked at the hands of men who hated my husband turned on me, twisting and tightening until every fiber of my being ached.

I groaned and tried lifting my hand to grip Michael's vest, only to realize I couldn't move it. I stared down at my other arm, but only managed to twitch my index finger.

"H-h-help m-me," I slurred.

Michael's mouth moved into a flat line. "Gave you a little something to help you sleep. Me and Angel'll get this place cleaned up. You need to rest now."

I tried to shake my head, but nothing in my body was under my control anymore. More blood pulsed from between my legs, but the pain was gone.

The carousel in my head slowed, and I was whisked away to a place where I felt as though I was floating. I had just decided I would stay forever when I looked up and saw Cobra standing just outside the bathroom doorway.

"I had to get another taste, sweetheart." He unbuttoned his jacket with a grin and stalked toward me. As he did, his head morphed into that of an actual cobra. I was momentarily distracted from the transformation because, despite the beating he'd doled out, his suit was still in pristine condition.

Not even one wrinkle.

Angel turned to him with a nod and went back to sweeping up the glass. The halo above his head tilted as he bent over, and he straightened it with a growl. "Try not to make such a mess this time, yeah?"

Cobra flipped him off, never taking his eyes off of mine. "I'll do whatever the fuck I want. If you're lucky, I'll consider letting you watch. What do you think, Celia? You want Angel to watch as I fuck you deep?"

I began screaming, reopening every wound until my mouth and throat filled with blood. It flowed from my nose and mouth, cutting my scream off into a gurgle.

Michael massaged my shoulder before ripping the towel down. "You be as loud as you fuckin' want, Celia. Ain't no one around to interrupt us."

He began fumbling with the zipper on his jeans while I lay propped helplessly against the side of the bathtub. Angel swept another pile of glass into the trashcan and straightened his halo before meeting my gaze.

"Sorry, Celia. Grey should've paid us more. You were a debt... that's all you've ever been. That's all you'll ever be. You want us to keep your secrets, pay the price."

"Open up, doll," Michael gripped my chin in his hand, squeezing until the bones gave. Only he wasn't Michael anymore—this was Comedian. He looked exactly the same, but I knew the difference.

This was the monster that hurt Mikey.

"No, no," Cobra snapped through his fangs. "That's not how we play this game, is it? I go first while you watch."

"Fuck that," Comedian growled. "Her old man kept a secret from me, didn't he, Celia?"

I shook my head. "I'm s-sorry—"

My words cut off as he shoved himself into my mouth, gagging me. I struggled to take a breath, but Comedian showed no sign of letting up, even as I began to vomit. His fists tightened in my hair, tethering me to him.

"Oh, sweetheart, you're just as good as I remember," Cobra taunted at my back as he ripped me wide open again. He was going to strike, over and over, filling my body with his venom.

Tears poured from the corners of my eyes, and the room grew dim. Still, I fought. I knew it was futile as I battled the waves surrounding me, trying to push myself above the water long enough to take a breath.

The numbness set in as the toxins took over and my body relaxed, dragging me down into the depths of oblivion. I'd always expected death to hurt, but it came as a welcome embrace.

CHAPTER FOUR

Grey: November 2000 (Age: 36)

I jumped out of the truck we'd taken from one of the New Mexico bikers, the dormant grass crunching under the heels of my boots as I raced across the front lawn. The drive down the mountain had been a white-knuckle experience, with Slim taking the icy switchbacks at full speed while I pleaded with him to go faster.

"Grey!" Bear called after me. "Wait a minute. We don't know what we're walking into here."

Didn't we?

I turned around. "One of us does."

Slim had been the one to take the call from Comedian just outside of New Mexico, but had refused to tell me anything about Celia's condition other than she was alive. His face had gone as white as a sheet, and it hadn't escaped my attention that he kept his foot mashed against the accelerator, even when the governor kicked in.

The driver's side door opened, and the man in question slowly climbed out to face me. "Jamie—"

"I'm goin' in there, Slim. Ain't one of you gonna stop me."

The alcohol had worn off hours ago, leaving me with panicked thoughts and a shitload of adrenaline. I would have torn the house down brick by brick to get to her and not even broken a sweat.

He nodded. "No one's tryin' to stop you, but you need to know what we're up against. Hawk rolled over, and now every club around knows you ain't with the Reaper. He wasn't working alone either."

The implication of his words hit me dead in the eyes. I'd had every piece of my exit strategy in place... save one.

Her.

I had listened to the wrong people and left my family alone with someone who'd betrayed them—convinced myself they were safer here than they were with me. Celia herself had begged me not to go. But, as usual, I did what I wanted.

My boots hit the front porch, and I took a deep breath, suddenly reliving every fucking second of my nightmare. I knew what lay on the other side of the door.

It was always the same.

Only this time, I wouldn't wake up in my wife's arms.

Richard jumped up from the recliner when I threw open the front door before falling onto the coffee table with a yelp. "G-Grey? You're dead. You died. We were at your funeral."

His words tumbled together, and he ran the back of his hand over his swollen eyes, trying to compose himself. "I didn't know who else to call. I didn't know—"

Out of habit, I checked behind the door, silently breathing a sigh of relief upon seeing that the space was empty. The carpet was free of stains and didn't squish beneath my boots.

This wasn't like before.

As I glanced around the room, nothing appeared to be out of place. I could almost believe that it had all been a bad dream.

Almost.

"I'll deal with you later. Right now, I need—"

Angel stepped out into the hall, closing the bedroom door softly behind him before crossing the room. "You need to shut the fuck up," he stated, his voice low and even. "She's resting."

His eyes flashed with anger, but the sight of bloodstained clothing distracted me. I was a scared sixteen-year-old kid again, standing in the same spot where I had rocked my mother's dead body in my arms. "Is she?"

I didn't know what I was asking. She wasn't okay, that much was obvious, judging by the state Angel was in.

Richard watched warily as Bear and Slim filed in behind me, still firmly planted on the coffee table with his hand over his mouth.

Angel's jaw tightened as he walked over to me. "I didn't know she was still here in town, Jamie. All alone. That don't sit right with me."

"Yeah? Well, get in line behind Dick. You two can speak your piece in a minute. Right now, though, I'm goin' to see my wife." I strode toward him, mistakenly assuming that he was raising his arm to let me pass.

The force of the blow from his fist sent me stumbling back a step, and I clutched my eye before growling, "What the fuck was that for?"

Bear let out a low whistle but made no attempt to intervene.

"C'mon, Richard," Slim stepped in. "Let's get some air and give these two some space, yeah?"

Ol' Dick slid his ass right off the coffee table and disappeared through the front door with Slim without so much as a goddamned word, leaving us to our showdown.

Angel straightened his fingers before clenching them into a fist again. "That's just a fraction of what I want to do to you, Jamie. You deserve to have your ass beat over this shit."

I blinked, trying to clear my vision. "I did what I thought was best."

"Don't sugarcoat this—not with me. You sacrificed your family for the club. You know who that sounds like?"

I shook my head and bit out, "Don't you fuckin' say it. I ain't nothin' like my old man was."

Angel laughed bitterly. "Nah, you're right. You let other men beat your Ol' Lady for you—"

I was on him before he finished talking and we went down in a heap. "You motherfucker," I roared. "You know what she means to me—"

Despite his age, Angel landed a blow under my jaw that left me sprawled out on my back, panting for air. His boot came down against my chest as I moved to sit up, pinning me against the carpet.

"Now, you listen to me, you piece of shit," he snarled, spit flying from his mouth. "That woman in there is as close to a saint as your mama was, and I'm covered in her blood because you left her and your kids unprotected—"

"I had Hawk—" I tried, only to be cut off again.

"Hawk ain't you, don't you get that? You leave your family with anybody else, and they're as good as dead. Now, I want you to listen for once in your goddamn life before you barge in there thinkin' you're the hero. Can you do that?"

When I nodded, Angel removed his boot and knelt beside me. "She's in bad shape, Jamie."

I pushed myself up into a sitting position, unable to look away from the bloody print left behind on my chest. "How bad?"

"Bad enough that the girls are gonna be stayin' with Richard and Norma for a while. Doc checked her over—she's got broken bones… a concussion—"

"Was she—did he?" I choked on the words, knowing the ways we broke our enemies, but not wanting to believe it could ever happen to her.

Angel paused and looked over at the bedroom door before quietly answering. "No."

"Thank the saints," I breathed out. "Can I see her?"

His lips pursed as if he wanted to say something else. Instead, he just gave a jerky nod and led me into the bedroom.

This was what happened to bad Catholics.

It was my only thought as the door opened to reveal a scene that would be burned into my memory for the rest of my life. The floral scent of Celia's perfume was gone, replaced with the strong stench of sweat and blood.

I'd dealt in blood since the night I sent my old man to meet the Reaper. I could look at any pattern and instantly recognize the type of weapon that had been used.

Drips were common during fight nights. Broken noses, busted lips; run-of-the-mill stuff. Cast-off patterns, or spatters, were typical with interrogations when we'd bring out the kill-lights or our fists to get what we needed.

Blood spray was the byproduct of a severed artery, usually a slit throat, whereas guns created a mist-like spatter.

I knew what the patterns on the walls meant, but it didn't stop my hand from coming up over my mouth in horror. I'd seen grown men vomit up their own blood and never lost a second of sleep, yet my legs tried to buckle beneath me when I saw where my wife had gotten sick on the carpet.

I had spent years learning how to break a body down to where it had become routine, but it sure as fuck didn't stop me from crying out something unintelligible as I passed the bathroom. Shards of glass coated the countertop and floor from where the mirror had been shattered.

I thought I knew so much, but none of it prepared me for the moment I finally laid eyes on her. The nightmare that had plagued me for years was nothing compared to the real thing. Even a sick fuck like me hadn't been able to dream up the level of violence that had been done to her.

Celia lay propped up against a mountain of pillows in bed, wrapped in her favorite fluffy pink bathrobe and shaking like she was having a seizure. Her jaw was clamped down, and she stared right through me with eyes that were glassed over.

She was here, but she wasn't.

My girl.

With her right eye swollen shut and lower lip split down the middle, her beautiful face was almost unrecognizable. The black and purple bruises trailed down her cheeks and throat before disappearing underneath the robe. Chunks of hair had been torn out, leaving behind bloody patches along her scalp.

This had been an interrogation.

My chest tightened at the sight of her and the bloody handprints along the wall leading into the bathroom where she'd tried to pull herself up. She'd been left helpless because of me.

Because I'd been so damn convinced my plan was foolproof.

Angel was right—I might not have swung my fists, but I'd done this to her all the same.

CHAPTER FIVE

Grey: November 2000 (Age: 36)

My eyes darted back and forth over the destruction before landing on Celia again, and I saw what I had missed before. Comedian, holding my wife's bandaged hand in his like Florence fucking Nightingale.

When he whispered something in her ear, rage flooded my veins and turned my vision red until I could almost hear the snap of his bones beneath my fist.

"Don't touch her," I growled, fighting to stay in control. He pretended to be a goddamn saint whenever she was around, but I knew the truth.

He might not have had a hand in what happened to her, but I was beyond giving a fuck. He was touching her like she was his. I sucked in a breath, forcing myself to remember that my real enemy was not the men who had dropped everything to get to her.

Even if one of them was a sadistic fuck who had gotten off on abusing my son.

I would send Hawk and anyone else who had a hand in hurting her screaming to the Reaper soon enough.

Comedian placed Celia's hand back in her lap before addressing me. "Had to give her something, Pres. She was in a bad state."

I raked a hand through my hair. “She’s drugged?”

“It should be wearin’ off shortly. She didn’t need to deal with that...” Angel cleared his throat. “Didn’t seem right.”

Comedian dropped his eyes back down to her. “Not like she’s much better now. Poor thing keeps crying out like she’s being attacked again.”

I pushed the fury back down to the darkest parts of my soul. I would save it until the day Hawk was on his knees in front of me.

“Speaking of not doin’ good, you look like shit. Were you in a fight?” He asked, letting his fingers trail across her swollen cheek.

I swore my molars were going to crack under the pressure. I stalked forward and gently lifted her off the bed and into my arms before growling, “Get. Out.”

Celia’s head fell against my chest and she let out a muffled groan, causing the lump in my throat to expand until it hurt to swallow.

I was holding my entire world. My arms tightened around her body, and I shot Angel a desperate look.

“Let’s give them a minute, yeah?” He pointed toward the door, saving me from caving Comedian’s face in. “Jamie?”

“Yeah?”

“Just—” Angel’s mouth fell into a flat line. “Just stay strong for her, okay? Don’t let her see you fall apart.”

The scent of bleach stung my nostrils as he passed, leaving behind more questions than answers.

I sank down onto the comforter without loosening my grip while her body continued to shake and tremble. It reminded me of the night she showed up at *Leather & Lace*. I shed blood for her then, but it hadn’t been enough to keep her safe.

“N-n-no!” Celia cried out suddenly, her body going rigid with fear. “I’ll b-be quiet.”

“I’m here.” I squeezed her shoulder as her foot came up, weakly kicking at air. Her toes were stained with blood, and I was once again struck with the need to hurt someone until they looked like she did.

“I don’t know where Jamie is,” she moaned.

I pulled her into my chest, and this time, she latched onto my shirt like I was her lifeline. A tear slid down her cheek, and I gently pressed my mouth to it. "I'm here, princess. Ain't leavin' you ever again."

Celia blinked, her pupils still dilated, as she fought to come back from wherever the drugs had taken her. "Jamie?" Her teeth chattered, causing the cuts around her mouth to ooze. "I'm s-sorry."

"Don't you fuckin' apologize to me, darlin'. I—"

With a low groan, she leaned forward and looped her arms around my neck. "N-no—all my..."

Instead of finishing her sentence, she tightened her grip, forcing my cheek down against the top of her head. The moan that came out of her was long and low-pitched, to where it almost didn't sound human.

"Celia? Baby, what hurts?"

She slumped back in my arms, panting. "Everything."

Doc had missed something.

I stood up, having decided I'd risk it all to get her help. I'd pay off a goddamn hospital if that was what it took.

"No... please," she mumbled, prying my hand away from the belt of her robe.

"Gonna get you checked over, princess. You need a doctor." A real one, I silently added.

She shook her head. "Mmmm... fine."

"You ain't fine."

I watched as her chin slowly dipped down toward her chest. Her hold on my neck loosened. Sweat ran down her forehead, triggering the strangest sense of déjà vu, as if I'd been through this before with her.

My right hand grew damp, and I adjusted her before moving it up to rest on top of her thigh. As much as I wanted to let her sleep, I had to know how bad it was.

"Please," she begged, as I pulled at the opening on her robe, her lips connecting with the skin of my throat. "Don't."

I stood paralyzed next to our bed, trying to decide the best course of action. Before, I would have fought her for control and demanded she listen to me—ultimately doing what I wanted.

But this wasn't like old times.

We were in uncharted territory.

Fight gone, I lowered her back onto the bed in defeat. For the first time in a long time, I didn't know what to do. I didn't know how to fix her.

I settled her head against the pillows and reached for the comforter when I realized the palm of my hand was coated in blood, not sweat.

The belt on Celia's robe had come undone, and with the drugs running through her veins, her reflexes were slow. It took several attempts before she finally pulled it closed again.

More than enough time for me to see what they had done to her.

My knees buckled beneath me, and I gripped the bedpost to steady myself. Where there weren't bruises, there were bite marks—from her tits to her exposed belly. Several were covered in dried blood from where the fuckers' teeth had broken through her skin.

I clenched my jaw and squeezed the wood until it creaked and groaned beneath my hand. This was more than an interrogation.

My breath came in short, panicked bursts, and I forced myself to turn away from her when my vision blurred. My nostrils flared with each measured exhale, but this time, there was no reining in my emotions.

Tears that had once been prayers now fell in apology for all the ways I had failed her and my girls.

It had finally happened.

Past and present collided, leaving me feeling as if I'd stepped out of my body, forced to watch helplessly as my wife endured my sins.

I gasped and choked my way through my next breath, releasing the sob that had been lodged in my throat since I'd gotten the news. I had made a similar sound the night Ma was killed.

Just like in my nightmare, I wanted to run—not from her, but to find the men responsible. Like some fucked up version of a Greek hero, I wanted to go to war for her before coming home to kneel at her feet, presenting the heads of our enemies like a goddamned offering.

I was no hero, though.

And none of it would make a damn bit of difference after what she had endured. We were a goddamn tragedy—there was no happy ending. There never had been.

I caught sight of my reflection in the vanity mirror and released my stranglehold on the bedpost.

"Jamie?"

Keeping my back to her, I nodded. "Yeah, princess?"

"The light makes my head hurt." Her voice cracked, right along with what was left of my heart.

Another tear ran down my face as I walked over to the window, but I swiped it away and took deep breaths until I felt like I was in control again. I wanted to drop to my knees and atone for my sins, but she didn't need my shit on top of what she was already dealing with.

Lost in thought, I turned the wand on the blinds until the room darkened, ignoring the clicking sound until the damn thing snapped off in my hand. I laid it on the windowsill before glancing back to see if Celia had noticed.

"Are you leaving?" she finally asked, breaking the silence.

I flexed my fingers, debating my options. The monster in me craved a good hunt, but the broken woman in my bed called to my heart. "Need to find the men who did this to you, princess."

"Right now, I just want you to lay with me."

When I made no attempt to move away from the window, she added, "Please."

I toed my boots off and climbed in next to her, pulling her back up against my chest. "I'm so sorry, baby," I wept into her hair. "So fuckin' sorry."

She let out a soft exhale but didn't move. It was if her body had given up the fight. When she finally spoke, her voice was no more than a whisper. "Tell me a story, Jamie. Something with a happy ending."

I had never been known for my stories. Sure, I could vomit up the shit I'd read about in comic books over the years, but Celia had always been the storyteller.

"I, uh, I ever tell you how the club got its name?" I asked, pulling the comforter up over her shoulders. When she didn't answer, I continued. "C'mon, princess, I figured with your Greek mythology smarts, you'd know all about this."

The back of her head shifted against my collarbone as she looked up at me. "I know what a phoenix is, Jamie."

"Yeah, Wolverine told me about them when I was a kid, but I wasn't too impressed with a bird that lived for a few hundred years before burning up into nothing." I waited for her to correct me, but she stayed silent, curled up against my body.

"He had to explain to me that when it burst into flames, it was reborn. Damn thing rises from the ashes, stronger than before. Just like you, darlin'. These assholes think they've won, but the club's gonna wipe 'em out, just like anyone else who's stupid enough to stand against us."

"You can drive out a nest of snakes, but if you don't kill every last one of them..." Celia's voice trailed off in a soft exhale.

I froze. "Where'd you hear that?"

It was impossible.

We'd killed the Serpents—wiped out every single officer the night they took out Dragon. On the off-chance one of them had survived, why in the hell had they waited fourteen years for revenge?

Her lashes fluttered, and she lowered her gaze down to my chest. "Doesn't matter. They took the money. You'll never find them now."

I lifted my head up off my arm. "What did they say, Celia? Where were they going? The cash I gave you—that was what? Four grand?"

Her lower lip quivered, and she dropped her forehead to my chest with a wince. "No. It was more. A lot more."

With a sharp cry, her body contorted, and I tightened my grip, reminded again that the idea that she had been safe here had always been just that. An idea.

An illusion.

Something I'd been too stupid to recognize.

More tears leaked from the corners of my eyes and fell onto her robe before disappearing into the fleece. I always saw myself as her protector, going up against her parents and Betsy, but hadn't been here when she'd needed me the most.

"Jamie?" Celia gripped my wrist. "I did something stupid..."

The thrashing of my heart inside my chest was the only sound in the room. I held my breath, waiting for her explanation, but she was lost to the drugs again.

I brushed my hand across her forehead, relieved to find her skin cool to the touch. Whatever they gave her, though, was still in full effect, leaving me to wonder how much of our conversation she would remember later.

Celia's left eye popped open again, focused on the bedroom door. "Did you know that the paint doesn't go to the baseboard on the wall behind our bed?"

I tucked a strand of bloody hair behind her ear with a frown. "I, uh, I didn't know—"

Angel interrupted with a soft tap on the door. "Hey, how's she doin'?"

Celia shifted with a groan. "I'm doing better."

"Yeah? You don't seem better." His eyes narrowed before he looked over at me. "Lucy's here."

"Lucy?" Celia called out. "She came all this way?"

He nodded. "Just to see you, doll."

"Hey, Celia," Lucy said, as she stepped out from behind Angel. Her eyes widened as she approached the bed, darting from one wound to the next in horror. Instead of running away, she shifted a massive bag up onto her shoulder and forced a small smile. "I brought you some things."

"C'mon, Jamie. Let's give them a minute," Angel began, but I cut him off.

"Ain't leavin' her."

His jaw clenched. "You've been in here with her for hours now. She needs to rest, and we got things to discuss."

Celia released her hold on my wrist as she moved away. "I want you to go, Jamie."

I squeezed her shoulder. "Celia..."

"If you have something you need to do, go do it. I don't want you here."

The order was like a knife to my chest, but I deserved every bit of her rejection.

Lucy's lips pursed as she took in the exchange. "We'll get you cleaned up—"

"No. Just give me something to sleep. Please."

Reluctantly, I rolled out of bed. As I bent to retrieve my boots, I studied the wall. The light blue paint looked the same as it always had. Not one bare spot to be found.

The lack of missing paint left me questioning how much of what Celia said was the truth, and how much was the result of the drugs. Maybe I'd slipped up and mentioned another club over the years, and in her current state, she had latched onto it.

I didn't want to consider the alternative—that long-dead enemies had resurrected themselves and come for my family.

CHAPTER SIX

Grey: November 2000 (Age: 36)

I left Celia with Angel and Lucy and stepped out onto the back porch. Bear and Comedian stood by the rusted cast-iron smoker, deep in conversation. Slim sat with his hands steepled under his chin in one of the lawn chairs. The three looked up, clearly waiting for news.

I tapped a cigarette from the pack and lit up with shaking hands. After taking several desperate drags, letting the nicotine hit my brain, I finally managed, "Serpents. Hawk was working with the fuckin' Serpents. Can someone explain to me how the fuck that's possible?"

The screen door slammed shut behind Angel. "If you'd sit the fuck down, we can."

I raked my fingernails down my jawline with a growl. "Sit the fuck down? Jesus fuckin' Christ! We need to find them!"

"That's what they're hoping for," Slim stated flatly. "It's what you've always done, and most of the time, it's paid off. One of our own rolled over and joined up with a Serpent and a member of Los Dictadores... why? Why them and why now?"

Los Dictadores?

Another group that, as far as we'd been concerned, had been wiped out.

"Hawk patched in after the war with the Serpents," Bear said. "It don't add up."

I took another drag, pausing at the deep rumble of exhaust pipes coming down the street, before slumping against the bricks. "Wolverine's here. We got anyone else?"

Angel cautiously walked over to where I stood. "Every brother is on his way here right now. Don't go runnin' into this with your dick out. We need a plan—"

"They beat her," I ground out with a stream of smoke, hands trembling again. "They—they used their fuckin' teeth, and you want me to sit back and let 'em slip away?"

He took a step back and looked to the others for help.

"Grey, ain't no one tellin' you to let them get away with it." Slim stubbed out his cigarette on the sole of his boot before standing up. "We need to find out who knows you're alive. You go after them like this and—"

"What if it was Lou?" I spun toward Bear. "Or Molly? You expect me to believe that you'd all sit on your asses and wait to come up with a plan? Fuck, Comedian, I think even you'd agree with me here."

He nodded. "You're fuckin' right, and those pricks will be screamin' for mercy long before I'm ready to send them to the Reaper, but Slim and Angel got a point. We need numbers—"

I flicked the ash from the cigarette and took another long drag. "I don't want 'em breathin' the same air as her..."

Bear rested his arm against the smoker, nodding along. "We fucked up, Grey. Before, I mean. With the Serpents, it was a goddamned ambush, and we were lucky to have made it out of that alive."

"You're welcome," Slim stated flatly as he lit up another cigarette, knowing his sniper skills alone had gotten us out of that one.

"Yeah, fuck you, Slim. What I'm sayin' is that we made mistakes... just took a few years to catch up to us. What is it Wolverine always said?"

"Better to leave your enemy thinkin' you're weak while you come up with a strategy than to run in and get your goddamn head blown off. Is that the one?" Wolverine asked, before stepping out of the early evening shadows.

I shook my head with a bitter laugh. "Yeah, you'd know all about that, wouldn't you? With Molly, we sat back and formulated a plan—oh, shit. No, we absofuckinlutely didn't!"

"That was different—"

"How in the fuck was that different, old man? Because unlike my Ol' Lady, Molly was stupid enough to involve herself with gangbangers? And not only that, but let one of them knock her up?"

Bear pushed off the grill and stalked toward me. "Watch your fuckin' mouth, Grey. We're tryin' to help."

With a curse, Angel stepped in between us. "Can we at least agree we need a fuckin' plan and go from there?"

I nodded with a smirk. "Yeah, just as soon as Wolverine takes responsibility for this shit. Have you seen her? Have you seen what they did to her?"

His brows shifted together. "How in the fuck is this my fault? Way I see it, the club kept your ass out of a federal prison. That's your problem though, Grey. Always assumin' you're somehow above everybody else. Maybe take a good long look in the mirror the next time you want to point fingers."

I cracked my neck and launched myself forward with a roar, slamming into Bear as he moved in front of Wolverine. "You think I don't? I can't even look at her right now without seeing every wrong decision I ever made!"

Slim pulled me back before turning to Wolverine. "Celia told Angel and Comedian that one of the guys was from Los Dictadores and the other was a Serpent. If that's true, then we all have blood on our hands."

Wolverine stumbled back, panting. "Jesus fuck. Jamie, I—"

"They're goin' to die... all of them. Anyone who had a hand in what happened to her." Realization struck, and I paused. "What the hell am I sayin'? Bear, you're in charge now. Do whatever the fuck you want."

I stubbed my cigarette out against the bricks and rubbed at my eyes, wincing when my knuckles came in contact with the bruises Angel's fist had left behind.

Defeated, I made my way back inside, stopping at the kitchen sink to catch my breath. I made the decision to hand over the keys to the kingdom. Nothing I could do to change it now.

I let my head drop onto my forearms, somehow knocking over a drinking glass with my elbow. "Fuck," I muttered, before searching for a dish towel to mop up the mess.

After checking several drawers, I found one and swiped it over the counter before scanning the kitchen with a frown. The sink was overflowing with dirty dishes, something Celia never would have allowed.

It didn't make sense.

"Jamie?"

I slowly turned to face Angel. "You said the girls didn't know anything had happened, right?"

He nodded. "Richard said they were still asleep when he showed up. They had no idea."

"What time did this happen?"

"Early mornin'? I couldn't get much out of her."

I was overthinking things. Maybe she had just been tired and left it for the morning. Hell, I'd been up for over twenty-four hours—anything was possible at this point.

"The bite marks..."

Angel gnawed at the corner of his lower lip, following my stare. "What about them?"

"It doesn't strike you as odd? When have we ever done that to someone we wanted to get information from?" I took a deep breath and forced myself to say it. "There's something you're keepin' from me. Just put me out of my misery... please."

That was the thing about love. It had torn down my walls, only to leave me defenseless in the end—begging for answers to questions I didn't have the balls to ask.

Whatever Angel said was only going to send me into a downward spiral. It was already taking everything in me not to drink myself into a stupor.

"I bet Lucy's finishing up. Me and the guys are gonna stay on watch... why don't you get some sleep?" He clenched his jaw and kept his eyes trained on my boots. "We're gonna take care of this."

"Thank you... for being here for her."

He squeezed my shoulder and led me back to the bedroom. "She's gonna be okay, kid."

I nodded and pushed the door open. Celia lay on her side in one of my old sweatshirts, fast asleep.

My clothes were still in the dresser drawers. Just another cruel reminder of how close we'd been to freedom. Tonight should have been a celebration.

Lucy hurriedly closed her bag and stood up. "I gave her a little something to control the pain and help her relax. How are you holding up?"

I bit down on the inside of my cheek and shook my head. "Don't worry about me, Luce. Is she—does she need a hospital?"

"She just needs to rest so her body can heal. Um, I heard Wolverine's bike—"

"He's out back."

Celia's lashes twitched against her cheeks, leaving me to wonder what it was she was dreaming about.

Was she seeing the men who'd hurt her or imagining the girls and me? Maybe there wasn't enough good left to outweigh the hell she had endured. I brushed a damp curl back and kissed her forehead.

"Did she shower?"

Lucy tightened her grip on the bag as if she was afraid someone was going to take it from her. "I gave her a bath. If you're good with her, I'm just going to find Wolverine... you should try to sleep."

Everyone wanted me to sit or sleep, but I couldn't. The ticking from the clock on the nightstand was a reminder that the bastards who had done this to my family were still out there. Each second that passed was another missed opportunity for vengeance.

I suddenly found that I didn't care if every MC in the country knew I was alive. There was no more hiding... no more running. I hadn't wanted a war back then, but now?

Now, I'd kill any motherfucker who got in my way.

"Jamie?" Lucy tried again.

I shook off my thoughts and nodded to her. "Go on. I'll stay with her."

The blue paint on the wall continued to taunt me as I kicked off my boots, leaving me with the nagging feeling that there was still something I was missing.

After ensuring that Celia was still asleep, I walked around to the other side of the bed and knelt down, my knees crackling in protest.

I was twenty-two when we went up against the Serpents for the first time, and twenty-six when we ambushed Los Dictadores.

Thirty-six might as well have been a hundred, with the miles I'd put on my body since then.

Instead of sitting with the club and coming up with a plan to end the men responsible before they made it out of the state, I was crawling around on bloodstained carpet, searching for missing paint like a fucking idiot.

"Fuck me," I groaned, before reaching up to switch on the bedside lamp. Shadows danced across the walls as I shifted onto my forearms, but besides a few cobwebs, nothing stuck out.

I spread my arms out at my sides and lowered my head until my chin was resting against the carpet while contemplating again why I'd felt indulging Celia's hallucinations was necessary.

My shoulders ached from the position, and I stretched just as a flash of something under the nightstand caught my eye. Ice flooded my veins, and I froze, straining to get a better look before shifting forward.

There was the missing paint, clear as day. It hadn't been some drug-induced illusion, after all.

I rocked back a few inches, and the wall appeared to be blue again. When I rolled my hips forward again, the bare spot came back into view, and everything suddenly clicked into place.

Angel refusing to look me in the eye...

Lucy's wariness...

"Oh, Jesus," I whispered, mashing the back of my hand to my mouth to stifle the sob. Cold sweat ran down my back as images invaded my mind. I knew I would never feel a fraction of the physical pain they put her through, but emotionally, I'd just been shoved down a garbage disposal.

It hadn't been just a beating.

They had taken something from her—something we would never

get back. It didn't matter if I hunted every last one of them down. They had scarred her from the inside out, and those marks would never fade.

How could we ever come back from this?

I bolted into the bathroom and fell to my knees in front of the toilet, unable to shake the image of her being violated.

I'd done that to her.

Just as much as them.

As my muscles spasmed in grief, my body purged what my mind never would. The darkness I'd tried to hide for years resurfaced, stronger than ever before.

Mikey.

Celia.

Katy.

Dakota.

How had I ever believed that I deserved them?

I was a killer—had been since the night I sent my old man to the Reaper. As much as I'd wanted a family, I had always known that a depraved fuck like me would never get a happily ever after.

Helplessness ripped the air from my lungs with the realization that I had never been a husband or a father.

Not really.

My tears fell soundlessly against the toilet seat as everything I thought I knew came crumbling down.

Instead of fighting it, I surrendered and let the monster fully consume me. A jagged piece of mirror on the tile reflected the madness in my eyes.

Maybe I hadn't been her protector, but I sure as fuck planned on avenging her. I swiped the back of my hand across my mouth before pushing down the handle and letting the last traces of my softness circle the bowl before disappearing completely.

According to the official records, Jamie Quinn had been dead since October 18, 1996. I left his body lying on a bathroom floor, surrounded by broken glass and his wife's blood.

CHAPTER SEVEN

Celia: December 2000 (Age: 28)

"Celia?" Lucy rubbed my forearm. "It's time to wake up and eat."

I kept my eyes closed, feigning sleep with a deep inhale. I'd been awake for hours, listening to the faint sounds of Fleetwood Mac coming from one of the other rooms.

With the music came memories—Jamie crooning Pink Floyd to a fussy Kate as he rocked her in his arms. The way my chin seemed to fit perfectly against his shoulder as we swayed back and forth across the living room carpet.

For the first time, I understood how people became addicts. The drugs that Lucy had given me over the last couple of weeks kept me in a suspended state of reality. In my world, Jamie chose to stay so we could be a family.

We were safe there.

I never wanted to leave.

The music faded into white noise, but I kept my eyes closed, unwilling to face the truth. Even with people coming and going regularly, I was alone.

I had been told my girls were safe, but didn't know where they were. Bikers filled my house to remind me constantly of the hell they were going to bring to Hawk and the others, while conveniently leaving Jamie's name out of it.

Maybe they feared suddenly alerting me to the fact that he'd never come home, as if I wasn't painfully aware of his absence with each day that passed.

Early on, I prayed for a miracle. I begged and pleaded for a second chance, all while knowing what the steady flow of blood between my legs meant. I prayed that Jamie's love for me would somehow outweigh what I had done.

I wanted his forgiveness so badly that, in my drugged state, I had convinced myself he'd rushed home—completely devastated and blaming himself.

My prayers stopped when I realized they were nothing more than delusional fantasies. God and the saints were saving their miracles for someone more worthy. My husband had finally given me the separation I had demanded for the better part of two years.

This was my purgatory.

"Celia, come on. Rise and shine."

Maybe it was for the best.

He would never have to see what I'd become.

I reluctantly opened one eye and then the other before meeting Lucy's concerned gaze.

"There you are. Thought you were going to sleep the rest of the day away." She pulled a bowl off the nightstand and held it out for me. "I saved you some of my potato soup—"

"No, thank you." I pushed it away.

Lucy sighed. "Celia, you have to eat something."

The mere thought of food turned my stomach, and I shook my head before sitting up. "Not right now. I need to shower."

"But you already took one this morning."

I kicked my feet over the side of the bed, swaying slightly as the room spun around me. Lucy placed a steadying hand on my arm, and I reached up to squeeze it before finding my footing. "I'm good. I'll just wash up and then try a little soup."

"Okay." She led me toward the bathroom. "Let me just see if one of the guys can reheat it while I help you bathe."

"No," I snapped. "I just—I just need a minute alone, okay? You take care of the soup, and I'll be out in a minute."

I had no intention of eating a bite, but was willing to say anything just to buy a moment's peace. I pushed the bathroom door closed and briefly let the back of my head rest against the wood before turning the lock.

The drawstring on my sweatpants had become knotted, and it took several tries before I got it undone. I kept my focus on the ceiling, ignoring the tremors in my hands and the pain in my ribs as I pulled Jamie's old sweatshirt over my head.

Once my breathing returned to normal, I padded over to the shower and turned the handle all the way to the left. The old pipes hummed to life, and I leaned against the bathroom counter with a sigh. Someone had replaced the mirror. It didn't matter that all traces of blood and glass were gone. I still saw the destruction in my reflection.

The cuts had scabbed over, and the bruises had faded from a vivid dark purple to a subtle yellow, but not every wound would heal. After eyeing the door again, I slowly turned toward the mirror and gently peeled back the bandage on my hip.

At first, the strange markings had confused me. It wasn't until I looked at it in the mirror—greeted by the diamond thirteen—that I realized what had happened.

I had been branded.

Just like the Ancient Romans had signified ownership over their slaves, I was left with a permanent reminder of what I was.

A victim.

The steam billowed out of the shower, fogging the mirror to where I almost believed I looked normal again. I stepped under the showerhead, hissing as it rained lava down over my skin.

"Cry," I commanded, moving the soapy loofah over my delicate skin. Each rough scrape sent pain reverberating down into my toes, but my eyes remained dry.

With a wince, I spread my legs and forced myself to watch as I dragged the sponge through my folds. "Cry," I growled, even blinking for good measure. "Just cry."

My heart raced as the sensation brought violent memories to the surface, and the edges of my vision swam in black. The bleeding may have stopped two days ago, but I still saw the stream running down the inside of my thighs. I could still feel the twisting knife of pain from a body that had failed to protect even the most innocent.

The sponge slipped from my hands as I dropped to my knees on the floor of the shower. "Cry, goddammit!"

What was wrong with me?

"Celia?" Lucy tapped at the door. "Are you okay?"

I reached up and shut the water off with a soft groan. "I'm fine. Getting out now."

I adored Lucy, but her constant hovering was suffocating me. It didn't matter how much I protested, or how many times I insisted I was okay on my own. She refused to leave.

I just wanted to get lost in my thoughts for a while—to sift through my feelings until I figured out why I hadn't shed one tear since the night they took everything from me.

What I didn't need was to be told when to eat or drink as if I was a child. I craved the ability to use the bathroom or shower without someone pacing on the other side of the door.

I towel dried my hair and pulled it up into a bun before slipping back into Jamie's shirt and my sweatpants. Lucy was waiting on the bed and jumped up the moment I opened the door.

"I picked out a dress for you. Thought you might like to put it on and go sit out back for a little while. The sun feels really nice right now... it's hard to believe it's December." She rambled, wringing her hands together.

The dress was one Jamie had bought for me not long after Kate was born. He had been in Black Hawk for a rally and saw it in a store window.

I stared down at it, waiting for the rust-colored material to dredge up what I had been unable to in the shower.

Nothing.

I was completely and utterly broken.

"I'm feeling a little dizzy," I lied. "I need to just sit for a second."

Lucy sprang into action, leading me back into bed and fussing with the pillows until she had me surrounded with them like an infant. "I had Angel reheat your soup. Let me just grab it—"

I pulled the comforter up over my head. "I'm good, Luce. Just gonna sleep it off."

"But you have company... I just thought you might—"

I could feel her frustration, but I didn't want to dress up so that one more Ol' Lady could tell me how sorry she was to hear about what happened before giving me a casserole.

I should have been wallowing in grief and self-pity over what they had stolen from us that night. Instead, white-hot rage coursed through my veins, knowing the three of them were still out there.

The soft strains of music began again, and I closed my eyes, feeling the lyrics deep within my soul. The tempo was slow, giving every indication that it was just another sad song.

It seemed those were the only ones worth playing.

Stevie's voice moved to a dramatic howl that left goosebumps on my skin, and for the first time in my life, I understood her perfectly. The fiery passion in her words wasn't mourning or even her feeling sorry for herself.

It was a declaration of war.

There wouldn't be a fairy tale ending or some neat resolution where the club was concerned.

Hawk.

Cobra.

Manny.

They had come looking for Grey, and just as soon as I was healed, I was going to go looking for them.

CHAPTER EIGHT

Celia: December 2000 (Age: 28)

"Mama, can you check again?" Dakota whispered. "I saw Loki hiding under my bed."

Kate rolled onto her side with a dramatic huff. "I tried telling her, but as usual, she wouldn't listen."

"What? Pops checked every night for me. You can never be too careful."

I gripped the bedpost and knelt down, grinning at the assortment of comics stacked messily underneath. "Oh, Dakota's right. There is a Loki under the bed."

I stood up, holding the comic over my head in victory. "Here we are. One Loki, just as you demanded. I think he was trying to infiltrate Asgard again."

Dakota snatched the comic from my hand with a giggle before placing it face down on the nightstand. "Hey, Mama? Do you think it would be okay if I wrote a letter to Santa tomorrow?"

Kate made another sound of exasperation. "Santa's not real, just like ghosts aren't real. Only a dummy would believe in that stuff."

Not even home for twenty-four hours, and it was apparent that their relationship had not improved during their time away.

"Kate, be nice to your sister," I warned, before turning back to

Dakota. "Santa is real, and if you want to write him a letter and ask for something special—"

"It's not that. It's just that Nan took me to the mall to visit, and already I left a letter, but I told him to bring my gifts to their house because I didn't know how long you'd be gone." Her voice grew small. "I just don't want him to go to the wrong house."

"You should just have them delivered there... at least Nan has a tree up." Kate gestured toward the hall. "Our house isn't even decorated. Besides, she's probably just gonna leave again."

Dakota's head whipped around to face me. "That's not true, is it? We're not going to go back to Nan and Pop's house, are we? You won't leave us again, will you?"

I sucked in a startled breath and shook my head, earning an eye roll from Kate that I decided I was better off ignoring. As if losing her daddy hadn't been enough, she had been yanked from her bed and moved to my parent's house with no explanation.

My daughter had become a full-blown cynic at ten.

It wasn't fair.

Nothing about our lives had gone the way I planned.

I waited for the telltale prick of emotion when Dakota's body plowed into my sore ribs and she buried her face against my neck, holding me in a death grip.

As usual, there was nothing but anger.

These men hadn't just stolen something from me. Their actions had left my girls scared and distrustful.

"Why don't you both get some sleep and we'll work on decorating the house tomorrow?" I helped Dakota back under the covers and kissed the top of her head.

"Love you, Kota-Bear. I'm glad you're home with me."

Her mouth stretched wide in a yawn. "Love you too, Mama."

"I love you, Katydid."

She yanked the blankets up over her head and rolled away. I knew I deserved every bit of her anger, but it didn't make it hurt any less.

My father was sitting in the recliner, watching a football game, when I came out of the girl's room.

"I'm surprised you're still here. Thought you'd be gone by now." I bent to retrieve Dakota's tennis shoes from under the couch and moved them over by the front door, knowing she'd be looking for them in the morning if I didn't.

He pressed a button on the remote, and the television screen faded into blackness. "I need to talk to you."

"Am I in trouble?" I asked with a raised eyebrow. My father had never been the disciplinarian. That task had always fallen to my mother.

"Sit," he directed, pointing to the couch. "Look, I'll just come out and say it. I'm not sure the girls are safe with you anymore, Celia."

I sank down onto one of the cushions, more out of shock than obedience. "What do you mean? Did you not see the entire army of bikers camped outside? If they're not safe—"

"You led those men here!" His voice rose as he jabbed a finger in my direction. "I told you they were dangerous—in fact, your mother and I even tried warning you about Jamie—but you refused to listen and look at what happened!"

There it was.

Eleven years of mistakes and blame placed solely at my feet.

My ribs protested the sudden shift from sitting to standing, and I clutched them in regret before stalking toward my father. "You think this is all my fault?"

"Sweetheart, you're an adult. It's time to act like one and admit that your gambling has put the girls at risk. I just worry—"

"My gambling was to keep the lights on because, as Mother so eloquently put it, I chose to live like garbage and shouldn't come to either of you looking for a handout. What would you have had me do, Daddy? Let my girls go hungry?"

He ran a hand over his face. "I didn't know things were that bad..."

My chest heaved up and down with each ragged breath I took. The blood drained from my face and arms and pooled in my belly, leaving me nauseated. "They were, and I did what I had to... for them."

"Your mother and I just think the girls would be better off living with us—"

Ignoring the stiffness in my fingers, I yanked him forward in the chair by the collar of his shirt. "You what?"

He stood up and backed away, breaking the contact between us. "Now, don't get upset, but we could keep them safe—"

"Like you kept me safe?" I bit out. "It's easy for you to point the finger at me and accuse me of being an unfit mother, but let's not forget how this all started, Daddy. Had you not been in over your head with drugs, I never would've been taken by the club in the first place."

The rage that had been clogging my veins spilled over into my words. "I would've gone my entire life blissfully ignorant of Silent Phoenix. I could have been ten times the woman I became, but you snorted away any chance at a future for me!"

I watched as his shoulders slumped forward and the anger fled his face. "Celia, I—"

"Get. Out," I growled as I threw the front door open. Comedian jumped up from the porch swing as my father reached for me, quickly moving in between us.

The hurt he had inflicted penetrated deep into my bones, but my body still refused to give in to the tears. "Leave," I demanded. "And don't you even think about taking my girls. Are we clear?"

"Celia..." He took a step forward, only to be stopped by the wall that was Comedian.

"Let's go, old man."

I watched as Comedian led him back to his car before closing and locking the door behind me. My body trembled and shook from the adrenaline that had been dumped into my system.

I thought surviving that night was going to be the hardest thing I had ever done. I was wrong. It was going to be getting up, day after day, and fighting.

Fighting to keep my girls.

Fighting to regain their trust and keep them safe.

Fighting to hold on to what little humanity remained.

"Cry," I whispered to myself, but just like my prayers, my demand went unanswered.

CHAPTER NINE

Celia: December 2000 (Age: 28)

I found the pack of cigarettes hidden behind a bag of frozen peas in the freezer and snagged the flashlight from the junk drawer before stepping out onto the back porch.

"Looks like you finally kicked ol' Dick to the curb," a voice slurred from behind me. "I wondered how long that'd take."

I yelped as images of Cobra flooded my mind before swinging the flashlight wildly, connecting several times with solid flesh.

"Jesus fuckin' Christ, Celia! It's me!" Jamie roared. He quickly pried the weapon from my grasp before tossing it out into the dead grass.

My body twisted away as he came into focus, still convinced there was a threat. Maybe there was, and I had just been too blind to see it.

"Goddammit," he growled, rubbing at his jaw. "You tryin' to knock my teeth out?"

The plastic around the pack of cigarettes crinkled loudly as my fingers tightened against it. "You—you just popped up out of nowhere."

"Pretty sure I've popped up like this before, and gotten a much better reaction," he grumbled.

"That was before—" I stopped, the implication of my words

hanging heavy in the air, like an early morning fog. "Why are you here?"

"Why am I here? Fuck, Celia, why do you think I'm here?"

I willed my fingers to stop trembling as I pulled a cigarette from the pack and lit up, remembering with the first drag why I had taken up smoking to begin with. I was also reminded of why I'd quit.

Him.

It was all because of him.

"I don't know, but you can show yourself out like Richard did," I stated flatly before slowly lowering myself onto a lawn chair. Judging by the penetrating ache in my chest, my brief stint as Rambo had just set back my recovery.

Jamie grabbed the other chair and dragged it over next to mine. "Ain't leavin', princess."

I exhaled a stream of smoke with a bitter laugh. "No? How ever will the club survive without you?"

"I'm out. Turned it over to Bear and walked away."

For the first time since that night, I was grateful for the dark, as I was sure shock was written all over my face. It was bittersweet—being given the one thing I had craved for eleven years at a point when it no longer meant anything.

Jamie fidgeted with something on his jeans before plucking the cigarette from my hand and taking a long drag. "Say somethin'."

"Why now?"

He absently stroked his beard before admitting, "I ain't done a lot right when it comes to you and the girls. I wanna be here to protect you—"

I abruptly stood up, wrenching the cigarette from his hand before pacing along the edge of the patio. "I think it's been proven that you can't protect me. You can't protect anyone. Showing up a month later doesn't change that."

The chair toppled over onto its side as he cut the distance between us. It was only then that I realized he was swaying unsteadily on his feet.

"Are you drunk?" I asked, just as he snapped, "I've been here the whole damn time!"

We both fell silent, taking in the other's words.

"Maybe I am drunk." He moved closer, and I stepped back until I came into contact with the brick siding.

"Why?" I whispered.

He lowered his forehead to mine, and I inhaled, breathing in the familiar scent of leather and cigarette smoke, along with the overwhelming stench of hard liquor on his breath.

"Why am I drunk, or why have I been here?" His arm hooked around my waist, drawing me up against his body. "Either way, it's the same answer. You."

His hand was like a vise against my injuries, the agonizing pressure stealing the breath from my lungs. Mistaking my gasp for something I was no longer capable of feeling, he tipped my face up and sucked my bottom lip in between his teeth.

So fuckin' good.

I jerked away, my head connecting painfully with the bricks at my back as I fought my way out of the cage he'd put me in. I thrust my knee into his groin, and he stumbled back with a groan.

"Don't touch me," I croaked, before doubling over with a ragged breath. With the waves of nausea came the flashbacks and an overwhelming sense of helplessness. My throat tightened, and I clawed at it, fighting to get air into my lungs.

"It's okay, darlin'," Jamie ground out through clenched teeth, before crawling over to where I knelt against the cold concrete.

Each gasp and wheeze was another sharp reminder that I wasn't okay. I would never be okay.

He kept his distance, but gripped my wrists in one hand. "I got you, princess. You're safe now. You're safe."

Jamie had been my safe place for as long as I could remember, but that was before.

Before Hawk's fists.

Before Manny's taunts.

Before Cobra's mouth.

Even with the sweatshirt between us, my skin sizzled from the heat of him. Hands that had held mine as I brought our daughter into the world were now searing and unwelcome against my body.

"Let me go," I whispered, keeping my gaze averted. "Please."

He dropped my hands immediately and rocked back onto his heels. "Jesus Christ, darlin'. What'd they do to you?"

I pulled the sleeves of the sweatshirt down over my hands. "It doesn't matter—"

"It does, goddammit." His voice broke, and he swiped the back of his hand over his eyes. "Please tell me."

"Are you crying?" The full weight of his grief settled over me, leaving me desperate for the cigarette I'd lost in the scuffle.

I wondered what it meant that Jamie was no longer the leader of Silent Phoenix. If his plan had been to abandon the club and come back home, then maybe my father was right.

My girls would never be safe.

As long as he was here, we would be vulnerable to another attack.

"Should've been here to protect you."

Three years ago, I had begged him to stay.

For me.

For the girls.

Now that he knew the depths his enemies would go to, he wanted to listen. Letting him back in would only turn the girls' world upside down. Not only that, but he couldn't even look at me with anything other than guilt and regret. Every time I stared into his blue eyes, I would be reminded of the violence I endured because he'd gotten cocky.

I would be forced to battle my demons and his.

All while the men who abused me got away with it.

With a deep breath, I steeled my spine and got to my feet while he remained on his knees beneath me. "I think you should go..."

"Don't do this, Celia." His hands connected with my knees. "Let me fix it."

Ignoring the ache in my chest, I raised my chin and said the only thing I could—the one thing that would save us all. "I'm not sure if they told you when you got here, but I paid my debt. You didn't need to come back."

He was on his feet in a second, towering over me. "Don't," he warned. "Don't fuckin' say it. You were never a debt—"

"Yet you collected. Not only that, but you reminded me constantly that we were nothing. So, as I said, I think you should go. There's nothing for you here."

Jamie was close enough that I could see the tears as they formed and spilled over onto his cheeks. It only left me with a sense of jealousy.

Why wasn't he broken like me?

"Darlin', you don't mean that. We built a life... a family—"

"I built a life and a family while you were off with your club," I hissed. "You don't get to come in now to be a part of it. I want you to leave—"

"No, goddammit! This is important—"

"The only things that are important to me are inside that house. Go back to your club, Jamie." Avoiding his eyes, I turned toward the door. I wanted nothing more than to run inside and hide out in my bed, but I had to be strong.

"Just like that, huh?" I looked back as he ran a hand through his hair and began pacing again. "You're gonna file for divorce after eleven years? Like it didn't mean shit to you?"

I took a deep breath, fighting to hold on to my resolve. "I don't need a divorce..."

"Thank Christ."

"You're already dead, so I'll settle for being a widow. It's over." I hurried inside, ignoring the painful sound of him gasping for air.

He didn't come after me.

I walked the house—too keyed up for sleep.

I alternated between hoping he'd believed my lies and wanting to take back my every word. The tremors that had been confined to my hands now spread throughout my entire body until I lay shaking on the couch.

I had torn open his chest and ripped out his heart under some delusional idea that I was saving us.

All of us.

At the angry rumble of Jamie's bike firing up and speeding off into the night, I let out the breath I'd been holding since walking away from him.

He was gone.

I didn't know how long I laid there, haunted by my actions and second-guessing my decision before I decided to get some sleep.

A shudder passed through my body as I stared into the dark master bedroom. Without the drugs to numb me, I was a coward who was suddenly afraid of the dark and had been sleeping on the couch.

I snagged an afghan off the back of the recliner and wrapped it around my shoulders before going into the girls' room.

The sound of their deep breathing filled the air as I settled into the old armchair where I'd nursed and kept them safe. It gave me peace. I might not have been able to save myself, but they would come out of this unscathed.

In the end, that was all that mattered.

Jamie would go back to the club and hunt down the men responsible, and I would fight to be the mother they deserved. I closed my eyes, seeing Jamie's tears.

When was the last time I'd seen him cry?

It had to have been Kate's first birthday when Mikey had stayed over. He'd always kept his heart under lock and key, but in those rare moments of emotion, I realized just how good he really was. And I'd fallen in love with him a little more.

What if I'd broken him?

If my plan backfired, then I'd just sent my husband into a suicidal downward spiral by taking away everything he loved. What if the club wouldn't take him back?

No.

I couldn't let myself consider the possibility.

Because, if I was wrong, then we were all dead.

CHAPTER TEN

Grey: June 2001 (Age: 37)

"Jesus Christ, Grey."

I rolled over, blinking against the sudden brightness streaming in through the open door. "If you're wakin' me up this early, your ass better have brought coffee."

"Coffee?" Slim laughed. "It's five o'clock in the fuckin' afternoon, dickhead. Bear got some intel on the Serpents. Club's just waitin' on you. Get up."

The pounding in my head demanded I sleep off the hangover before doing shit, but I'd spent the better part of six months trying to find the fuckers who laid hands on my wife.

I peeled myself out from under the damp sheets, stumbling over my boots and last night's clothes as I took in the unfamiliar room. "Where the fuck are we, Slim?"

"Motel, just outside of Pearland," he answered before looking up at me. "Fuck! Put some goddamn clothes on!"

My cock jutted up against my belly, clearly not giving a damn that morning wood was typically reserved for the morning. It didn't matter that she'd ended things between us. Every day I woke up harder than a fucking rock, with the image of her in my head.

That was all it took.

It was just like the old days. I should have been impressed that an old fuck like me could walk around with a constant hard-on without the help of a little blue pill.

Comedian had tried sending me whores, but I refused to touch another woman. I'd made a vow, and if that meant I spent the rest of my life jacking off six or seven times a day to thoughts of her like some teenage boy, so be it.

"You hear me, fucker?" He turned around. "Jesus Christ, Grey! The fuck is wrong with you?"

I watched, mesmerized, as my hand moved up and down my shaft like it didn't even belong to me anymore. "It's doing it all by itself, Slim. Polite thing to do would be to let it finish."

"You ain't hungover—you're still strung out. What the fuck did you take?"

My hand continued stroking as I sauntered over and took a swig from the half-empty bottle of tequila on the dresser. I scanned the room, just as curious as Slim to see what I'd done.

The weeks and months since leaving her had been spent finding new and creative ways to fuck myself up. If I did it just right, I'd buy myself a few hours where I didn't see her broken body.

I didn't have to watch her self-destruct just from me touching her or see the message they'd sent in the form of blood and bruises.

The numbness kept me sane until it was time to kill again. Then, and only then, did I allow myself to feel it. We may not have found the three responsible, but the trail of bodies left in my wake told me I was getting closer.

My eyes landed on the bag of blow sitting on the nightstand at the same time Slim's did.

His jaw tightened, and he shook his head. "I'll never understand why in the hell Bear allowed the club to vote you back in as Pres. You're a fuckin' train wreck, you know that? And if there's anyone who should be completely fucked in the head, it's still not you—it's her!"

He was right.

Somehow, she had found the strength to go on where I woke up alone every day, reminded of the fact that I'd failed at the most basic of tasks—keeping her safe.

Whatever remained of my high faded, and I dropped, bare-assed, onto the bed with a groan. "You heard from Wolverine or Angel? How's she doin'?"

Slim tossed me the jeans from the floor. "Ain't discussing your Ol' Lady while your dick's hangin' out."

It took talking my cock down and falling into the wall twice before I got the denim on. "Okay. I'm fuckin' decent. You happy now?"

He sat in the beaten-down armchair and lit up a cigarette. "Wolverine helped her get a job—"

"A job?" I interrupted. "Why? She has the bank account he set up. There's more than enough in there for her and the girls to live comfortably."

"She ain't used one cent of that money, Grey. He found her a job doing the back-office stuff for a bakery—it's one of ours, but I can't recall the name. Anyway, she don't know the club's runnin' it." He took a long drag and ran his hand over his face.

It didn't make a damn bit of sense. If Celia was hellbent on doing something outside of the house, she could have used the money and taken college classes while Kate and Dakota were in school.

I frowned. "Wait. It's summer. Where are the girls?"

Slim looked down at the threadbare carpet. "They—well, there's no easy way to say this, but she and the girls moved in with her parents. I guess they're keeping them while she works."

"What?" I began pacing the shitty motel room. "Why the fuck would she go there? She hates her parents! I gave her the goddamn house... the car... money."

"She's selling the house. Wolverine said he didn't blame her—hard to feel safe in a place like that."

"So, she thinks she's just gonna sell my childhood home and I'm not gonna have shit to say about that?"

Slim exhaled a cloud of smoke in my direction. "The fuck you gonna do about it, Grey? According to the authorities, you're dead. And, in the great state of Texas, everything passes on to your widow. You don't get to say shit about shit."

I eyed him warily. "Don't call her that. Don't fuckin' call her that word."

"What? A widow? That's what you made her, right? When you walked out on her and the girls—"

"That's enough, Slim," I growled. "Don't make me tell you again."

He ran his tongue over his teeth with a grin. "Oh, yeah? How many times have you gone up against me and won over the years?"

With a heaving chest, I stumbled over to the nightstand and took a bump of blow while glaring up at Slim, silently daring him to stop me.

"Goddammit, Jamie." He stabbed the cigarette out in the ashtray and stood up.

"Ain't a fuckin' line, Slim. Just takin' the edge off."

"Takin' the edge off? The edge off of what?"

The pain in my head lessened, and I stood up straighter, finally feeling in control again. A line was for forgetting, but a bump was good for just existing. "Excuse the fuck out of me, but you're the one who barged into my room, droppin' the family shit on me before I was fully awake—"

"You asked about your Ol' Lady first, asshole." His gaze softened. "After what she went through, she deserves to move on, Grey. If she feels it's best for her and the girls—"

My fist struck his jaw with a satisfying smack, the momentum sending me staggering past him and into the dresser. The tequila toppled off and landed on its side, distracting me just long enough for Slim to react.

He barreled into me like a freight train, and we both went down in a tangle of limbs. I blocked his first punch—the coke in my bloodstream convincing me I was invincible.

Unfortunately, the feeling was brief as his second, third, and fourth hits were all painfully accurate.

I clutched my gut just as he swung again, connecting with the side of my head. The throbbing that had all but disappeared only moments ago now returned with a vengeance.

"You gettin' sick of old men kickin' your ass yet, or you wanna keep goin'?" he asked with a snarl.

When I remained silent, he glanced a warning blow off my ribs. "Last chance, asshole. I don't give a fuck if you're Pres or not. It was a fuckin' cheap shot, and your ass is gonna pay."

I closed my eyes and nodded. "Fuckin' hell, Slim. You're supposed to slow down in your old age—"

"Quit the drugs. We clear?"

My stomach churned from the adrenaline and the effects of his fists, leaving me ready to hurl on the carpet. I worked on getting my breathing under control before answering. "Slim, why are you even here? Thought you went Nomad."

Using his hand, he shifted his jaw from side to side before popping it back into place. "Seems without Wolverine and Angel around, I'm the only one who can talk any goddamn sense into you. I guess that makes me your handler. Now, get up and get your ass in the shower. We got things to discuss."

I got up and slammed the bathroom door shut behind me like a bratty child. So, maybe my drinking and using had gotten a little out of hand. I was still doing spades better than most of the fuckers around me.

Comedian had fucked off on a week-long bimbo bender after Betsy and Mike disappeared before sampling every drug we sold. Hell, when Bear found out Molly was knocked up, he'd promptly attempted to drown himself in vodka.

But, oh no.

"John 'Fuckin' Killjoy' Greene can't let me escape reality for one goddamn second," I grumbled to myself as I stepped under the showerhead.

The water pressure was shit, raining lukewarm water down on me like a weak stream of piss one second and stripping the skin off my back the next.

By the time I worked the soap into a lather, my cock was demanding attention again. With a grunt, I slapped a palm against the tile wall to steady myself before taking it in my fist.

Instead of conjuring up one of my usual fantasies of Celia, I kept coming back to Slim's confession. Imagining her doing the books wasn't working, so I tried picturing her decorating cakes before the rational part of my brain took over.

I saw her, as if she was right in front of me, wearing nothing but an apron. Her hair fell across one shoulder as she looked back at me before leaning over the long metal table in front of her.

In a fantasy that felt more real than anything I had experienced over the last six months, Celia reached back and untied the apron, giving me an even better view of her perfect ass. When she slipped it over her head and tossed it aside, I began pumping my cock in desperation. She ran her tongue over her lower lip before hopping up onto the table and spreading her legs, inviting me in.

This was the best high I'd ever had.

I imagined positioning her on the edge of the table until her ass was damn near hanging off before burying myself to the hilt inside her tight pussy.

My teeth scraped over the white substance that coated her nipples, and I decided it was powdered sugar, not blow. My girl was good enough to eat.

More.

Vivid scenes played out in my mind, each one hotter than the last. I spread cake frosting on her belly and sucked chocolate sauce off her clit until the pressure in my spine increased, and I couldn't hold back any longer. I let out a low growl as my dick jerked against my hand, coating the tile in front of me.

Shame immediately flooded my body, and I let out a ragged breath before dropping my chin down to my chest. I was so far beyond fucked up that there wasn't even a word for it.

It felt wrong imagining her like that, knowing what those bastards had done to her.

Knowing that I'd caused it.

I shut off the shower just as there was a quiet knock at the door. "Grey?"

"Yeah, Slim. I'll be out in a second." I wrapped a towel around my waist and stared into the mirror until the truth was staring back.

The king of death and the goddess of life.

She'd never belonged with me.

I just hadn't wanted to see it back then.

I saw it now though.

CHAPTER ELEVEN

Mike: June 2001 (Age: 18)

"You can't surf for shit. Didn't you say you grew up around the water?" The kid laughed, pushing his damp dark hair out of his face as I struggled to get back on my feet.

Since getting my license two years ago, I had been making the drive from Beaumont to Galveston anytime I was free. Unfortunately, the kid in front of me was here about as often as I was. He worked at *A-Frame Surf* on Seawall and had sold me my first board.

Maybe I stretched the truth when I said that I'd grown up on the water. There had been a playa lake near our house, so that counted for something, right?

Mom and I had been down here for going on six years. Almost five whole years without my father in the picture. Grey had shown up in the middle of the night, lifting my lanky thirteen-year-old body out of bed and carrying me outside to an unfamiliar truck. I had been half awake as he settled me into the backseat but pretended to be asleep as he spoke in low tones with my mother, before drawing out a map of where she needed to go. When she cried, he had pulled her into a hug.

"Betsy, he won't find you—I'll make sure of it. He's goin' on a run for the next three nights. Once he gets back, we'll pretend to look into it, but he'll never be in the same town as you or Mikey again."

At the time, I thought he was protecting us from the bad guys. It wasn't until we had gotten settled in our new home that I realized he was protecting us from my father. I hadn't seen the point of it, really. I had already witnessed the murder of two people—how much worse could it get? My old man was hell bent on me turning out just like him and working my way up in the club, while Grey still didn't think I was cut out for club life.

Almost overnight, my mom had become a new person. Thanks to Grey, we had a house and enough money to ensure we never worried about a thing. For the first time in my life, she was focused on making friends and even joined a women's church group.

One rainy Saturday, while up in my room doing homework, I heard something strange. When I crept downstairs, I found my mother humming in the kitchen as she baked pies. Flour coated almost everything, but she had a big smile on her face. I must have stared at her for what seemed like hours, certain that aliens had abducted her. I couldn't recall the last time I'd seen her smile so freely.

Not long after our arrival in Beaumont, we got word that Grey had been killed. There weren't a lot of details included in the anonymous letter—just that he'd been gunned down by a rival club member. We were informed that he'd left us money, which was wired over to us days later.

My mother had dropped the letter onto the kitchen counter and promptly disappeared for the rest of the evening. I'd sat on the stool nearby, reading the words over and over until I knew them by heart. I didn't cry—I knew he wouldn't have wanted me to fall apart. He'd have tucked a finger under my chin and told me to be brave for my mama. I remember wondering if Katy and her baby sister, Dakota, were being brave like me.

It was until lunchtime the following day when my mother emerged from her bedroom, eyes bloodshot. She hadn't said a word before pulling me into her arms and rocking me on the couch. I think she was afraid that my dad would find us without Grey there to misdirect him.

"You gone deaf from that fall, Mike? I'm talking to you." I tried to recall the kid's name—Patrick. Or was it Roy? Either way, the guy had been a royal pain in my ass from day one. Rich little shit, thinking he owned the beach.

"Hey, don't listen to him, Mike. The guy's a poser." My best friend, David, panted as he dragged his board up on the damp sand beside us. He shook his head like a dog, sending sprays of water in every direction.

His mother and mine had met through the Bible study group at church. They'd introduced us when I was thirteen and he was fifteen and we'd been inseparable ever since. His dad, John, was in construction and reminded me a lot of Grey—down to the tattoos on his arms.

David was the most unassuming person I'd ever met. He didn't ask about my life in Lubbock. He just wanted to know if I had any good video games. After that, I was in.

He graduated and began working for his dad, but we still hit the beach together every chance we got. I'd graduated a couple of months ago, so I knew my days of freeloading off my mom were coming to an end. I had to enjoy every last moment of it.

"Hey, Mike—you looked good out there," Sadie tossed over her shoulder as she walked past with her board tucked under her arm and my heart immediately started pounding in response. She could've walked past and told me I couldn't surf for shit and I still would've been following her like a damn puppy.

I bit the inside of my cheek to keep from grinning. "Yeah? You almost kept up with me this time."

Roy/Patrick made a noise of disgust and stormed off down the beach. Sadie watched him go before turning back around to face me. "You sure talk a good game, but could you ever back it up?"

David shook his own head in laughter before heading toward the seawall. "You're on your own here, dude. I'll meet you back at the truck."

"There's not much I'm afraid of, if that's what you're asking." I snatched my towel up off the beach and casually tossed it over my shoulder. *Smooth, Mike. Nice and smooth.*

Sadie's hair was starting to dry and the salt from the ocean left it with a slight wave. "Alright, tough guy. You got a longboard?"

Without missing a beat, I responded, "I can get one. Why? You takin' me on a date?"

She shook her head. "Let's just see how you do with this before we get ahead of ourselves. Meet me here at six-thirty tomorrow morning?"

I agreed, still completely unaware of what I'd just signed up for.

CHAPTER TWELVE

Mike: June 2001 (Age: 18)

"C'mon, you motherfucker." I panted as I paddled in front of the perfect wave. I'd been getting my ass kicked by these all day—not at all what I needed when I was trying to impress Sadie.

Tanker surfing.

That had been her big challenge. We chartered a boat for over six hundred dollars to take us out a few miles, chasing after ships in the channel. I'd convinced David to come out with me, only to try to back out when we pulled up and saw Patrick/Roy waiting with Sadie.

It turned out that his first name was Patrick and his last name was Roy—I only discovered this when the driver of the boat introduced himself as Captain Roy... Patrick's dad. He was actually an alright guy and had been running chartered tours like ours for decades. He spent a long time going over the safety instructions before we ever left the harbor. I lied, saying that I was an experienced surfer.

Ten hours later, I was cursing my big mouth. I'd been battered by wave after wave all fucking day. Even Captain Roy had caught on to my lies a few hours in. I'd gotten an earful from him about how I was putting everybody in jeopardy, including him, every time I went down early. I guess with all the ships crossing, there was a chance of his boat getting swamped or pulled into the ship's current.

I'd sucked down a bottle of ice cold water while nodding at the appropriate times. Patrick, Sadie, and David had all managed to get a few hundred yards in each run, while I rode after them in the boat with Captain Roy.

This was my wave, though—David had tried giving me a few pointers each time we got back in the boat together and I think I finally had it down. If I ever wanted to see Sadie naked, I needed this to go well.

When the wave reached me, I jumped up into a low squat, using my arms to steady myself. Once I realized I wasn't going under, I stood up straighter, just keeping my knees slightly bent, with my right leg leading. I wanted to throw my fists toward the sky, while giving a war cry, but I needed to keep my arms still to avoid wiping out.

After a few minutes, I knew I had it and tentatively raised one arm in the air. I hoped Sadie was seeing this—she had to go out with me now. David let out a whoop from a few yards behind me, and I grinned. I'd gone at least a few hundred yards, which was the longest I'd ever stayed on a board.

"You're nothing but a kook, Sullivan, and Sadie ain't going anywhere with you!" Patrick's words caused my jaw to clench and the smile to leave my face.

I turned on my board to find him, only realizing my mistake when the wave forced me underwater. I'd lost my balance because of that asshole. Pain shot through my right calf and my vision blurred as I pushed my way back up to the surface.

Patrick was already a good twenty yards ahead of me by the time I broke through the water. The sea had pummeled me all day, but this wave had been like a brick wall. My leg throbbed, and I tried stretching it out as I waited for Captain Roy to circle back around with the boat. Maybe I'd torqued a muscle when I fell. I pulled myself back up onto the board and that's when I saw it. My lower leg was bleeding heavily—the wave had thrown me into an oyster reef. I just knew it. The bay was full of them. If that hadn't been enough, Captain Roy had warned us about them damn near every chance he'd gotten.

I tried propping my leg up on the board, well aware that a bleeding leg in the ocean was an invitation to predators. My nerves kicked in just as Captain Roy drove up with the boat. I knew I was going to have to pull myself back in, but my right leg was quickly becoming useless.

I paddled over and somehow managed to get myself up and back into the boat. Captain Roy was over to me in a second. "Shit, kid. Looks like you got a leg full of oyster reef when you fell. You had it too —if you wouldn't have turned your entire body, you would've stayed up."

I bit my tongue, resisting the urge to tell him about what a prick his son was as he poured bottled water over my wound, cleansing it as best he could.

"You're gonna need stitches. Let's get the others and get you to the emergency room."

I groaned and let my head fall back against a cushion. "Can't you just superglue it? Or wrap it up?"

He shook his head grimly before tossing me a towel. "You're losing a lot of blood. It's best not to wait around, hoping it'll stop." He sat back down and directed the boat toward the others.

Sadie's smirk faded the minute she pulled herself up and saw my leg. "Oh, Mike. You poor thing!"

I kept my face stoic. "It's just a scratch—Captain Roy wants me to get it checked out, but I'll be fine."

She set her board aside before sitting down next to me, taking my hand in hers. I would've bailed off my board a lot earlier had I known I'd get this treatment.

David climbed up next and his brow wrinkled. "What the hell happened to you?"

I shrugged. "Made friends with the ocean floor—I'm good." I unwrapped the towel to show him I was fine as blood pumped steadily from my wound. Maybe I should've been more worried—I was starting to get dizzy.

Patrick was the last to get back on the boat. His face paled when he saw Sadie's hand in mine. I winked at him. "Some wave back there, man."

He nodded absently before sitting down across from us, his eyes never leaving our hands.

Once we reached the harbor, Captain Roy made a big fuss of

getting me off the boat and back to our truck. After arguing that we didn't need him to drive us to the hospital, he went back to settle things up with the boat. David helped me into the bed of the pickup truck. "You gotta sit back here. I don't want blood all over my seats."

I agreed and tried to get comfortable against the metal.

"You got room for one more?" Sadie asked as she climbed over the tailgate.

I nodded, my mouth dry. I wanted to remember the way she looked at this moment—with the sunlight hitting her face and highlighting her blonde hair. That's when I knew I must've lost a lot of blood—her tits were practically falling out of her swimsuit top and I was hung up on her hair.

Patrick insisted on joining us as well, but David had him follow us in his Jeep, leaving me and Sadie to ourselves.

I was going to owe him big time for this.

CHAPTER THIRTEEN

Mike: July 2001 (Age: 18)

Either the emergency room was having a slow Saturday night or the nurses were afraid I was going to create a river of blood through the waiting room, because they wasted no time in getting me back to a room.

An hour later, I'd been disinfected and diagnosed with a pretibial flap laceration—medical speak for a fucked-up shin. The doctor explained that they'd have to use Steri-Strips to close the wound, as the skin was too thin for stitches. Then, to add insult to my injury, she told me I had to be off of it for at least the next few days and out of the water until it was completely healed.

I punched the plastic bedrail in frustration. I'd just gotten somewhere with Sadie—it was crucial that I be back out on the water tomorrow or risk losing her to Patrick.

Fucking Patrick.

He was probably cozying up to her in the waiting room while they worked to close my leg up.

"I called your mom." David shut the curtain behind him and walked over to the bed.

"And?" I asked. Knowing my mom, she was probably sick with

worry and headed up here. Just what I needed for Sadie to see—Mikey's mommy taking care of him.

Well, this day had officially gone to shit.

David grinned. "She said she'd expected something like that with all the 'surfing experience' you had. Then she gave the nurse her insurance information and told me to make sure you got home safely."

I frowned. "She's not coming down here? Was she drunk?" My mom wasn't a drinker—not even close—but that was the only plausible explanation for why she hadn't flipped out.

He shook his head and rocked on his heels. "She sounded fine. Don't get me wrong, she was worried, but we're basically grown men now."

I agreed as the doc finished up. "Okay, Mr. Sullivan, we're all done. I'll get you a prescription for pain medication, as you're going to be hurting a lot over the next few days."

They gave me a card for a follow-up appointment in a few weeks—probably wanted to make sure my leg hadn't rotted and fallen off by then. That'd just be my luck.

Once everything was squared away, they wheeled me out into the waiting room, where Patrick and Sadie were waiting. She jumped up when she saw me, while Patrick glared right through me.

"Are you going to be okay?" She leaned down and stroked my arm. I was disappointed to see that she was wearing a hoodie now—I'd declined IV pain meds so that I'd be alert enough to appreciate the view this time around.

That'd been pointless, obviously.

"Well, the doctor had some pretty specific instructions in order for me to heal." I bit the inside of my cheek to keep from smiling.

Her brow furrowed in concern. "Like what?"

I sighed and looked down. "Well, I've got to stay off of it and keep it elevated. She also said I was going to need a date with you—that part was crucial. I could lose my leg."

"You've gotta be fucking kidding me," Patrick muttered to himself.

I shook my head. "I'm dead serious, Patty."

He balled his hands into fists, but remained seated on the plastic chair.

Sadie pressed her lips into a flat line. "Is that right? Well, who am I to go against doctor's orders?"

David glanced down at his phone. "You need anything from your truck? I gotta get home—I'm helping my dad early tomorrow morning on a job."

I hadn't even considered that I wouldn't be able to drive myself home. Maybe someone would pick it up and get it back to me tomorrow.

"Shoot, what time is it? I was supposed to be home by eleven!" Sadie turned to David.

"It's ten fifty. We can give you a ride home first and then get the stuff out of your truck, Mike."

Patrick stood up and stretched. "Why don't you run Sadie home, David? I can take Mike to his truck and then we'll meet you."

I rolled my eyes. *Yeah, right.* Since when was Patrick helpful?

David frowned. "Are you sure?"

Patrick clapped him on the back. "Absolutely—you get her home and I'll help Mike get whatever he needs. That way, everyone gets home on time."

I was all set to protest when Sadie leaned down and pressed her lips to mine. "Call me tomorrow." Then she and David were running out to his truck, and the words died on my lips. Patrick could take me to prom at this point and I wouldn't care.

We drove in silence, and I replayed that kiss repeatedly in my mind. So, I couldn't drive, but maybe Sadie could come to my house. I could get rid of my mom for a few hours.

Patrick made a left when he should have gone right and I looked over at him. "You missed the turn, Patty."

He didn't respond and continued out of town.

"Yo, Patrick. Harbor's back that way. You don't have to take me home yourself."

I wasn't scared, but tense. I'd willingly gotten into a vehicle with a guy who hated me. Patrick pulled into an empty parking lot and killed the engine.

"Get out."

I stared at him. "You're joking, right? I can't walk, thanks to the shit you pulled earlier."

He pulled the keys from the ignition and jumped down, slamming the door shut behind him. I opened my door and stepped down with my left leg. *What did he expect me to do—hop over to him?*

"C'mon, man, let's talk about this."

He came up so fast that I didn't even have time to process it before his fist was in my face. My jaw popped from the force and if I hadn't grabbed the door handle, I would've gone down.

"I told you to stay away from Sadie, but you didn't listen. Here's a reminder." His fist hit my stomach, and the force knocked the air from my lungs.

The memory hit me as I leaned over, gasping for my next breath.

"You're gonna have guys that want to kick your ass—it's just part of being a man. Your mom wants you to run and find a teacher or another adult, but I ain't raising no pussy. You gotta fight back." This had been said when I was ten, after I'd gotten my nose bloodied by a sixth grader on the bus ride home.

My father had come in after my mom cleaned me up and told me to stand. *"Put your fists up, Junior. Let's see what you got."* I brought my fists up, just like they did on television. He began making quick jabs along my ribs and it didn't matter how much I moved my arms, I couldn't block him. My eyes had welled with tears, but I knew crying would only make things worse for me. When he knocked the air out of me, I'd remained upright, arms still held out in front of me.

"No, no, no—don't lower your arms. Keep your right arm up, ready to strike. Use your left arm to block body shots. Watch the other guy—his eyes are gonna go where he's aiming. Don't waste your time with body shots. He's just tiring himself out. When he least expects it, drive your fist under his chin, just like in baseball when you swing it out of the park. Give it everything you've got..."

Patrick came at me again and, despite the throbbing pain running from my jaw down to my leg, I held him off. He took a step back, panting. His eyes were completely unfocused, and I knew I wouldn't get another opportunity.

I let go of the door handle and put weight on both legs. Then I swung my fist up under his chin with every bit of strength I possessed.

His eyes rolled back and he went down immediately. The back of his head connected against the curb with a loud crack.

I'd done it.

I'd torn my shin open again, but I'd done it. I'd taken my old man's advice and come out of the whole thing no worse for the wear. I opened my mouth and rotated my jaw back and forth—well, only slightly worse than I was before.

My phone rang.

"Mike, where are you? I'm down by your truck."

I turned away from Patrick and looked over at the sign hidden among weeds. "The fucker jumped me, David. We're at that old strip club, *Captain's Quarters*. You're gonna have to come get me—my leg's torn open again."

He cursed and then told me he'd be right over. Patrick made an odd sound. I hobbled over to him, hoping David made it here before the prick woke up. I didn't think I could take him on again in the shape I was in.

Headlights illuminated the parking lot when David pulled up. He surveyed the scene with a low whistle. "Holy shit, you knocked him out?"

I nodded. "Should we move him back into his Jeep?"

Patrick made a gurgling sound, bloody foam leaking out of his mouth. I'd never knocked a guy out before, but I was pretty sure that wasn't normal. We'd only taken a couple of steps toward him when he started convulsing violently.

I looked at David in horror. "Fuck! What do we do?"

Patrick's body shook for another minute before it finally came to a stop. My shoulders relaxed, and I took a deep breath.

"Thank God."

David leaned over him. "Uh, Mike? We've got a problem—he's not breathing."

I pushed through the pain and hunched down next to David. "What do you mean, he's not breathing? Why isn't he breathing? Fucking do something, David!"

He shot me an incredulous look. "What the fuck am I supposed to do, Mike? How hard did you hit him?"

I grabbed onto Patrick's shoulders and shook him, but got no response. Blood ran from the side of his mouth and I knew I was in deep shit.

David started pacing. "We could drop him off in the ER—explain what happened. You're gonna have to get your shin fixed up again."

I nodded. "Okay, let's get him in the back of your truck."

We lifted him up and carried him back to the truck, while I prayed Patrick would sit up in our arms to tell us to fuck off and that the whole thing had been a joke.

He took the turn toward the hospital. "Stop!" I yelled, and he slammed on the brakes. "We can't take him. They'll arrest me!"

He stared at me incredulously. "What the hell are we supposed to do then, Mike? Leave him in the back of my truck?"

I pulled my phone from my pocket. "Just give me a second." The phone rang three times before someone finally picked up.

CHAPTER FOURTEEN

Grey: July 2001 (Age: 37)

"Why are you so goddamn cheerful?" I snarled, as I passed Comedian coming up the stairs with a plastic ice bucket in one hand and a bottle of whiskey in the other.

He stopped whistling and grinned down at me from a few steps above. "Life is good, Pres. Life is good."

My own smile faded. "Is it?"

I wanted to knock the smirk off his face. Bear's tip on the Serpents had been worthless. By the time we made it to League City, all traces of them were gone. It was like they'd never even been there. No matter what we did, we were always going to be one step behind.

"C'mon, Grey," Slim urged, steering me over toward my bike.

I straddled it, watching Comedian as he made it to the second-floor landing and entered a room. "The fuck has he got to be happy about?"

My wife and daughters were living with two people I hated. And unless the Serpents were going to suddenly appear, ready to surrender, I didn't see any part of our lives that could have been considered good.

Slim rubbed his neck. "You ain't gonna like it."

"What?" I asked distractedly, taking in the cracked windows and missing shingles on the roof of the motel. I didn't even know why we were still here. The place was a complete shit hole. It was a wonder it hadn't been condemned.

"Betsy's back."

Two words that had me climbing off my bike and heading for the stairs. "I'm gonna fuckin' kill 'em both."

"Grey," Slim jogged up behind. "Just wait a goddamn second. She thinks you're dead—"

I gripped the railing, not missing the way it moved with my body. "She's about to be. How many times did I warn her not to come lookin' for him, Slim?"

"Mikey ain't a kid anymore. Hell, we just watched him graduate a couple months back."

I looked up at the door. "What am I supposed to do? Let her come after Comedian like a junkie in need of a fix? Me bein' alive is the least of our worries if she keeps hangin' around. You know that, right?"

Slim placed a hand on my shoulder. "Let's go grab a beer and some grub at the bar across the road. If you still feel like killin' the two of them after... then I'll help you bury the bodies. Let's just think about it first."

I kicked a patch of gravel with the toe of my boot before following him across the nearly deserted highway. The white and yellow stripes had long since faded, making the area seem like a ghost town.

Given the abundance of big rigs and motorcycles in the bar's parking lot, the only people stupid enough to be out this way were truckers and criminals.

Luckily, we managed to stay out of each other's way just fine.

The bell above the door jingled, and every head turned in our direction. Upon seeing who it was, most looked away again almost immediately. The only ones who maintained eye contact were the ones who shared the same patch.

Bear held up a shot glass, but Slim waved him off and led me to a booth in the back. After ordering us a couple of pitchers of beer, he sat back and watched me. "David's been teaching Mikey to surf. Kid's complete shit at it, but keeps showin' up."

The corner of my mouth lifted, and I took a swig from my pint glass. "Sounds like his old man, doesn't it? Reminds me of the time we went to the lake house with Phantom."

I made a sign of the cross and added, "God rest his soul. Thought we were just gonna spend the weekend fishin', but he dug out the damn water skis."

Slim grinned. "Jesus, I forgot about that. You were awful. My old man said you must've been part fish with the way you kept going under. It's funny... I thought he was invincible back then. I guess in the end, he handled everything but a bad heart."

We slipped back into silence, drinking our beers and remembering a time when shit wasn't complicated. It sure as hell hadn't felt that way at the time, but at least back then I'd known how to fix things. Donald wanted to beat on my mother? I'd step in and take it for her.

Problem solved.

Faking my death was supposed to have ended the threats. Instead, the Donalds of the world had gone after the easiest target.

Her.

"What are you thinkin' about?"

I picked at the cracked Formica. "It seems a little fuckin' obvious now, but don't you think our lives were easier then?"

Slim put the menu down. "You know the guys used to give me shit for settlin' down right out of high school. Some even tried to say that Lou was forcin' me into marriage. There were a couple of times I wondered if maybe I should've fucked around with other girls, just to be sure I was makin' the right decision—"

"Did you?" I was genuinely curious. I'd given him hell a few times, but never once thought I'd gotten under his skin. It always seemed he knew exactly what he wanted—a patch... Lou... even David. If Slim made a decision, he stuck with it, for better or worse.

He shook his head. "I couldn't. She was it—then and now. Why would I want to go back to bein' an insecure teenager, knowin' what I do as a thirty-nine-year-old man? For that matter, why would you? You were dealt a shitty hand, but ain't no way was your life better without Celia or your kids."

"I lost every single one of 'em, Slim," I said softly, keeping my eyes on the table. "You tell me how that's better. At least with Ma, I knew how to keep her safe. The enemy was one man, and I gladly took those beatings. Now, I don't even know who to trust or how in the hell I'm supposed to fix any of this."

The waitress walked up and took one look at us before slinking away again.

"We fix it by trackin' these fuckers down and sendin' 'em to the Reaper." He ran the tip of his index finger around the rim of his empty glass. "The rest we'll figure out together."

Suddenly aware of the quiet, I looked around the bar at my brothers. Bear and Torch were deep in conversation at a table near the door; most likely discussing their weapons strategy. Others sat on bar stools or gathered around the three tables that had been pushed together to form one.

The mood was somber, as if they were just as pissed as I was over us not having one damn lead on the Serpents.

I'd been so preoccupied with Celia that I hadn't had time to think about what leaving the club would've meant for me. These were men who'd offered to go to battle for me, no questions asked. They'd kept watch over my daughters while Celia was recovering, and not once had I worried that they'd turn on me.

I might've come into the world an only child, but the men around me were my brothers, in every sense of the word.

It could've been the pitcher of beer I'd downed, or maybe I'd never sobered up from the last time. Either way, now seemed as good a time as any to turn into a sentimental jackass and drag my sins into the light.

"They raped her, John."

He blew out a sharp breath and dragged a hand through his hair before bringing it back to rest against his forehead. "They—you're sure? I mean... fuck!"

I squeezed my eyes shut and pinched the bridge of my nose. "Say we do find 'em, it doesn't change what happened to her. I can't fix it."

"No, you can't fix it, but if we destroy the threat, it gives Celia at least a fightin' chance at recovering."

The muscle in my jaw tightened. "How in the hell am I supposed to look her in the eye and promise to protect her when I've already proven I can't do shit to keep her safe?"

Slim sat back, draping his arm over the back of the booth. "You don't." When I flinched, he shook his head. "What do you want me to say? That you can show up like before and fix everything with your dick? Think about it, Grey. She's always been the one to come after you—"

"That ain't true! I went after her when Betsy took her to Vic's... and when I found out she was hurt..."

I wracked my brain, trying to come up with another instance.

"Isn't it? You only go after her when you're tryin' to fix the shit you caused in the first place. When have you ever shown up for her? Not to gain somethin' or get her to fall in line, but just for her?"

CHAPTER FIFTEEN

Grey: July 2001 (Age: 37)

I opened my mouth to argue, only to realize he was right. It had always been about me. Even that night on the patio had been about me selfishly thinking I could be the one to put her back together.

Instead, I'd only hurt her more.

"You've gotta keep showin' up, but ultimately, it's her decision. You can want her to choose you from now until the world ends, but if that's not what she wants, you've gotta be okay with walkin' away."

I swiped the pint glass off the table with the back of my hand, sending shards of glass across the wood floor. "I ain't ever walkin' away, asshole."

"Good," Slim dryly noted over the ringing of his phone. "Glad to see you're gonna be mature about this. Now, my kid's callin'. You think you can keep your temper in check for a goddamn second?"

I shrugged and watched in amusement as our waitress reappeared, wide-eyed and holding a broom. "Bumped it with my elbow."

She nodded shakily and began sweeping it up, keeping her eyes on the floor.

Slim flipped me off and answered the phone with an easy grin.

"Hey. You're still in Galveston? Thought you were gonna help me out tomorrow mornin'—he what? Shit. How bad is it? You call Betsy?"

At the mention of her name, an electrical current of awareness raced through my body, and I mouthed one word.

Mikey.

He held a finger up with a nod. "Tell me where his truck is. Just leave the key in the wheel well, and I'll have someone swing by and get it. Yeah, call your mama and let her know. Love you too, kid."

My heart was lodged somewhere in my throat as I waited for him to break the news. It didn't escape my attention that this was the second time someone else had gotten a phone call meant for me.

"He's gonna be fine," Slim immediately said. "Busted his leg open surfin' and they had to take him to the ER to stitch him back together."

I flopped back against the booth with a relieved laugh. "Jesus, he really does take after his old man."

Instead of seizing the moment and giving me shit, Slim dropped a wad of cash on the table and slid out of the booth.

"Where are you goin'? Thought you said he was fine." When he didn't respond, I jumped up and followed him outside. "Slim! Goddammit, Slim!"

He stopped in the middle of the highway and faced me. The vein in his neck pulsed rapidly, and his hands clenched into fists. "I was wrong!"

Seeing that we had an audience, I waved everyone else back into the bar. "Get back inside. None of this shit concerns you."

"All these years I thought I did the right thing by tellin' you to forget the kid—"

"Keep your goddamn voice down," I hissed, as I approached him. "You did what you thought was right."

He shook his head. "No, I did what I thought would keep the club together. See, I had it in my head that Betsy was a good mother."

"Well, she ain't awful—just thinks with her cunt instead of her head."

His chest heaved up and down. "I say we go with your original plan. Kill 'em both and say they died."

I stared at him for a beat before forcing out a laugh. "Thought you wanted me to think about it."

"No." He shook his head. "Killin' them is the best option."

"And your reason is..."

"David called Betsy to tell her about Mikey hours ago, and you know what she said? Make sure he gets home safely. She'd rather get dicked down than be a mother. Jesus fuck, how many years were you fightin' with her to stay gone, but she just kept runnin' right back to him?" He yanked his .40 from the holster. "Let's go."

There was nothing I wanted more than to send Betsy to the Reaper for the multitude of shit she'd pulled over the years, but Slim himself had reminded me that Mikey was a man now. If she wanted to fuck away every remaining brain cell she had with the man who'd beaten her senseless on more than one occasion, who was I to judge?

My boy would leave soon for college. If he was smart, he'd never go home. I joined Slim on the stairs. "Guess I should start by thankin' you—"

"Don't. Your life was fuckin' chaos from the beginning, and you deserved better." Knowing I wasn't going to let him kill the mother of my son, he returned the gun to his hip. "You all deserved better."

I clapped him on the shoulder with a smile. They did. I, on the other hand, had been reaping what I'd sown since the night I killed my old man.

Slim didn't bother knocking. He turned the handle and waltzed into the motel room like he owned the joint. Betsy lay face down on the mattress, her dark brown hair spread out like a fan across the comforter. My heart stuttered in my chest because, from where I was standing, she almost looked like Celia.

Comedian stood at the side of the bed, thrusting into her body like a man possessed. The maniacal look in his dilated eyes further confirmed that he was strung out on something.

Initially, I assumed he'd killed her until she began rocking back, meeting his thrusts with soft moans and pleads for more.

Jesus.

The two of them really did deserve each other.

Comedian finally looked over at us, not once slowing down as he growled, "The fuck do you two want? A turn? You'll have to wait until I'm done."

Betsy's head came up off the bed, and I took sick pleasure in watching the blood leave her face when she saw me. "G-Grey? You're alive?"

She scrambled across the bed, leaving Comedian alone with his still very hard cock in his hand. No wonder Slim had lost his shit on me a few days ago. Seeing another man stroke his own dick felt almost menacing in a way. At least in the clubhouse, the lights were low, and the music was loud enough to drown out the sounds of fucking.

"For the love of god, put your dick away." Slim turned to Betsy. "Where's Mikey?"

Keeping her eyes on me, she planted a hand on her hip. Her tits bounced from the movement, and I tried to decide if they were as big as Celia's. I couldn't remember if I'd even used my mouth on them the one time we were together.

"Mike is not a child who needs a babysitter, Slim. He's perfectly capable of—"

A robotic musical tone began playing from the phone on the nightstand, and she turned her back on us to grab it. I let my eyes wander down her backside before remembering how much I despised her. I wouldn't have touched her again for all the money and drugs in the world.

I had to be in a dry spell if I was getting hard looking at Betsy Sullivan. If she'd had her way, I wouldn't have ever had Katydid. Fuck, I wouldn't have had Celia or Dakota either. Regardless of what little time we'd had as a family, I'd take it over not having had them at all.

My cock backed down immediately, and I swiped a hand over my face, fighting to focus on the one thing we'd come up here for.

"Hello?" Betsy answered the phone like she was working a goddamn telethon, giving absolutely no sign that she'd been test-driving Comedian's cock only moments before.

He stood in the same spot, glaring at the phone pressed against her ear. "Betsy," he snapped before pointing down. "On your knees. You wanna be a fuckin' brat, I'll treat ya like one."

Slim's eyes rolled back as he shook his head. "Fuckin' hell, Comedian. Give it a rest."

"Where are you? I can be there in thirty. Cline Nature Sanctuary near Stewart Beach. Got it." She placed the phone back on the nightstand and calmly said. "Mike's in trouble—"

I took a couple of steps forward before catching myself. "What kind of trouble? Is he hurt?"

She shook her head and whispered, "I don't know; he didn't say. I just have this feeling that it's bad, Grey. Like really bad."

Comedian hurriedly threw on his jeans and boots, searching the sheets for his t-shirt and kutte. "Where's my boy?"

My back teeth connected painfully.

Slim was right. We should've just killed them.

CHAPTER SIXTEEN

Mike: July 2001 (Age: 18)

We sat on the side of the road until headlights illuminated the back window. Most teenage boys wouldn't have called their moms to bail them out, but if there was anyone who could understand what I was up against, it was Betsy Sullivan. She hadn't even bothered to ask for anything other than my location. Must have been the residual effects of thirteen years spent living with my father.

"David?" I tried, waving a hand to snag his attention. He spun a silver ring on his right ring finger, blindly staring through the windshield into the dark. "David!"

He jerked out of his stupor and turned toward me in shock, as if he'd forgotten I was still in the truck with him.

"My mom's here. She'll know how to fix this. Don't worry."

There was a light rap on the passenger window and I turned, expecting to see my mother's face. Instead, I was met with the face of a man I'd hoped to never see again in this life.

"Dad?" I croaked before reluctantly opening my door.

"Hey Junior, your ma said you needed help. What's goin' on?"

Just like that.

As if he hadn't been out of the picture for the last five years.

"She called you? *You?* Of all the people she could've recruited—she chose you?" My voice grew increasingly louder until I was all but shouting in his face.

David leaned across the seats and jerked a thumb toward the back of the truck. "The problem's back there."

My old man's focus shifted over to David, and he squinted against the dome light as if trying to place him. "You John's boy?"

He nodded, and my father shook his head before stepping around to the bed of the truck, muttering, "Thought so."

When Patrick's body came into view, he let out a low whistle. "What the hell do we have here?"

I climbed out and limped over to meet him. "Guy jumped me—I only hit him once though—he fell back and cracked his head."

He looked at me with something that could only be described as pride. "Got him with an uppercut, yeah? One and done, just like I taught ya."

I shrugged. "I guess—I just need to know what to do. Do I take him to the hospital? Call his dad?"

My dad reached over and hit Patrick's side with the back of his hand. "Why? He's dead, son."

I ran my hands through my hair in frustration. "Jesus, fuck. What am I gonna do? I'm gonna get arrested." Blood poured from my reopened leg wound, and I leaned down to clutch my knees, fighting to stay conscious. I was so screwed right now.

David's voice cut through the silence. "Did you say dead? He's dead? Like dead, dead? Are we sure he's not just unconscious?" His face looked almost green in the headlights of my father's truck, and I knew he was seconds away from puking.

My father surveyed both of us for a minute before gesturing to his truck. "Get what you need out of your truck and head back to the house. Where's his vehicle parked?"

"He's parked at the old *Captain's Quarters*. Wait, what about David's truck? We can't leave it here."

My father laughed and pointed down at my leg. "Junior, your leg ain't gonna stop bleedin' unless you get it taken care of. Your ma's back at the house. She'll get you fixed up and David's truck will be waitin' out front in the morning. Sound good?" He gripped my shoulder and squeezed lightly.

I stared up into his eyes and nodded, feeling choked up. "What about," I pointed to the bed of David's truck, "him?"

I sighed as David leaned over and hurled.

My father chuckled. "Damn, kid, you gonna make it?" David gave a small groan before retching again. "Guess not. Look, I'll take care of this fuckin' mess—you get home to Betsy and don't tell anyone shit. Got it? You left the hospital and went straight home."

I nodded, still trying to wrap my mind around him being here.

He squeezed my arm again. "Damn proud of you, son. You did what you had to do. Let me take care of it for ya, okay?"

I nodded again, my throat tight. "Thanks—I, uh, I owe you for all this."

He ruffled my hair and helped me into his truck. Suddenly, I was eleven years old again. Just a kid, desperately seeking approval. He led David back to the truck and gave him the keys.

"You boys drive safe. I'll take care of this."

David started the truck, but left it in park. "Mike, you killed a guy. We have to go to the police. And your dad? When the hell did he show up? And how does he know my dad? Oh god, I can't be a part of this!"

I leaned over and shifted the truck into reverse. "David, you need to drive us back to my mom's." He hit the brakes, so I tried again. "David, c'mon. Just get us back to Beaumont."

"I helped you—I'm an accessory to murder!" He began hyperventilating. I was going to have to calm him down if we wanted to make it home in one piece. At the rate we were going, he was liable to drive us right off the ferry and into the ocean.

"David, look at me. This is all on me. If the shit hits the fan and my old man can't fix it, I'll take the fall. But if we pull it off, I'll owe you one. Anytime, day or night."

He drove around his truck and got us back on the road before somberly replying, "Like I'll ever cash in on that favor."

CHAPTER SEVENTEEN

Grey: July 2001 (Age: 37)

Slim and I sat with our bikes idling in the shadows, about a hundred yards behind Comedian's truck. He'd jokingly said he was taking the cage because he couldn't stash a body in his saddlebag.

I hadn't laughed.

In fact, I'd spent most of the ride fighting off the sick feeling in my gut. First Celia. Now Mike. It was like dominoes. One had fallen, sending the others toppling onto their backs.

"I know you wanna be up there, but he don't know you're alive and I'm not sure now's a good time to drop that shit on him," Slim noted before his eyes narrowed. "Oh, fuck."

"What?" I craned my neck, struggling to see what was up ahead without drawing attention to myself. Not knowing what had happened or why Mikey needed help had me on edge and ready to snap.

Suddenly, Slim looked a little green. "I think that's David's truck."

"Go. Make sure he's alright."

He shook his head and dropped his fist against the instrument panel. "And what? Reveal to him that his daddy's a biker? I'm just as fuckin' trapped as you right now."

The three moved around to the bed of David's truck, but we were too far back to hear what was being said. Comedian pointed toward his own before helping Mikey over to the passenger's side. I couldn't see the wound on his leg, but judging by the way he was limping, it appeared to be quite the injury.

After getting him situated, Comedian led David around to the driver's side, leaving me to wonder if he was hurt or just sick over whatever had happened. The truck fired up but remained parked.

"C'mon, David," Slim pleaded quietly. "Just fuckin' drive off."

Finally, the brake lights kicked on, and the truck backed up before disappearing into the night. We rode up to find Comedian leaning against the tailgate with a shit-eating grin plastered across his face.

"What'd I say, boys? Life is good." He dropped it to reveal the body of a kid who couldn't have been much older than Mikey. The ground quaked beneath my feet as my worst fears were confirmed.

Slim brought his fist up to his mouth with a shake of his head. "The fuck? Who is this?"

Comedian punched the sole of the kid's sneaker with a chuckle, making his body jolt like a puppet on a string. "He's dead, so I don't guess it matters much now, does it? By the way, your boy don't handle murder real good, Slim." He slammed the tailgate shut and turned back, his smile suddenly gone.

"It's funny. I spend five years tryin' to find my wife and kid, and I could've just asked you."

"You think I keep up with David's friends in between runnin' a business and helpin' the club? That's a fuckin' laugh," Slim stated flatly.

"Don't you?" Comedian pushed off the truck. "Thought that was the requirements of bein' Daddy of the Year, or whatever the fuck it is you seem to think you are."

I continued staring at the kid's body while they snarled at each other like rabid dogs. Comedian caught Slim's shoulder and began shoving him back toward the tree line.

Deciding I didn't want the hassle of dealing with three bodies, I stepped in between them with a terse, "We need to focus on cleanin' this shit up."

"I'd hate to think you knew somethin' about this, Pres."

I lowered my chin and glanced down at him. "You really think that I was concerned with where your kid was while I was in the middle of a goddamn war? Now, Slim and I are out here cleanin' up the mess he made. If you've got it under control, we'll leave you to it."

His shoulders relaxed, and he nodded. "No, you're right. Just seems like they were right under my nose the entire time... maybe I just didn't look hard enough. Sorry, Pres." He turned back to Slim. "And you too, I guess."

Slim's nostrils flared as he panted, murder written all over his face. "Yeah, thanks for that, fucker."

"I'm only goin' to ask this once, but what the fuck happened here?" I sighed, trying to distract the two of them from thoughts of killing each other.

I knew what it looked like, but a small part of me still refused to accept it.

The grin returned to Comedian's face. "Asshole tried to jump my boy. Solid uppercut and the kid went down. One and done... I taught him that."

As if on autopilot, I climbed up onto the tailgate. A trail of dried blood ran from the kid's ears, nose, and mouth. I doubted they could've saved him even if they'd tried.

The countless times I'd lost sleep worrying about keeping Mikey safe had been for nothing. He could've been raised in a fucking convent.

It wouldn't have changed a damn thing.

Comedian might've been the monster in front of him, but I'd always been the threat. The evil that lived in me had been passed onto my son, settling into his soul and taking root.

I took one last look at the kid's face before hopping down onto the asphalt with clenched teeth. "Where'd it happen? We need to take care of the vehicle... check for security cameras—anything that could lead the cops back to Mikey, or David, for that matter."

Slim agreed. "They've got their whole lives ahead of 'em. Comedian?"

He slammed the tailgate shut, still grinning. "Yeah, yeah. We'll fix this right up for our boys. Kid's car is at Captain's Quarters, the old strip club just back that way." He pointed behind us.

"You know what's funny? Betsy was always spouting off nature and nurture bullshit when Mikey was a kid. Said that genetics were stronger than environment. I taught him how to defend himself though... me; not his mother's weak genes. I made him a man."

There was so much pride in his voice that it was easy to overlook the fact that everything he was saying was complete horseshit.

Slim watched me closely as we climbed back onto our bikes, no doubt seeing me for what I really was; what I'd always been.

A fuck up.

The bright yellow Jeep abandoned in the deserted parking lot of a boarded-up strip club might as well have had a flashing neon sign above it with as much attention as it was going to get come morning. The three prospects we'd brought with us sat with their bikes idling around it, like guard dogs.

Knowing what was at stake, I pushed my grief down and slipped into my more familiar role as Pres. "Slim, call Chop and make that vehicle disappear. Tell him I'll pay double if it's broken down before daylight."

"Grey," he began. "Are you—"

"In a fuckin' hurry?" I snapped. "Little bit, yeah. Call Bear. I need every man here right now. These prospects ain't gonna cut it."

When he made no attempt to move, I added, "Or call Lou and tell her she'll be makin' weekend trips to Gatesville to talk to David through plexiglass. Your choice."

He yanked the cell phone from his pocket with a curse and stomped back toward his bike.

Comedian scanned the empty lot before pointing up toward the single light pole. "Camera. If they got one there, there's bound to be more."

I nodded. "Slim's callin' everyone in. We're gonna need a boat and a place to break down the body."

"Leave that to me. Really appreciate you doin' this for my boy. I know he ain't a patch—"

He wasn't.

It wasn't a life I'd ever wanted for him, but this changed things. Wolverine had seen what I was the night I sent Donald to the Reaper; he'd known that I needed to be controlled.

Same as Mikey.

I came back to the conversation as Comedian threw in, "If we get inside the club, should be a way to wipe the surveillance."

"No."

He cocked his head to the side and glared at me with cold eyes. "No? The fuck you suggest we do then? We have to destroy those tapes. You wanna call Torch in to burn the place to the ground? What's your plan?"

I'd lost Celia and the girls because I hadn't held on tight enough. Mikey would either end up dead or in prison if I didn't hold on with both hands.

The poison that flowed through my veins ran through his. I'd created the monster, and it was my responsibility to keep it in chains.

I wasn't willing to lose another person I loved.

God help me, I knew what I had to do.

"You work on gettin' that boat. I'll take care of the tapes."

His lips pulled back as if he was about to question my orders when Chop's crew pulled up.

"Right on time," Slim said, by way of greeting, as he ended a call. "You know the arrangement. Nothing left that can be traced back to us."

Comedian snagged one of the prospect's bikes, kicking up stray rocks on his way out. Slim was still deep in conversation with Chop's crew over by the kid's vehicle and didn't notice me digging in my saddlebag.

I climbed into the bed of the truck, taking advantage of their momentary distraction. The shutter on the camera clicked, bringing with it a sense of peace.

This wasn't about getting him into a kutte.

Just like Wolverine, I wouldn't force this life on anybody. Still, it didn't mean I wouldn't do for him what the club had done for me.

Once upon a time, I'd vowed to keep him safe. Now, more than ever before, Mikey needed me to uphold my end. Whatever the cost, we'd face his demons and find a way to control them.

Together.

CHAPTER EIGHTEEN

Grey: October 2001 (Age: 37)

"Told him I'd vouch for him and everything," Comedian slurred before falling back against the couch cushions. "With the two of us, the club can't lose."

I stayed silent and knocked the bottle of tequila back, welcoming the burn as it slid down my throat. We'd been lying low just outside of Lajitas—in a clubhouse that straddled the border. After dumping the kid's remains out in the ocean, we rode out just as the feds moved in and began combing every grain of sand on the beaches.

I'd planned to go back once shit died down and tell Mikey the truth.

About all of it.

Unfortunately, Comedian had gotten there first. His offer to wipe the surveillance tapes that night hadn't been some half-assed attempt at being a good father.

It was leverage.

I should have known that he was up to something when he secured a boat in record time and insisted again on being the one to erase the footage. I agreed because, by that time, the shock had set in. My only thought was on how to protect Mikey.

The pictures were to keep him in check, a visual reminder of what could happen if the monster was unleashed on the wrong people.

When I found the videotapes, I realized Comedian would never let Mikey move on. He was going to take my son's mistake and exploit it for his own gain.

Keeping a tight hold on the neck of the tequila bottle, I stumbled outside and away from the sounds of celebration. I was going to be forced to watch my son walk down the same path that I had.

There was no victory in that.

It was just another reminder that I'd failed.

I slipped around to the side of the clubhouse and into the shadows before retrieving the plastic bag from my pocket. Slim had warned me to quit using, said it fucked with my judgment, but being sober hadn't done me any real favors lately either.

"Thought I might find you out here."

I dropped the bottle into the dirt and took a bump before responding. "It's like you just know to go where you're not wanted, Betsy."

There was enough moonlight coming through the trees overhead for me to see her lips as they pushed into a pout. "C'mon, Grey. Don't be like that. I wanted to thank you for helping Mikey out—"

I ignored her praise, fighting the urge to send the entire bag up my nose. Instead, I settled for another hit. "This is what you want for him? Goin' nowhere but Hell?"

Pain flashed in her eyes, and she looked away. "I want him to have a choice, the same as you, but—"

"But what? How's he doin' with all this? Does he—is he—" I blew out a frustrated breath. "Is he like me?"

Her eyebrows moved together as she frowned. "I don't know what you mean. What's wrong with you?"

It took me by surprise. Either she hadn't been paying attention over the years or living with Comedian had completely fucked her sense of good and evil.

"I'm a killer, Betsy," I bit out slowly. "A fuckin' monster. So, I'll ask again. Is our boy like me?"

She took a hesitant step back, eyes darting side to side, searching for a way out of the conversation. "Mike—he's a good kid. You and I both know that he didn't mean to kill that boy. And despite what Comedian thinks, he doesn't want a patch."

My throat, still raw from the liquor, tightened at the admission. "What does he want?"

"To go into law enforcement."

Despite the situation, my lips curved up into a smirk, and I chuckled.

"I'm serious, Grey," she hissed. "Maybe he was scared straight or something... I don't know. It doesn't matter now, though, does it? Michael said he made his choice when he took a life. In by blood, out by blood."

My smile faded. "Don't recite the goddamn club mantra to me. I'm still the Pres. I call the shots, and I decide who wears the patch and who doesn't."

If we put it to a vote, the other members would probably be more than happy to see Sullivan's boy patch in. I just had to keep it from coming to that.

Instead of backing down, she jutted her chin up at me, looking so much like Celia that it knocked the air from my lungs. I cut the distance between us and took her face in my hands before the rational part of my brain reminded me that the woman in front of me wasn't fit to wipe my wife's ass.

I released her and backed away while she watched with amusement. "Still trying to run from this, after all these years. Why? We were good together once—"

The blow and tequila were playing tricks on me, forcing me to see Celia's face everywhere I looked. I raked my hands through my hair in frustration. "Once was bad enough. I'm Celia's—from now until I take my last breath. What part of that ain't stuck yet? Jesus, you really fucked away all your sense—"

Her palm cracked across the side of my face, and I clenched my hands into fists, aching to retaliate.

"Why? Why her, Grey? You've been saving yourself for a woman who didn't waste any time moving on when she thought you were dead. She's not some saint—why can't you see that?"

I planted my palm against her chest and shoved, sending her stumbling back. "And you are?" I snarled. "You don't know a fuckin' thing about her."

Betsy straightened and stalked back toward me triumphantly. "Really? At least I stayed celibate for my man. Even when we were apart."

With a growl, I leaned in again. "Are you not counting all the times you threw yourself at me the minute his back was turned? You know he ain't ever been faithful to you—"

"I know she had another man's baby in her belly the night she was beaten," she snapped with a vicious smirk.

I fought to get air into my lungs before carefully asking, "Where'd you hear that?"

It wasn't true.

This was just another way for her to manipulate me. The only trouble was that her old man had gotten to Celia long before I had. If anyone knew what really went down, it was him.

She mashed her lips together before admitting, "He was drunk—said he didn't realize there would be so much blood. Look, I'm sorry that it happened to her. No one deserves what she went through."

"Blood?" Every muscle in my body contracted, leaving me vibrating with tension.

Betsy nodded. "From the miscarriage. I guess she wasn't that far along... maybe a couple of months. I'm sorry I had to be the one to tell you—I thought you knew."

You want a baby, princess?

The blood on her robe.

"Jesus, fuck," I muttered to myself. Despite what Betsy thought, it hadn't been another man's baby in Celia's belly.

It had been mine.

There was a reason things had felt strangely familiar that night. Because I was right. I'd been through it before.

Just not with Celia.

The reality of the situation barreled through me, and I let out a low growl before storming into the clubhouse with Betsy right on my heels.

"Grey—he said not to—"

"Comedian!" I roared over the music and drunk bikers, the vein in my forehead throbbing to the point of rupturing. I didn't want to believe that my men would keep something like that from me.

The clubhouse fell silent, magnifying the sounds of my ragged breaths. Comedian stood up slowly, keeping a hand on the gun at his hip. "Pres, everything okay?"

"Did you know?"

He looked past me to Betsy, confirming the truth as the color drained from his face. "Shit. Grey, I can explain—"

My eyes stung, and I pinched the bridge of my nose to keep my emotions from spilling onto my cheeks. "You—you knew she was pregnant?" My tone betrayed me—giving away the helplessness I'd tried so hard to hide.

Bear stepped into view, staring daggers down at Comedian. "Pres asked you a question. It'd be in your best interest to answer."

"We did what we could for her, but it was too late. She asked us not to tell you—said with what happened to your ma—"

His words dealt a death blow to my heart, but I refused to break down in a room full of bikers. I ran my tongue over my trembling lip with a smirk. "See, that's funny. I could've sworn you rode in my club. Bear, ain't that the way it's always been?"

"Pretty sure it is, Pres."

I nodded. "And since when did we discuss club business with Ol' Ladies, Bear?"

"Since never," he replied icily. "The shit that went down with Grey's Ol' Lady shoulda never crossed your tongue, Comedian."

"But she was knocked up by another man!" Betsy snapped. "Who cares who he told? Just focus on what really matters."

"Shut the fuck up, Betsy," Comedian pleaded.

Bear traded a look with Torch, and he nodded, before downing the rest of his beer and making his way over to her.

"Betsy," I said, as Torch locked an arm around her bicep and began dragging her to the door. "Baby was mine."

Her eyes widened in horror, and then she was gone.

I turned back to Comedian. "I'm sure I don't have to tell you how this looks, right? Wasn't too long ago that Hawk rolled over on us."

His jaw clenched, but he nodded. "Ain't ever laid a hand on your Ol'

Lady, Pres. Ain't ever gonna turn on the club. It was a mistake keepin' what happened from you—"

The list of shit I couldn't fix only seemed to grow longer, and I damn sure wouldn't go out surrounded by family, but fate had presented one opportunity that I sure as fuck planned on taking.

I tightened my posture as I walked over to stand in front of him. "A mistake that's gonna cost ya, I'm afraid. Bear, relieve him of his kutte."

Comedian's nostrils flared as he stripped it off and tossed it to Bear. "Do you know what she said as she bled out on the bathroom floor? She apologized and said it shouldn't have been us dealin' with her. As if she was something that needed to be dealt with—nothin' more than garbage. She could've asked for anything at that moment, and I would've given it to her."

I squared my shoulders and cracked my neck just as Bear's fist struck Comedian's mouth. "Think it's time for you to shut the fuck up."

He straightened and wiped the blood from his mouth with a grin. "So, that's it? I'm out?"

I wanted to knock his teeth down his throat. He'd been there for my wife, and I hadn't. It should've been me.

He'd known how bad it was and kept it from me while pissing away the opportunity to be a father to a kid I would've laid down my life for.

Life had been kind to Comedian.

Where was the justice in that?

"No," I finally responded, surprising even Bear. "Told you years ago that if your Ol' Lady couldn't keep my girl's name out of her mouth, I'd knock you back down to prospect. Well, guess what, asshole? I wasn't lyin'."

His eyes narrowed, but he nodded. "Fair's fair."

"You can earn your patch, same as the other prospects. Oh, and your boy ain't ever gonna wear a kutte. I've cleaned up after him once, and I ain't doin' it again."

Comedian spat blood onto the concrete. "What's he supposed to do, then?"

I clenched and unclenched my fist. "According to his mama, he wants to go into law enforcement." Before he could interject, I added, "Let him. You never know when it might benefit the club."

He gave me a blood-stained grin in response.

If I had it my way, the club would never once need to lean on Mikey. But my way had led to this.

To death.

To destruction.

It ended tonight.

CHAPTER NINETEEN

Grey: October 2001 (Age: 37)

"Make sure he and his Ol' Lady are on board," I directed. "Bear, you're in charge."

If I wanted, I could've forced him to pass Betsy around the club as punishment, but knowing her, she would've enjoyed it.

Mikey was going to be okay; I'd made sure of it. That had to be enough.

I sucked in lungfuls of air when I stepped outside, grateful for the rare chill left behind from the late afternoon thunderstorm. The clubhouse sat right on the border, in the middle of Big Bend; the park I'd always thought of when someone mentioned the Wild West.

When I was a kid, I'd imagined myself patrolling the river-carved canyons on horseback, searching for bad guys to wrangle up. As an adult, I knew that there were no good guys left in these parts. We were all villains, searching for a place to hide.

The cooler weather reminded me of the night Katydid had come into the world. I'd held Celia's hands as she panted through each contraction. The minute the pain let up, she'd dozed off against my arm, completely unaware of the sweat that ran down her face.

Just like the night she'd lost our baby.

The tears I'd been holding back now fell in rapid succession;

causing my entire body to jerk as I fought against the sharp pain in my chest.

I staggered around the back of the clubhouse and toward the river, knowing it wouldn't be long before they came looking for me. The muddy brown water of the Rio Grande flowed just feet below me.

One wrong step in the dark could send me hurtling off the edge of the rock overhang. If the flow was high enough, I'd be swept away. If it wasn't, I'd end up waist-deep in silt with a broken leg, just as stuck as I was now.

Celia, what if you get knocked up?

What would happen if I did?

The ache in my chest became unbearable, and I fell to my knees with a cry. I wanted to rip through the tattooed skin covering my chest; to break apart my rib cage and let my heart fall into the water with my tears.

I didn't know how long I sat there, bawling like a scared kid, before pulling the cell phone from my back pocket. I dialed, knowing exactly what I was going to hear.

"Jamie?" Angel yawned. "Everything okay?"

"No." I cupped my forehead with my hand and hiccuped through a sob, making no attempt to cover it up. "She was pregnant?"

He sighed and shifted against the phone, probably rolling over in bed. "Yeah, kid. She was."

The confirmation only pushed me closer to the edge of that overhang, ready to stand up and launch myself into the rushing water below. "I," I choked. "I ruin lives. Donald was right about that, wasn't he?"

"You been drinkin'?"

I nodded and sniffed. "A little. Mikey's a murderer, Angel. Just like me. And Celia—I bet she was so scared. It shouldn't have been you—seein' her like that."

"Jamie," Angel said slowly. "Where are you right now?"

I swiped the back of my hand across my eyes. "Don't matter anymore."

"Are you near water? Listen to me, remember that time I took you and your mama fishin' off White River? How many did she catch that day? Put us all to shame."

I pulled the phone away from my ear, letting my finger hover over the red end call button. I knew he meant well, but I didn't need one more distraction. "Love you, Angel. I'm sorry I fucked it all up. I wanted to be like you when I was a kid. Instead, I turned out just like my old man."

"Jamie—"

"Just—just take care of them for me." I mashed the button, and the phone went silent again.

I roughly ran a hand over my face before dialing again.

"Lo?" he stated flatly, as if the actual greeting required too much effort.

"Mikey?" My voice was thick from all the tears I'd shed, sounding nothing like the man he'd known as a kid.

"Who is this?"

"I—" I mashed my fist against my lips. "I'm so sorry, buddy."

"Buddy? Jarrett, pumpkin, is that you? Still pissed that my Oilers whooped up on your Hurricanes? A bet's a bet, asshole. Pay up."

I smiled despite myself before hanging up. He sounded like a typical teenage boy. Maybe, even with all the mistakes I'd made along the way, I'd given him a fighting chance at a normal life.

There wasn't a doubt in my mind that he was going to try to call me back using reverse caller ID. Unfortunately for him, my phone was untraceable. He'd never been content with loose ends as a kid; everything had to be wrapped up nice and neat.

He'd make a damn fine detective someday.

My hands shook as an image of Celia infiltrated my mind, and I dropped onto my ass with a heavy sigh. She was lying on my bed at the clubhouse, looking up at me from under those thick lashes—hair nothing more than a wild mane of curls. My daughter was in her belly, and everything was right in the world.

It was the memory I'd held onto with everything I had left. It would be the one I took with me when the Reaper showed up. That, and the sound of her voice as she said my name.

One more call.

One last time.

My heart raced as the phone rang, leaving me feeling like a kid calling his crush. It wasn't too far from the truth. She'd always held a power over me I couldn't explain.

"Hello?" a girl's voice breathlessly whispered.

"Katydid?" How did she sound like a grown woman? She was only eleven, for Christ's sake.

"Who is this?" she asked sternly, and I pictured her as a toddler, face scrunched up in annoyance.

I swallowed down the lump in my throat. "When'd you get so big, Katy girl?"

She'd never be a baby again. I'd wasted all that time running away, thinking that things would just go back to the way they'd been before when I eventually made it home again.

Life didn't work like that, though.

There'd be no tea parties for Spiderman or demands for one more story. I'd never get back the time with them that I'd lost. I rubbed at the back of my neck, realizing I'd fucked it all away for a patch.

"Daddy?" Her voice went soft.

I sniffed. "Is your mama there?"

There was a brief scuffle as Kate begged, "No! Give it back! It's my daddy! That's my daddy!"

"Kate?" The phone dug into my ear as I strained to hear my daughter's voice.

"Why are you calling here?" Richard demanded over Kate's screams before lowering his voice. "Sweetheart, this isn't your daddy. It's a wrong number—"

"Wait! Don't hang up. I just need to talk to Celia. Need to hear her voice... please."

He went quiet for so long that I became convinced he'd hung up, only to pull the phone away to see that we were still connected.

"Richard," I croaked. "Please."

There was a heavy sigh before he wrecked what was left of my heart. "Celia isn't here, Jamie. She met someone, and he's good for her. She and the girls are happy. Why can't you just accept it and move on?"

I wanted to beg him for a way to reach her, to talk her out of it, but

Slim was right—she deserved a good life. And if I couldn't be the one to give it to her, I could at least go out knowing she was happy again.

"Just—just tell her I'm sorry... for all of it."

Everything inside of me screamed for release as I tossed my phone into the flowing river and retrieved the gun from my hip. I shoved the barrel up underneath my chin and took a deep breath.

"You're doin' it wrong," Slim calmly stated before coming to stand beside me. "You'll blow your jaw off, but not much else. Best way to do it would be to stick it in your mouth with the barrel angled up."

I lowered it and turned to him. "You came here to give me tips? Ain't gonna make any attempt to stop me?"

He lit up a cigarette with a shrug before offering me one. "Figured you'd made your mind up already. No sense talking you out of what you think is best."

I clenched my jaw and shoved the gun back into the holster. "Why the fuck are you even here? Thought you were headed back to Beaumont."

"Call it a hunch or a sixth sense, but I made it as far as Fort Stockton before turnin' around. Angel called me as I pulled up to the clubhouse, claimin' you were gonna end it. When he mentioned hearing water, I knew where you were. Don't mean I don't think you're a goddamn pussy, though."

The muscles jumped under my skin as I lit up the cigarette. "I'm a pussy? You got any idea the shit I've been dealin' with? Not everybody gets a fairy tale like you, dickwad."

"Fairy tale?" Slim laughed. "You really believe that's what I got? You've got no fuckin' clue—"

I smirked. "Yeah, name one of your problems. Didn't make the church bake sale? David missed curfew?"

He lowered himself down next to me and watched the river before admitting, "I stopped counting Lou's miscarriages after the seventh one."

"Jesus," I breathed. "I had no idea—"

"Yeah," he cut in. "Because I didn't lose myself in the bottle or get strung out on whatever the club was sellin'. That's your problem, though. You love wallowin' in your own shit. Yeah, you were raised in a fucked-up environment. But at some point, you gotta man the fuck up, Jamie."

I rubbed my swollen eyes and took a drag. "We ain't all you—"

"No, and thank Christ for it. My girl needed me to be strong for both of us, and I was. You would've ended it and left her alone. I mean, look at you! Fuckin' pathetic. You ain't doin' this for any reason other than you can't handle their pain. Guess what, asshole? It's your motherfuckin' job to be their provider!"

I felt the vein pulsing in my neck and snapped, "She was pregnant and lost our baby because of me. Because I fuckin' failed at my job as her husband, John! Mikey killed someone because I failed at being a good father. They're better off without me."

He nodded. "Maybe they are because it's always been all about you. Your wife is beaten and raped, and you're hung up on how much it hurts you. Your boy makes a mistake that most people go to prison over, and you're mopin' about what kind of dad you were? You don't wanna end up just like your old man, then change it! Jesus Christ, just harden the fuck up!"

I jumped up, ready to fight. "I am my old man! Whatever was in him runs through my veins, the same as it does Mikey's!"

He stood up and squared off with me. "Then do it, Jamie. Put a bullet in your brain so that it fixes things for you. Who gives a fuck how the rest of us are, right?"

I couldn't punch or kick my way out of the situation because, as much as I hated to admit it, he was right. Instead, I dropped back down to my knees with a cry. "How'd you do it? How'd you fix it?"

Slim ran his hands over his face before kneeling beside me and placing a hand on my shoulder. "You don't fix it. Some things can't be undone, no matter how hard we want them to be. Best we can do is pull ourselves up by our bootstraps and be a rock for them."

"Dick said she moved on—found someone else. What good am I gonna be to her now?"

She would've been better off had she never met me.

"I'd be wary of anything her old man told you. He's had it out for you for years. And even if she moved on, so what? I don't think for one second that Celia's taken the time to fully accept what happened to her. She's not in the right frame of mind to do anything. But there will be a day when she lets herself feel it, and your ass better be there to help her grieve."

He lit up another cigarette. "This is what I was tryin' to tell you. Your feelings don't matter because it didn't happen to you. So, you can be a selfish prick who ends it because shit hurts too much, or you can choose to be better. That means you give up the drinkin' and drugs, though."

I laughed. "So, give up the only things that have kept me going?"

His mouth flattened into a thin line before disappearing behind his beard. "They ain't kept you goin'. They've slowed you down. You couldn't protect them before. Jamie, this is your chance to redeem yourself. There ain't a doubt in my mind that if you had a clear head and a solid plan, you'd wipe the motherfuckers off the map tomorrow. Ultimately, it's your choice, though."

I'd been digging my own grave for as long as I could remember, but instead of dropping a handful of dirt onto me and walking away, Slim had reached down and pulled me out.

Just as I was ready to give up.

As usual, he was right. If I wanted to see my girl smile and hear her laugh again, then I had to fight for it with everything I had. Completely sober. She deserved a man who was strong enough to slay his own demons before coming for hers.

I might have lost my way, but it was suddenly clear. Never had any other choice but her.

Celia.

I chose Celia.

CHAPTER TWENTY

Celia: November 2004 (Age: 32)

The phone rang again, its shrill noise assaulting my ears. When I made no attempt to pick it up, Molly raised her eyebrow and walked over to it.

"You gonna get that?" She checked the caller ID. "I don't think he's taking the hint."

I stayed where I was and scraped a plate over the trash can before shaking my head. "Nope."

Rock bottom had been moving in with my parents at twenty-nine. An arrangement that had lasted all of two months. As if discovering that my mother had been withholding food from Dakota and shaming Kate for developing breasts wasn't bad enough, the house hadn't had one showing.

According to the realtor, rumors of a murder having taken place inside the house scared any potential buyers off. It didn't matter that there wasn't an ounce of truth to it. The damage had been done.

I almost found it amusing that the same neighbors who hid behind curtains and brick walls whenever I walked out onto my porch had gone out of their way to ensure I couldn't leave.

So, I stayed—trapped in a house that held nothing but pain and memories of Jamie.

"How many times a day is he calling?" she prodded, earning herself a dramatic sigh. "What? You can't avoid him forever, Celia."

I'd talk to my father again, just as soon as Hell froze over. I knew he meant well, but he'd enabled my mother's behavior for far too long.

Initially, I'd seen their home as a safe place to hide out and heal. I slept in my old bedroom with Kate and Dakota on either side of me, protected from the world outside.

Then the cracks began to show. My mother made several comments regarding Dakota's weight, but backed off when I intervened. I stupidly thought that was the end of it, only to find out later from Kate that on the nights I worked, Dakota was being deprived of food.

Any chances of us talking through our issues ended when I overheard her telling Kate that tight shirts were for girls looking to get groped.

I knew if we stayed, the girls would grow up just like I had, thinking that their bodies were little more than something to be admired or used by a man.

We moved home that same day, but the effects had lingered for months after.

"Hello, earth to Celia." Molly waved a hand in front of my face. "You in there?"

"I have nothing to say to him. Has Bear mentioned anything about the club or what they're up to?" I asked, in dire need of a subject change.

She handed me a serving spoon to add to the sink before hopping up onto the countertop. "Are you asking about the club, or Grey?"

Even though a part of me had been dying to know how he was, I'd avoided saying his name for the better part of three years.

Whenever I pushed for information on the whereabouts of the men who hurt me, I was given little more than vague responses. If anyone knew where Hawk had gone, they were under strict orders from Jamie not to tell me.

As if I didn't have a right to know.

I should have moved on. It was evident that what little affection remained between us had died that night on the back porch. Something held me back, though. I'd made a vow to love him until death—a promise that I was incapable of breaking.

Until I could look at our daughters and not feel as though my lungs were collapsing when I saw his smile on Kate's face or his vivid blue eyes in Dakota's, I wasn't ready.

"The club, obviously." I waved the dishrag flippantly before wiping down the stovetop. "I couldn't care less about Grey."

Molly's eyes narrowed, and she brought a hand up to rest against her hip. "You sure about that? Because you can't even say his name without blushing. It's pretty disgusting."

As if on cue, my cheeks heated. "Really? What if I told you I'd met someone?"

"Bullshit," she coughed into her hand. "And to answer your question, Ol' Ladies are still cut off from knowing jack shit about what the club's doing or not doing."

I nodded and tossed the rag back into the soapy water. "I figured as—"

"Doesn't mean there aren't other ways of getting information, though," Molly continued with a sly grin. "There was some type of altercation outside of a bar in Colorado Springs—pretty sure there were some Serpents on the wrong end of a barrel. I don't know if any of them were yours, though."

Bile moved up into my throat, and I shook my head. "Don't call them mine ever again. Does Bear know that you've infiltrated their inner circle?"

Her grin widened, and she blew on her lacquered nails before buffing them against the front of her shirt. "Who said Bear didn't know?"

"See, now that's disgusting."

"What? This pussy is so tight it just squeezes the information right out of him," she said, waggling her eyebrows up and down suggestively.

That's a good girl. So fuckin' tight.

I released a shuddered breath and stared around the kitchen in confusion while my brain worked to identify the threat.

"Are you okay?"

I ran a soapy hand over my forehead with a shaky nod. "Just got a little too warm. Feels like it's mid-July, not November... whatever."

"November nineteenth."

My blood ran cold, and I paused, hovering over a sink full of dishes with a coffee mug in my hand. "N-November nineteenth?"

Saying the words aloud did nothing to calm my fears. It only made them more real.

Molly nodded slowly before gasping in recognition. "Oh my god, sweetie, I didn't even put two and two together. Are you okay?"

"I'm fine. It just surprised me. That's all." My hands moved the dishrag over the mug as if on autopilot.

Four years.

The money they'd taken from me had been more than enough to keep them off the radar. They were still out there; and despite the club's best efforts, we were still no closer to finding them.

Our baby would've turned three in July. Would they have had Jamie's blue eyes or my green ones? It was devastating, losing a child so early into a pregnancy. There was no casket or urn—no stone monument that proclaimed my baby's existence to the world.

No one had even known I was pregnant and, given that most of the people in my life thought Jamie was dead, it wasn't as if I could talk about it.

So, I buried the secret deep down, along with the memory of what happened that night. I wanted to forget and move on, but every year, on July fourteenth, I found myself thinking about what kind of person our baby could've been.

Had that night never happened, would things have turned out differently? Would Jamie still have chosen to walk away from the club for good as my belly swelled with his child?

The sadistic part of my brain often chimed in, wondering if he would have stayed had he known about the miscarriage.

It wasn't fair.

Everyone had moved on but me.

A chill ran the length of my spine, urging me to run and hide. Instead, I placed the cup on the drying rack and forced my hands back into the murky water to retrieve a plate.

They weren't coming back; I knew that.

They'd gotten what they came for.

At the noise behind me, I let the plate slip from my hands and back into the water with a small shriek. My fingers closed around the only weapon I was going to find.

"Mama!" Kate stepped back with a cry of alarm, eyes welling up with tears. "It's me! I just needed a drink!"

Suds dripped from the edge of the steak knife onto the floor, but I refused to let it go.

"Celia?" Molly wrapped an arm around my shoulders and led me away from the sink. "Your mama is just exhausted, Kate. We need to get her to bed."

Kate nodded shakily, keeping an eye on me as she found and filled a glass with water. "Goodnight, Mama. Goodnight, Molly."

Molly kissed the top of her head. "Goodnight, sweet girl."

I released my death grip on the handle and placed it on the counter. Even though I knew I was safe, I made sure that it was still within reach.

"Are you still going to class?"

"Yeah. Every Tuesday night," I answered distractedly, keeping the knife in my sights.

"You ready to earn your blue belt yet?" She pushed. "Little Ricky is about to move up to green. Bear said it won't be long now before he can take him on."

My fingers twitched, aching for a weapon. "Yeah. I'm going to test soon. Are he and Bear getting along any better?"

She shrugged. "Depends on the day. I thought telling him about his real dad was a good idea. That side of the family had been dying to meet him, and it seemed like he was mature enough to handle it. Instead, it just drove a wedge between the two people I care about the most."

"He'll come around. He just needs time."

"And what about you? What do you need?"

Three men. Dead.

I smiled. "I've got everything I need right here with the girls. I'm fine."

"Sure," Molly snorted. "You just confused your fourteen-year-old for an intruder, but other than that, things couldn't be better, right?"

I blinked slowly as the room came back into focus and the feelings of imminent danger dissipated. This one had lasted longer than usual. "Did you leave Little Ricky alone?"

Her eyebrows drew together, and she cocked her head to the side. "Remember? I told you he was staying with his abuelita. God help us all. The woman cannot say no to him."

"Right. Sorry."

"C'mon." She took my hand and led me into the living room. "Sit. I wanna know how you are... really."

"I told you, I'm fine—"

She mashed her lips together and shook her head. "I wouldn't be. I'd either never get out of bed or spend all my time contemplating how to kill them. It's okay to not be okay."

"It's getting late." I pushed her hand off my knee and stood up. "Dakota will be up at the crack of dawn."

"I was thinking..." Molly gnawed at the corner of her lip. "It might be nice to have a sleepover... like old times. What do you think?"

A sleepover meant I wasn't alone.

It also meant that I wouldn't be able to stay up and check the locks on the windows and doors every hour without looking like a crazy person.

Wolverine may have had the bathroom window replaced and a high-tech security system installed, but I trusted my method.

Being alone in the house at night still made my skin crawl, but it was where the girls were most comfortable. So, I set aside my feelings and distracted myself with late-night talk shows and reruns.

"You don't have to stay—"

"Please." Molly's eyes widened. "I miss my best friend. Even when I had to leave town, I always thought that I'd come back, and we'd pick up where we left off, but you're not the same girl you were before."

I studied the clock on the mantel, letting myself get lost in the monotonous ticking. "And you think you're the same girl you were in high school? The rebel? It's easy to get hung up on how I've changed, but maybe look in the mirror."

"We just want to help you, Celia. You say the word, and I'm there."

It must have run in the family. If it wasn't Lucy pushing me to find a therapist, I had Molly guilting me for not smiling as much as I used to.

"For the last time, I am fine. Now, if it's okay with you, I need to shower." I left her sitting on the couch and forced one foot to move in front of the other until I was standing in the master bathroom.

Goosebumps broke out across my skin as I pulled the blinds closed, raising the hair on my arms. I kept my eyes on the inside of the clawfoot tub. Once, I'd made the mistake of looking and had been convinced that my reflection was someone else looking in.

I turned on the taps to the shower, comforted by the grumbling sounds from the pipes. Maybe it was just as well that the house didn't sell. My sanity seemed to rely heavily on routine.

My jeans were the first to go, followed by the oversized sweatshirt that fell to my knees. It was always the same. I'd strip down and stand in front of the mirror while the water heated, searching for marks that had long since faded.

Physically, I was completely healed. It didn't matter. I still felt their hands and teeth on my skin. So I stood, night after night, searching for wounds that were invisible to anyone but me.

My fingers traced the brand on my hip, the nails slipping over the raised scars left by Cobra's ring.

"Cry," I taunted, as the woman in the mirror studied me with narrowed eyes. "Cry and get it over with."

Instead of the sadness I'd been seeking for four years, rage bubbled up to the surface. I stared until the vision blurred and the woman in front of me no longer looked afraid. She looked haunting.

She was a specter; a war goddess, ready to take down any man who dared stand in her way.

Then, and only then, did the tightness in my throat subside, allowing me to breathe.

CHAPTER TWENTY-ONE

Celia: December 2004 (Age: 32)

The cars in front of me moved at a snail's pace through the school parking lot, much like how I imagined rush hour went in Los Angeles.

It would have been faster to park a few blocks away and jog to the parent pick-up line.

I'd been late leaving the bakery and had gotten caught at every red light along the way. To make matters worse, the sky that had been threatening rain all day chose that moment to open up.

"C'mon," I snapped at the dashboard in frustration. "Just get your kid and go. It's not hard."

Every day, there were the parents who refused to park and instead used the drive-through lane as their own personal valet while they sherpa-ed their child into the school or hosted a mommy get-together on the sidewalk.

I checked the clock, knowing Dakota was going to be livid.

She'd finally found other fourth-graders who loved comics as much as she did, and today was their first official club meeting at the library. Given the way the line was moving, she was going to be very late.

I impatiently drummed my fingers against the steering wheel as the car in front of me shifted forward a mere three inches, while halfheartedly singing along with the song on the radio.

A flash of a smile caught my attention, and I jolted up in my seat, checking the rearview mirror. I knew that grin. I saw it in every one of my nightmares.

Manny.

I spotted the back of his dark gray hoodie, stopped just feet behind my car. I dropped the gearshift from park into reverse and was just letting off the brake when a small boy came bounding up to him.

The man draped an arm around the child, and they disappeared into a sea of umbrellas. The car behind me tapped their horn as the line began moving again, and I shifted into drive.

What was wrong with me?

I could have killed a random father in front of his kid, and everyone else's because of his smile. Maybe Lucy and Molly had it right. I needed professional help.

There was just the minor issue of figuring out how to talk about what happened with a complete stranger when I hadn't been able to discuss it with people I'd known for years.

Dakota spotted my car and took off toward me, the backpack on her head acting as a makeshift umbrella.

"Where have you been?" she exclaimed before climbing into the backseat. "Barry said four o'clock sharp. No late-comers."

I turned the radio down before pulling out. "Well, it's the public library. It's not like they can keep you out. How was school?"

She dug around in her backpack before meeting my eyes in the rearview mirror. "Fine. We had to write a paper on where we're going over Christmas break, so that sucked."

"Dakota Mae, do not say that word," I chastised, before turning up the windshield wipers. The rain was coming down faster than the desert sand could absorb it, flooding the surrounding streets. If it kept up, I'd need a boat by the time Kate's school let out.

"Sorry. It blew. Better?"

A large truck went flying past, sending a wall of water onto the car and obliterating my ability to see through the windshield. I ground my teeth together and increased the wiper speed again. "For the love of all the saints, Dakota. Can you not right now?"

"Fine," she grumbled, pulling a comic from her backpack.

Except for the soft squeak from the windshield wipers moving over the glass, the rest of the drive was silent.

We pulled up in front of the library, and I turned around with a wide grin. "Only five minutes late. If Barry has a problem with that, he can come visit with me."

Dakota shook her head and opened the door. "You're not even scary, Mama."

"I could be—"

"No," she insisted. "You cried that one time a mouse got caught in the mousetrap. Plus, you don't even have any superpowers. You're like a fairy princess."

"Fairy princess? Couldn't I at least be Thor's sidekick?"

She closed her eyes and shook her head in disappointment before climbing out. "Thor doesn't have a sidekick. Pick me up at five, okay?"

I gave her a thumbs up. "You got it, crazy."

"Oh... I almost forgot. Your friend told me to give this to you." She placed a large manila envelope in my hand. "He said it was important."

"My friend?"

With a shrug, she slammed the door and leaped over a puddle before jogging up the steps into the library.

The rain pelted the roof of the car, and I shivered despite the warmth from the heater. Jamie's warnings from over the years came rushing back, leaving me with a head full of worst-case scenarios.

Anthrax.

A bomb.

It wasn't until I glanced up at the clock that I realized I'd spent ten minutes turning the envelope over in my hands while imagining all the ways in which it might kill me.

The sound of my nervous laughter was magnified in the silence. "You're being ridiculous. Just open it."

I pinched the metal prongs together and carefully lifted the flap before emptying the contents onto my lap.

A picture.

I studied it with a frown, wracking my brain for a memory that wasn't there. Was it a middle school yearbook photo sent home for me to review? If so, why had they blown it up so big? And why had they given it to Dakota?

In it, Kate stood against the side of the school, hand shielding her face from the sun as she talked to a friend. I flipped it over and sucked in a startled breath, my chest heaving in panic.

Wonder if she'll cry when I break her in...

Fear took over, and my foot slipped off the brake pedal. The car rolled forward several feet before I regained control and shifted into park.

"No, no, no," I growled, letting the picture fall to my lap. It hadn't been a hallucination. Manny had been at the school; within arm's reach of Dakota.

Images of them being forced to endure what I had flashed through my mind and my breaths turned shallow, leaving me clawing at my throat as I fought for air.

With clammy hands, I fumbled around for my cell phone, sending my purse and everything in it rolling across the floorboard.

"Molly," I whispered when she answered, instinctively flinching as someone slammed a car door nearby.

What if he'd followed me here?

"Celia, what's wrong?"

Like a drowning victim breaking the surface, I sucked in a ragged breath while scanning the parking lot. "He was at the school! The library has Dakota, but Kate—I can't leave her."

"Can you give me just a second?" she asked someone in the background before coming back on. "Where are you? I'm coming. Take a deep breath in..."

"I'm at the library near Broadway," I choked.

"In and out, nice and even," Molly said, before laughing softly. "Jesus, I sound like a porno."

I caught sight of my reflection in the rearview mirror while she attempted to keep me calm. My cheeks were flushed from the heat blasting through the vents, yet I continued to shake and tremble.

My desperate pants turned to wheezing, and I reached up to pinch my forearm, digging my fingernails into the sensitive flesh until I felt like I could take a full breath. It was going to leave bruises, but pain seemed to be the only thing that could bring me back to the present.

"Celia?"

I exhaled slowly; my limbs weak with exhaustion. "I'm here. I'm okay."

"Good. I'm pulling up behind you."

Seconds later, she was rapping at the passenger window before climbing in. She took in the items strewn across the floorboard. "Wow, I love what you've done with the place."

Deciding that there was no sense in delaying the inevitable, I thrust the manila envelope into her hands. She studied it, looking about as confused as I imagined I had before flipping it over.

"Oh, dear god." She turned to me with wide eyes. "Celia, we need to call the club—"

"No." I shook my head. "Think about it, Molly. It's been four years. Why now?" It was the one thing I kept coming back to. If they were going as far as threatening my daughters, they were doing it for a reason.

"You think they want a war?"

"They want Grey—it's what they've always wanted. If I go to the club, then I'm playing right into their hands. We've got to be smarter."

Raindrops that had gotten caught in her hair now ran down her face, and she distractedly reached up to brush them away as she asked, "Don't you think that if Grey knew about this that he'd handle it? Bear, Torch... they'll all back him. You can't just let them get away with this."

"I'm not letting them get away with anything." I gnawed absently on a fingernail. "We're going to kill them."

Molly's head jerked back, and she let out a rough bark of laughter. "Sorry, I could've sworn you just said we were going to kill someone."

A plan had begun to take root in my mind, leaving me wondering why I hadn't thought of it sooner. Not so long ago, she'd asked me what I needed.

Catharsis.

I needed to purge the anger I'd held onto for four years.

"What?" I asked coldly. "They came after my daughter to get to my husband. I'm not letting it happen. End of story."

"Celia... after all this time, why are you still hellbent on protecting him? He knows these men—"

"Not like I do. If they're willing to provoke him like this, then they must think they have an advantage. What happens when the club goes up against them and loses? Are you willing to kiss Bear goodbye, knowing it might be the last time you see him alive?"

Molly mashed her lips together with a quick shake of her head. "No, but I don't see how you think two Ol' Ladies are going to take down an army. If the club can't kill those assholes, then how will we?"

I was tired of being weak.

A strange sense of calm settled over me. The night it happened, I'd put it all on Jamie to fight alone. Maybe that had been a mistake. I was just as much responsible for what happened as he was.

"They're counting on me alerting the club. They'll be so focused on the men that they'll never see us coming. I refuse to live the rest of my life in fear. What about you?"

She let her eyes move over the picture again before looking up at me. "I'm in."

Taking them out would either fix what they'd broken in me or turn me into a monster.

I found I was okay with either.

CHAPTER TWENTY-TWO

Celia: December 2004 (Age: 32)

"You're sure he'll come back?" Molly asked through the speaker of my cell phone.

I placed it in the cupholder and inched the car forward in the pick-up line, studying the face of every parent and teacher that walked by. "He'll show. He's taunting me now."

Two weeks.

It had become a twisted game of *Where's Waldo?* as I searched for his face in the crowd. That was the problem with men like him. They got cocky and made careless decisions, never imagining a woman could fight back.

Initially, my plan had been to take his son before Molly gently reminded me I was no better than they were if I did.

So, I waited patiently for him to reappear, and he didn't disappoint. Once, he'd even gone as far as waving to me before disappearing.

The breath burst from my lungs, and I jumped at the sound of loud tapping against my window. Fighting against every one of my instincts, I slowly turned to face him.

Manny lifted his fingers to his mouth and blew me a kiss with a wide grin before walking away.

"Was that him?" Molly whispered through the phone.

I gripped the steering wheel until my knuckles were white. "Y-yeah. That was him."

"What's he wearing today?"

Glancing at the side mirror, I replied, "Gray hoodie. Same as yesterday... and the day before that. He should be headed right toward you."

Manny had scoured the school grounds for bikes and leather vests, yet he seemed to miss the bright red Chevy Cavalier that trailed a few cars behind his every day.

Initially, I'd wanted to be the one to follow him, but I had Dakota with me. Plus, he knew what I drove. It was better for him to think I was weak and afraid.

Molly had insisted that she could use her own car, but knowing how dangerous the men were, I'd pulled my old car out of storage and had her snag some spare license plates from Bear's body shop. There was nothing on that car that could be traced back to either of us.

There were a few seconds of tense silence before she excitedly exclaimed, "Got him! He's getting into the same black sedan as before. Am I following him again? If so, you're gonna have to get Little Ricky to jiu-jitsu."

Dakota hitched her backpack up onto her shoulder when she saw me and began making her way over.

I grinned and waved to her before looking down at the phone. "Just make sure he goes back to the motel. Then meet me at the house. I'm ending this tonight."

"Tonight?" she all but screeched. "We're not re—"

I ended the call just as the back door opened and Dakota climbed in.

"Hey, baby girl. How was school?"

She pushed her glasses up onto the bridge of her nose and leaned forward in her seat. "What's wrong? Why are you smiling like that?"

"Nothing's wrong. Can't I just be happy to see my Kota-Bear?"

"Don't call me that. I'm not a baby," she protested with a frown as she buckled. "And you don't look happy. Just crazy—like Hela."

"Who's Hela?" I asked, checking the rearview mirror for any signs of Manny. My fingers itched to dial Molly for an update, but the last thing Dakota needed was a reason to worry. She and Kate managed just fine on their own.

"Hela, Mama." At my blank stare, she rolled her eyes and sighed, "We've been over this like a hundred times. Have you never picked up one of Daddy's old comics and flipped through? She's only the goddess of death and one of Thor's biggest enemies."

I stopped at a red light and turned to face her. "She's what?"

"Thor's biggest enemy? Well, not as much as Loki, but she still causes—"

"No," I interrupted. "The one before that."

Dakota's blue eyes momentarily widened in confusion until she realized I was genuinely curious about her favorite subject. Then, the corners of her mouth turned up in a big grin. "The goddess of death part? Yeah, that's pretty cool, right?"

"So cool." I turned back to face the road with a wince, needing a cigarette like I needed my next breath. She looked so much like her daddy that it took my breath away.

She went quiet again, so I prodded. "Goddess of death has a nice ring to it..."

"I mean, it's neat except for the minor issue of her helping Loki bring about the events of Ragnarok. Did you know she built her ship, Naflgar, out of the fingernails of the dead?"

Jamie would've lived for conversations like this, where I felt like she was speaking a different language.

"Fingernails? Okay, that's it. I've changed my mind. I was all set to become the goddess of death and defeat Thor, but I'm not doing arts and crafts with fingernails. That's where I draw the line," I said with a laugh, feeling lighter than I had in years.

I'd wasted years weaving crowns from flowers and hoping for neighborhood barbecues while forgetting that I'd always felt most alive on the arm of the god of death.

Maybe this was what I'd needed all along.

Dakota continued discussing how Hela tried and failed to defeat Thor while we waited to pick up Kate, and I found I didn't mind. I wasn't thinking about what to make for dinner or worrying that I'd left a door unlocked.

It felt like before.

Before Jamie faked his death.

Before Hawk began stealing from me.

Before the night I wanted so badly to forget.

If I couldn't bring their father home, the least I could do was resurrect their mother. I didn't want to be the girl who hid inside anymore. I had to get back to the woman who'd driven to a biker clubhouse in the middle of the night and demanded to speak to the Pres.

She was still in there. I knew it.

"Mama... Mama... Mama," Kate repeated from the passenger seat, waving a hand in front of my face.

"Sorry, zoned out for a second."

"She's still imagining a ship made of fingernails," Dakota giggled from the backseat.

Kate's nose wrinkled up. "Gross. Who would do that?"

I shook my head. "The goddess of death, apparently. Now, what were you asking?"

She shot a quick glance to the back seat, her eyes sparkling mischievously. "I was just thinking that you shouldn't have to cook dinner tonight. You're probably exhausted from working so hard..."

"Mmm-hmm..." A pop song came on the radio, and I began humming softly while tapping my fingers on the steering wheel to the beat.

Kate continued watching me earnestly, and I fought against the smile playing on my lips when I caught Dakota's inquisitive stare in the rearview mirror.

"You know, that's a good idea. I've been waiting for the day that you and Dakota would take over. I can sit back and watch my favorite show while yelling into the kitchen every five minutes to see if it's ready."

Dakota sank back down in her seat with a huff as Kate's shoulders fell. "I was actually—I mean, we were thinking it might be nice to just pick something up. That way, no one has to waste time cleaning up the kitchen—"

"Kate." I patted her leg. "You can stop now. We're picking up a pizza for dinner, and that's final." The grin returned to both girls' faces, and Dakota raised her fist in victory when we pulled into the parking lot.

We cranked the music on the drive home, the three of us belting out the lyrics like we were on stage. While Kate and I thumped our fists against our chests dramatically, Dakota squeezed her eyes shut and held her pretend microphone in a death grip.

I would've stopped time itself if it meant they could stay young and carefree forever. As that wasn't an option, I'd have to settle for knowing that the men who hurt me would never lay a finger on either of them.

If I had it my way, no man would ever raise a hand to them.

Dakota saw the motorcycle parked in the driveway before I did and began bouncing up and down in her seat. "Is that Angel? This really is the best day ever! I can't wait to fix his hair!"

"What's wrong with his hair?"

"Nothing's wrong with it, but he lets her take it down and brush it out like they're playing beauty shop," Kate explained while I parked, as if she was too grown up for such things.

"It's not a beauty shop. It's a superhero transformation center. When his hair is down, he looks like Thor. Well, like an old man Thor. I mean, his hair isn't blond, but it's long."

"And?" Kate pressed.

"And... he pays me five bucks just for doing it," Dakota finished sheepishly. "What? I didn't tell him to, but he said I have a natural talent."

She could have put his hair up in pigtails, and he would've given her the money all the same. Except for Lucy and Wolverine, no one loved those girls like he did.

When we moved out of my parent's house, he filled in as babysitter on the nights I worked late. Initially, I thought he was just doing it to help me until I saw how he was with them. He got just as much, if not more, out of it.

He stood up from the porch swing with a wave, and Dakota threw the car door open and went racing toward him. Kate stayed where she was, staring out the window.

"What's the matter, Katydid? You don't want to spend some time with Angel?"

She shrugged. "It's just that I'm almost fifteen, and other girls my age are babysitting. It doesn't seem fair."

I knew it was coming. By the time I was her age, I'd sat for half the kids in the neighborhood. If anyone was mature enough to stay home alone, it was Kate.

Unfortunately, the world preyed upon young girls and made them hard. By the time I discovered it at seventeen, it was too late. The darkness sank its talons into me while I was distracted by pretty words on the lips of a man in a leather vest.

"You and Angel have fun together, right?"

"Yeah, I guess," Kate admitted. "Sometimes he brings his old records, and we sit and play them, but I just feel like I'm old enough to stay alone."

It was apparent that she wasn't going to fall for a distraction, leaving me with only one option. I'd never be able to give her the real reason, so I settled for a version of the truth.

"Okay, it's time I let you in on a little secret, but you have to swear to never tell your sister."

She offered me her pinky finger. "I swear."

We linked them before I continued. "I've known for a while that you were old enough to watch your sister by yourself. It's just—it's Angel. You know he's all alone, and at least when he's here, I don't have to worry if he's getting a good meal. So, can you humor me, at least for tonight?"

With one hand on the door handle, she looked back at me. "I'm sorry, Mama."

I pulled the keys from the ignition and waved my hand. "No need to say you're sorry—you didn't know. We'll have some pizza, maybe see if you can talk Angel into renting a movie—"

"That's not it. I'm sorry because you're so quick to take care of everybody else, but there's no one to take care of you."

CHAPTER TWENTY-THREE

Celia: December 2004 (Age: 32)

The woman in the mirror was a stranger.

I hid my dark hair underneath a platinum blonde wig that trailed down over my shoulders. The greasy makeup that Molly had expertly applied made me look like a siren but felt as if it was caked onto my skin.

To complete my look, I wore sky-high heels and a dress I'd found at a second-hand store that dipped down low in between my breasts, leaving little to the imagination.

"I look like a whore."

Molly stood up on her tiptoes to look over my shoulder. "Yeah, you do. I'd pay good money for you, too. I think I might have some cash in my purse. Hang on."

"No, I'm serious." I tugged on the hem, struggling to make it reach the top of my thighs. I hadn't worn a dress since the night of the blackjack game. "I don't feel comfortable being this... exposed."

She dropped back onto her heels with a sigh. "I know, but we've been watching this prick for weeks now. He has a thing for breaking tiny blondes with huge tits and not much in the way of clothing. You fit the bill, but if you've changed your mind and would rather call in the club—"

"No, it needs to be me." I stared through the windows that overlooked the garage. Molly had insisted that Bear's body shop was the perfect place to hide out and get ready, yet I kept waiting for one of the bikers to bust us. "What does Bear use this apartment for, anyway?"

Molly gnawed on the corner of her finger. "You really wanna know the answer to that question, or should we move on to something else?"

With a grimace, I quickly responded with, "Something else. You know you have a problem, right?"

She threw her head back with a cackle. "A problem? It's only a problem if you're not getting any, which you most certainly are not. Don't tell me your last time was with Grey. Because if it was, you, my friend, are the one in need of a dicktervention."

The memory barged in uninvited, leaving my skin crawling. I clenched my hands into fists and focused on my reflection in the mirror until the whore gave way to the warrior.

The fog of numbness settled over me again.

I'd let myself feel it. Just as soon as they were dead.

She looked down at the floor. "I'm so sorry—"

My breathing gradually evened out, and I relaxed my shoulders before looking up at the clock on the wall.

"Don't be sorry," I snapped. "I'm so sick of everyone being sorry. I just want to get this over with so that I can go back to my life."

"Absolutely. Where's your gun?"

Heat flooded my face as I admitted, "I, um, I didn't bring it."

"What do you mean, you didn't bring it?" She narrowed her eyes, hands already moving up onto her hips. Any minute now, she was going to use her mom voice on me.

"Well..." My voice cracked, and I cleared my throat. "There's actually a really good explanation. A gunshot is going to attract the attention of every man in that motel. According to the cleaning lady, the windows don't open. So, obviously, I'll need to find a quieter method for... all that."

With a heavy sigh, Molly sank down onto one of the worn beanbag chairs. "That makes sense, but how exactly were you planning on handling 'all that?'"

I pulled the bodice of the dress away from my body to reveal the boning knife hidden in my corset bra. "With this."

She dropped her head down into her waiting palm with another sigh. "We're dealing with hardened criminals here, and you're bringing a knife to a gunfight. Literally. Please tell me you have a backup plan."

"The knife is my backup plan." Her head shot up hopefully. "I'm going to lead with jiu-jitsu, disarm him, and then just..." I gestured toward my throat with trembling hands. "Just do the... thing."

"Jesus Christ, Celia. When you said you were ending it tonight, I sort of thought you had some foolproof plan in place."

I straightened the dress. "It is foolproof! Tony said I was quickly becoming one of the best students in my class. I can take down men twice my size—"

"We need to call the club. Grey was ready to kick my ass for bringing you to *Leather & Lace* for fight night. Can you imagine what he'd do to me if I let you get yourself killed?"

"You really think he cares what happens to me now? I threw him out, Molly. Four years ago. Have you seen him around anywhere? Because I sure as hell haven't."

I snagged the small purse from the table and headed toward the door. "Either you're helping me or running to the club to tattle, but you can't do both."

"I want to help you," she pleaded. "But think about the girls, Celia!"

"Did you already forget the threat against Kate? I am thinking about the girls. I'm doing this for them."

She followed me down the stairs. "Celia, what happened to you that night? I want to help you, I do. But I can't if you won't open up to me."

Molly meant well. I knew she did. But giving my demons a voice wouldn't help anyone. Once she realized she wasn't going to get an answer out of me, she let it go and got in the car.

We'd decided on our drop-off location after following Manny for a week. He and his friends congregated every evening in the parking lot of a sleazy by-the-hour motel just off the interstate, blocks from where the local prostitutes gathered. Wanting to keep the list of potential witnesses at zero, we found a spot in between the two, near a towing company.

"It's not too late to back out," Molly blurted as she pulled up to the curb. "I just mean, I don't want you to feel like this is all on you."

The dome light kicked on as I opened the door, illuminating a face that had gone white as a sheet. She looked as if she was going to be sick at any moment.

"Hey." I reached across the console to squeeze her hand. "It's going to be okay. If I'm not back within an hour, you have my blessing to call in the cavalry."

She looked at the glowing green numbers on the dash and then back at me. "One hour. Please be safe."

"Who knows? He might be in the mood for a brunette tonight, in which case, I'll be back sooner than you think." I laughed, even though the thought left me feeling hollow inside.

This had to work.

I didn't have a backup plan.

As I teetered down the block, it quickly became apparent that I would never master wearing heels. Nothing about my movements screamed grace or sexiness. If anything, I resembled a drunk toddler.

Two hookers crossed their arms over their chests and moved shoulder to shoulder as I approached. The blonde one on my left chose to be the spokeswoman. "What the fuck do you think you're doin'? This is our corner."

I pulled a wad of cash from my purse. "I'd like to rent it for the night."

Wolverine had been pushing me to use the money in the bank account he helped me set up; money that I knew came from Jamie.

I finally listened.

She took the cash and quickly counted it before letting out a low whistle. "Holy shit, girl. This is five grand. Why you turnin' tricks when you got cash like this?"

"Revenge," I stated flatly. "Are we good?"

They both nodded in awe and took off, presumably before I changed my mind. I noted they looked like supermodels strutting a runway as they disappeared from view, leaving me to wonder if there was a class somewhere I'd missed.

A sane person would've been nervous when the familiar black car pulled up to the curb. Instead, I was strangely excited.

When he rolled down the window, I stumbled over, knowing from our surveillance that he was going to order me to get in. Despite what I'd learned by watching *Pretty Woman*, there were no questions regarding price per hour or how much it would cost him for the entire night.

Several of the girls who'd gone with him hadn't been seen since. It made what I was about to do even more important.

I climbed in before realizing that he hadn't said a word. He looked me over for several tense seconds before running his tongue over his lip ring.

"Fuck. You're a dime piece."

I didn't know what a dime piece was, but given that he hadn't thrown me out of his car yet, I could only assume it was something positive.

I took my lower lip between my teeth and blinked slowly as I looked up at him, something that had never failed to turn Jamie on.

He reached across and gripped my thigh. "You're quiet. I like that." When I stayed silent, he leaned over and whispered in my ear. "I bet I can make you scream, though."

Scream, Ma. Get those girls awake, and we'll show them a good time.

My leg muscles tightened under his fingers; as if my body remembered what my brain pleaded for me to forget and was urging me to run.

"It'd be nice if someone could," I joked softly, hoping he didn't hear the shakiness in my voice or notice that my fingernails were now embedded in the skin above my knee.

Manny sat back with a wide grin as he mashed the accelerator against the floorboard. "Oh, you're fuckin' perfect."

CHAPTER TWENTY-FOUR

Celia: December 2004 (Age: 32)

None of the men loitering in the motel's parking lot wore leather vests. It didn't make them any less menacing, though. In the weeks we'd spent watching, I hadn't seen Cobra or Hawk once, leading me to believe they were using Manny as bait to draw Jamie out into the open.

Then, and only then, would they move in.

He pulled around to the front, near a room I'd seen him enter and leave countless times, taking up two parking spots as he straddled the faded white line.

"Upstairs. Room two-twenty. Marcus is gonna check you for weapons."

How had Molly and I missed that detail?

Ignoring the beads of sweat that trailed down my spine, I shook my head and pushed my lips into a pout, letting my fingers roam over my breasts. "What if I just want your hands on me?"

The mere thought made me want to vomit. My performance had been too over-the-top. There wasn't a snowball's chance in hell he'd buy it.

Manny clenched his jaw, and I waited for the fist that was inevitably coming.

Proving that men like him only thought with what hung between their legs, his eyes followed the movement of my hand, nostrils flaring as he whispered, "I bet you're already wet for me, aren't you?"

I giggled and opened the door, sounding like a creepy animatronic bear the girls had growing up when its batteries were low. "Why don't you take me upstairs and find out?"

With a growl, he jumped out, all but dragging me up to the room. When he reached for the light switch just inside the door, I covered his hand with mine. "Get on the bed."

The street lights were one thing, but there would be no hiding who I was if he flipped that switch. His hand shot up and tightened around my jaw, and I realized I'd made a mistake. If I wanted to make it out of this alive, I had to think like he did.

"Let's get one thing straight, bitch. I make the rules. We clear?"

I nodded as the overhead light kicked on. "I under—"

He spit into my open mouth and grinned. "You do now."

Adrenaline flooded my body, and I dug my fingernails into the palm of my hand to fight it.

His eyes narrowed on my face, and he cocked his head to the side. "Wait a minute, I know you—"

"I don't think so." My heart hammered against my ribs, but I refused to take my eyes off of him. I'd been sucker-punched once before. This time, I was going to be ready for him.

His lip ring clicked against his teeth as he exclaimed, "I got it! You work at that bar over in the District. Shit, what's it called? *The Sink? The Tub?* Man, I can't remember. All I know is that my buddy, Fernando, fucked you in the bathroom, yeah?"

"Oh my god!" I sighed with relief. "Yes."

"I knew it, Ma."

It was surreal.

He'd gone out of his way to threaten my daughter and taunt me through car windows. But the same man who'd beaten and brutalized my body four years ago didn't seem to recognize me when I was standing right in front of him wearing a cheap wig.

Maybe I was the only one forced to relive the events of that night every time I closed my eyes.

The same fists that had broken my nose and split my lip now fell open in trust as I slipped the straps of my dress down over my arms.

I observed him from under my lashes as he stumbled back into the armchair beside the bed before working the thin material of my dress over my breasts.

A part of me tried to pretend it was Jamie. The other fought to remind me of why I was here.

This wasn't about gratification.

It was penance.

The mouth that had once left marks on my flesh fell open in awe as I tugged the dress down to my hips. He impatiently unzipped his jeans and began moving his hand up and down his already hard shaft.

Ignoring the empty feeling in the pit of my stomach at the sight, I shimmied out of the dress and stood before him in nothing more than heels and lingerie.

Manny's gaze trailed over my body appreciatively, and my mind descended into hell, replaying every agonizing moment in slow motion.

He'd done this—turned me into someone I no longer recognized.

I kicked off the heels and strode toward him, and he looked up with a drowsy grin, mistaking my rage for lust. "Right here, Ma." He thrust his hips in the air. "Let's see if that cunt is as tight as Fernando says it was."

Fuck me, doll. I'd be inside this cunt every day if I could.

The acid in my stomach moved up, burning my throat, and filling my mouth with a bitter taste. I swallowed past it and forced my body down onto the chair, knowing as I straddled his lap that the only thing separating us was a thin scrap of lace.

His hand moved beneath the waistband to cup me, and I exhaled loudly through my nose. My skin was in flames under the weight of his palm, but before I could pull away, his other hand came down like a weight against the back of my neck, guiding my mouth down over his.

His tongue began its brutal assault on my mouth, rough and unyielding against my lips. My resolve crumbled, and I sagged against his chest in defeat. Coming after him had been a mistake—I was too far gone.

Cry.

The word echoed so loudly in my head that I could've sworn it was being screamed at me through a loudspeaker.

Cry, and let him break you again.

Cry.

Cry.

Cry.

"No!" I roared, bucking my head back until I broke the contact between us. In the half a second it took for Manny to realize there was a problem, I'd freed the boning knife from my corset and pressed the tip of the blade against his throat.

"The fuck?"

I wanted to scream my name into his face and see the recognition in his eyes before I tore apart his flesh and reminded him of what he'd stolen from me.

My body.

My child.

My husband.

Grief expanded like a lump in my throat, preventing my words from escaping; but I hoped he saw the hatred in my eyes as I sank the blade into the soft flesh underneath his jaw.

Just like countless times before with beef and poultry, I made my cut, but my hand placement was all wrong, and I ended up dragging the knife backward across his throat.

As I did, blood began to flow from the wound—nothing like my experience with cutting up a whole chicken. By the time I realized I hadn't gone deep enough, Manny's hand was already latching onto my wrist.

One opportunity, and I'd blown it.

Blood trailed down the blade and over the fist I had clenched around the handle, shocking me with its warmth. The metallic stench flooded my nostrils just as a drop fell onto my thigh, spreading out like fingers. Agony stole the breath from my lungs, and I no longer saw his blood.

I saw my own.

"You fucking cunt!" he roared in my face.

I barely heard him over the pounding in my head. The back of his hand connected with my cheek, sending me sprawling onto the carpet.

The pain didn't even register.

All the ugliness I'd tried to keep hidden surfaced. I felt every bit of it. I watched in horror as the wounds reappeared on my body and the last piece of Jamie spilled out from between my legs.

I clawed at my throat and wheezed through a shallow breath while Manny circled me, like a lion going in for the kill.

He snagged my dress from the floor and held it to the wound on his throat before demanding, "Who sent you?"

When I stayed silent, he went for my hair, yanking the wig so forcefully that I came up off the carpet before it released from my scalp.

"Holy fuck, Ma. You gotta be the dumbest bitch alive. Needed another taste, huh? I'm gonna get another go at your ass, and then—"

He latched onto my real hair and began tugging until I was back on my feet beside him. "I'm gonna make you watch as I fuck your girl bloody before slitting her throat. And, unlike you, I know how to work a blade. Nod if you understand."

As he jerked my hair violently, making my head bob up and down like a marionette, something inside of me snapped.

I took a deep breath and closed my eyes, hearing Tony's voice loud and clear. I brought my hands up to cover Manny's and instinctively drove the heel of my foot into the side of his knee. He let out a small gasp of surprise before releasing me.

Time seemed to slow, and I reopened my eyes just as he began pulling away from me.

All he needed was one good hit to regain the upper hand. One blow to the side of my head, and it wouldn't matter how much training I had.

I slipped my right arm around his and covered his hand, effectively caging him under my armpit before bringing my left hand up to latch onto his forearm.

Knowing it was my last chance to save my family, I turned suddenly and dropped into a squat, forcing his arm across my body. Keeping both of my hands on his wrist, I used my weight against him and pressed down on his elbow, straining the joints and ligaments until he groaned in pain and began struggling to break free.

I'd never gone beyond a person's pain threshold with an arm-bar before. Typically, my opponent would tap and that was the end of it. This wasn't a game, though. If I released my grip now, Manny would fulfill every one of his warped promises.

With that in mind, I dug my toes into the carpet and sank all of my weight into the move. Eventually, the joints would give. If I was lucky, the bones would snap too; giving me a fighting chance.

Bits of wood flew toward us as the door was kicked in. The room plunged into darkness as men entered, and I realized that I'd never considered what would happen to my girls if I didn't succeed.

I should have taken my chances with the gun.

Manny moaned loudly as I put my weight on his elbow again. If I was going down, I was going to inflict as much pain on him as possible before they took me out.

A rough hand latched onto my hair, forcing my face up toward the ceiling. "Sorry, sweetheart, but Pres said no witnesses." He ground up against my backside. "I'd love to take my time with you, too."

Familiarity pierced the veil of panic as his arm tightened around my throat. I knew that voice. I released my hold on Manny and tried using my stance to free myself from his unforgiving grip.

He kicked my legs out from under me and lifted me higher until the tips of my toes just grazed the carpet. The sounds of struggle were muffled in my attempt to get oxygen.

"Michael," I croaked, clawing blindly at his arm. "Comedian—"

Instead of going dark, everything became brighter, and I squinted against it, only to see the man I'd been trying to protect glaring back at me.

"Jesus Christ, Celia," Jamie growled. "What the fuck are you doin' here?"

At the sound of his voice, moisture pooled between my thighs. Proving that I was beyond saving, it had taken four years and Death himself to make me wet.

CHAPTER TWENTY-FIVE

Grey: December 2004 (Age: 40)

Comedian relaxed his hold, and Celia stumbled forward on the carpet, coughing violently. My arms instinctively came up to catch her, but she planted her bloody palms against my chest and pushed off.

"Where is he?" she croaked, scanning the room with eyes that were wild—with rage? Lust?

I didn't know.

We'd had to rely on a former stripper turned madam to get a lead that finally paid off. Three of her girls had disappeared around the same time she noticed an increase in bikers in the area, and she'd confronted Comedian, convinced my club was behind it.

The fact that I'd heard about the encroachment from a whore instead of a hang around hadn't set well with me. If another club even sneezed in our territory, it was their job to let me know.

"Answer the fuckin' question, Celia," I demanded through clenched teeth. "Why are you here?"

"Go to hell, Grey." Her chest heaved up and down with each ragged breath she took, pulling my attention back to her tits. Tits that were covered by nothing more than some see-through lacy shit that pushed them up under her chin.

Torch sucked air through his teeth at her insult and dropped his gaze down to the stained carpet. Bear scratched an invisible itch on his neck and studied a cheap painting on the wall, clearly waiting for the explosion.

There was a time when I would have demanded she show me respect in front of my men. A time when I would have dragged her kicking and screaming back to the clubhouse. As it was, it was taking everything in me not to shed my kutte and wrap it around her as a reminder to anyone stupid enough to look.

She laid eyes on the gangbanger, and with a low growl, stalked over to where my newest patch, Crossbones, held him.

He looked up at me helplessly. "Pres?"

What I needed to do and what I wanted to do were miles apart, but I had to stick with my original plan where she was concerned.

No matter how much it hurt.

"Couldn't do it yourself, could you, Ma?" He spit in her face, and I stepped forward, only to be met with Comedian's arm.

He appeared to be oblivious to the tension in the room as he watched her with something like admiration before muttering, "Let's see what she's got."

Crossbones held the prick's arms back, and Celia drove her knee into his groin with a vicious smirk.

He doubled over with a quiet grunt before cackling. "You put up more of a fight with Cobra—"

Something came over her at his words, and she raked her fingernails down the sides of his face with a scream, driving her knee into his gut repeatedly, before retrieving a boning knife from the carpet.

The blade was all wrong for what she was trying to do. It wasn't effective. She was exerting too much energy and would have exhausted herself long before the asshole was close to death.

If we were ever forced to resort to hand-to-hand combat, we stuck with trench knives. The brass knuckle handle provided better stability and control.

Bear met my stare and shook his head ever so slightly, urging me to call it off. Rage flooded my veins, and I nodded. It had gone on long enough. She should have been at home with our daughters, not holed up in a shitty motel room like some half-naked hit woman.

Her hand shook violently as she pressed the blade to the superficial wound at his throat, and I moved toward her. "Celia—"

"Better listen to your man, Ma. He's the one in—"

"You stay quiet, and I won't cut out your tongue," she forced out through clenched teeth before digging the tip of the blade into his skin. "Good and quiet."

I waited for her to finish it, but she stood frozen, the breath bursting in and out of her lungs. Torch's boot caught the edge of the bed as he moved closer, and she flinched before bringing her elbows in close to her body as if trying to become smaller.

My men looked at me, and I held up a hand, signaling for them to wait. Her green eyes widened when I moved closer, darting back and forth between the gangbanger and me.

"Can't do it, can you?" he taunted. "That's okay, Ma. I'll still hold up my end of our agreement."

I jumped in surprise when Celia snapped and drove her fist into his jaw with a quick, high-pitched burst of laughter.

It wasn't a laugh of amusement, but one of sheer panic. The woman in front of me wasn't my wife. She was little more than a wounded animal that had been cornered.

Crossbones' jaw clenched, and he tightened his grip, only holding himself back on my orders. "Pres?"

Ignoring everything I knew, I latched onto her upper arms and pulled back, feeling the vibrations of her body beneath my palms. Keeping my voice low and even, I said, "I need you to come with me, darlin'."

She jerked out of my grasp and angled her chin up at me, proudly displaying a split lip and the beginnings of a bruise forming across her cheek. "You need to leave. I'm in the middle of something."

"In the middle of somethin'? Like what? Gettin' yourself killed? Fuckin' Christ, Celia!" I ran my hand through my hair, fighting to calm down.

I'd save my rage for the gangbanger, taking my time to make his death slow and painful. By the time I sent him to the Reaper, I doubted there'd be much left of him.

Her nostrils flared. "I was doing just fine before you barged in—"

"You weren't," I stated flatly. I nodded to Crossbones, and he released the gangbanger to me. He immediately cradled his left arm, so that was the one I latched onto as I dragged him back over to her. "What possessed you to come here?"

"Why do you think she was here, *hijo de puta*?" he spat. "She needed another taste—to be reminded that she's nothing but holes to be filled—"

This time it was Comedian who stepped forward and drove a fist into the guy's gut, silencing him. He went to his knees with a loud exhale. I took advantage of the position and caught his left arm on the way down, forcing it over my thigh until I felt the bones give beneath my hands and heard the snap.

Bear raised an eyebrow in question as the gangbanger collapsed near my boots with a moan. Initially, we'd agreed to be in and out, saving the torture for when we were back at the clubhouse. That was before I knew she was here, though.

Ignoring his pointed stare, I knelt over the gangbanger with a grin. "You see what I did there, Celia? You hyper-extended his arm. I broke it."

His eyes rolled back in his head as I forced his jaw up, exposing his mangled neck. Feeling generous, I decided to let him sleep it off for a few minutes. With days, maybe even weeks, of torture in store, he needed to keep his strength up.

"Pres?" Comedian interrupted, but I continued.

"Looks like you tried to slit his throat, but you didn't get the blade deep enough. You were using the wrong knife—"

"Pres?"

"Now, it's obvious you came here to kill him, but he's still breathing. So, you tell me where you had it all under control—"

"Grey!" Comedian snapped, and I jerked my head up.

Celia had backed herself into a corner near the bed, wincing as she examined her fist. She cradled it in her arm, panting like she had when she was in labor with the girls. It was her eyes, though, that stopped me in my tracks—staring through me to an enemy no one else could see.

I'd taken it too far.

"Get him out of here," I demanded. "Get everybody out of here!"

Bear hauled the prick to his feet, digging his fingers into the skin of his broken arm until he was wide awake and screaming.

I waited until they were gone before approaching her. "Celia, princess, can you hear me?"

She responded with a deep breath and a jerky nod. "It's just my hand—"

"Is it broken?" I held my palm out, and she reluctantly placed it in mine. As I ran my thumb lightly across the raw knuckles, her nipples tightened beneath the sheer lace. And my cock, which had been hard since laying eyes on her, strained against my zipper, begging for release.

God, I wanted to fuck her.

I tried to adjust myself discreetly before checking her over, but she caught it, and her tongue darted out to lick along her lower lip. It only made me harder.

"You're uh, you're gonna be sore..." My voice trailed off as her nipples peeked through the sheer lace, and I fought to get myself back on track. "But it doesn't... it doesn't feel like anything's broken."

Celia's chest rose and fell rapidly, and I worried she was slipping away again. She'd obviously developed some strong coping skills, but maybe being alone in a room with me was bringing back bad memories.

With a slow smile and slight tremble, she brought her palm up to rest in the center of my chest. I held my breath as the other one moved up to cup my jaw. Her touch was electric, sending a jolt straight to my cock.

She slipped her hand beneath my kutte and fisted the t-shirt, all while watching me with those wide green eyes. As much as I wanted to lose myself in her body, I held back, letting her navigate.

"Jamie," she whispered, and I couldn't help myself. I reached out and let my hand trail through the dark curls on her head.

Her breath rasped out as a flush worked its way up her chest and, just like a book of matches near a can of gasoline, she moved up against me and ignited a spark.

CHAPTER TWENTY-SIX

Grey: December 2004 (Age: 40)

Our mouths collided roughly, reopening both of our wounds. I sucked the iron from her lips—a man starved for the taste of her. Fingernails dug into my chest as her hands moved almost frantically over my muscles, gripping me like a lifeline.

I fought to take a breath, knowing it was too much, too soon.

I needed to pull away, but at her soft exhale, I palmed her ass and dragged her up into my arms. Her legs wrapped tightly around my waist, her thighs holding me in place while she rocked against me.

My mind shut off as I walked us over to the floating vanity near the A/C unit and set her down on top of the worn laminate counter. The antique mirror above it had gone cloudy, giving the appearance that we were surrounded by fog.

With a soft moan, she slipped her tongue between my lips, and I forgot why kissing her was a bad idea. I forgot why I'd fought against it for so long. That first time her lips connected with mine, I'd been a goner.

I blinked against the sting of tears as I was taken back to that afternoon in my office at *Inked on Broadway*.

When shit went south, I couldn't even look at that couch without being reminded of everything I'd given up for the club.

My hands slipped beneath the waistband of her lace panties and roamed over her ass as she pulled my lower lip between her teeth.

Goosebumps spread over her skin when my fingers brushed across a rough patch of skin near her hip, and it was like flipping a switch. One minute she was grinding against me, and the next, she was struggling to get as far away as possible.

She scrambled down off the counter, and toward the wall, pushing both palms out. "Wait!"

I nodded with a rough exhale and took a step back, waiting for her to make the next move. It was vital for her to feel like she was in control. I knew that, but it was damn near impossible to keep my hands to myself.

"I'm... I'm not sure what's wrong with me." Celia moved toward the mirror again, studying her reflection before meeting mine. "I'm sorry."

"What are you apologizin' for? You don't owe me a fuckin' thing, princess. I'm sorry."

I'd keep apologizing for that night until the breath left my body, even knowing that it wouldn't change a goddamn thing.

She gave me a shaky nod before turning back to the discolored glass in front of her. "I just..." She sighed. "I just feel strange."

"Strange?" I asked carefully, moving behind her until I was close enough that my cock brushed up against her, but not enough to leave her feeling trapped. Keeping my eyes on her reflection, I pressed my lips to the side of her neck before whispering, "How?"

Her teeth sank down onto her lower lip with a muffled groan as she turned to face me. "I... I'm incredibly turned on right now. It's like hitting Manny gave me this high. That's weird, right?"

I shook my head.

It would've been weird to anyone else but me.

The realization that I might've turned her into something like myself left me feeling sick.

"Why'd you come here?" she whispered. The lost expression on her face turned into one of anguish, and I wanted to drop to my knees at her feet—to beg for forgiveness. For answers. For anything that could fix the two of us.

"I came for you."

She gave me a shaky nod and reached between us, working the panties down to her thighs. "Maybe you came for this." Her movements were the same as before. If I hadn't known the truth, would I have seen the terror reflected in her eyes?

Or would I have missed it, just like I had everything else?

Her panties were soaked, and it took every ounce of strength I still possessed to pull away. "Princess, I ain't fuckin' you in a shitty motel room."

"I never imagined there'd be a day you'd turn down sex," she said with a shaky laugh. "I must be losing my touch." Her knees buckled, and she stumbled, turning to catch herself on the counter.

I didn't laugh; didn't even crack a smile. My eyes were glued to the circular mark on her hip. It wasn't flat like a scar but raised up. The pattern seemed strange until my brain reversed it, and I realized what it was I was seeing.

A lucky thirteen encased within a diamond.

As if raping and beating her hadn't been enough, the motherfuckers had branded her.

"Jamie?"

I stroked her skin with the pad of my thumb. "He do this to you?"

Celia bit down on the corner of her lip, looking like she was seconds away from crying. I wasn't sure what I expected, but when she turned back and wrapped her arms around my waist, I knew that wasn't it.

She buried her face in my chest, and I did the one thing I knew how to do with her. In front of a grimy mirror, we held each other. The feel of her body up against mine only reinforced my decision to kill anyone who'd played a role in what happened that night. I held onto her like she was my salvation.

And she had been.

Even if she didn't know it yet.

"I want to be the one to kill him," she said softly, and I could've sworn I'd heard her wrong.

"Celia—"

She stepped out of my embrace with a shake of her head, and I realized she hadn't been close to tears. Even as her nostrils flared, her cold eyes remained dry. "Don't try to talk me out of it, Jamie."

"Princess, I ain't lettin' him spend one more second near you—"

She jabbed a finger into my chest. "That's not your call to make."

"Ain't askin' for your permission," I snapped. "He laid hands on you. Now, he's gonna deal with me. That's the way it goes. Did you drive down here?"

Crossing her arms over her chest, Celia stared up at me through narrowed eyes. "Like you don't already know."

I cocked my head to the side and pinched my lip. "What the hell are you talkin' about? You think if I knew a goddamn thing about you bein' here that it would've gotten as far as it did?"

Had I known she had plans to become an assassin, I would've intercepted her before she ever made it to his room. Fuck, I would've stopped her before she ever left the house. My world and her world were never meant to mix.

Celia's hand moved up to her hip. "Right." Her lips curled up into a cruel smirk. "I'm supposed to believe that Molly didn't call you, and you just magically knew to show up here? She and I had an agreement. One hour."

"Molly?"

Oh, Bear was going to have a field day with that one. I doubted Molly would be able to sit for a week.

My neck cracked as I looked up at the water-stained popcorn ceiling before shaking my head. "Molly knew about this? You recruited Molly for this plan? This ain't a game, Celia! You go up against these guys and they will kill you!"

"And what about you?" She moved closer, standing toe to toe with me. "Do you think you're immune?"

I knew I wasn't, but if anyone deserved to be on the front line, it was me. I swallowed and stared down at her feet; my mouth suddenly dry. "I fucked up, and you got hurt. I couldn't live with myself if it happened again. Why can't you let me handle this?"

"Because I can't!"

Celia was the only one who pushed me, the only one who dared to stand up to me and fight for control. When she didn't elaborate, I threaded a hand through her hair, lightly tugging her up against me. She lowered her eyes to the floor, forcing me to tighten my hold until her chin lifted.

She watched warily as I brought my other hand up to rest at the base of her neck, her throat bobbing up and down in a nervous swallow. "Let me go."

My girl was bold, I'd give her that, but she knew nothing about the underworld I called home. The path I'd been on since I was sixteen led to one place, and I wasn't willing to drag her down with me, even if she was my greatest weakness.

I nodded. "I will. Just as soon as you let go of this idea that you can take these guys on your own—"

Her lips curled up as she bared her teeth and snarled, "You're just stupid enough to get yourself killed, aren't you? What makes you think you can stop them? If it weren't for me, you wouldn't have even known where Manny was!"

"If it weren't for you?" I chuckled, having moved past anger and into amusement. "That's fuckin' cute. Wrong, but cute."

I'd tried patience and gentleness, but her goddamn stubbornness pushed me beyond rational thought and ignited my temper. I was hanging on by a thread, and I knew that if it snapped, she'd never recover. The monster would devour her whole.

She sucked in a breath, her eyes brimming with homicidal rage as she dragged her claws down my face. "They want you dead! Don't you know that?"

I released her hair and grabbed her wrists, stopping the assault. "And why the fuck do you care? I chose this life, princess!"

With a deep breath, she dropped her hands and backed away. Any relief I may have felt was gone the minute she opened her mouth.

"You may have chosen this life, but I was forced into it, and I'm not willing to sit at home. You want me to believe that you've got it all under control, but you don't. You're still running into situations without thinking them through."

She was starting to sound like Wolverine. Instead of listening, I studied my wounds in the mirror. The red streaks started just below my eyes and disappeared into my beard.

She'd done worse.

Didn't mean she wasn't gonna pay for it. I'd let her push me past the point of sanity. Fuck niceties. Now, I wanted to fight.

"Explain to me how tracking a gangbanger's movements is considered 'running,' Celia. Way I see it, me showin' up here saved your ass—"

Her chin raised defiantly, and I was almost convinced she didn't need to be handled carefully. What she needed was to be taken over my lap before I fucked the opposition out of her.

"They were baiting you, Grey. And if they were bold enough to do that, then they must think they've got the numbers to take you."

"Baiting me how?" I ignored her use of my club name, focusing instead on the idea that the men who hurt her would be stupid enough to do it again.

The green eyes that had been narrowed at me in anger now widened in surprise, as if realizing she'd revealed more than she wanted.

"Celia," I tried again. "Baiting me how?"

Her arms went around her torso, holding herself together before she quietly admitted, "He—Manny—showed up at Dakota's school a few weeks ago. He gave her a photograph of Kate. They were going to use her as bait to get to you. I wasn't going to let it happen."

Saliva flooded my mouth, and I clenched my hands into fists, relishing in the sound of my knuckles cracking under the pressure. "How?"

Her eyes flashed with something, but it was gone as soon as she blinked. "There was a message on the back of the picture—"

"Do you have it?" She shook her head, and I pushed. "Where is it? What'd it say? Goddammit, Celia! Just fuckin' tell me!"

I'd take Manny to the brink of death and then bring him back. Maybe I'd do it over and over again.

"I wonder if she'll cry when I break her in..."

My nostrils flared, and she watched in silence as I began pacing the room. "Motherfucker!" I growled. "I'm gonna rip his dick off and force it down his throat. Then I'll move onto his hands—one digit at a time."

"It should be me—"

"Absofuckinglutely not," I bit out. "Ain't lettin' him breathe the same air as you ever again. Call Molly, tell her you need to be picked up." I crossed my arms over my chest, signaling the end of our discussion.

Her mouth fell open. "Don't you treat me like a little girl! It's too late. I've seen your world, and no matter how hard I try, I can't forget it."

Lust flooded my veins as I thought of all the ways I could prolong death, keeping the gangbanger alive for as long as I saw fit. It didn't matter which god he prayed to. By the time I was done with him, he'd be begging for my forgiveness... for my mercy.

"Maybe you've forgotten, but you don't make the rules, darlin'. You're lucky I've got work to do, or I'd be takin' a hand to your ass and haulin' you out of here myself. What do you say to that?"

"What do I say?" she spluttered. "Go to hell, Grey! That's what I say to that! You can't just lock me away like I'm helpless!"

I absolutely could and would if it came to it. No one would ever touch her or my girls again. She began working her panties back up over her hips, but not before I saw the wetness clinging to the inside of her thighs.

My girl still wanted me.

The real me.

That was all I needed to know. The rest was just details.

CHAPTER TWENTY-SEVEN

Grey: March 2005 (Age: 41)

I stepped into the dark room with a wide grin. "You know what today is, *amigo*?"

Manny watched me with bulging eyes from the wall he was propped up against, arms tied up behind his back. A rope ran from his bound wrists and up over a metal beam near the ceiling, keeping him tethered like a leash. It must have been a bitch trying to find a comfortable position. If I had to guess, I'd say he wasn't getting much rest.

"C'mon," I prodded. "Don't get shy on me now. No guesses? Fine, I'll tell you. It's the first day of spring! You believe that shit? Time flies when you're havin' fun though, right? How long have we been doin' this now—three months?"

When he stayed silent, I kicked him with the toe of my boot before tugging the rope, hoisting his body up into the air. His arms hung suspended behind his back, transferring all of his weight to his shoulder sockets. He groaned and expelled a stream of snot from his nose before fighting to take a breath.

"You remember what this is called, *amigo*? No?" I loosened my hold on the rope, letting him drop a few inches, before stopping him with a sudden yank.

"Sss-tttt—"

"Ssss-tttt... the fuck you tryin' to say? We been over this. Strappado. Shit, can you imagine if I didn't watch the History Channel? I'd be runnin' out of ideas on ways to keep you entertained, *hombre*."

Manny lifted his head to stare at me, the hatred rolling off of him in waves. In all honesty, I hadn't meant to keep him alive as long as I had. No matter what I did to him, he would never give up Hawk or Cobra.

I knew that. Still, I forced him to stay alive.

When he refused to eat or drink, we brought our club doctor, Eli, in and hooked him up to an IV. He'd been on the verge of death more times than I could count, but there was just something that held me back and kept me from sending him to the Reaper.

"Now..." I wound the rope around a hook on the wall, securing him in the air, before retrieving a CD from my bag and popping it into the player. "Let's play a little game. You tell me where your buddies are, and I'll..." I paused and lit up a cigarette, leaving him to dangle while I decided his fate.

Initially, I thought that it'd get old, but anytime I found myself ready to give up or thinking that maybe I'd gone too far, I imagined my girl's broken body.

The monster inside of me had been well fed for months, and I slept better than I had in years.

I took a long drag. "How about this? You tell me what I want to know, and I won't cut off another tattoo."

Somber music filled the space, and I exhaled a stream of smoke toward his face with a smirk. "I told you how I ended up with this music, right?"

He bucked against his restraints but stayed quiet.

"I didn't? Well, I was in a real bad place after I saw what you did to my girl, Manny. Strung out and fucked up don't even begin to cover it. When I was tryin' to get clean, someone suggested meditation."

I took another drag with a low chuckle. "It's hard to imagine, yeah? So, I go down to the record store, and I'm fuckin' lookin' everywhere for somethin' to help me center myself or some bullshit, and the clerk recommends Tibetan chants. Really thought I'd listen and find my inner peace, but Jesus Christ, it is creepy as fuck! Who am I kidding? You know—you listen to it every night."

"K-k-kill m-m-me," he whispered through cracked lips.

I stubbed my cigarette out on his forearm with a shake of my head and immediately lit up another. "No can do, *amigo*. Who would I spend my days with? Tell you what, though, you tell me where your buddies are, and I'll consider your request."

In the early days, he'd bragged about the things they'd done to Celia, about the things he wanted to do to my girls. Maybe he thought I'd lose my temper and give him a quick death. The old me would have put a bullet in his head and been done with it, but the clean and sober version had all the patience in the world.

I was in control.

The cigarette dangled from my lips as I pulled the knife from my pocket and opened it up, letting the back of the blade trail over his chest. "Tick-tock, *amigo*. Time is runnin' out."

The door beside me opened, and Wolverine stepped inside, eying Manny with a look of disgust. "You ain't cracked yet? How much longer you wanna drag this out?"

"He ain't gonna give up his brothers," I said, before poking the tip into the center of a tattoo on his abdomen. "I like this one. A tiger with a snake in its mouth. That's somethin' you don't see every day."

Wolverine moved in to inspect it. "I'll be damned. That reminds me of someone else's. What was that prick's name? Chris? No, that ain't it. Shit, Grey, you remember?"

"Yeah. Carlos. It's funny that you joined *Los Dictadores* and got your gang ink, but you still got no fuckin' clue what it means."

"It doesn't mean shit," Manny croaked.

Wolverine held out his hand, and I placed the knife in it. There was nothing I loved more than watching him carve someone up. I'd seen him retrieve colors on more than one occasion, with a precision that couldn't be matched.

"See," he noted casually, as he slipped the blade under the skin. "That's where you're wrong."

Manny's nostrils flared, and he groaned as Wolverine lifted the edge of his tattooed flesh before continuing. "Back when I ran the club, *Los*

Dictadores worked hand in hand with the Serpents. There was an incident involvin' payment, and suddenly, *Los Dictadores* was out.

"Turned out, another MC had issues with them, too. Knew to strike when the iron was hot, though, and they approached the gang to form a partnership. The Outlaws and *Los Dictadores* even redesigned their club ink to reflect the change."

The skin was peeled away from his body, rolling up like a sheet of paper as Wolverine moved the blade.

I stepped forward and gripped Manny's face in my hands. "How fuckin' stupid do you have to be to join up with your gang's number one enemy? And not only that, but to protect them? If you don't think they would've rolled over on you the first chance they got, then you need to look long and hard at what it was they had you doin'."

Wolverine made his final cut, and the tattoo fell away from the skin. I caught it in my palm and held it up for Manny to inspect. "You forgot what it was your gang used to stand for, so we relieved you of your colors. Tell me where to send it."

I loosened the rope and lowered him back down to the concrete floor. He forced his head back and looked up at me, blinking slowly.

It was the same every time.

Wolverine nodded toward the hall, and I followed him out, but not before cranking the music up. After wiping the blade on his jeans, he handed it back to me and crossed his arms over his chest. "He ain't gonna survive much more, Grey."

I nodded. "I know. I was hopin' we'd be able to get somethin' out of him. I'm sick of chasin' these guys."

"I hear ya, but if he was gonna break, it would've happened long before now. Best we can do is find a place to drop his body that would send a message loud and clear." He tilted his head to the side. "How are you holdin' up?"

"Me? I'm fine. I could do this all day. Fuck, if we needed to keep him alive for years, I'd do it—"

He grinned. "Ain't questionin' your abilities when it comes to torture, son. I wanna know how you are—you seen Celia?"

"I see her every night. You know that."

"Campin' out in the backyard ain't the same as seein' her. I'm worried about her." He tapped the side of his head. "She ain't been herself in years, but ain't a doubt in my mind that if anyone could reach her, it'd be you."

I'd planned on waiting to approach her until all the threats were eliminated, but still hadn't worked out what exactly I'd say after she'd made it clear she never wanted to see me again the last time. In hindsight, locking her in the motel room until Molly arrived to pick her up hadn't been my best idea.

At the sound of a wail, I tore my eyes away from Wolverine and looked back toward the door with a shake of my head. I hadn't seen Celia cry in years, yet Manny seemed to do it almost every day.

"To be honest," I admitted. "I don't have a plan. For any of it. I thought that I'd finish them off and then go to her, but I just don't know."

Wolverine scratched at his beard with a slow nod. "You ever stopped to think about what she wants?"

It was all I thought about.

My last encounter with her had fucked with my head for days. How was I supposed to regain the upper hand while making her feel like she was in control? It was impossible.

"Old man, I think about what she wants every second of every goddamn day. Don't mean shit if those fuckers are still out there, though."

Manny's groans of pains blended with the chanting into one perfect soundtrack of torture.

"Have you ever asked yourself what's kept you from killin' the gangbanger? You've had the opportunity to send him to the Reaper, but you pull back. Why is that?"

"We've been over this. I don't know—"

"Think," he interjected. "What does your girl want more than anything right now?"

Other men in my position wouldn't have wasted time with hypothetical conversations, but Wolverine was like Slim in that he always seemed to know how to break through to me.

Realization dawned, and I looked up at him incredulously. "You're serious? You want me to hand him over to her to finish off?"

"Normally, I'd be against an Ol' Lady dolin' out any sort of punishment. This ain't their club, and they don't call the shots. But the way I see it, you can kill two birds with one stone here. Club don't even have to know it was her."

My fingers curled into fists at the thought of him being close to her again. But Wolverine had presented the perfect solution. I'd had the answer staring me in the face for the past three months.

I ran my tongue over my teeth with a grin.

I suddenly knew exactly how to get my woman back.

CHAPTER TWENTY-EIGHT

Grey: March 2005 (Age: 41)

The light switch in the laundry room flipped on, sending a stream of light across the backyard and directly into my eyes. It was the only room in the house without blinds and one she seldom entered at night.

After checking my watch, I sat up in the hammock and watched as Celia carried an armful of laundry over to the washer. The sight of her messy curls and sleep-scarred face left my cock aching, but it was the look of fear on her face that had me up and moving toward the back door without another thought.

The lock was engaged, and it took some searching before I found the spare hidden beneath a garden gnome in a nearby planter. The sound of the door opening seemed magnified in the silence, and I held my breath as I crept toward the laundry room.

I didn't want to startle her. I just needed to know she was okay. The washer was shaking violently when I entered the empty room, and I belatedly remembered that I was supposed to have replaced the suspension springs on it a few years before. It slammed into the side of the dryer with such force that an entire army could have entered the house and I doubted Celia would've heard it.

First thing tomorrow, they'd both be replaced.

The nursery door was closed, and I paused just outside, fighting the urge to go in and see Kate and Dakota. I realized the vision of them in my head was all wrong. Kate was a teen, not a toddler, and given what I'd heard about Dakota, me calling her a baby would end bloody.

I'd come for their mother, though.

Light spilled out from around the master bedroom door, and I silently pushed it open before entering. The bed had been stripped down to the mattress, and the floor was littered with uncovered pillows.

My pulse raced as I scanned the room for Celia before spotting her in the bathroom. She sat in the tub with her back to me.

"Cry," she stated, in a voice that sounded nothing like hers. She repeated the word, and I watched in horror as she picked up a razor blade and ran it sideways across her arm. Blood welled to the surface and trailed over her skin, but she didn't even flinch. "Cry."

"Celia?" I rushed in, only to be knocked flat on my back. I blinked until my vision cleared and looked up into the eyes of a stranger.

The softness I'd seen in glimpses the last time we were together was completely gone, replaced by a hardness that only came from surviving the unthinkable.

"Why are you here?" she demanded, digging the blade into my throat. Every nerve ending in my body went haywire at the feel of her naked body on top of mine, even as my brain tried reminding me she had a weapon.

"Why are you doin' laundry in the middle of the night?" I croaked, struggling to move. I managed to sit up, only to be knocked back to the tile in a way that didn't seem physically possible.

"Asked you a question, princess."

She snorted and shifted forward, right up against my cock. "I asked you first. Why are you here?"

I swallowed and propped myself up on my elbows. "I'm pretty goddamn stubborn, so it took me a little longer, but someone once told me that when you love someone, you go after them. I saw the lights kick on in the laundry room and wanted to check on you—"

Her palm came down on my chest, forcing me back to the tile as she hissed, "You broke in? This may come as a shock, but you don't live here anymore! You can't come and go as you—wait, how did you know I was in the laundry room? Are you stalking me now?"

"Not stalkin' you. I've been sleepin' in the hammock. Wanted to stay close in case you needed me."

"You—you've been spying on me? I thought I was pretty clear in that I didn't want to see you again."

I remained pinned in place under her thighs. Lying still would've been the smart thing to do. Instead, I thrust my hips up, watching in amusement as the denim of my jeans brushed up against her pussy, forcing a gasp from her lips.

I was nothing but pent-up aggression and sexual frustration. Frustration that was growing stronger the longer my wife used her body to hold me in place. "What happens when you get tired?"

Her green eyes narrowed. "I won't."

The corner of my lip turned up in a soft smile. "Darlin', you need to be able to put a man down—not give him thoughts of fuckin' you."

I dropped my gaze down her body, driving home my point, and not missing the way her pink nipples puckered under my stare. Something like a whimper crossed her lips before she stood, breaking the contact between us.

"You should go," she said flatly, refusing to meet my eyes.

I rubbed the back of my head as I sat up. "You want me back outside, I'll do it. But I ain't leavin'. I don't give a fuck how long it takes to prove to you that there ain't nothin' more important in the world. Before I go, though, I wanna know why you're cuttin' yourself."

Her hand dropped to the wound on her arm, covering it. "It was an accident," she lied.

"And since when do you wash sheets in the middle of the night when no one's sick?"

"Jamie," she pleaded. "Just stop. I had a nightmare... just a stupid dream."

Trauma could manifest itself in a variety of ways. And while Celia's coping skills were impressive, her mind was filled with land mines of bad memories. She might have known how to avoid them during the day, but night was a different story.

"Your mind..." I trailed off, realizing that by saying anything more,

I'd be revealing what I knew. "It, uh, it fucks with you sometimes. I've been there a time or two."

She retrieved her robe from where it was thrown over her vanity chair and wrapped it around herself before sitting down. "You have?"

I walked over to her and knelt, ignoring the stab of pain in both of my kneecaps. "You know, I ain't really opened up to you about my life. It always felt like you had this idea of me—that you saw me as a good person. And maybe I thought it'd be better if you never knew who I truly was."

Her eyes widened, but she moved in closer, silently urging me to continue.

"I told you that my ma and I had a rough go with my old man, and her losin' the baby only made things worse." At the mention of the word baby, something like grief flashed in Celia's eyes, and she reached for my hand.

"What I, uh, never told you is what happened the night I patched in. I was a sophomore in high school and used to spend all my time with Slim at Phantom's body shop. It was easier than bein' at home and watching Ma self-destruct or gettin' in the way of my old man's fists."

I paused, struggling to say the words; to give a voice to the pain that I'd held onto since I was sixteen. "Slim told me one night that Donald had gone against the club. From what he'd overheard, they were gonna take him out. I rushed home, ready to tell Ma to pack her bags, but I couldn't find her anywhere..."

Celia's fingers tightened around mine, and I took a deep breath. I'd only told the story once before, to Wolverine, while sobbing like a baby. "I found my old man in the kitchen, drunk and covered in blood. After runnin' through the entire house, I found her. Right where I'd come in. She'd been behind the front door the entire time—"

"Oh, Jamie," she breathed.

I saw my mother's lifeless eyes staring through me and shuddered. "She'd never even had a chance. The worst part is that it didn't even hit me how much I still missed her until I found you. She would've loved you, Celia. And the girls. Ain't a doubt in my mind she would've spoiled the shit out of 'em—Mikey too."

The tears fell to my cheeks as I blinked, and she brought a hand up to brush them away, watching me with a curious expression. "I never imagined... you and Angel have always been so tight-lipped on it. I guess I just assumed she'd passed, but never like that. And you were only sixteen?"

Her eyes softened. "You must've been so scared. What happened to your father? Did the club handle it? Is that why you patched in?"

I scratched at my beard, studying our linked hands while wondering how she was going to take the next part. "I handled it," I choked. "Went back into the kitchen... and lost it. I hit him for hurting her... for hurting me. I beat him to death and never once regretted the decision. Wolverine showed up, and I thought I was a goner, but he surprised me. Allowed me to patch in; gave me an opportunity to have a family."

She nodded, and it dawned on me that I'd just revealed the monster and she hadn't run. If anything, her grip on my hand had gotten tighter. She lowered her head toward her lap before looking up at me from under her lashes. "What was it like?"

"I was just a scared kid—"

"No." She shook her head. "What did it feel like to hit him?"

"It felt really fuckin' good," I admitted. "That was when I realized there was somethin' wrong with my brain."

Her fingers moved underneath my chin, bringing my eyes up to meet hers. "Wrong how?"

"I liked killin', princess. I still love it. Ain't no other high quite like it."

Her throat bobbed up and down in a swallow, and I knew I'd said too much. She was going to throw me out, and I couldn't say I blamed her.

"I feel that too," she quietly admitted, and my heart damn near stopped. "I can't stop thinking about the night I went after Manny, and how good it felt to be in control. Sometimes, I dream about killing him. Like, if you hadn't shown up..."

"Someday, I'll teach you everything I know." I wasn't ready to admit that Manny was still alive.

Not yet.

Celia's head jerked back in shock. "You will?"

I gnawed at the corner of my lip and nodded. "You got just as much reason to go after these guys as I do."

Maybe it was all the result of trauma. I'd been turned into a monster because of what happened to my mother, and Celia had been turned into one because of me and my actions.

To survive, we needed each other.

"What does that mean, exactly?"

"It means..." I brought her fingers up to my mouth, placing a kiss against each knuckle. "That when the time is right, I'll teach you how to kill a man properly."

She moved her hand behind my neck, trying to bring my mouth up to hers, but I pulled away, pressing my lips to her forehead instead.

When I released her hands and stood, she let out a soft sigh of disappointment. I turned away, fighting a smile because it wasn't what she thought.

My wife was still wearing her wedding ring. I would have missed it had the diamond not scraped against my neck. She hadn't had it on that night at the motel.

It was a sign.

That she hadn't given up on me.

On us.

If I wanted to see it on her finger for the rest of my life, then I had to be different. I couldn't go after her like I had before—using her body to satisfy my own needs.

Until there were no more secrets between us, I'd hold back on what I wanted and just focus on helping her heal.

She needed me to be her rock.

Her protector.

CHAPTER TWENTY-NINE

Celia: March 2005 (Age: 33)

I stubbed my toe on the small stereo sitting in the middle of the living room floor and muttered a soft curse. "Kate! You can't just leave your stuff lying on the floor. It's going to get broken!"

She looked up from the magazine in her hand with a roll of her eyes and coldly replied, "I'm listening to it."

Dakota watched the exchange with raised eyebrows before leaping up from the couch and disappearing down the hall to their bedroom.

"Mary Katherine, do not roll your eyes at me—"

"Where are you going?" she asked, looking me over.

"I'm not going anywhere, but you, on the other hand, are going to be grounded if you can't pick up your stuff."

She frowned. "But you're wearing a dress. You haven't worn a dress in years."

The brick-red dress had been gathering dust in the back of my closet. I couldn't explain it. I'd had a dream that Jamie and I were on a beach, walking hand in hand, and stopping to gather seashells. I'd been wearing a chiffon cover-up that just reached the tops of my thighs, and he couldn't keep his hands off of me.

It didn't matter that I'd never been anywhere tropical alone, much less with him. It felt so real.

When I woke up, I wanted to recreate the feelings the dream had conjured up. I wanted to feel sexy again. Wearing a dress had seemed like the answer.

"Maybe I just felt like wearing a dress, Kate," I stated, before pointing toward their bedroom. "Clean up. Now."

I jerked my head toward the front window at the sound of a motorcycle and fought a smile, feeling like a teenager again.

The night he'd shown up, I'd had a nightmare. Cobra had come back, but this time, Kate walked in as he assaulted me. The carpet fibers had dug into my palms as I dragged my body toward her, but it didn't matter how fast I moved. I never got any closer.

I woke to sheets drenched in my own sweat and urine, still hearing her screams of pain.

Jamie was the last person I'd wanted to see, but the only one who seemed to bring down my walls. Learning the truth about what had happened to his mother reawakened feelings in me I thought were dead.

Since then, I found myself creeping out of bed in the middle of the night to watch from the laundry room window as he slept in the hammock, wishing I was brave enough to invite him inside.

I jumped at the sound of the doorbell and pulled myself from my fantasy to answer it. Angel held up a hand in greeting and smiled, as if he was reading my mind.

"Angel. Hi." My cheeks flamed in embarrassment.

"Hey, I'm here to pick up the girls."

I frowned. "Pick them up for what? Did we set something up and I'm just forgetting?"

He opened his mouth just as Lucy pulled up in her big SUV. "Hey," she called through the open window. "Are they ready?"

Wolverine climbed out of the passenger seat and walked Angel's bike into my garage as I struggled to remember what day it was.

"I'm sorry. I feel like I forgot to write something down on my calendar. Y'all will have to remind me."

Angel grinned. "We said we were takin' the girls to the lake this weekend. Remember?"

I shook my head. "When did we plan this?"

Dakota squeezed past me and went flying off the front porch. "Aunt Lucy, I got my bag packed, but I just remembered..." she paused to catch her breath. "I don't have a fishing pole. Can I still come?"

"Wait a minute," I protested. "Everyone knew about this trip, but me?"

"Yeah," Kate stated flatly from behind me. "Surprise."

"The girls mentioned having a long weekend, and we thought it'd be fun to get away for a few days. I could've sworn we talked about this," Lucy said with a wince.

"Well, I don't have a bag packed, but if you'll just give me a minute—"

Wolverine emerged from the garage with a shake of his head. "Sorry, Celia, you ain't goin'. Only got room for the girls and Angel this time around."

"I could drive my own car."

Angel shook his head. "Nah, that piece of shit would never make it up to the cabin. You stay here and enjoy a weekend off."

Kate lugged a large suitcase out onto the porch and handed it over to Angel while Wolverine retrieved Dakota's stuff from inside. I stood, dumbfounded, feeling like the world's worst mother.

"You don't want me to go? You're sure?" I pleaded.

Dakota shook her head. "Nope. We're good. Bye, Mama."

Kate sighed dramatically and wrapped an arm around me. "You should be happy. Now, you can clean the whole house without anyone messing it up again."

"But—"

Angel wrapped me up in a bear hug, whispering, "Ain't one thing gonna happen to either of them on my watch. You deserve a weekend. Don't fuckin' clean. Don't lift a goddamn finger. Just relax."

I nodded and watched as they climbed in and drove off, unable to shake the feeling that there was something they weren't telling me.

The house seemed too quiet without the sounds of the girls' bickering. I paced from room to room, picking up stray hair ties and socks while wondering if maybe I'd been too hard on them. The trip had obviously been a way for them to get away from me.

Why else would they have left on Easter weekend?

I was so caught up in second-guessing my every parenting decision that I almost missed the knock at the door.

"Oh, thank the saints," I muttered, all but racing to answer. It was an early April Fool's Day joke. Dakota had been plotting ways to trick me for weeks now, but I hadn't ever imagined she'd go as far as a fake trip.

My hand fell uselessly from the doorknob when I opened it, because it wasn't the girls.

It was Jamie.

Or someone who used to be Jamie.

His long, dark blond hair was gone. There was just a little bit of length left on the top, but the sides had been trimmed above his ears. The beard that had always been a wiry mess was now cut and groomed to perfection, but that wasn't what had my knees buckling beneath me.

My biker was wearing a suit.

The man who'd insisted on a leather vest and jeans for our wedding was standing before me in a light gray suit and tie. I'd grown up around men in suits, and while Jamie's wasn't custom, it molded around his muscles perfectly.

It was like looking at a stranger.

He thrust a bouquet of Indian paintbrush flowers into my hands with a nervous smile. "Hey, Celia."

"You got a haircut," I responded dumbly.

He scratched at his jaw, the grin on his face widening. "I did. Like to take you out, if you're free."

I blinked slowly, expecting to wake up at any moment. This wasn't real. Instead of pinching myself, I prayed that I'd be able to stay in the moment forever.

"You know," I bit down on my lower lip with a grin. "My schedule is suddenly wide open. Would you happen to know anything about that?"

"Not a fuckin' clue," he said with a smirk. "I, uh, I got my bike out front." He gestured toward the driveway behind him.

I tried to hide my excitement and fear with a casual nod. I'd never been on his bike. By the time we'd decided on a relationship, I was pregnant with Kate. From there, our lives had gone in separate directions, and any alone time we had was reserved for one thing.

He reached for my hand and carefully led me down the steps as the neighbor sitting on his porch across the street lowered his newspaper to watch. I doubted they'd recognize him. I barely did. I hiked up my dress, and he helped me onto the back of the bike before leaning down until his mouth brushed against the shell of my ear. "Fuckin' love your dress, princess."

I fought against the quiver in my thighs and gripped the metal beneath my seat. He took the flowers and tucked them into the saddlebag before climbing on. My body instinctively moved down the hard leather seat to his back. Keeping my dress bunched up in my lap, I wrapped my arms around his waist and held on as the bike fired up with a rumble.

Vibrations moved straight through my core, and I clenched my legs around him with a muffled groan as he pulled out onto the street.

The wind in my face almost stole my breath as it lifted the hair off my shoulders, whipping it wildly around my face. I squeezed my eyes shut against the stinging slap with a manic grin.

It felt like coming home.

I pressed my cheek against the center of his back and watched as we blew past farmers just beginning to plant their crops, the brown fields and green tractors blending together into one.

Exhilaration flooded my veins, and I found I was almost disappointed when he slowed to turn down a dirt road. Unlike the rest of the desert landscape, we were now surrounded by trees stretching at least sixty feet in the air.

"Pecan orchard," Jamie shouted over the bike before making another turn.

We passed a large red barn before pulling up in front of a modest Folk Victorian farmhouse with a large covered porch. Its steep-pitched gabled roof with decorative trim reminded me of the houses I used to draw as a child.

He shut the bike off and turned back to me. "You like it?"

My body felt as if it was still vibrating as I climbed off the bike, causing me to stumble slightly as I made my way up the worn steps. "Like it? It's gorgeous. It even has a porch swing! Will the owners care that we're here?" I asked, while looking through the front window.

"The owner is here."

I looked back at him in surprise. "You live here?"

The corner of his mouth turned up slightly. "Well, not lately, no. Been campin' outdoors more."

My fingers trailed over the wooden porch swing, and I kicked off my sandals before sinking down onto it with a contented sigh before declaring, "If I lived out here, I'd never leave. It's so quiet and peaceful."

Jamie leaned against the railing, watching me with an unreadable expression on his face. When he stayed silent, I added, "How'd you find it?"

"It was Angel's," he said, retrieving the pack of cigarettes from the inside of his jacket. He tapped one out and offered it to me.

I shook my head. "I quit."

He lit up and took a long drag before asking, "Since when?"

"Since Dakota found my pack in the freezer while looking for Sundae Cones. She got Kate involved, and I received quite the lecture on the dangers of smoking."

"I wish I could've been there to see that." Jamie stared off into the orchard.

"So, Angel used to live out here?"

"Well, he bought the house for me and my ma. Was gonna move us in once the club took care of my old man. When he lost her, he refused to come back, and it sat empty."

"Did you know it was here? Back then, I mean."

He shook his head. "Not until about three years ago. I got sick of stayin' out at the clubhouse, and he told me about it. Wolverine and Bear helped me fix it up, and I've been out here ever since."

"Oh." I nodded to myself before getting up, keeping my back to him as I moved over to the porch steps. "Is this where you've been the whole time?"

It shouldn't have upset me. I'd pushed him away; I didn't get a say in where he went afterward. I guess I'd always assumed he would've become a nomad, moving from place to place as he tracked down the men who hurt me; not living alone out in the country.

"Come on." He hopped off the railing. "Got somethin' I wanna show you."

I pushed my hurt feelings aside and let him lead me around to the back of the house, where a gingham blanket was spread beneath a massive oak tree. The red cooler on top had kept it from blowing away.

"What's all this?" I asked, brushing the hair back off my forehead.

He stripped the suit jacket off and directed me to sit before proudly announcing, "I made us lunch."

No matter how much I wanted to stay mad at him, I couldn't fight the smile that crept onto my face when he pulled out bologna and cheese sandwiches and bags of tortilla chips.

A sharp pain pricked the base of my nose, the feeling almost foreign. I hadn't been able to cry in years, yet was close to it because of lunchmeat.

I quickly turned away as a burst of laughter broke free from my chest.

"What?"

"Nothing." The sound of my high-pitched voice caused me to snort, and I slapped a palm over my mouth and doubled over.

"Celia," Jamie said calmly. "The fuck are you laughin' at?"

"It's—I just—" I gasped for air and tried to compose myself before slumping over again with a wide grin.

His hands moved up under my armpits, and I rolled onto my back, fighting to escape the tickling. "I'll stop," I begged. "I will!"

He propped himself up onto his forearms and looked down at me with narrowed eyes. "You were expectin' somethin' fancy, right? You're disappointed?"

I trailed my fingers through his short hair and looked up at the heavy clouds rolling in. "Do I look disappointed?"

"Why'd you laugh?"

I realized then that it wasn't anger, but worry, in his eyes. It was apparent he'd gone to a lot of trouble to set the entire day up; even recruiting Angel and Wolverine to help. He'd mistaken my amusement for condescension.

"Hey," I squeezed his jaw. "I wasn't laughing at you. It's just that I haven't gotten emotional in years and seeing this—" I gestured around us. "I just can't believe you did all of it for me."

He rocked back onto his heels. "You haven't cried?"

"Not since they..." I realized what I was about to say and smoothed my dress out before sitting up. "It's just been a while."

"Why?" His stare seemed to move through the sugarcoated facade I presented and into my soul. The sandwiches and chips lay forgotten in between us as I took in his question.

"Why were you out here?" I snapped, bracing myself for the blow-up. "All this time? You could've been chasing—you should've stopped this!"

Jamie ran his tongue over his teeth and nodded. "I could have, but I had to get clean and sober first."

CHAPTER THIRTY

Celia: March 2005 (Age: 33)

My mouth fell open. "You... you relapsed?"

Had I known that?

He'd been drunk the night he'd surprised me on the patio, but had I known then what it meant? So much of the early years after the attack were shrouded in a fog, details becoming nothing more than blurs.

"I was in a bad place. Drugs... booze... whatever I could do to make it not hurt, I did. Mikey got into some trouble, along with some other shit, and I couldn't fuckin' take it. If it hadn't been for Slim..." His nostrils flared as his voice trailed off.

I crawled over and climbed onto his lap. "What did Slim do? Is Mikey okay? Jesus, are you okay?"

His arms came up around me, and my heart raced in my chest as he recounted the events leading up to his decision to get sober. My chest ached at the realization that, because of my actions, I'd almost lost him for good.

The very thing I'd feared had come to pass, all because I pushed him away. I'd put the gun in his hand by being too proud to admit the truth about that night.

"I moved out of the clubhouse and stayed here with Slim as I detoxed—which was a fuckin' nightmare. Threw up everything but my toenails and all I wanted to do was sleep, but couldn't, so I stayed awake, roaming the house like a fuckin' zombie."

Without thinking, I dropped my head and pressed my lips to the corner of his mouth. He stiffened and lowered me back to the picnic blanket before moving away.

As if there was some part of him that knew it was all my fault.

The first drop of rain landed on my arm, quickly followed by another, and Jamie sprang into action, tossing the food back into the cooler and tugging the picnic blanket over our heads as we raced up the back steps and into the house.

Air conditioning blasted my drenched skin, sending goosebumps across my arms. The inside of his house wasn't what I expected. I'd imagined it looking like a bachelor pad, with folding chairs and card tables, but he had actual furniture.

Several black and white pictures hung on the wall behind the couch, and I moved closer to study them. A woman with blonde hair that trailed down to her waist stood in front of the house I now lived in, with a baby propped up on her hip. "Is this—"

"My ma." He watched intently, waiting for me to say something else.

"She was gorgeous, Jamie. And look at how little you were..." Images of the child we'd lost entered my mind, and I clenched my jaw before turning back to the photographs.

His boots moved across the hardwood floor away from me. "Just gonna throw these in the fridge. Make yourself at home."

"Oh." I followed him. "Where's the bathroom? I need to dry my hair."

He kept his back to me. "End of the hall. Take a left."

The rain battered the windows and lightning streaked across the dark sky as I walked through the living room. I took my time meandering down the hall, stopping to look at pictures of my husband before life had made him hard.

I closed the bathroom door behind me with a soft click and studied my reflection in the mirror. Mascara trailed down over my cheeks from the sudden shower, and I hastily swiped it away before leaning closer.

Why was he pulling away from me?

Was it because he blamed me for his relapse? Or had he only found me desirable when he was intoxicated?

I snagged a peach-colored towel and ran it through my damp hair with a frustrated sigh. If either were true, then he wouldn't have shown up on my doorstep in a suit.

It didn't make any sense.

He was still banging around in the kitchen when I came out, so I chose to explore the bedrooms. The first one had sunshine yellow walls and a small wooden desk but was otherwise empty. I decided the second one was the master, with its king-sized bed and dark wood nightstands. The faint smell of cigarettes and leather lingered in the air, confirming my suspicions.

I ran my hand over the faded white quilt, wondering if he'd brought anyone over. Listening for the sound of his boots, I quietly slid open the dresser drawers one by one, looking for signs that there was someone else.

There had to be a reason he was keeping his distance, and I wasn't leaving this room until I found it. I pushed the bottom drawer closed and stood up, surveying the rest of the room.

A quick glance under the bed yielded nothing out of the ordinary, as did a check of one of the nightstands. I blew out a frustrated breath and tiptoed over the other, gently tugging the top drawer open.

Books.

The drawer was packed with books. *I Can't Get Over It: A Trauma Survivor's Workbook. Love and PTSD. Rape Recovery Handbook. Born Silent: Healing After the Loss of a Child.* The titles jumped out at me, one after another, and I clutched my stomach in pain before backing away slowly.

He knew.

A choking sound had me whipping around in horror before I realized it was coming from me.

Without thinking, I kicked off my shoes and bolted. The screen door slammed shut behind me with a loud crack, but I didn't turn around to see if I was being followed.

Rain pelted my body, weighing my dress down with every step, yet I put one foot in front of the other, forcing myself forward. My feet kicked up mud before tangling in my skirt, sending me sprawling into a puddle with a grunt.

"Celia!"

I clawed at the soft earth, fighting to get back to my feet, before being lifted by strong arms.

"What the fuck are you doin'?" He brushed the rain from his forehead with a frown.

"You—" I raised a shaking hand. "You have those books!"

He mashed his lips together and nodded, and the weight in my chest grew heavier.

"No!" I shook my head, ignoring the tingling in my limbs. "Why would you have those?"

Jamie crossed his arms over his chest and looked away.

"Goddammit!" I slapped at his arms, sending sprays of water up toward our faces. "Tell me why you have them!"

I'd sworn Angel and Comedian to secrecy. I remembered that much. There was no way he could have known.

"You tell me why I have them!" he roared over the thunder; eyes wild with rage. "You. Tell. Me!"

I dropped my palms and stepped back. "What do you want from me, Jamie?"

"We lost a child, Celia!" He ran the back of his hand over his eyes, his tears mixing with the rain. "What do I want? I want you to react, goddammit!"

"Stop!" I held my palms up weakly. "Please stop!"

"No! You wanna pretend it never happened, but I'm fuckin' dyin' here!"

"You think I'm pretending it never happened?" I let out a guttural roar. "July fourteenth, Jamie! Our baby would be turning four on July fourteenth. So, don't you accuse me of acting like it never happened!"

The cords in his neck strained as he mashed his lips together to stop them from trembling. "You said you never cry," he forced out through clenched teeth, angrily brushing more tears away with the back of his hand.

"I can't." I tried swallowing past the sudden lump in my throat. "If I do, then I'll never stop. I did this to us!"

"How?" he demanded. "How in the fuck is any of this your fault?"

It wasn't fair. He'd been reading books on how to help me, and I was the one responsible for all of it. I wasn't worthy of his sympathy. "I pushed you away—"

"And you had every fuckin' right to. I was strung out, and you deserved better than that!"

I shook my head, dragging my hands through my soaking wet hair in frustration. "No, Jamie! You deserved better! They all know you're alive because of me... because of the things I did!"

"Whatever you did was because I left you and the girls on your own. Ain't gonna hold any of it against you—"

When he tried reaching for me, I backed away. "Money started going missing, and the electricity got shut off. I didn't know what else to do!"

His eyebrows drew together in confusion, but I continued before he could say another word. "At first, it was small amounts. I assumed I'd gotten careless and misplaced it. Then, it was enough that I couldn't pay the bills. Hawk said he'd tried reaching you—"

"I never heard a word from him. Trust me, if I had, I would've—"

I nodded. "I know that now. I should've told you, but I was naïve and stupid. I turned to gambling; thought that I could win the money back, and it'd be like it had never happened. Someone broke in not long after you brought money the last time and took all of it. Hawk got me into a high-stakes blackjack game..."

A sour taste filled my mouth at the memory, and I dug my fingernails into my arm to keep from getting sick.

"What happened?" he asked quietly.

"I won." My voice cracked. "Two hundred and fifty thousand dollars. I had a plan too—I was going to open multiple accounts and spread it out. I didn't know then, but two of the men at the table were working with Hawk. They waited until my father left and..."

A wave of dizziness washed over me, and I stumbled back, righting myself just before I went down in the mud again.

The muscle in his jaw ticked as he clenched his teeth, and I lowered my head in shame.

"I'm sorry."

My head jerked up at the apology.

"I am. None of this shit would've happened had I not left. It's been on your shoulders too long, princess. Time to let it go."

I pursed my lips together. "Don't do that. Don't minimize what I did."

He moved closer and reached for me again. This time, I didn't pull away. His arms tightened around my waist and my palms clenched into fists. "You did the best you could, and you've been so brave for so fuckin' long. It's time for me to be brave for you. Let me take care of you."

"I don't deserve your forgiveness," I whispered, my eyes stinging with unshed tears.

"Ain't nothin' to forgive, darlin'. Just let go."

"I—I can't," I weakly admitted, resting my chin against his chest.

He ignored the raindrops running rivers down his face and nodded forcefully. "You can." He shifted until I was at arm's length in front of him. "Forgive yourself."

I broke away with a pant. "The girl you loved before is gone, and I don't know how to get her back..."

"And I ain't the same man that you left on a porch almost five years ago."

He dropped down into the mud, staining the knees of his slacks brown. "So, we'll start over. Together. I've known the truth of that night, and it didn't change jack shit for me. You're all I want... you're all I'll ever want. Can you say the same?"

I nodded immediately, and his shoulders relaxed. "Celia... cry."

At his command, something opened up inside my chest. The grief I'd felt over losing our baby had been locked away for five long years, but Jamie had been the key. Instead of running from it, I let my head fall back in an anguished scream as the first tear fell onto my cheeks.

The numbness faded away, and I forced myself to feel every

memory as it bubbled to the surface until I was on my knees in the muck beside him, gasping for air. "It hurts." I clutched at my aching throat. "God, it hurts so much, Jamie. I can't—"

He nodded and pulled me into his arms, rubbing small circles across my back. "I know."

"I'm sorry. I'm so sorry!" I wept for the secrets we'd kept, and the life we'd never had. Fighting against the tightness in my throat, I let my body release all the pain the only way it could.

"Shhhh..." He cradled my body, gently rocking us back and forth as the storm raged all around us. "That's my brave girl."

The feeling of security that I'd been searching for since the night our lives changed returned under his touch. He tightened his hold with each strangled exhale, holding me together.

When the sobs turned to hiccups, Jamie lifted me in his arms and carried me back to the house. He kicked off the motorcycle boots I hadn't noticed under his slacks, never once loosening his grip.

As we passed the pictures on the wall in the hallway, I realized the dreams we'd started out with had become nightmares.

But we were still here.

We were still fighting.

CHAPTER THIRTY-ONE

Celia: March 2005 (Age: 33)

"So much for a nice afternoon picnic," I noted, from the couch. The storm hadn't let up, and I watched in fascination as the porch light illuminated the droplets of water as they trickled down over the gingerbread trim.

The shirt he'd let me borrow while our muddy clothes were being washed fell almost to my knees, yet I continued tugging it down over my chilled skin.

Jamie retrieved another blanket from the hall closet and brought it back to wrap around my shoulders before going over to mess with the record player. His suit had been replaced with a plain white t-shirt and jeans, and as my eyes trailed down his body, I wondered if he still went without underwear.

I should have been exhausted.

My head ached, and my eyes were swollen from my tears, but I was oddly refreshed. I'd thought that relief would only happen with the deaths of the men who hurt me, but it had come in the form of forgiveness.

A second chance.

"You warmin' up now?"

I nodded, feeling the heat of a flush work its way up my chest. Purging my pent-up emotions had also left me open for new ones—namely lust. "Are you?"

"Oh, yeah. I'm good now." He padded back over to the couch with a grin, and I tried to recall the last time I'd seen him with bare feet; the last time I'd seen him completely relaxed.

Organ music filled the room, and I frowned in confusion before realizing what he'd put on. I brought my hands up over my mouth, muffling my giggle before exclaiming, "No! Really?"

Jamie's lips twitched as he leaned toward me, waggling his eyebrows suggestively before crooning, "Well, I guess it would be nice if I could touch your body. I know not everybody has got a body like you..."

We were no longer sitting in his living room, but perusing stacks of records, searching for our favorites. This time around, though, I knew exactly what I wanted. There'd be no mistaking it for Stockholm syndrome or living in fear of someone finding out.

Jamie Quinn was it for me.

Always.

I shrugged the blanket off my shoulders and launched myself at him, knocking him back against the couch as I straddled his lap.

"Kiss me."

His hands came up around my backside, and I took pleasure in watching as his eyes widened when he realized I wasn't wearing panties.

"Celia—"

I silenced his objections with my lips, relishing in the feel of his hands digging into my soft flesh as he pulled me closer with a rough growl. His body was hard beneath mine, and I rocked against him with a groan before tangling my fists in his hair.

When I nipped his lower lip, sucking it between my teeth, his hand came down hard against my backside with a reverberating smack. I let my head fall back with a loud exhale, knowing without a doubt that I had just soaked the front of his jeans.

As if I hadn't already been wet.

His thumbs pressed into my skin, and I realized he wasn't drawing me in, but pushing me away.

"I'll be right back." He shifted me over to the middle couch cushion and disappeared down the hall, leaving me painfully aroused and thoroughly confused.

"Jamie?"

The bathroom door slammed shut in response, and I ran my fingers over my puffy lips, trying to determine where I'd gone wrong.

I hadn't been intimate with him in five years, but I was reasonably certain I hadn't lost my touch. Lightning arced across the sky, and I drummed my fingers idly against the back of the couch, watching the raindrops race each other down the glass.

We were together in the middle of nowhere for the entire weekend, and I didn't want to waste another second apart. I stood up and stripped the t-shirt over my head before stalking down the hall, the sounds of running water growing louder the closer I got to the bathroom.

Praying he hadn't locked the door, I turned the handle and breathed a small sigh of relief when it opened. Steam billowed out from the top of the small glass shower, and I leaned against the vanity, watching as the hot water cascaded over his muscles. Muscles that hadn't come from a gym, but from breaking down men like Manny.

I'd seen a small preview of his strength in the motel, and it had left me with a fluttering in my chest and a strong desire to run my hands over him in reverence.

He slapped a palm against the tile while the other moved furiously up and down his shaft. "Celia," he whispered, letting his forehead drop. "Fuck."

I kept my eyes on him as my own hand moved in between my legs. The feelings of disgust that normally welled up, leaving me nauseated, were gone. My teeth sank down onto my lower lip as I circled my clit, wishing it was his fingers touching me.

With a deep breath for courage, I pushed off the counter and stepped into the shower with him.

"Celia." His hand fell away, and he backed into the corner, trapped. "I can't."

Water ran into my eyes, and I blinked against it before gesturing toward him. "It looks like you can. Why are you running from me?"

"I can't be soft with you, princess. And that's what you need—"

I lowered myself to my knees and looked up from beneath my lashes before reaching for him. "What I need is you."

He shook his head and tried to step around me, but I moved, wrapping my hand around his shaft with a gentle squeeze.

"Fuck, you gotta stop."

My tongue darted out to lick the moisture beading along the tip. I knew he'd never force me—maybe that was what had my body in flames with desire. "Please."

"Stop—I can't."

I pulled back and let him help me to my feet. He tried reaching around me to shut off the water, but I stopped him with my arm. "Wait. Just hear me out, please."

I fought against my own fears to admit, "My body healed physically, but I still have the memories of what they did to me that night, Jamie. I still feel them inside me, and those scars don't fade. Please don't push me away."

He swallowed and nodded. "I ain't been with any woman since you. Do you know how many times I've jerked myself to thoughts of your body, only to feel sick after? I read the books and as much as I fuckin' wish it was, it ain't me that you need."

I brushed the water from his beard and moved until my breasts were up against his chest, pushing my body for a reaction.

Safe.

Every fiber of my being radiated with the thought. I would never feel safer in anyone's arms but his. I lifted onto my tiptoes and whispered against his lips, "A book doesn't know me. I need my husband. No one else but you."

"For fuck's sake, Celia," he growled, letting his fingers skim along my ribs. "You want me to stop? Tell me now."

I shook my head. "Please don't stop."

His hand came up to rest lightly against the base of my throat before he guided me back up against the tile. Teeth scraped against the sensitive flesh of my neck and moved down my chest as he lowered himself to his knees in front of me.

I brushed the wet hair off my forehead, looking down to watch as he moved to one of my breasts, teasing the nipple with his tongue before pinching it between his thumb and forefinger and guiding it into his mouth.

Pleasure flooded my body, and I arched my back with a moan, giving my body up to him in offering.

His free hand moved down to cup between my legs, and he released my nipple to ask, "Who's in charge here, Celia?"

"Y-you," I answered shakily, fighting to keep my legs beneath me.

Jamie moved away until he was crouched directly under the showerhead.

"Come back," I begged, running my hands over my breasts. "Please."

His nostrils flared, and he moved closer, trailing his fingers across my belly and down to trace the moisture on my lips. My body shuddered at the contact, and I ground shamelessly against his hand. His middle finger plunged inside me, and he slowly pumped it in and out before asking again. "Who's in charge?"

My mind was beyond rational thought and only focused on relieving the ache between my thighs. "Y-you are. Don't stop."

Again, he pulled himself from my body and moved away. "Ain't touchin' you until you say it, Celia. Tell me who the fuck is in charge right now?"

I studied the intense expression on his face, and my lips parted in surprise. "Me?"

"Who's in charge?" he demanded again.

"Me," I repeated, stronger this time. "I'm in charge."

He leaned in and licked my slit with a grin. "That's my good girl. You're in charge, princess. You want me to stop, I'll stop."

I shook my head, actively aware of my heart pounding out a steady rhythm in my chest. "I don't want you to stop."

"Thank Christ," he muttered before thrusting his finger back inside my body. I sought to find something to hold on to along the tile before settling for his hair. My fists tightened around the newly shorn locks as he flicked his tongue across me, pushing me to the edge.

I just needed... "More," I panted. "Please."

He added another finger and lazily moved them both in and out of my body while fisting his shaft in the other hand. "What else do you need?"

"Your..." Black spots danced across my vision. "Mouth."

"It's all yours, darlin'."

He sucked me in between his teeth, giving me just the right amount of pleasure and pain to send me over the edge with a loud cry. My hips bucked furiously against his face as I rode out my orgasm in a mix of moans and pants before blinking drowsily down at him.

A wide grin stretched across his face. "God, I missed your taste."

I clenched my thighs around his fingers, aching to come again. "Please..."

He rocked back onto his heels. "What do you need?"

"I need your..." I stopped myself from saying it and pointed down where his shaft jutted up against his abdomen.

His eyes narrowed. "My what?"

"You," I groaned, feeling my cheeks heat. "I need you."

"Now, see..." A wicked grin played at his lips. "You've got me. I wonder if there's something else you might be meanin', though. All you gotta do is say it."

"You're an asshole," I ground out, fighting to hide my grin.

"You got a filthy mouth on you, wife. Tell me what you want."

Knowing two could play his game, I lowered my hand down to my breast, tweaking my nipple in between my fingers just like he had. "Oh," I moaned, watching his face contort into one of pure, unadulterated need.

"Say it," he forced through clenched teeth. "Fuckin' say it, please."

I licked along my top lip. "Let's see... I've got this hand." I squeezed my breast.

"And this one..." I moved the other between my legs. "Do I need anything else?"

He began jerking himself off with abandon. "For the love of all the saints, tell me you want my cock."

My teeth sank down onto my lower lip before I admitted, "I want your cock, baby."

With another low growl, he lifted me up and buried himself to the hilt inside me. The men who'd used their bodies to hurt me were gone. It was Jamie's hands holding my hips in a death grip as he drove himself into me, chasing away the memories of that night with every thrust.

He brought his mouth down to mine while keeping his eyes open, and I knew he was watching for signs that I might be slipping away.

I stayed in the present, letting each stroke drive me closer to madness before coming with his name on my lips. He was no longer a biker Pres, and I was no longer a victim.

We were nobodies, learning to navigate each other's bodies again while staying safely hidden away from the cruelness of the world.

His tongue sought entrance into my mouth, and I parted my lips, letting him in fully. My defenses were down, and any urge to fight him was long gone as we let the friction between us take over.

I kept a death grip on his shoulders, the muscles in my body losing tension as he drove himself into me. The blood drained from my face, and a scream ripped from my throat as I came before his fingers dug into my backside and he yanked me up, spilling his seed onto my belly.

His heart pounded so forcefully that I felt it in my own ribs, each of us fighting to draw air back into our lungs and come back down from wherever it was we'd just gone. "You okay?" Jamie gasped.

When I nodded shakily, he let his forehead rest between my breasts, pressing a soft kiss against my sternum. The water had gone cold at some point, and I shuddered against the chill before drawing him closer.

He reached out and shut it off with a soft chuckle, keeping a tight grip on me as he moved us onto the tile. "Let's get you warmed up."

Bypassing the plethora of bath towels, he strode out of the bathroom and toward the bed in the master bedroom, ripping the comforter back before lowering me into it. I wrapped my fingers around his wrist as he settled in at my back, pulling him around me like a blanket.

"I missed you," I whispered, and his arms tightened around me in response. The sounds of our heavy breathing drowned out the sounds of spring rain on the window, and my eyes grew heavy with fatigue.

I drifted off to sleep knowing that while my biker didn't know how to be soft; he had given me the one thing I hadn't even realized I'd needed.

Control.

CHAPTER THIRTY-TWO

Celia: March 2005 (Age: 33)

I awoke to a completely dark bedroom and the soft sounds of snoring behind me. Slipping out from under the sheets, I padded into the bathroom to relieve myself.

The rain had finally stopped, and I listened as a pair of coyotes yipped to each other from somewhere out in the orchard.

My eyes were still swollen from crying, and I blinked blearily against the overhead light, trying to let them adjust. With a yawn, I tore several sheets of toilet paper from the roll, wincing slightly as it came into contact with my sensitive skin.

A flash of color caught my eye, and I froze before slowly lifting the tissue up.

Blood.

I was bleeding.

A soft whimper escaped past my lips as panic tightened like a vise around my chest. There was a low thud from the bedroom, followed by the heavy tread of Jamie's feet racing across the hardwood.

"Celia?" He opened the door, hastily rubbing the sleep from his eyes. "What's wrong?"

I shook my head. "I just—I—"

"Hey, it's alright. I'm here." He walked over and knelt beside the toilet, taking my hand in his while somehow remaining oblivious to the fact that we were both still completely naked.

"It's nothing. I just saw some blood and freaked out. Sorry to wake you—"

"You on the rag, or..." He trailed off and looked up at me helplessly. "Fuck, I don't know."

I mashed my lips together. "I think that... it's just—this is really awkward—"

Suddenly wide awake, he moved in front of me. "You okay, princess? Do you need me to call a doctor?"

Mortified didn't even cover it.

My face heated as I blurted, "I think it's just been a really long time since we've had... relations and there might've been some tearing. It's not a big deal and before this wouldn't have even been an issue, but—"

"You saw the blood, and it took you back," he finished for me.

I nodded. "I'm sorry."

"Don't fuckin' apologize..." He grinned. "Well, I take that back. You called what we did 'relations.' I feel like I'm owed an apology for that one."

He swatted my thigh and stood up. "Come back to bed."

I let him get to the door before admitting, "I could watch you walk away all night."

Jamie looked back over his shoulder with a grin. "You starin' at my ass?"

He flexed his muscles when I nodded, and I chuckled before adding, "I like your ass... a lot."

"Got a dirty mouth on you, darlin'. I like it."

I almost expected to see the old me reflected in the mirror above the sink as I washed my hands, but the warrior met my gaze instead. I stared until her lips curved up in a playful smirk, bringing with it the realization that the girl Jamie fell in love with was still in there. She just wasn't as soft as she used to be.

He was sitting up in bed when I returned. "All good?"

I pulled the covers up around my body and settled in at his side. "All good."

"Today's been a lot for you." He stroked my shoulder, and I brought my head down to rest against his chest.

"You know," I said, my jaw stretching wide with a yawn. "I can't remember the last time I slept this well. I have this weird routine where I get up every hour and check all the locks. Then, it's like every little noise makes me jump."

His body tensed beneath mine, and I lifted my chin, straining to see him in the dark. "What's wrong?"

"Just thinkin'," he breathed. "Wish I would've been there for you—"

"You were," I cut in. "There were so many times I asked myself, 'Celia, would Jamie be scared of a cicada in the kitchen window?'"

His chest rose and fell in a deep belly laugh. "Fuck yeah I would. Those fuckers are nasty. And how many times did cicadas get in the house that you had to ask that?"

I punched his shoulder playfully. "I was using that as an example. It only happened once or twice."

"Hey, princess?"

"Yeah?"

He mashed a button on his watch, illuminating the face. "You know it's only nine o'clock, right?"

I sat up. "Are you serious? But I'm starving... I thought maybe it was close to morning." As if on cue, my stomach rumbled loudly, eliciting another chuckle from my biker.

"Not sure if you remember or not, but we kinda missed lunch." His hand connected with my thigh under the blankets, squeezing lightly. "C'mon, darlin'. Let's get you fed."

I'd been at war with my body for almost five years; hiding under baggy clothes and cutting myself open just to feel. Nothing would erase what they had done to me. But tonight, in front of the man I'd pledged my life to, I was completely comfortable in my own skin.

I didn't bother picking up the shirt on the floor as I followed him through the living room and into the kitchen. "Do you have eggs? I could make breakfast for dinner."

He gestured toward one of the stools near the butcher block island. "Sit your pretty ass right there, and I'll get ya fixed up."

In our relationship, I'd been the one in charge of meals, but watching him rummage through the kitchen cabinets while humming to himself felt normal. It was as if no time had passed at all.

I quickly realized why I'd always done the cooking when he held up the bright blue can with a triumphant grin.

"Spam?" My nose wrinkled, and I shook my head. "You don't have anything else?"

"You ever had a fried Spam sandwich?" he asked, pulling the tab back before dumping a flesh-colored block onto a plate. "It'll put hair on your chest."

"And that's something I would want?"

"Just you wait, darlin'. You're in for a treat." He cut it into thin slices and arranged them on a plate before grabbing a cast-iron skillet.

I watched him fry up the canned meat, convinced that there was no way I'd be able to eat a single bite and keep it down. Then, I smelled it, and the appetite that had fled around the same time the blue can appeared suddenly returned.

The oil in the pan popped, and Jamie jumped back.

I grinned. "You better be careful, or you might end up with burns in some pretty uncomfortable places."

He flipped before turning back to me. "I'm a pro, baby."

After several more near-misses with the hot oil, he snagged a couple of pieces of bread and carefully spread mayonnaise and mustard over them before adding the meat. He placed the entire thing in front of me like a chef would a food critic.

I bit into it as he sat down next to me, watching my face expectantly. "Well?"

"It's surprisingly good," I said around a mouthful.

"Surprisingly," he scoffed. "You country club types have been missin' out. Admit it."

"Fine. We've been missing out." We devoured our sandwiches, slipping into a comfortable silence.

"What are they like?"

"Who?" I asked with a frown. "Country club people? About like most, I expect."

"No, the girls. What are they like?"

"Oh." I finished chewing. "Well, Kate is a moody teenager. So, that's fun."

Jamie rested his elbow on the island, leaning in toward me. "But what does she like to do, though? Is she in sports or a club at school?"

The hope reflected in his blue eyes was almost childlike. He wanted to know our girls—all the little everyday things that I'd taken for granted over the years.

I thought about it. "Kate loves music. Nothing else breaks through to her quite like it. She's in the choir at school, but it's the songs on the radio that I catch her listening to late at night. Some days, I'm convinced that she feels things on a deeper level. Does that make sense?"

He nodded with a soft smile. "Complete sense. What about Dakota Mae?"

"Do you remember how she was obsessed with Thor when she was a toddler?"

"Oh, yeah." He laughed, rubbing at his forehead. "I had more silverware thrown at my face during that phase..."

My hands moved up between us as I animatedly described his children. "Well, it wasn't just a phase. She is a full-blown comic book junkie, but only with Marvel. Otherwise, it's no good. She helped start this comic book club that meets once a week at the library. From the sounds of it, all they do is argue. But every week, she's ready to go back and do it again."

He picked at the skin around his thumbnail. "When I came into the house a few nights ago, I saw the closed door and just immediately thought of it as bein' a nursery, but they ain't babies anymore. Don't matter if I wipe out every rival club in the country, I can't get that time back."

I had similar thoughts with Kate and Dakota—especially after losing the baby. I wondered if they knew how much I loved them and how proud I was of the young women they were becoming. There were the nights I lay awake, worried that my grief had impacted my ability to be a good mother.

"Before, you said that you had walked away from the club. What were you going to do?"

He ran a hand roughly over his face. "Doesn't really matter now, does it?"

I reached over and laced my fingers with his. "It does to me. You think I don't imagine how different our lives could have been?"

"You do?"

"I do. Just last night I had a dream that we were on a beach together—"

"A beach?" His mouth turned up. "What kind of beach? Like a clothing-optional one?"

"Sorry to disappoint, but it was not a nudist beach. You were wearing black swim trunks and an unbuttoned shirt, and I was wearing a bikini under this see-through cover-up thing."

"Did we seem happy?"

I thought back on it and smiled. "We did."

His grip tightened around my hand. "Maybe I'll take you to a beach someday, princess."

"I'd like that." I spun the ring on his left hand before pulling back in surprise. "You're still wearing it."

"Been on my finger since our wedding day. Noticed you were wearin' yours, too."

"I am." My gaze dropped to my hand. "Do you remember that day in the cemetery?"

He paused, considering my question. "Yeah. Greek mythology and, uh, the constellations, right?"

I nodded. "You asked me a question before leaving, and I said that maybe someday I'd tell you..."

The blood drained from his face, and he swallowed. "I asked you what Persephone wanted. More I think about it, the more I realize she would've been better off had she never met him."

It was easier for him to pretend we were talking about fictional gods and goddesses instead of ourselves.

"Would she have, though? Stuck tending a garden for the rest of her life? Doing everything her mother commanded?"

Jamie pulled his hand back and stared down at his empty plate. "Least then she would've been safe..."

I shrugged. "If anyone knew what it meant to eat those pomegranate seeds, it was Persephone. She knew, and yet, she did it anyway. Don't you see that?"

His head cocked to the side. "What are you sayin'?"

"She could have stayed in the garden, safe from the world for the rest of her life, but she would've spent every second wondering what lay beyond." I smiled up at him. "Hades never took Persephone, Jamie. She went willingly and chose to stay in his world."

"You didn't know what you were gettin' into then..."

I held up my left hand. "I know now. Still, I chose to stay. The day I take it off is the day you'll know I've given up on us."

A slow smile spread across his face. "Then I'll fight every day to ensure it stays on your hand."

CHAPTER THIRTY-THREE

Grey: March 2005 (Age: 41)

I kept one hand on Celia's shoulder and the other over her eyes as I led her around the back of the house. "Okay, keep 'em closed. Shit, watch out for that puddle."

"I can't see anything, remember?" Celia noted dryly.

There was so much I still wanted to show her around the property. Initially, I'd planned on saving the tree for last, but yesterday had changed everything.

Sixteen years later, and she was still mine.

It was something I'd never take for granted again.

"Okay." I took a deep breath and dropped my hand. "Open."

She stared up at the pink flowers spanning the length of the tree limbs before turning back to me. "It's beautiful. Has it always been here?"

"I planted it." My voice began to shake, and I cleared my throat before trying again. "When I got sober."

"Look at you, babe. Biker, gardener, master of Spam. It's like there's nothing you can't do," she said, running her fingers over the thin bark with a grin.

"It's just—" I could do this. I just had to say it. "I planted it for the baby."

"What?" The smile faded, and her hand moved up, covering her mouth and nose.

I nodded, suddenly wondering why it had seemed so important to bring her out here. "Slim saved my life when I wanted out. Reminded me of my purpose, and when I got clean, he was the one who suggested I plant somethin' so I'd have a place to visit... to pay my respects."

Celia's eyes filled, and she began blinking rapidly.

"It didn't seem right to pretend like it never happened," I choked, fighting against the tears that I knew were going to fall at any second. Sobering up had turned me into a fucking crybaby.

"It was like there was nothing to prove that he or she had even existed," she breathed.

I nodded and swiped a hand over my eyes with a soft chuckle. "For whatever reason, I imagined it was another girl, so I planted this because I wanted to see those bright pink flowers and be reminded of her every time I sat out on the back porch."

"Jamie—" Celia's voice broke, and she dug the heel of her hand into the center of her chest, fighting to speak through her tears. "Can you—can you just give me a minute?"

I bit the inside of my cheek and nodded before squeezing her hand. On the walk back to the house, I lit up a cigarette and took long, desperate drags before sinking down into a chair. It took everything in me to stay on the porch as I watched her body shake with sobs.

She knelt against the damp earth and placed her hands on the trunk as if she was praying. Early on, I'd spent my evenings in the same position, apologizing for the choices I'd made and the life I'd chosen to live. I begged for forgiveness and a way to make amends—to salvage what remained of my family.

Sometimes, a confessional wasn't a fancy box found inside a church. Maybe it was nothing more than a Texas Redbud sitting in the middle of a pecan orchard.

My cell phone vibrated from my pocket, and I pulled it free to see that it was the club. "What's goin' on?"

"Got an update on your gangbanger," Bear said casually.

"He finally decide to give up his friends?"

"Not even after I branded his ass," he chuckled.

I shook my head and looked up to make sure Celia wasn't headed toward me before hissing, "You branded him?"

"Yeah, shit gets boring after a few hours. All he wants to do is sleep. Went pokin' around in some of those abandoned units and found a fuck load of branding irons. Some asshole was into some kinky shit."

"Bear," I drawled. "It ever cross your mind that some asshole might've been a rancher?"

"You know, that actually explains the weird as fuck symbols. Anyway, he ain't gonna be with us much longer, and I know you got shit goin' on, but thought you'd wanna know. I'd be happy to put him down."

"I'll handle it." I stabbed the cigarette butt into the ashtray and immediately lit up another.

"You got it, boss." Bear ended the call, and I sat back with a sharp exhale. Things were moving too fast.

I'd wanted the entire weekend with her before dealing with him. For over an hour, Celia sat beside the tree, talking and crying, while I chain-smoked and tried to come up with what I was going to say.

She glanced at the overflowing ashtray with raised eyebrows as she climbed the porch steps before snagging the cigarette from my hand and dropping into the chair beside mine.

"Remind me to send Slim a fruit basket," she finally said, exhaling a cloud of smoke with a cough. "Thank you... for all of it. I mean it. I was convinced that I'd never survive if I stopped to let myself fall apart, but I feel more alive than ever. It's like being awake for the first time in years."

She passed the cigarette back over to me, resting her head on her hand as she stared out toward the tree. Her face was splotchy and streaked with tears, but to me, she'd never looked more beautiful.

What had taken me years, she'd figured out in a weekend, which meant it was time.

"Got somethin' you need to know."

"I'm not sure I can take much more today, Jamie," she said with a laugh. "I think I've cried all the tears I can."

"I know, but you deserve the truth—"

She cocked her head to the side. "About what? What's left that we haven't already discussed?"

"Manny," I stated flatly.

Celia's mouth twisted up, and she looked down, rubbing her palms along the skirt of her dress. "I hope you made him suffer..."

"Come here." I tugged her up and into my lap. "Look at me. I told you I'd teach you how to kill a man properly, but I wanted you to be ready. Unfortunately, time is workin' against us right now."

She fidgeted with an earring before bringing her eyes up to meet mine. "I guess I'm not following..."

"Manny's alive, Celia. But, according to Bear, he ain't gonna be with us for much longer. You say the word, and I'll show you everything I know."

Her mouth fell open. "What—how?"

I chuckled and tightened my grip on her thigh. "Club's got some damn fine doctors on its payroll. I wanted to kill him, fuckin' tried to several times. It's gotta be you, princess. Nobody else but you."

She sucked in a quick breath and let her forehead rest against mine. "Okay. I'm ready."

CHAPTER THIRTY-FOUR

Grey: March 2005 (Age: 41)

"Pres." Crossbones nodded to me as we approached the entrance to the storage facility. "Ma'am."

Celia nodded somberly, waiting until he was out of earshot before excitedly exclaiming, "It's like we're detectives who just arrived at the crime scene, and they're lifting that yellow tape for us to cross, right?"

I shook my head. "You realize that what we're about to do is illegal in all fifty states, right? I'd say that's about as far from bein' a fuckin' detective as you can get."

She shook her hands out at her sides and cracked her neck, like a boxer warming up in the ring. "Okay, let's do this."

"Celia?" Her green eyes met mine in question, and I pulled her to my side. "Just calm the fuck down, yeah? I ain't shown you a goddamn thing yet."

The heel of her sandal tapped nervously against the pavement as I unlocked the door, and I paused to look back at her until she stopped. "Sorry."

I tilted her chin up. "Were you this nervous when you went after Manny on your own?"

She shook her head. "No, but I was in a different headspace then. I never let myself consider what would happen if I failed."

"Hey," I stroked her cheek. "I swear to all the saints I wouldn't have brought you here if I couldn't keep you safe. He's tied up, so he ain't gonna lay a hand on you, but I need you to stay calm and follow my lead, okay?"

"Okay."

I flipped the switch, and the fluorescent bulbs overhead buzzed loudly as they began warming up. Celia jumped at the sound and pressed up against me, clearly still expecting the Manny from before.

"Where is he?" she hissed.

"Princess, if this place gets raided by the cops, you think I want the gangbanger strung up like a goddamn Christmas tree where anybody could see him when they walk in?"

She shook her head. "But where is he?"

"Imagine you're me. Where would you put him?"

I watched her eyes roam over the large metal building as she tried thinking like a criminal. "Someplace that wouldn't stand out. I'd look for a basement—preferably one that was soundproof, so that even if someone came in, they'd never hear him."

Fuck.

Hearing her describe her ideal torture facility left me rock hard. It didn't matter that I'd had her twice since our afternoon discussion on the back porch. My cock was ready for round three.

"Nailed it."

"I did?" Her eyes lit up in surprise. "Seriously?"

I tapped a finger against the tip of her nose before leading her through another door next to the back office. "My girl's a goddamn genius."

We reached the foot of the stairs, and she turned to me with a frown. "This is just a hallway. I thought you said he was down here—"

"He is. Last door on the left."

Celia released her hold on my kutte and moved closer to the wall, feeling for a seam. "Got it."

"Good girl. Now, before we go in, you need to know that he ain't the same man you faced in the motel. We've broken his body down, but forced him to stay alive."

"I'm ready," she said with a nod.

I opened the door, and she immediately reared back at the stench of blood and decaying flesh. Keeping my hand on her lower back, I walked us over to where Manny sat against the wall.

He blinked until she came into focus, a wide grin stretching across his face when he realized who it was. "Back for a third-round already, Ma?" he rasped.

A tremor passed through her spine, but she stayed silent and took another small step forward, studying him carefully.

"Your enemy will try to bait you into doing somethin' stupid. It could be they want you distracted while they make their move or, if they know they've been beat, they'll use it hoping to get a quick death."

Celia nodded to herself and pushed up the sleeves on the sweatshirt I'd let her borrow. "What do I do?"

We'd swung by the house long enough for her to grab an old pair of jeans, but she'd insisted on keeping her sandals. I figured it was a mistake she'd only make once.

"A gun is the fastest. Get the guy on his knees, press the barrel against his skull, and pull the trigger." I smacked my hand against the metal on the wall, imitating the sound and sending Manny scurrying back across the concrete like the cockroach he was.

"You're smaller than most men, though. Even if you got your hands on a gun, they ain't goin' to their knees without a fight. I calmly walked over and retrieved the trench knife from the old wooden table in the center of the room while she watched me intently.

"For someone smaller, a sneak attack is better. You had the right idea with usin' a knife before, but you needed one you could keep a sturdy grip on. Try this one."

Her fingers slipped through the rings on the brass knuckle handle, tightening as she turned her wrist back and forth. "This is much better," she breathed before handing it back.

"You've got the pointed tip, which is sharp enough to go in with little to no force. The tip should always be sharp enough that it slides right in. Because the blade itself is sharp on either side, you can come at your enemy like this..." I flicked my wrist backward and then brought it forward again. "Or like this."

"You find Hawk and Cobra yet?" Manny taunted. "Or should I ask your girls?"

Celia's lips curled in disgust, but she stayed where she was, waiting for my direction.

I placed the knife back into her hand and walked over to the wall, jerking the rope with such force that his body seemed to fly off the ground. Celia's eyes widened as she took in his flayed skin and a flush worked its way up her neck.

I couldn't read her.

He exhaled a groan of pain as I hoisted him higher, and I grinned. "*Amigo*, the grown-ups are havin' a discussion. Why don't you hang out, and we'll get ya in second."

"Celia," he panted, setting my teeth on edge. "You... found them... before..."

The monster thrashed against his cage of flesh and bone, begging to be set free. I should have cut his tongue out, but had held back, thinking he might actually give us something we could work with. If I didn't stay on guard, he was going to push her right into another episode.

Keep her safe.

The thought had been running through my head for years. I thought I finally knew what to do, but what I was about to show her was a gamble. There was no taking it back.

She'd either come out of it stronger or retreat into her shell.

"Jamie." Her voice was husky as she moved in front of me, but there was strength in the way she said my name.

"Fuckin' tell me who's in control right now." I scanned her from head to toe, searching for signs that an attack was coming.

Her chin jerked up, green eyes narrowing as she met my stare. "I am. Just show me how to do it."

Fuck, she was perfect.

I moved to stand directly in front of Manny. "You crossed my girl, which means you crossed me. You feel me?"

"She knows where they are," he forced out through cracked lips.

"Show me, Jamie," she demanded, bringing a smile to my face.

I'd forced Celia into the underworld I called home, never once imagining how it was going to affect her life. Back then, it hadn't mattered to me because what I wanted, I took.

End of story.

Women like my ma and Celia were easily broken. They were too good... too soft. The world didn't give a fuck about what people deserved, or I would have been in the ground a long time ago. But the two of them? They'd deserved so much better than they'd gotten.

My princess was a fighter, though. She'd taken on not only my enemies, but me as well. I'd sworn after Donald that nobody would force me to kneel, yet she had me living on my knees, happier than I'd ever been before.

"Who's in control?" I reminded her.

"Me," she repeated, moving to my side.

I jerked Manny's head back, exposing his throat. "You can do what you did before, but that requires a lot of strength. Remember Remington?"

Her lips parted, and an almost dreamy look crossed her face. If I didn't know better, I would have sworn she was turned on. "I remember," she breathed.

"I had to put everything into that." I forced Manny's chin down to his chest, causing him to cry out as I placed the tip of the blade against his head. "Now, you could go in at the base of the skull. Hold the blade flat and slide it in right here. Sever the spinal cord, and he's dead almost instantly."

"It's that easy?"

"Not quite. You gotta go in between the vertebrae and cut through the spongy shit to get to it. Some guys aim for the heart or lungs, but neither is guaranteed instant death. He still might have enough in him to take you down."

Celia crossed her arms over her chest with a pout. "Well, what am I supposed to do? Besides jiu-jitsu."

I hid a smile, remembering how effective her martial arts skills had been... in getting me aroused.

Releasing my hold on Manny, I took a step back. "There is one thing you could try that I think would work with your build..."

I pressed the tip of the blade underneath his chin where it met his neck. “His carotid arteries run on either side. That’s what you’re aimin’ for, but you gotta get the blade in about an inch and a half. You could go in from the side and pull the blade toward you, cutting through the front, or you could drive it in underneath his chin, using your momentum to drag the blade down toward his shoulder.”

Her gaze moved between Manny and me as I demonstrated both techniques before she took the blade from my hand.

“See which one feels more comfortable.”

It was surreal teaching my wife how to take a life. I never wanted her to have to use what she’d learned outside of this room, but knew it was absolutely necessary that I give her a way to defend herself.

“Cobra...” Manny struggled against the ropes, fighting to take a breath. “He wants her...”

“Who does he want?” she asked without hesitation.

“Y-you. He wants you. I... was supposed to wait. Girls... off-limits.”

The fuck?

CHAPTER THIRTY-FIVE

Grey: March 2005 (Age: 41)

Her eyebrows moved up toward her hair as she turned to glance at me, as if ensuring she wasn't the only one hearing his words. "It wasn't their idea to use my daughter as bait?"

Manny's tongue darted out before he admitted, "No."

That was why they hadn't come looking for him. He'd defied Cobra's orders and was a walking dead man by the time we found him at the motel.

Without another word, Celia thrust the blade just under Manny's right ear with a cry of rage and punched it forward, ripping his throat wide open and sending a spray of blood into the air.

There was no gurgle or cry of surprise. He was dead before her arm came down. Instead of stepping away from the blood, she leaned into it, jabbing the tip of the knife into his chest and dragging it toward his navel with a roar.

Again and again, the blade connected with his neck and chest until his head fell awkwardly to the side, almost completely severed.

"Celia," I said quietly. "It's over."

She shook her head and drove the knife into his belly again. "No, I can do it. I can kill him."

"Darlin'," I moved closer, keeping my palms up. "He's dead."

Her lips turned up into a defiant expression. "Not to me."

I'd felt something similar when I sent Donald to the Reaper. It didn't matter how many people I put down. Death had never given me the closure I sought.

"He ain't comin' back. Give me the knife." Her grip tightened around the handle, and I sighed. "Celia, you said you'd trust me. Tell me who's in control?"

"Me." Her shoulders slumped forward, and she released the knife into my waiting palm before dropping to her knees and vomiting.

I ran my knuckles up and down between her shoulder blades until her retching turned to dry heaves. She ran the arm of her sweatshirt over her mouth before rocking back onto her heels. "Let me guess," she muttered. "You've probably never thrown up after a kill."

My lips curved up into a smirk. "You guessed right. How do you feel?"

She took my hand and let me pull her back onto her feet before looking up at me with the stubborn expression I'd come to know and love.

My bloodstained goddess.

"I want to kill him over and over until it takes away the memories of what he did to me."

I nodded and led her out of the room. "Ain't no kill in the world that can erase that. Sometimes I close my eyes and I swear I can still feel my old man's fists on my ribs; can even smell the stench of liquor on his breath."

"What do you do?" Her hand curled around mine.

"I fight it—remind myself that he's gone. Now..." I turned to her once we reached the hallway. "You did good in there, but you and I both know that he wasn't any real threat. The next time might not be as easy, but you gotta be willin' to put him down just the same."

With a sigh, I added, "And if I'm tellin' you to do somethin', fuckin' listen. You can't act in rage. That's a damn good way to get yourself hurt or killed. I showed you exactly how to handle the knife, but you let your emotions cloud your judgment, and it showed."

Celia's lips mashed together for a brief second before she responded. "I was listening to you. I did exactly what you said—"

My frustration increased. "You're just lucky you killed him with your first strike. This ain't fuckin' karate where you can tap out or whatever it is they let you do. You fuck up like you did back there and it'll be like the motel all over again. But next time, I might not be there to save you! Are we clear?"

Where I'd expected an argument—or at the very least an outburst—she remained quiet, watching me through narrowed eyes.

"Celia," I pushed, needing her compliance.

"We're clear."

"Good." I'd just put my hand on the door handle leading upstairs when she swept my legs out from under me, sending me down to the concrete in a tangle of limbs.

"It's jiu-jitsu," she panted, planting her hands on my chest. "Not fucking karate. And, as you can see, it's highly effective."

She tugged the bloody sweatshirt up and over her head, lifting just enough to tug her jeans down past her wide hips, but not enough for me to move.

"Celia?"

"Don't move," she commanded, kicking her sandals off and freeing her legs from the denim. My heart thumped painfully against my chest at the sight of her tight nipples and feel of her pussy grinding against the front of my jeans. "Are we clear?"

The sound of her voice was muffled by the blood rushing in my ears, and she lowered her head, letting her teeth graze against my shoulder. "Jamie..."

I nodded, and her fingernails dug into the center of my chest. "Answer me."

"Understood," I bit out. She was using my words against me, but I couldn't say a goddamn thing out of fear that she'd suddenly stop.

I'd been wrong.

About all of it.

Killing Manny would never bring her peace, but I'd assumed it'd at least help with the next stage of her healing. Instead, I'd set her monster free and worked her up into a frenzy of lust.

Same as me.

Her delicate hands moved down to my jeans, yanking the belt

buckle away from my body as she worked to unfasten it. The sound of my zipper coming down was punctuated by the short bursts of air she was exhaling, and I ached to sink my fingers into the flesh of her ass, forcing her to let me lead. The only thing stopping me from making my move was the desperate need reflected in her eyes.

Freed from the confines of denim, my cock sprang up into her waiting hand, and she gave it a rough tug before rolling her hips forward. Her head fell back in a loud moan as she sank down over me, flooding the space between us with her juices.

"Fuck," I forced out through clenched teeth.

As if reading my mind, Celia reached for my hands, bringing them up to cup her ass cheeks. The truth from the books I'd read barreled through my mind.

Intimacy with a victim should be done in a well-lit setting where there are no reminders of the assault.

Any objections I had died on my lips when the muscles of her cunt clamped down around me like a vise.

My wife was fucking me on the concrete floor of a dimly lit hallway, less than ten feet from the rapist she'd just put down.

There wasn't a single book in the entire goddamn world that could help me navigate that.

"I need," she pleaded with a whimper. "I just—please..."

"Who's in charge here?"

"Me," she whispered, her teeth sinking down onto her lower lip, begging.

Knowing what she needed, I pulled my hand away before bringing it down in a punishing slap against her ass. She immediately tightened around me with a soft moan before bucking her hips, as if begging for more.

"Good girl." I brought my palm down again and again until the pleas became moans and her cream coated my cock. She came with a strangled gasp, and I gripped her hips, pulling her up and off of me.

"Celia," I groaned as my orgasm ripped through me, fisting my cock before coating her tits and belly.

Her eyes went heavy, and she leaned forward, placing her head against my chest with a contented sigh. She hadn't once questioned my decision to pull out.

Maybe we both knew that neither one of us would survive it a second time.

We were in the middle of a fucking war—a war that had been going on for years. If I wanted to keep her safe, I couldn't put her body at risk again. I'd failed her once. The breath would leave my body before I failed her again.

"Jamie," she whispered a few minutes later. "Are you awake?"

I chuckled as the concrete dug into my spine. "This ain't exactly a bed we're layin' on, princess."

Her palms moved to the floor, and she pushed herself up into a sitting position, a sly grin playing on her lips. "I can't believe we did it."

"You, darlin'." I brought my hand up over one of her breasts and squeezed. "It was all you."

"And we got a confession!"

I frowned, fighting to get the blood back up to my brain. Manny hadn't given us one goddamn thing. "Think you and I might be rememberin' things a little differently."

She shook her head, her grin widening. "No, he said I'd know where to find them. He was right, I do."

"How?"

"The same way I did before... at the blackjack table."

CHAPTER THIRTY-SIX

Celia: May 2006 (Age: 34)

I slammed the car door shut and jogged up the front porch steps with a wide grin.

"What do you think?" I asked, doing a little twirl under the porch light for the biker on the swing.

Jamie leaned back against it and looked me up and down before blowing a stream of smoke toward the yard. "I don't like it."

My grin faded. "The dress?"

"The fuckin' plan, Celia. We been chasin' underground games for over a year—danglin' you in front of their faces like bait. I can't fuckin' do it anymore."

"But I feel like we're getting closer—"

He shook his head. "No, we ain't. All we've managed to do is make your attacks worse. You tell me how you fightin' to take a goddamn breath in the middle of a game is us gettin' closer."

I wanted to believe that I'd left all the fear and hurt from that night out in the middle of the orchard, but I hadn't. He was right. The brokenness had only risen to the surface, rearing its ugly head at the most inopportune of times.

The faintest whiff from a cigar at the first game had left me hyperventilating in the bathroom, forcing the prospect-turned-bodyguard to call Jamie in.

During the games I managed to sit through, I found myself easily distracted and restless, convinced that I was being watched.

Whatever card skills I'd possessed before were long gone now.

"What are we supposed to do, then?" I snapped. "Let them get away again?"

He patted the empty seat next to him on the swing, but I stayed by the railing, keeping my arms crossed over my chest.

"Celia, your head ain't in the game. You're sloppy and unfocused—"

"I'm doing the best I can right now!" A small part of me was relieved that he was calling it off—that he was doing what I couldn't, before I remembered my anger.

"Who has the girls tonight?" It was impossible to miss the irritation in his voice, but it was laced with something else, too.

Worry.

"Angel. He was already planning on stopping by for dinner, so it worked out."

He took a long drag and gnawed on the corner of his lip before admitting, "There ain't a game tonight."

"What?" I laughed, but the sound was hollow. "But you told me to come out here—you said—"

Jamie stubbed out the cigarette and bent over, resting his elbows on his knees before cupping the back of his head with his hands. "Fuck," he growled. "Don't wanna fuckin' do this, princess."

"Then don't. I'll go by myself," I snapped before turning away. I hadn't even taken a step when I felt him at my back. His body moved behind mine, wrapping me up in a bear hug and sending flames shooting down my arms.

"Let me go," I fought to keep my voice steady.

It wasn't often, but sometimes, when he caught my shoulder or pulled me into his arms, I was struck with the realization that he was a giant. If he ever decided to use his strength against me, I'd be powerless to stop him.

He spun me around to face him before letting his hands fall away.

"Ain't lettin' you leave. You came all this way—let's play a game together."

"You wanted me to come out here so we could play board games?"

His bottom lip went between his teeth again, as if he was considering his options. "Not board games. Blackjack. Your skills are rusty. Only way to get better is to practice, yeah?"

"Are we playing for money? If so, I'm afraid you have me at a disadvantage."

Jamie scratched at his jaw. "Tell you what. Let's play for braggin' rights. Nothin' else. Main goal is gettin' you ready to play the tables again, okay?"

I was certain I resembled Kate as I halfheartedly shrugged before mumbling a bored, "I guess."

A blackjack table sat in the middle of the living room with two chairs on either side, and I looked up at him with a glare. "It looks like maybe you were planning this, Jamie."

"What can I say, darlin'? I wanna help you. Sit."

He took the dealer's seat and pushed a stack of chips over to me. "Each one's worth a grand."

I pushed two into the betting circle, and Jamie began shuffling the deck. I wasn't sure what he thought we were going to accomplish. We were in a controlled environment where I could stay one hundred percent focused.

He placed an ace and a two in front of me.

"Soft thirteen. And the dealer shows a four." He reached inside his leather vest and pulled out a cigar, popping it into his mouth to wet the head before holding it up in front of me.

"Now..." He flicked his lighter. "Most people don't know this, but you can't smoke one of these babies like a cigarette. You gotta ignite the end like this..."

I ran a hand through my hair and scratched at my throat as he slowly rotated the cigar over the flame. He took several puffs before pulling it back out for inspection.

"Sometimes, it don't light correctly, and you gotta do it again. Don't want it burnin' unevenly."

I grimaced as the smoke reached my nostrils, and my eyes began to sting. "Jamie," my voice was barely above a whisper.

"Soft thirteen, darlin'. Hit or stay?" He took another puff before exhaling the smoke rings toward my face.

Paralysis took the wheel, keeping me glued to my seat even as the first tear fell. My breaths became agonizing wheezes as I saw Cobra, sitting in the corner of my bedroom, watching and waiting for me in the dark.

You don't mind if I smoke inside, do you?

I jerked, pushing the chair back across the hardwood as I fought to get to my feet. Jamie calmly reached across the table and placed his hand over mine. "Look at me."

I reluctantly forced my eyes up to meet his, feeling like I was looking at a stranger. He'd been at that first game—had seen firsthand what the scent had done to me. "W-why?"

"Who's in control?" he gently reminded me.

"You," I said flatly, fighting against the emotion that was clogging my throat and obscuring my vision.

He tapped the deck of cards with his free hand and shook his head. "I ain't the one callin' the shots. You are. Now, focus. You gonna hit or stay?"

"I hate you," I choked, back to being the broken woman lying on a bathroom floor, praying for help.

Weak.

I'd thought he could be different this time.

Thought we could be different.

There was always going to be a chasm between us, though. Jamie had told me he couldn't be gentle with me; had insisted that he wasn't the man I needed. Yet, I'd stupidly convinced myself that I would make it work because I didn't believe that anyone would ever love me like he did.

"Hit. Or stay?" He questioned as he pulled his hand back, eyes flashing dangerously.

"Hit."

That was what he was doing, wasn't it? Pummeling a skull-shaped hole into my heart?

He dropped the card with another puff on the cigar. "Six. Brings you up to nineteen."

Turning his second card over, he added, "And four makes eight for the dealer." He dealt a third card and exclaimed, "An ace makes nineteen, princess. Push."

I ignored his smile. The bond that had connected us for seventeen years was stretched taut, ready to snap at any second.

"Why are you doing this?"

Jamie dropped his chin to his chest, blinking rapidly, before looking back up at me. It was then that I saw the tears. "Who's in control here?" He asked gruffly, before clearing his throat.

"Just tell me why you're doing this to me. Please."

"Let's go again."

"No." The chair legs squeaked loudly against the floor as I moved back. "I thought you cared… thought you loved me enough to never—I'm leaving. Don't call me—"

His hand latched onto my arm, tugging me back toward the table. The edges of my vision swam in black.

It was happening again.

Except, this time, it'd be worse, because it was him.

"Where are you right now?" Jamie asked, keeping me from slipping into unconsciousness. "What do you see?"

"I—can't…"

He dropped the cigar into the ashtray and moved around the table toward me. "You can. Who's in charge?"

"You are, don't you see that?" I roared, my face crumpling in anguish. "You're breaking me apart, just like they did!"

"What'd I say on the porch? Hmm? You remember me sayin' I didn't want to do this? What do you think I meant?"

I swiped a hand over my damp face. "I don't know, but I don't want to play this game anymore. I want to go home."

"You are home." He released my arm and lowered himself to his knees. "I'm tryin' to help you the only other way I know how. Close your eyes."

I shook my head. "I can't."

"C'mon, Celia. Do you trust me?"

Against my better judgment, I did as he asked, gulping back another sob.

"What do you smell?" It was apparent he was waving the cigar in front of my face, and I mashed the back of my hand to my lips, fighting the urge to vomit.

"I smell... him."

"Who?" he pushed.

"Cobra."

"What's he doin'?"

My skin burned red hot as I was forced back into Hell. "He—" I licked my lips. "He's in the chair in the bedroom, watching me." I clutched the front of my dress in my fist. "He tore my dress... and his teeth—"

My turn.

"What three cards did you just have?" he asked, blowing a puff of warm cigar smoke toward my face.

"I—an ace—" I tried picturing the table but could only see Cobra sitting in the dealer's chair, smirking down at me. I pushed myself. "T-two and a six."

"Good girl," he praised. "Now, think about what I had. Can you remember?"

I hiccuped loudly and his hand covered mine. "You had two fours and a—"

You're doin' great, sweetheart. Absolutely fuckin' perfect.

I cried out, bucking against the hand on mine. It was too much. Short bursts of air escaped my nostrils, sounding almost like panting.

Their panting.

I shuddered and slumped forward in the chair with a strangled gasp.

When I opened my eyes, I was in Jamie's lap on the floor. He tilted my chin up, watching me with eyes that were dark and unreadable.

"I'm sorry," I croaked. "I can't make myself be normal—I don't want to be broken like this—"

"Don't fuckin' apologize to me. You ain't broken. A broken woman wouldn't have gone after a gangbanger on her own. A broken woman wouldn't have forced herself to confront her own demons. Nah, you ain't broken, darlin'. You're a motherfuckin' warrior."

The cigar lay on the floor near his boot, and I stared down at it in disgust. I didn't want to spend the rest of my life cowering in fear. Pulling away from his grip, I reached for it with trembling fingers. "This isn't about the game, is it?"

"No," he said quietly. "By the time you sent Manny to the Reaper, he was broken down. Before that, though, he wanted me to know everything he'd done to you—everything he wanted to do to our girls. Hawk and Cobra will be the same."

I rolled the cigar between my fingers, fighting against the urge to throw it as far away from my body as possible. I felt Jamie's chest against my back, saw his legs on either side of mine.

He'd made himself a human shield.

For me.

"They'll try to trip me up... get me to do something stupid. You said that before..."

"They won't have to try hard. Everybody that's sat at a table with you knows that you ain't the same as before. That'll get back to them. If they know your weaknesses, they know how to break you." His arms moved around my torso. "They knew how to break me."

I was his weakness... and that night was mine.

Jamie had pushed me to cry—to grieve the things we'd lost, but he couldn't stop the war from raging in my mind. That was something only I could do.

"What do the books say about this?" He'd offered them to me several times over the last year, but I refused to crack the spine on anything that repeatedly used the word victim to describe me.

I was so much more than that.

I'd likened killing Manny to an addict getting a fix—leaving me feeling invincible.

Euphoric.

Desperate for my next hit.

Mistakenly, I'd thought the high would last, but the world was full of reminders, each one of them just waiting to knock me back down to the ground.

Jamie's body went rigid, and his grip tightened. "They suggested exposure therapy, but it's obvious you ain't ready, princess."

I took a shaky breath and turned to press a kiss to the corner of his mouth. It was time to face the demons head-on. "I'm ready. How does this work?"

CHAPTER THIRTY-SEVEN

Celia: May 2006 (Age: 34)

I jerked my head up off the pillow at the sound of raised voices coming from the living room and blinked at the clock.

It was just after eleven.

I'd hoped for another few hours of sleep before going to pick the girls up from school, but it sounded as if Angel had decided to hang out and catch up on his daytime television at the only volume he seemed to know—loud.

After driving me home, Jamie had retired to the hammock in the backyard. By the time I got up to get the girls out the door, he was already gone again.

Kicking the blankets off with a groan, I padded into the bathroom and studied my bloodshot and still-swollen eyes in the mirror before splashing cold water onto my face. Jamie ran on little to no sleep and looked like a million bucks. I did it and looked like the undead.

With rocks weighing heavily on my chest, I'd pushed myself past the panic and anxiety, reliving the events of that night into the wee hours of the morning.

When I started to slip away, Jamie would turn it back to blackjack, rapidly firing questions to pull me toward reality.

After back-to-back panic attacks and another fainting spell, he'd been ready to call it off, apologizing and insisting again that I wasn't ready.

It only made me want to fight harder.

My body screamed for me to run, but I stayed; inhaling the smoke from the cigar... tracing my fingers over a diamond thirteen ring and remembering how the hot metal had felt like a thousand bees stinging my skin.

The worst part was putting myself through the emotionally and physically draining exercises without fully knowing if they'd worked.

Voices reached a fever pitch as I left the bedroom, and I pushed my exhaustion to the side, ready to lay into Angel until I glanced toward the front door and realized it wasn't the television.

"Mother? What are you doing here?" I'd avoided her for the better part of five years, dealing only with my father when necessary.

She pushed past Angel. "Why are you still in bed in the middle of the day—why do your eyes look like that? Are you high, Celia?"

I pressed the pads of my fingers under my eyes and shook my head. "No, I'm just tired—"

"Where are the girls?" She forced her chin up, jerkily turning her head as if Kate and Dakota might pop up from behind the furniture at any second.

Leaving his post by the front door, Angel came over to stand at my side. My mother looked him up and down with a sneer. "I thought Dakota was joking when she said you had a vagrant living here—"

"A vagrant?" My voice shot up several octaves, and while Angel stayed silent, I could feel the rage coming off of him in waves. "First, as usual, you have no idea what you're talking about. Second, when were you around my daughter?"

She waved her manicured nails flippantly. "Your father and I have lunch with her once a week at school, and thank the saints for that because otherwise, I'm afraid we'd never see her."

Angel's hand on my shoulder was the only thing that kept me from launching myself at her. "There was a reason for that," I bit out.

"Apparently." The judgment in her eyes made it clear that she thought it had something to do with Angel. "She admitted that you'd been leaving her and Mary Katherine alone with a perfect stranger for quite some time now. I told your father that we've ignored your poor choices, but I can't sit back and watch you ruin their lives, too."

"Get out," I growled, stabbing my finger toward the door. "Get out and never come back here again. You are not welcome around me, and you are not welcome around my girls. What we do is none of your goddamn business!"

Instead of cowering, my mother brought her hand up to her mouth with a soft laugh. "Oh, but it is my goddamn business. You see, I hired someone to look into it, and this man..." she pointed at Angel. "Has quite the record. Let's see... there was drug possession—"

"It was weed," he interjected. "My arthritis gets bad and—"

She nodded condescendingly. I brought my arm around his waist, each of us keeping the other from losing control.

"Sure it is. And I'm sure the weapons charges were for a health reason too, right? Trafficking, was it? There were so many that it's hard to get it all straight. Anyway, that wasn't the most interesting thing I learned."

She paused dramatically, clearly waiting for us to begin taking guesses. "It's the fact that you belong to a notorious outlaw motorcycle gang. What happened, Celia? Lost one trash biker and needed another to take his place? Didn't you learn anything after they beat you up? You had so much potential when you were younger. Everyone just knew your smarts were going to take you somewhere amazing. Now, look at you."

The fire in my belly worked its way up into my chest and wrapped its tendrils around my heart, fighting to remind me of how far I'd come. My pulse pounded, leaving my head throbbing, but I refused to break in front of her. Not anymore.

Keeping a tight hold on Angel's shirt, I straightened to my full height and faced her head-on. "So, you figured out he's a member of Silent Phoenix. Good for you. It doesn't change a thing for me. I won't have you near my girls ever again—"

"See, I thought you might say that, so I talked to a good friend of mine. Do you remember Judge Lucas? He gave you a very sizable gift for your graduation." I briefly remembered the name, but instead of waiting for a response, she continued. "When it came to light that your new man friend had been convicted of child molestation, he agreed we couldn't push this under the rug. Not when the girls' safety is at stake—"

Angel broke free from my hold and stalked toward my mother, sending her scurrying back toward the sofa. "What did you just accuse me of?" he snarled. "Those girls are like granddaughters to me. I ain't ever touched them or any other kid, and you know it—"

"Now, you listen here." My mother raised her finger again. "I know every judge in this town—"

"Stop!" My lungs narrowed, shortening my breaths into pants. "You don't know anyone! If you've shown up here, hoping to intimidate me into letting you see my girls, you've failed!"

She perched against the back of the sofa; hands folded primly in her lap. "How do you think I kept your father out of jail when he barreled nose-first into a godless lifestyle? I didn't come here to intimidate you. I came here to tell you I'm taking the girls—"

As I fought to take a breath, Angel clenched his hands into fists and slowly approached her. "Over my dead body. Those girls belong with their mama. You had a chance to get to know them, and you blew it. Don't make me call their daddy in to handle you."

"Their daddy?" My mother snorted. "From where? The cemetery?"

"Jamie's alive," I stated flatly. "Didn't Daddy tell you?"

"He's what? No, that's impossible," she faltered, before regaining her composure. "Even if it were true, it wouldn't change things. I have an emergency custody order in my purse. The girls are going to be living with me and your father from now on."

"No," I ground out. "I will fight you with everything I have—"

"You won't. Because if you do, your friend here will be locked up on child pornography charges, and you know how they treat those men behind bars. He's no spring chicken either—"

"Celia, do it." Angel ran a hand roughly over his face. "I don't give a fuck where I end up, as long as I know they're safe with you."

"I wasn't finished," she snapped. "Celia, it's obvious you're strung out. God only knows on what. I doubt you'd fare much better behind bars either. You can't care for them—look at the state you're in. They'd both end up just like you—knocked up before graduation and forced into the same life—"

"That's enough," Angel growled. "You ain't threatenin' her. You wanna lock me up? Fine. I got people on the inside, same as I do on the outside. But leave Celia out of this."

My mother eyed him defiantly. "I'll take down your entire gang. Maybe it'll come to light that you weren't trafficking weapons, after all. Maybe this entire time, you've all been running a child prostitution ring—"

I was going to lose them.

CHAPTER THIRTY-EIGHT

Celia: May 2006 (Age: 34)

Angel yanked his gun from a hidden holster on his hip and brought it to her head. "Maybe I'll put you down right here—"

Her throat bobbed up and down in a nervous swallow before she found her voice again. "That might've worked had I not alerted several friends of mine that I was coming here. You might want to check out front. I bet they'd be interested in hearing that the leader of a gang they've been tracking for years faked his death."

With every shaky step toward the front window, the ache in my chest intensified, the pressure leaving me gasping for air. Two squad cars sat in the driveway, drawing the attention of every nosy neighbor on the block.

"There are cops outside, Angel—" My voice cut off in a sob, and this time, I didn't fight it. "How can you do this to me? To them? I'm doing everything to keep them safe!"

"You're leaving them to gamble!" My mouth fell open, and I didn't miss the triumphant grin on her face. "Yes, I know about that. Several prominent friends of ours have spotted you at the casinos, throwing your money away."

I'd never once gambled in a casino, only underground games. If my mother's friends had seen me, I could fathom a guess as to how they'd risen to a position of power.

"I can't lose them," I begged.

"Then you and all of your outlaw buddies can enjoy prison together. I wonder how the girls would react to that being on the news. What would their friends think?"

She pushed off the sofa and adjusted her linen slacks before heading for the door. "You'll drop them off by four o'clock sharp today, or I'll have the entire police department in your front yard, and they can watch as you're placed in handcuffs. Your choice."

The front door slammed shut behind her, and the uncontrollable shaking in my body grew until I was down on the carpet, clawing at my throat and feeling as if I was going to die.

Angel sank down to his knees and pulled me into his arms, giving me permission to fall apart. My hiccupping sobs were punctuated only by my gasps for air. This was worse than the pain I'd endured last night. This was the kind of hurt that consumed a soul.

I would have taken on a thousand Cobras for them—let them break my body apart again if it meant my little girls were safe. I'd thought that afternoon in the orchard was my breaking point, but it was here.

The dam inside my chest broke open, and the pain that I'd carried for six years came rushing out in the form of tears. Every drop was a cruel reminder that life would never be what I wanted it to be—no matter how hard I fought.

"I got you, girl," Angel murmured, rocking me back and forth like a small child.

"I—can't," I whimpered. "I can't—lose them."

He sniffed. "I let Jamie know... he'll know what to do."

The tears eventually stopped, leaving me numb again. I kept my head down, focusing on a small blue stain on the carpet left behind by Dakota's marker. It didn't matter how many times I said that they were only to be used at the kitchen table. Any given day I could walk in and find her happily coloring on the floor.

"How do I do it? How do I tell them they can't live with me anymore?"

"You don't."

I jerked my head up to see Jamie standing at the back door, chest rising and falling rapidly.

"You're here," I whispered.

"Got here quick," Angel stated flatly. "It ain't good, kid. What she doesn't have on us, she's willing to get her rich friends to say she does."

"She's going to take them," I whispered. "And I can't do anything to stop it."

Angel got to his feet and stomped toward the door.

"Where the hell you goin'?" Jamie snapped.

"Ain't fuckin' sittin' around twiddling my thumbs. I'm gonna reach out to Wolverine and see who we know. Then, I'm bustin' my girls out of class and takin' them for ice cream and a movie. Fuck what that cunt says!"

The door slammed shut behind him, rattling the glass in the picture window.

"Come here." Jamie lifted me into his arms and walked down the hall to our bedroom. After placing me on the bed, he rocked back onto his heels. "Tell me everything."

His blue eyes seemed to darken more with every word I said until his body was taut with fury. I scrambled back toward the headboard when he went for his gun, checking the chamber and clicking various things into place.

"Uh, Jamie? What are you doing?"

"Gonna blow their brains out, darlin'."

I swallowed. "Well, she sort of accounted for that and has police protection—"

"Jesus fuckin' Christ!" he roared before shoving it back into the holster. "I've always had the right people in my pocket until now. And if she had this kind of power all along, why the fuck didn't she use it to keep you away from me?"

Regardless of what my mother thought about me, I knew the things I'd sacrificed for my daughters. I knew the lengths I would go to just to keep them safe.

Why hadn't my parents done the same for me?

Until now, I'd been holding back in my struggle to stay in control—

to stay present. The severity of what she was about to do hit me, and I slumped against the pillows behind me—feeling myself slipping away again, back into the darkness I'd desperately fought to escape.

My mind had become a narrow hallway with no clear exit, churning my stomach with the realization that I was trapped.

"Celia?" He was right in front of me, but his voice sounded as if it was miles away.

I was pulled from my stupor when the backs of Jamie's boots connected with my slippers, sending him stumbling into the dresser. A bottle of perfume fell to the carpet and rolled toward the wall, and I watched it curiously before looking up at him.

He carefully studied my face with an unreadable expression before storming into the bathroom to turn on the faucets above the tub.

"What are you doing?" I asked calmly.

He grabbed the bottle of bubble bath and flipped it upside down, squeezing until it was empty before tossing it onto the tile with a growl. "What's it look like I'm doin'? I'm takin' a bath."

I mashed my lips together in an attempt not to laugh as I watched my biker run himself a bubble bath. "You don't take baths. Like ever."

"Maybe I do now."

I nodded as if it made all the sense in the world before making my way over to him. "How is that going to help us, exactly?"

He stripped off his leather vest and t-shirt before whipping them onto the vanity. "Won't, but you're slippin' away on me. That, and it'll stop me from goin' over there and killin' 'em both with my bare hands."

"Believe me, I wish you could. But the people she knows want nothing more than to take down the club—"

"Fuck the club!" he roared, and I shrank back against the doorway. "Fuck all of it! Jesus fuckin' Christ, just when I think we're close to bein' together again, everything goes to shit. I'm so fuckin' sick of not havin' my family under the same roof, and that cunt—" The muscles strained against his skin as his chest heaved.

With a growl, he reached for the drawstring on my pants, letting them fall to the floor. I stepped out of them like an obedient child before he went for my shirt, carefully peeling it up over my head until I stood like an offering before the god of death.

"What are you doing?" I asked quietly.

"Bringin' you back to me," he panted. His eyes looked almost feral. "You need to relax, and I need to not shed blood right now."

Bubbles began to flow over the side of the tub, like the head on a beer poured way too fast. He'd added enough soap for twenty baths, but I wasn't about to tell him that.

I checked the temperature and shut the taps off before stepping in. "You coming?"

Jamie ran a hand over his face and nodded before stripping out of his jeans and joining me. I settled between his legs with a deep sigh and he gripped my shoulders, tugging my back up against his chest and sending another cascade of bubbles down onto the tile.

The fog lifted, freeing me from the endless loop of pain running through my head. "Do you feel any better?"

"Not one goddamn bit," he replied icily, palming my breasts in his massive hands. His fingers dug into the flesh, kneading in a way that was somehow intimate without being sexual.

"I can't lose them, Jamie."

He inhaled deeply. "Believe me, princess, if I thought I could send 'em both to the Reaper without anyone immediately lookin' to you, I'd do it."

"How can they just take them from me?" I choked. "I know I haven't been the best mother, but—"

"The fuck you sayin', Celia? You're a goddamn saint. Ain't no one could've done a better job with them."

I sat up suddenly and held my breath, waiting for the answer to come to me, refusing to believe it had been that simple to rip away my entire world. When it didn't come, I slumped forward, resting my forehead against the lip of the tub.

How could she have been that cruel?

"Lift your head, darlin'. It ain't over yet," Jamie gently reminded me.

"I wish it was," I mumbled.

"I'll fix this."

CHAPTER THIRTY-NINE

Celia: May 2006 (Age: 34)

He couldn't.

At four o'clock sharp, after countless phone calls to every club ally in town, I dropped my girls off at my parent's house.

With rage flowing through my veins and hate reflected in my eyes, I met them on the porch and handed over the two beings most precious to me in the entire world.

Kate was sullen, refusing to give me a hug goodbye as she went to stand at my father's side. She hadn't spoken a word since I told her the news. My apologies fell on deaf ears, and I died a little more inside with the realization that they could never know the truth.

Long blades of grass tickled the tops of my feet as I stood frozen in their front yard. Numbness settled like a blanket around my shoulders, almost convincing me I was doing the right thing.

"I just don't want to say goodbye!" Dakota wailed in despair, clenching the bodice of my dress in her fists, and I realized that this was my point of no return. By walking away, I would forever be a villain in her book.

Their memories would be overwritten with the narrative that their mother had chosen gambling over her own children. A single line that would sum up what they thought of me.

All because I hadn't known how to defeat the very people who should have loved me like I loved those two little girls. I pressed a kiss to blonde hair drenched in tears as my father ripped her from my arms.

Her screams of despair echoed all around me, piercing my armor and leaving me fighting to stay on my feet as I climbed back into my car.

Alone.

A masochist until the very end, I forced the car into drive and lifted my eyes to the rearview mirror; watching as Kate buried her face against my mother's neck, unable to look at me for a moment longer.

I was convinced nothing would pierce the veil of darkness that had settled around my heart until Dakota lifted her tear-streaked face and reached her hands out for me. A pained scream broke free from my chest, and I collapsed against the steering wheel in a fit of crippling sobs.

I'd left my babies on that porch, along with what remained of Celia Quinn.

CHAPTER FORTY

Mike: January 2009 (Age: 26)

I cranked up the speed on the treadmill as I asked into the phone, "Are you working late again?"

David laughed. "What do you think? I gotta get this business off the ground or my old man's gonna be busting down my door to get his money back."

A shapely ass on the elliptical in front of me caught my eye, and I momentarily forgot about David and his money problems. Jesus, I loved working midnights. By the time I got off and made it to the gym, I had all the hotties to myself.

I had fulfilled my dream of becoming a cop. A little ironic, considering what had happened with Patrick, but I was hellbent on staying on the right side of the law.

With Patrick's face plastered on damn near every billboard along the Gulf Coast, David had been anxious to get the fuck out of Dodge. We compromised and ended up in west Texas, renting a shitty little house in the college district. I went to college and got my sociology degree while David followed in his old man's footsteps by starting his own construction company. John had loaned him the money to get it off the ground, and David had jumped headfirst into being a business owner.

Even more surprising than my decision to become a cop was the fact that my father seemed to want the very same thing for me. Gone were the plans of me joining up with the Silent Phoenix MC. Not long after the Patrick Incident, he'd shown up, offering me a kutte and a chance to prospect for the club.

When I told him I was thinking of a career in criminal justice, he'd gone quiet. He scratched at his beard as he thought it over before a grin spread across his face. *"My boy—a cop. At least one Sullivan will make something of himself."*

Seemed he was just full of surprises. Gone was the asshole who'd beaten my mom within an inch of her life for cooking chicken incorrectly. In his place was a man who rarely raised his voice and showed a genuine interest in his wife and son.

"Hello? Mike, are you still there?"

I looked away from the blonde and her ass. "Yep, still here. Thinking of a way to get your ass to unwind. I worked all night and here I am at the gym, fresh as a fucking daisy. Surely, if I can pull a midnight and still go out, you can too."

The blonde slowed her pace and tried to discreetly peek at me over her shoulder. I winked, and her cheeks immediately flushed pink before she spun back around, giving me a marvelous view of that ass again.

"Fine," David conceded, and I grinned.

"*Nick's* at eight, dick. Don't flake out on me again."

He laughed. "10-4, asshole."

My shift had begun at eight the night before. I'd pulled over a car with a broken taillight, broken up a bar brawl between two drunken frat bros, responded to a burglary, and then dealt with a fuck ton of paperwork to top it off.

I went into the academy right after getting my degree. My father had supported me throughout school, but made it clear that if I didn't get into the academy, I'd be on my own. Like I said, he was nothing like I remembered.

After FTO, I drafted to midnights, where I'd been residing a bit impatiently for the last four years. I enjoyed midnights—it was a hell of a lot better than working days where paperwork was the highlight of your shift.

I just wanted to be a detective—to track my cases from start to finish. As it was, I'd bust someone, only to turn around and hand it over to the investigating detective. I wanted the ability to control my cases until they were solved.

There'd been rumors for months that CAP (Crimes Against Persons) had an opening they were looking to fill. I'd applied to pick up extra shifts, knowing it made me look better to the higher-ups. I just needed official word they were looking, and I'd make damn sure that I was first in line for an interview. Until that day, I'd be pulling midnights.

"So, you're a cop?"

I looked away from the television screen mounted on a metal crossbar in front of me and down at the perky blonde with the great ass.

It was too easy.

Seriously, the badge was a pussy magnet.

I could say anything and they'd fall hook, line, and sinker for it. I paused the treadmill and grinned like there were a hundred paparazzi cameras in my face. "Why? You in need of some help?"

She licked her bottom lip—lips that had been injected with god-knew-what until they were perfectly pouty. I wouldn't mind seeing them wrapped around my cock. She widened her eyes as if she read my thoughts. "I might be. Are you free, officer?"

I cleared the machine before she even finished talking and hopped down. "For you, sweetheart? I just might have some time to kill."

CHAPTER FORTY-ONE

Mike: January 2009 (Age: 26)

"See? Aren't you glad you came out tonight?" I slapped David on the back and took a long swig from the bottle of Guinness in my hand.

It was an unseasonably warm January night, so I decided we should hang out on the patio at Nick's.

He looked between me and two of the guys he worked with. "Yeah, I'm not sure that this was 'unmissable' as you so eloquently put it—and what the fuck is going on with your eye?"

I reached up and patted the puffiness before grinning. "Well, it turns out that *Little Miss Aren't You Going to Frisk Me* from the gym was very much married. Her husband got off early—ensuring that I didn't get off at all."

David's two work buddies cracked up while he shook his head. "Mike, again? Jesus, put a leash on your damn dick. You should've stuck with Sadie. She was good for you."

He didn't get it. Being with Sadie had been a nightmare—she was constantly breaking down over Patrick's disappearance and wanting to talk about it. Frustrated, I'd turned to someone who knew the whole story—my father. David was out because he'd made me swear to never bring up that night again.

I was desperate for advice and, in his own twisted way, my father knew just what to say. He bluntly told me that women were good for keeping a bed warm, but that they demanded something a man could never give—monogamy. He'd gripped my shoulder and told me that men like us would never be content to live with our balls in a vise.

I'd wanted to write the whole thing off as bullshit, but he had a point. I'd been happiest when I was inside of Sadie. Any other time, though, she drove me up a fucking wall. Breaking up with her had been a good decision. Now, I kept girls around long enough to keep my dick happy before sending them on their merry way.

It was a suitable arrangement for all parties.

I took another swig of beer. "Yeah. You might be right on the leash thing; I'll probably need a muzzle as well. He's a vicious son-of-a-bitch." Everyone laughed, and I continued, "As for Sadie, I could only watch her pine after Patrick Roy for so long before I cut my losses and moved on. Hard to compete with a dead guy, don't you think, David?"

His face paled at the mention of Patrick's name, but before he could respond, a flash of blonde appeared near him.

"Oh, heads up," I called out as the blonde and her drink fell into David's arms. He didn't even seem to be aware of the fact that she'd doused him in some fruity cocktail as he knelt down and freed her foot from the deck.

"Are you okay?"

The pint-sized blonde kept her head down and stammered, "I-I-I'm fine. Thank you." Then she looked up and froze. Yeah, he had that effect on women.

Bastard.

He flashed her a big smile. "I think the only casualty was your drink, which I'm now wearing."

David's buddy, Pete, looked to me for answers and I shrugged. He wasn't normally that talkative with people he didn't know. In all honesty, he was kind of a grumpy asshole most of the time.

The blonde's eyes drifted down his body, and I shook my head. Brazen to be eye-fucking him with a bunch of his buddies at the table.

She shook her head and muttered, "I'm so sorry about your shirt and for falling on you. I'll let you get back to your evening. Again, I'm really sorry," before turning to walk away.

I was all set to dive back into our conversation when he reached out and grabbed her hand. "Wait, at least let me buy you another," he lifted his shirt up and smelled it, "*Malibu* and pineapple?"

Holy shit. He was into her.

She smiled again. "Shouldn't I be buying you a drink?"

At that, he stood up and put his hand on her back. "Beautiful women should never have to buy drinks." She walked toward the bar and he turned back to us. "Don't wait up, fellas."

Pete and Eddie raised their eyebrows and then went back to their pitcher of beer. Not me, though. I couldn't recall one instance in the last thirteen years where David went off with some woman, abandoning boy's night.

Me? I pulled shit like that all the fucking time. Not him, though. In the past, when I'd asked him why he didn't put himself out there more, he'd laughed and told me he didn't want to waste time with the wrong woman.

It had sounded like that psychobabble bullshit they spoon fed us at church camp growing up. I didn't want to think of him as naïve, but my old man had cheated on my mom almost the entire time they'd been together. Who was to say that David's old man hadn't done the very same thing? John might have just been better at it. Hell, even Grey hadn't seemed like the faithful type.

David and the blonde came back out onto the patio, choosing to sit as far away from our table as possible. I could sit and watch the two of them for a few more hours or I could go. I was tired anyway—dealing with Vanessa's husband hadn't been in my plans for the day.

It was Vanessa, right?

Maybe it was Veronica.

I threw a twenty down on the wrought-iron table and made my excuses to Pete and Eddie. I'd barely made it out of the parking lot when it hit me.

Victoria!

That had to have been it. Damn, it would've been more helpful if she'd been screaming her own name instead of just mine.

Violet?

Vivien?

V—*What the fuck is this guy doing?*

The sedan in front of me had a taillight out and was weaving in and out of cars like it was a damn NASCAR race.

It was most likely a drunk driver.

And I was most likely not going to make it home any time in the foreseeable future.

The sedan veered to the right, banking its tires up on the curb before over-correcting and swerving back into the middle lane.

Time to call for backup.

I hope David was just living it up because, while he was off getting laid, I was going to be stuck under a mound of paperwork thanks to the dickhead in front of me.

Some guys had all the luck.

CHAPTER FORTY-TWO

Grey: January 2009 (Age: 46)

It was just after three in the morning when I turned off toward the orchard. The dark thoughts that had been running through my head only seemed to intensify as I hit the end of the driveway, and I killed my bike before walking it toward the house.

Maybe the extra time alone would give me a solution to the problems that kept stacking up.

"You were gone a while," Celia said from the porch swing.

The sound of her voice sent my heart racing, to where I expected it to burst from my chest. "Jesus, Celia! You tryin' to give me a heart attack?"

"You're the one sneaking up to the house like a kid who missed curfew."

I popped the kickstand on the bike and joined her on the porch. "Fair enough. Why you up so late?"

"Couldn't sleep. Did you find any underground games?"

"No," I lied.

Cobra and Hawk could wait.

The nightmares that Celia had fought so hard to overcome had returned with a vengeance since we lost our girls.

Every second I'd spent fixing up the farmhouse, I imagined what it would be like to have my girls with me. Since that afternoon in the orchard, things had felt like they were moving too quickly, but my plan had always been to propose again.

I was going to get down on one knee—do it right the second time around.

The ring had felt like it was burning a hole in my pocket, but the timing never seemed to be right. I didn't want Celia distracted with finding Cobra and Hawk or worried about the girls having to switch schools.

It didn't matter, though.

Norma stepped in and ripped the life we were supposed to have away from us, and the house that I'd moved us into when Celia was pregnant with Kate had turned into a graveyard of bad memories, sending her spiraling out of control.

There was no proposal... no ring.

I called the club in, and we packed it up before moving her out to the farmhouse. At first, she'd kept the attacks at bay by staying busy with repainting and decorating.

I'd thought she was getting better.

Until she proudly led me into the spare bedroom one evening, and I realized most of her efforts had been spent recreating the girls' bedroom from the previous house.

"I just want them to feel at home here like I do," she'd said with a soft smile.

I'd sworn to myself then that no matter how long it took, I would find a way to bring my family back together—my entire family.

And I'd gladly kill anyone who stood in my way.

"What's wrong?"

I sighed and shook my head. "Crossbones got arrested a few hours ago while movin' shit for the club."

She rubbed my arm. "I'm sure you know someone who can make those charges disappear."

My molars ground together. "Mikey arrested him."

"Oh."

I nodded. "Yeah. It's a fuckin' shit show."

Back in the day, Silent Phoenix had an agreement with the local police department. They stayed out of our way, and we continued doing whatever the fuck we wanted.

It had worked out nicely.

Until now.

"Could Comedian talk to him—"

"You think he's gonna listen to a goddamn thing Comedian has to say? Kid's been fightin' to get away from him his whole life."

More and more, I found myself wondering if my kids being raised by psychopaths was some form of divine retribution for all the sins I'd racked up in my lifetime.

I thought back to club gatherings we'd had when Mikey was still a kid. He'd always been quiet, not once doing anything that would have drawn attention. Sometimes, he'd disappear with other kids his age, but for the most part, he'd always kept to himself.

It was funny how some things changed, but others stayed the same. Mikey had moved into our backyard but was still doing everything he could to keep himself off Comedian's radar.

Celia stifled a yawn and crossed her arms over her chest. "What happens if you can't get him out?"

I ran my tongue over my teeth. "He was smugglin' blow and semi-automatics. If that were to get out, or if the fuckin' thing went to trial, we'd all be screwed."

Mikey's actions had created a logistics nightmare for the club—one that would trickle down to the people we did business with. If any one of them got cold feet, it would throw a wrench into our entire operation. All it took was one motherfucker flapping his gums to bring the entire house of cards down.

I should have been proud. My son had chased his dreams and become a cop. He wanted to rid the world of crime.

Unfortunately, he was doing it one biker club at a time.

Bear had been the one to break the news to me, along with the fact that our drugs and weapons were now residing in an evidence locker.

"Then you're going to have to do it."

I cocked my head to the side. "Do what?"

She shrugged. "If you want to operate the way you used to, you need him on board. It's time to let him know you're alive."

"You want me to stroll up to the kid's front door and say what, exactly? 'Hey Mikey, remember me? Guess what, I'm not dead. Oh, and can you call off the investigation into my club?'"

Her lips moved into a flat line. "Well, maybe not quite like that, but yeah. You need him—"

"He wouldn't do it. Not in a million years, Celia. He was gonna be one of the good guys, don't you remember?"

"Look around you, Jamie! There are no good guys!" She stood up and began pacing the length of the porch. "Even if there were, it wouldn't matter. The bad guys win every time."

"What happened today, baby?"

Her eyes filled, and she turned away. I stood up and slowly walked over to her. "You went to the school again, didn't you?"

"I just don't understand how Manny stayed under the school's radar," she whispered. "The minute I get within a hundred feet of my daughter, I've got the superintendent in my face, demanding that I leave the grounds."

"Darlin', we been over this," I said carefully. "Told you to talk to me first before you do shit like this. Your bitch of a mother took our kids. Don't think for a second she wouldn't press charges and put you behind bars."

"I know, but I had to try. Did you see Kate?"

I nodded, my jaw tightening. "Yeah, waited outside her dorm and saw the prick she's been seein'. Shut that shit down—"

Her eyes widened. "You killed him?"

"He ran into one of his buddies in the parking lot—talked about wantin' to fuck her. She's only nineteen, for Chrissakes. Too fuckin' young to be thinkin' about that."

"So, you killed him?" she asked again.

"Jesus, Celia. Didn't kill him... just gave him a nice warnin'."

Giving me a smirk, she threw in, "With your gun?"

I pulled her into the crook of my arm and walked us back toward the swing with a grin. "The hell is wrong with you?"

She waited for me to sit down before stretching out across the swing, letting the back of her head rest against my chest. "You said

Kate's too young to be thinking about sex. You remember I was seventeen, right?"

Several of her dark curls lifted in the breeze and landed against my lips. I brushed them back down before answering. "You were too fuckin' young. If you'd been my daughter—"

"Oh," she giggled. "Is this some role play thing you wanna try now? Want me to call you daddy?"

Jesus.

"Not unless you want me to bend you over my knee and tan your ass."

She lifted her chin until she was looking up at me before tapping a finger against her lips as if considering it.

"Celia," I warned. "Don't fuckin' call me daddy."

She pushed her lips into a fake pout before asking, "Are you planning on chasing every one of Kate's boyfriends off?"

"Maybe. I got a prospect keepin' an eye on her for me—"

"Keeping an eye on her, how?" she interrupted with a raised eyebrow.

"Not like that." I reached out and swatted her thigh. "It's Jeremy. Damn near got a hard-on when I told him we were sendin' him to college. Asked if he could major in business or some shit like that. Told him as long as he kept my daughter safe, he could study to be a fuckin' astronaut for all I cared."

"What if—" she paused. "What if Mikey could keep an eye on her, too? On both of them?"

I considered it. "And how would you suggest we talk him into it?"

"Who says you have to talk him into anything?" She gnawed on her lower lip. "You know I love Mikey like he's my own, but the club covered up a murder for him. And if I remember correctly, you hold the evidence that's keeping him out of prison."

"Celia..." I brought my fist up to my forehead. "I swore I'd never make him choose this life."

"You're asking him to keep your men out of jail—not to patch in. You scratch his back by keeping what he did under wraps, and in return, he does the same for you."

As much as I hated to admit it, it was the best option we had.

"You know, he always thought you hung the moon," she said, watching me carefully. "Maybe this is your chance to get to know him again. He deserves to hear the truth, maybe not right away, but someday, when the timing is right. He's a part of our family."

The truth was that, despite my best efforts, I was going to condemn my son to the life of an outlaw.

Just another promise I'd failed to keep.

CHAPTER FORTY-THREE

Mike: January 2009 (Age: 26)

"C'mon Junior, up and at 'em." My father yanked the comforter back, and I bolted upright.

"What the fuck are you doing here? Who let you in—David?"

He rolled his eyes. "Junior, you wanna tell me what you did last night?"

I groaned and fell back against my pillow. "Do you mean before or after the fifth of El Toro? If it's after, I gotta be honest, things are still a little fuzzy."

He sneered. "El Toro? You might as well have had a New Jersey Turnpike. Jesus Christ."

I blinked blearily and smacked my lips. Yep, it still tasted like something died a violent death in my mouth. "Is that the one with butterscotch schnapps?"

"You're thinking of somethin' else. A New Jersey Turnpike is when you take the bar mat and bar rag and make a shot at the end of the night. You look like you've been lickin' a bar floor—but that's not the reason I'm in your motherfuckin' house at seven o'clock in the morning. You decide to play cop after the bar last night?"

I took a deep breath to keep from hurling. *People actually drank the contents from a bar mat as a shot?* God, that sounded like a bacterial infection just waiting to happen.

"Junior, answer me."

I closed my eyes and tried to recall last night's events. David had gone off with some woman he met... I stayed for a bit longer—drove home... shit. I'd called for back-up on a suspected drunk driver. Along with the guy failing field sobriety tests, the car itself was a fucking goldmine. We popped the trunk and quickly realized it had a false bottom in it. Underneath was a hefty stash of cocaine and semi-automatic rifles.

I sighed and looked at my old man. "We busted a guy for drunk driving and, uh, we found some other stuff while searching his vehicle."

He rocked back on his heels. "Yeah, you busted Crossbones. Now your ass is gonna have to fix this shit before it gets worse."

I laughed even though it felt like an ice pick was being driven into my skull. "Okay, sure. I'll just hop in my fucking time machine and go back to last night."

His jaw clenched, and he clamped a hand around the back of my neck before hauling me out of bed. "Get the fuck up! Let's go."

I tried to maneuver myself out of his grasp, but it was obvious that I was going to have to put more effort into working out at the gym and less into fucking the women there if I wanted to take my old man in a fight.

He dragged me down the hall and into the living room before unceremoniously dropping me onto my ass. I scrambled up onto my feet, ready to fight, when I saw I had another visitor.

My mouth slackened and I rubbed my eyes in disbelief. I had alcohol poisoning, that had to be it. The bottle of tequila had been in the back of the liquor cabinet. I couldn't recall when David and I bought it. It was tainted, plain and simple.

"Alcohol poisoning. Or I'm still drunk," I mumbled the words to myself and stared down at the palms of my hands, as if they held the answer to my hallucination.

The figment of my imagination stood up and came over. "Do you need to sit down, Mikey? You're looking a little pale."

I shook my head. "You're dead—they said you died. Oh my god, I'm never drinking again."

My father laughed. "Junior, calm the fuck down. Grey, tell him why we're here so we can get the hell out before the roommate shows up."

He'd died, hadn't he?

That's what the letter had said. After getting on the force, I'd looked into his case. He was missing and presumed dead. After October 18, 1996, James "Grey" Quinn had simply ceased to exist.

I sank down onto the couch and put my head between my legs. The combination of the hangover and shock had me on the verge of puking or passing out—I hadn't decided which.

"There we go." Grey patted my back. "So, I guess I should start by saying that I'm alive and let you know you arrested my road captain last night. I'm gonna need you to get the charges dropped."

My stomach rolled at the thought of helping them. I'd worked too hard to get where I was. It didn't matter what happened with Patrick. I'd gone straight, and I wasn't prepared to do anything that would jeopardize my career.

"I can't do it, Grey. It's out of my hands."

My old man cackled again as he stretched out on the couch across from me. "That ain't the way to make friends, Junior. Now, I believe the Pres issued an order. Don't make him repeat it."

Sweat trickled down my spine. I thought my old man had supported what I was doing with my life, but he'd clearly planned on using me to draw attention away from the club the entire time.

I shook my head. "No, I won't do it. I worked too hard for this. If I got busted tampering with evidence, I'm not just looking at losing my job. I'm looking at time in a federal prison. Do you get that?"

Grey ignored me and looked over at my father. "Show him what we've got."

He pulled a phone from his pocket and began scrolling through it. "These pictures look familiar to you, Junior? Because I gotta be honest—they don't look real good for you."

He scrolled through them, and my stomach dropped to the floor. I was fucked. Bastard hadn't shown up that night in Galveston to help me out of a bind. He'd shown up to blackmail me. Patrick's empty eyes stared at me throughout the various photos. He'd gotten not only the body, but David's truck and license plate in them. He could pin the whole thing on my best friend.

My old man stifled a yawn. "Got some surveillance from that old strip club, too. Guess the owners had some break-ins not long before you showed up for fight club." He switched screens and there it was, in grainy black and white, me committing a murder. If that got released to anyone, David and I wouldn't see the outside of a prison cell ever again.

I jumped up and began pacing. "You just show up from the dead and expect me to drop everything and help you? I was just doing my job, for Christ's sake. How was I to know he was one of yours? He wasn't wearing a kutte. Can't we just agree from here on out that I won't arrest your guys and we chalk this up to a minor mistake?"

Grey remained seated. "Things got complicated, and the club decided it was best if I went dark for a while, at least until things calmed down. It got the feds off our asses, along with a couple of clubs that seemed to have forgotten their place. If shit goes south again, I won't hesitate to remove myself from the equation to keep the club intact.

"As for this? It ain't a minor mistake, Mikey. I'm out a fuck ton of money thanks to LPD confiscating my merchandise and my man. That leaves a lot of loose ends—loose ends that could lead every goddamn agency in the country to my doorstep. And that really chaps my ass."

My father, who until that point had appeared to be fast asleep, opened one eye. "He really hates having his ass chapped, Junior."

This was it.

Until now, I'd labeled what happened with Patrick as some sort of freak accident. If I refused to help them, they'd release everything. No jury in America would ever see what I did as anything other than cold-blooded murder. If I helped them, then I was a dirty cop. Not only that, but if I got caught helping them, I'd still be looking at spending time in prison.

I was damned either way on this.

"How do I know you won't release the evidence you have even if I decide to help?"

I'd directed my question to Grey, but he looked to my father to answer. The old man reluctantly opened one eye again and fixed it on me. "You know, there's about to be an opening for a detective in the—oh, what's it called? The Crimes Against Persons division. I hear it comes with a nice paycheck, too."

I reached my hand out for the wall to steady myself. It was what I'd wanted, but it came with a steep price—my morality.

Grey chimed in, "It's a good gig, Mikey. With the club behind you, you'd be damn near invincible. Anything you want, we can get. You scratch my back, I'll scratch yours."

I wasn't about to go down for a damn mistake I made as a teen. "Count me in."

CHAPTER FORTY-FOUR

Mike: January 2009 (Age: 26)

"Okay, now you do it to her. That's fuckin' hot." I propped my arm up behind my head and leaned into the headboard.

Alright, I may have fallen into the headboard.

I was celebrating.

I had my freedom.

I had a motherfucking promotion.

And I had two lovely sorority girls from the house across the street going down on each other right in front of me.

My life was good.

Getting the charges against Crossbones dropped was easier than I imagined. I all but walked the evidence out the front door and into one of Grey's vehicles. I made that shit disappear. Then I absolved my sins in the holy waters of *Don Julio 1942*. I was in the big-time now—I needed a tequila that was on my level.

The girls moved up into my lap, having grown bored with each other. The brunette kissed her way down my chest and onto my waiting dick, while her friend thrust her tits in my face.

Yep. Life was beautiful.

"Hey Mike, you home?" David called from the living room.

"In here, man." I was in a giving mood. Maybe I'd share one of the girls with him. So, I was banned from ever telling him about the MC, but I could help him celebrate life outside of prison on a subconscious level.

The door opened. "Hey, got someone I want you to—"

I raised the half empty bottle of tequila up in a toast before bringing it down to my lips. "Which one do you want?"

His mouth fell open. "Goddammit, Mike. What the fuck is this?"

A tiny blonde head appeared and moved around from behind him before he could stop it. It was the girl from last night—it might as well have been last year. So much had changed in the last twenty-four hours. She took in the debauchery on my bed with wide eyes, but I thought I detected a brief glimpse of lust before she ducked back.

David followed her. "Beth, come back. Honey, he's an asshole."

I sighed. "Party's over, girls. You gotta go."

This was the second time in twenty-four hours that I'd been cock-blocked.

The brunette's lips slid off of me with a soft pop, and she grinned. "You sure about that? I think someone was getting close."

I shook my head. "Nope, not even in the vicinity of close, sweetheart." I patted her head. "You get a little more practice and maybe we'll get there. I'll call you."

Her friend had already begun pulling her clothes on, while—*what the fuck was her name?* BJ? *Yeah, that seemed right*—while BJ pouted on the bed.

Tits McGee looked down at her inside out shirt and then over to me in confusion. She'd been tripping on some strong shit when I called them over. "But, Mike? You don't, like, have our numbers? How will you call us?"

I swiped my badge up off the nightstand. "I'm a cop, sweetheart. Remember?"

She'd already forgotten she just lived right across the street, it appeared. That was a good thing, given my track record lately.

Tits McGee nodded jerkily and whispered softly, "Right. Cool."

BJ crossed her arms over her chest and huffed loudly. "I just don't get why we can't stay. Doesn't your roommate want to join us?"

I thought about the wide-eyed blonde running from the room.

"You know, I think he's gonna pass on the sex tonight. C'mon, up. Out, out, out."

I stood up and swayed heavily as the floor moved beneath me like waves. Somehow, I managed to get my boxers on while remaining semi-upright.

BJ stomped toward the door while Tits McGee grinned like an idiot at every object we passed. I was fucked up—she was somewhere way beyond that.

I walked out into the empty living room and threw the front door open. David's truck was still sitting in the driveway, so he was somewhere on the property. "Okay, there ya go, ladies. Tits, BJ, have a great night."

BJ turned back around on the porch. "Wait. That's not our na—" I slammed the door and locked it before she could finish.

"Nice, Mike. Real fucking nice. I bring Beth here to meet you and you're smack dab in the middle of an orgy." David stood in the doorway to the kitchen, frowning.

I offered, "Well, it was more of a ménage than an orgy." His gaze darkened, and I began talking faster. "What I mean to say is that I am very sorry and it will never happen again. Now, where's this girl of yours?"

David relaxed and pointed toward the back door. "She's out by the fire pit. Now, before you fuck this up royally, I really like her. Okay?"

I nodded and fell into the wall. It took me several tries before I was able to get back on my feet. "Yep, got it. Don't embarrass you."

He grabbed my arm and led me into the kitchen. "Jesus Christ, Mike. Did you not bother sobering up after last night?"

I shook my head. "I'm celebrating. Got a promotion at work—you're looking at Detective Sullivan." Then I pushed myself off of him and threw up in the sink.

"David? I think I'm gonna head home. I've got training at my new job on Monday... gonna turn in early."

Wasn't today Saturday?

Was I supposed to be at work?

I took a long drink from the faucet before turning around. Beth's eyes widened again, but she was polite enough to extend her hand toward me. "Hello, I'm Elizabeth."

I wiped my hand on my boxers before shaking hers. "Mike. Pleasure to meet you."

She was way out of my league—David's too, for that matter.

He stepped in and pried her hand from mine. "Alright, let me walk you out to your car." He turned to me. "I'll deal with you later."

I nodded and waited until they walked out before rinsing my mouth under the faucet again. I really needed the room to stop spinning for a fucking second so I could regain my bearings.

"So, are we gonna discuss the real reason that you've gone off on a two-day bender?" David shut the front door behind him and walked over to where I stood hunched over by the sink.

I shrugged. "Turns out, I'm not real good at celebrating within reason. I gotta work on that. So, enough about me—tell me about this girl."

Please, for the love of God, don't ask me anything else.

David's entire face changed once I mentioned Elizabeth. That was definitely a new one for me. The guy had two expressions—surly and *don't fuck with me*. Sure, he'd smile from time to time, but he didn't give that shit away freely.

"She's... I don't know, man. She's just perfect." He grinned and stared off into space.

"She must be something for you to have gone off with her for the last two days." I sounded jealous, which I wasn't. I'd had BJ and Tits keeping me company.

His grin faded. "Gone off with her? Mike, I've stayed here alone for the last two nights. I'm sorry you were too shit-faced to notice, but Beth isn't that type of girl."

That wasn't right. He hadn't been home when Grey and my father showed up... had he?

"Uh, I was up and sober early Saturday morning and you were nowhere to be found. Care to explain that?" A bead of sweat formed near my hairline.

David grabbed a chair from the small table in the corner and sat down. "Mike, I'm really starting to worry about your drinking. I told you when we went out Friday night that I had a job Saturday morning. It's one of the reasons I didn't want to go in the first place. You really don't remember me being here at all this weekend?"

My shoulders dropped. He hadn't overheard anything. I didn't exactly believe that Grey and Co. would just let David walk away if they thought he knew something. "No, I'm good. I just forgot and you know I'm a sound sleeper, so if you were in and out, I don't remember hearing you. That's it."

His eyes narrowed. "That's it?"

I nodded and tightened my grip on the sink as the floor started shifting in and out of focus again. "Yep, all good here. You want me to grab you an ice pack?"

"Why would I need an ice pack?"

I forced myself to keep a straight face. "Because your new girl? Most definitely a virgin. And I'd bet my next paycheck your balls are so damn blue that they're bordering on indigo."

He smirked. "Nice—how long did it take you to come up with that?"

I belched, and tequila rose in my throat. I swallowed and held my breath for a few seconds to keep from hurling again.

That was close.

"David, seriously, I saw the way she looked at the girls earlier. You've got yourself a virgin. Mark my words. Have you tested her gag reflex yet? That might be a good place to start—you know, get her good and warmed up."

He laughed, but not really in a humorous way, before shaking his head. "I don't care how drunk you are, Mike. You are two seconds away from getting your ass kicked."

I held my hand up as my body slumped forward. I was starting to think that Tits and BJ had poisoned me. *What other explanation was there?*

"You know, it's probably a good thing that she's with you. Your dick's so small that losing her virginity will be practically painless."

David jumped up out of his chair, knocking it over, before taking two steps over to me. He shoved me back into the cabinets, sending the drawer knob painfully close to my ass. “Don’t you fucking talk like that about her. You hear me? She’s off limits to you.”

I laughed even as his face turned a lovely shade of red. “Calm your nuts. All I’m saying is that you can ease her into it... make it easier for guys like me later. Ya know?”

His fist was the last thing I saw as it came flying at my face.

CHAPTER FORTY-FIVE

Mike: May 2010 (Age: 27)

"So, then I yelled, 'Come on in!'" David's father, John, shook his head and ran the flat of his palm across his throat. I looked over at David and Elizabeth, but the two of them looked like they were preparing for a bomb to go off.

I belatedly noticed David's grandparents in the crowd and realized that, while my speech had been great for the bachelor party, it would not go over well in a wedding toast where children were present.

I cleared my throat and the microphone gave a little scream of protest. "When I first met Elizabeth, I was far from being my best, but that's the thing about her. She came into my life at a low-point, but never once judged me for it. She has a way of always finding the best in people—hell, if it weren't for her, I'm not sure David would have stuck with me. We all need a partner in our lives who sees the good when we can't. David is lucky enough to have found it in Elizabeth. And, if he ever forgets that—well, you have my number. Raise your glasses to Mr. and Mrs. Greene!" I tipped the champagne back amid cheers and clapping.

Well, I'd pulled that speech out of my ass.

Thank god it had worked.

"Boy, I swear you're gonna get your ass beat with that story," John noted dryly as I stepped up to the bar.

I shook my head and sighed dramatically before ordering a beer. I had to keep myself away from the liquor for the rest of the evening. The three shots before the ceremony had apparently been more than enough. "Tough crowd we got here tonight. If they were expecting hearts and shit, they should have picked a different best man, yeah?"

John chuckled. "Damn, son, you should write greeting cards. You're so fuckin' poetic."

I tipped my beer in his direction. "Thank you, good sir. I always knew you had good taste."

A squeaking sound drew our attention back to the center of the ballroom. Jess, Elizabeth's matron of honor, was attempting to give her speech, but kept dissolving into unintelligible blubbering mid-sentence. She pointed to a picture of David and Elizabeth that was on the projector before making some more squeaking noises and tears.

"C'mon now. They can't be falling for this shit." I looked over at Elizabeth, who was nodding her head and crying along with her. David looked to be on the verge of tears himself.

"Looks like you're not the master of ceremonies tonight, Mike," John observed, before winking at me. "I liked your toast, though. It showed a lot of heart for a self-proclaimed man-whore."

As if on cue, an older woman sidled up next to me at the bar. "Nice speech. Although, I think I'd prefer to hear the original version. Care to enlighten me?"

She had to be pushing forty, but she'd had her tits and face done, giving the illusion she wasn't a day over thirty-five. I could have committed to her, but the night was young and I was at a wedding—the one event where women were made painfully aware of their singleness and were reckless enough to pounce on the first guy that looked their way.

That was where I came in.

The woman in front of me was a solid seven, but at an event like this, I wasn't whipping out my cock for anything less than a ten. Last night, I'd had the waitress from the rehearsal dinner on top of the ice machine on the second floor. I'd waited until she was busy cleaning up before telling her how hard weddings were since my wife had left me. I'd slipped my room key into her hand and that was it.

At home, I stuck with the cop script. But here I was looking to change things up. *So, what if I was feeding them a line?* These women were desperate and eager to please. Who was I to deny them their fantasy? Tonight, I was Jack, a depressed widower.

"Maybe I didn't make myself clear," the woman purred before slipping her hand beneath the waistband of my linen pants, her voice dropping to a whisper, "I want to be fucked."

"Whoa there, Sandra. Okay, I'm cutting you off."

I looked up and locked eyes with my ten. She was stunning and a redhead—I'd never had a redhead before. I wondered if the carpet matched the drapes before she removed Sandra's hand from my pants. "I'm so sorry."

John shook his head, laughing, and moved away from the bar as I turned on the charm.

"Don't be sorry, darlin'. It led to me meeting you. I'd say it's been a good night."

"You hear that?" Sandra slurred, "He wants me. You can go, Lauren. I'll take it from here."

She moved to step back, but I grabbed onto a lock of her hair, holding her in place. "I meant you, darlin'. Think you can get this one to bed and come back to me?"

I watched in amusement as her chest flushed red before the color moved up into her cheeks. Thank god for pale skin. It was a great barometer.

"S-sure," she stuttered, "Just give me a few minutes."

CHAPTER FORTY-SIX

Mike: May 2010 (Age: 27)

I was waiting by the front entrance with a bucket of beer when she got off the elevator. She looked around the lobby, and as she spotted me, I swore she jumped up to a twelve.

"Hey there. What's the plan?" The breeze coming off the ocean lifted her hair up around her face as she approached me.

I had an uncontrollable urge to wrap it around my fist and kiss the hell out of her. I shook my head to clear my thoughts. I needed to stay in control. So, I offered her a beer. "Thought we'd grab a few drinks and take a walk on the beach. How's that sound?"

She looked back toward the reception hall. "Won't they wonder where we are?"

Ah, a wedding virgin.

"Darlin', they're surrounded by family members who want to discuss the most boring of wedding details. I doubt they've even noticed we've snuck out." I held my hand out, and she didn't hesitate before taking it.

I led her across Seawall Boulevard and down to the beach. There were still a few chairs left from the ceremony and we made our way over to them. "So, Red. Tell me about yourself. What brings you to Galveston? And you can't tell the truth."

She set her beer down in the sand and kicked off her sandals. "I can't tell the truth?"

I nodded. "Nope. Make it up. Bonus points for creativity."

She grinned again and bit the corner of her lip in concentration. Damn, I was rock hard.

"Okay," she said, clearing her throat. "My name is Charlotte. I'm an art dealer in Dallas. I was told that I had to get down to Galveston and check out Salvadore Goya. He's a young painter that's generating a lot of buzz in the art world. He could be the next van Gogh. His work is exquisite; you can see his passion in every stroke of the brush. Your turn."

My mouth went dry. She was good.

I wanted her to stroke my brush.

I nodded. "That was okay, Red. Now, watch a pro. My name is Jack and I'm originally from California. I grew up on the water with a board in my hand. People said I had to get down to Galveston and try tanker surfing—" An image of Patrick falling toward the curb crept in and I stopped mid-sentence.

Charlotte prodded my thigh with her hand. "C'mon, don't stop in the middle. Remember? Bonus points for creativity."

I swallowed past the lump in my throat and nodded, trying to play it off like I was just trying to think of good material. "Right, where was I? Oh yeah, so I'm here and ready to try tanker surfing tomorrow. Care to join me?"

Where the hell had that come from?

First, I thought of Patrick, who hadn't crossed my mind once in the last nine years. Then, I invited her out tomorrow? I was a one and done kinda guy. There were no second dates.

Her eyes widened in surprise. "Oh, well, I'm actually leaving in the morning. Gotta get back to work—unless you weren't really asking me and it's part of the game—never mind, I'll shut up now."

I chugged the rest of my beer and cracked open another one before responding, "Yeah, I was just gettin' into character. I've actually got to head home early tomorrow, too."

Charlotte extended her hand. "I win. Pay up."

I smirked. "And what makes you think that, Red? Maybe I'm not done yet."

She shook her head, keeping her palm open in front of me. "You said you're originally from California, but I gotta be honest here. That Texas accent is way too thick for me to believe you. My story was better... ergo, I'm the winner."

I scratched at my beard and settled in deeper on my chair, letting my toes dig into the sand a little more. "Is that so? Well, darlin', I guess it's time to give you your prize."

She bit down on her lower lip and smiled expectantly. God damn, this woman would be my undoing tonight. "I'm ready," she whispered before closing her eyes, while continuing to hold out her hands.

I was out of my chair and on my knees in front of her so fast that I kicked over my beer in the sand. Then I bypassed her open hands and went straight for her mouth. I balanced my arms on either side of her and dove in headfirst. She exhaled a little sound of surprise before her hands went around my back and took hold of my shirt. Her lips tasted like the beer we'd been drinking, along with a hint of salt coming off the ocean.

She moaned as I slipped my tongue past her lips, tightening her hold on me. I didn't usually waste a lot of time kissing—didn't really see the point to it, but her mouth just begged for attention. I nipped her lower lip, and she moaned again, encouraging me to continue. It was like a game of hot or cold. The warmer I got, the more vocal she was.

I moved my hand up and cupped her jaw, drawing her in even closer. She reciprocated by wrapping her legs around my waist and pulling my body up against hers. I caught a flash of underwear as her dress rode up.

Was it a thong?

Boy shorts?

Were they green like her dress? Why wasn't there more moonlight so that I could solve this argument in my head?

Fuck me. This was going to be a one-night stand for the books.

She broke away, panting. "Um, should we? I mean, do you want to dance with me?"

Wait. What?

I thought we were moving to the bedroom, not the ballroom.

She exhaled shakily. "I just mean that I came all this way—it'd be a shame if I didn't get to dance at least once in this dress."

I thought about the repercussions of taking her back inside. With my luck, she'd end up being one of David's most cherished cousins and then I'd end the night with his fist in my face—which was par for the course with us. Still, I kinda wanted to try leaving my face intact for the night.

I pulled out my phone and logged into my music account. "I've got an idea..."

A guitar began playing on my phone, followed by Dierks Bentley crooning, 'Come a Little Closer.'

I put the phone down on a chair and crooked two fingers at her. She stood up and came over with a big smile, pulling her dress back down in the process. "Now, you've completely blown your cover."

I pulled her up against me and whispered in her ear, "Is that so? You'll have to let me know where I went wrong."

We swayed back and forth on the sand, some half-assed version of dancing, yet neither one of us seemed to care. She tilted her face up toward mine and whispered back, "You're playing country music. Now, I know you're not a California boy, Tex."

Her green eyes sparkled with amusement and I wondered if I would ever meet anyone as beautiful as her again. It didn't make a damn bit of sense, but it was as if she looked past every ounce of bullshit and saw me.

It was completely unnerving.

I pressed a quick kiss to her forehead and then tucked her against my shoulder, choosing to croon a few bars from the song instead of staring at her any longer. Those green eyes were hypnotizing. I didn't know what I might confess to if I stared into them any longer.

She sighed happily against my chest. "I like you, Jack. I can't remember the last time I had this much fun doing nothing with someone."

I stopped moving, painfully aware of just how little give these pants had. "Oh, yeah? Let me take you back to my room and show you how much fun we could have doing something."

Charlotte stepped back, and I was treated to watching her skin change from white to red again. "Don't you want to get to know each other a little more?"

I shook my head and closed the gap between us. "You know what I wanna know?"

Her lips parted, but no sound came out.

"I wanna know how you feel wrapped around me—how wet I can get you." I touched her lips. "I wanna know how loud you'll moan when I hit all the right spots."

She stuttered through another breath before nodding in agreement. "I want... I want you to have a drink with me first. And then, then I want all of those other things."

Damn this woman. Just when I thought I had her figured out, she threw me for a loop.

I cleared my throat. "You want a drink? You sure about that?"

She looked back over her shoulder at the event center. "Yeah—I know it's silly, but I just met you. And I've uh- I've never done 'this' before. I just need a minute."

Whoa. Back the motherfucking bus up.

This time, it was my mouth that fell open in shock. "You've never done this before? So, you're a—"

She waved her hand erratically. "No, not that. I just meant that I've never slept with someone I just met... not that we'd necessarily be doing a lot of sleeping, but you know what I mean. Oh god, I'm rambling again..."

Her voice trailed off, and I surprised her by reaching for her hand. "Hey, it's okay, Red. Let's grab that drink and you can tell me more about the art world. Do you own any phallic sculptures?"

She snorted with laughter. "Wow, I was not expecting you to go there. I guess I am a bit of a connoisseur when it comes to phallic sculptures. But really—what single girl isn't?"

I bit the inside of my cheek. She was something else—quick-witted and cute as hell. I gathered up the empty beer bottles and threw them away, while she grabbed her sandals and began walking back toward the event center.

"Hey, look at this!" She stopped in front of a beach bulletin board. "Horseback riding on the beach. I didn't know that they did this. I love horses."

I looked over her shoulder at the ad and shrugged. "Horses are cool, but have you ever ridden a beard?" Then I lightly bit the point where her neck met her shoulder, eliciting another giggle from her.

By the time we reached the event center, we were hanging onto each other as if we were drunk, but I'd never been more sober in my life.

She dusted bits of sand off of her dress and then looked over at me with a small grin. "You just have a little something right here. Let me help you." Her fingertips grazed my jaw, and I kept my eyes locked on hers, not wanting to miss a thing.

"Are we ready for that drink now?" I arched my eyebrows up and down suggestively and she bit down on her lip to keep from laughing again.

"Just give me a minute. I just want to freshen up in my room. It won't take long. I'll meet you back down here in five." Then she was gone, before I'd even had a chance to respond.

Five minutes.

She better not suddenly end up with cold feet or I, sure as shit, would comb every inch of this place to find her.

CHAPTER FORTY-SEVEN

Lauren: May 2010 (Age: 23)

I paced in front of the bathroom mirror, unsure of whether I wanted to vomit or do a victory dance.

"Oh my god," I groaned into my hands.

Was I the type of woman who could sleep with a man I just met?

He'd been so perfect out there, but what if that changed the minute I slept with him? I shouldn't have told him I liked him—I probably cursed myself by doing that. But, for a moment, he'd made me forget just how shitty my life was.

A knock sounded from the door between mine and my boss, Sandra's, rooms before she poked her head in. "Everything all right in here?"

She was gorgeous and blonde, and probably the only person who could tell you off with a smile on her face. And she'd obviously spent the last few hours sobering up.

I shook my head and splashed some cold water from the sink faucet onto my cheeks. If the decision was making me queasy, wasn't that a good sign that it wasn't for me?

I sighed. "I met someone. He wants to take me back to his room... for sex."

Sandra grinned and came all the way into the room. "Do tell."

When I first met her, I mistakenly assumed she was a patient coordinator or pretty face hired to make the pediatric dental office look good, but no—the company was all hers.

Dr. Sandra Mulloy showed up to work in designer blouses and heels in an industry where there was a high probability she'd end up covered in some bodily fluid before the end of the day.

Despite that, the woman oozed sexuality, somehow keeping it completely hidden away from our young patients. Sure, the occasional single dad would show up to an appointment and try to convince her to go to dinner, but she politely declined their offers every time.

Super classy.

Unfortunately, she turned up almost every Monday morning, complaining about the lack of sleep she'd gotten over the weekend and how sore she was, thanks to whoever the flavor of the week was. Luckily, the men never seemed to last longer than a week. There'd be the obligatory bouquet of roses that would be delivered to the office, and that was the last I'd ever hear about them.

At first, I expected HR to intervene and put a stop to it, before remembering that as the new office manager, I was HR, and bringing it up to my superior—her—would only result in me losing my job.

A job I desperately needed.

I told Sandra about my walk on the beach with Jack and the dancing. "It was the most fun I've ever had on a date, but I could see a future with this guy. I don't want to mess it up by sleeping with him so soon, you know?"

She shook her head. "Honey, you said he didn't give you a real name. That should've been your first clue that he doesn't see this going anywhere. Second, you're in your own room right now. That tells me you know you're not a one-night stand kind of girl.

"If you really saw yourself going through with it, you'd be down there with him. Not up here, telling me. A wedding is not the place to meet the love of your life. It's where you find someone to keep your bed warm for the night and then you both move on the next day. Is that something you could do?"

I thought back over the night and realized she was right. Fake names—made up careers. He'd been trying to get inside my panties from the moment I met him. Judging by how good he was, this was definitely not his first time.

"Oh my god," I groaned again into my hands, feeling more nauseated than ever.

She patted my back. "There, there. No use crying over dry panties. Let's get you into bed. That way, you can leave here tomorrow with your dignity intact."

I nodded and let her lead me over to the bed, sliding my still sandy feet under the covers and hugging the pillow to my chest.

Maybe when he saw I wasn't coming, he'd search the entire hotel for me. It'd be like a romantic movie. I'd felt a real connection to him—it wouldn't be totally crazy if he felt one too, right?

Sandra wet a washcloth and placed it across my forehead. "You get some sleep. We'll leave bright and early tomorrow so we can get back to the real world."

I agreed and closed my eyes, suddenly afraid to voice aloud that I never wanted to get back to the real world.

I wanted to stay in a world where Jack and I could dance on the beach and fall madly in love without any obstacles.

CHAPTER FORTY-EIGHT

Grey: May 2010 (Age: 46)

Slim met me in the hallway and slipped the room key into my hand with a wry grin. "Do I even want to know what he did this time?"

I ground my teeth together and shook my head. "I'm sure David could tell you a thing or two about the shit he's pulled lately."

He tugged at the collar of his dress shirt with another chuckle. "Well, if David wasn't tryin' to bow out of his own reception to run off and fuck his new bride, I might just do that. As it is, I'm liable to end up with a black eye."

"Fuck. I shouldn't have asked you to leave—"

"Oh, you absofuckinlutely should've. I'm wearin' linen pants and a shirt that's been stranglin' my muscles all goddamn day. Is Celia still with Lou? If so, meet us up in our room later. I got plans." He rubbed his hands together with a grin, and I took a step back.

"Ain't doin' a fuckin' orgy with you, Slim. No matter how much you love taking part in 'em at the club."

He clapped me on the shoulder. "Good to see that the drive down didn't fuck up your sense of humor." Before turning to walk toward the elevators, he added, "Oh, and I'll be sure to let everyone downstairs know that you're lookin' for some swingers' action. We'll get you fixed right up, Pres."

"Yeah, fuck you," I called before entering the room.

I'd come to Galveston to watch Slim's boy tie the knot, but after watching the drunken spectacle that was Mikey's best man speech, I realized taking a weekend off had been nothing more than a pipe dream.

He was more of a liability to me now than he was the morning Comedian and I showed up on his doorstep to let him know I was alive.

As Comedian had dragged him out of bed, I realized that the scrawny kid who'd been scared of his own shadow and couldn't surf to save his life was long gone. In his place was a bulked-up man-child who sank his dick into anything with a cunt. And if he wasn't doing that, he was buried in a bottle of tequila.

Just like his old man had been.

It seemed like the longer I stared, the more of myself I saw in him, and I wondered how long I'd be able to keep my secret.

When we confronted him with the surveillance footage and photographs I'd taken, he'd agreed to help us, but it seemed as if we had spent most of our time since covering his ass.

Quickly moving around the empty hotel room, I retrieved the weapons Mikey had stashed in the closet and nightstand. The last thing I needed was to walk out with a bullet in me. He'd taken off toward the beach with a redhead, but I knew I only had as long as it took him to fuck her before he was back.

Unable to resist, I opened the door of the fully stocked minibar and my mouth flooded with saliva, as if nine years of sobriety had just been for laughs. I cracked my neck and focused on each inhale and exhale before dropping into the overstuffed chair beside the bed and lighting up a cigar with trembling fingers.

Initially, I'd bought them to help Celia confront the demons of her past, but found that they kept me calm when I was close to losing control.

And right now, I wanted a drink... badly.

I straightened at the sound of a keycard being swiped against the door and took another puff to clear my head as the overhead light was flipped on.

"Holy fuck, Grey! Who let you in here?" Mikey kept his eyes on me as he moved into the room, no doubt going for guns that were no longer there.

He glanced at the nightstand and then back at me.

"Don't bother, kid. I already got that one." He nodded slowly before looking toward the closet. "'Fraid I got that one too. I came here to talk some sense into you—if that's even possible anymore. Have you fuckin' seen yourself? You're gettin' sloppy."

Ignoring me, he went straight for the minibar, and I clenched my molars as everything in me fought to join him.

After draining the small bottle of liquor, he squared his shoulders and faced me with a grin, reminding me so much of myself that it hurt.

"You think I'm getting sloppy? Then do your own fucking dirty work. Oh, yeah, you think you're a big guy running an empire from underground. You know what me and the rest of the goddamn world think? That you're a fucking pussy. You'll hide behind the club walls and let the world think you're dead so that you get off scot-free and the club's left holding the smoking gun. You wanna talk about me? Well, guess what, motherfucker? I wanna talk about you. Where the fuck do you get off?"

Something inside of me snapped, and I was on him before he'd even finished spouting off the bullshit he believed was the truth. Using his lapels as handles, I shoved him into the wall, wondering how Wolverine had dealt with this and not sent me to the Reaper.

"Only one of us in this room has any motherfuckin' sense for runnin' a club," I snarled. "And that sure as fuck ain't you, boy. No, you're too damn preoccupied with where your next lay and drink are coming from to see the big picture. Now, I'm shellin' out a lot of cash to someone who isn't putting the club first. You care to remind me why?"

There was no fear in his eyes, only lust for a fight, as he shoved me back. It was like looking into a mirror. I straightened my shirt and rubbed at my face, wondering why I was wasting my breath.

He was twenty-seven now.

The time for talking sense into him had come and gone years ago.

"You're damn right I'm not putting the club first. Wanna know why? Because I work for the city, asshole. My loyalty lies with the police department, first and foremost. If your club goes against that—well, then guess what, fucker? You're going against me, too. You're gonna need more than one detective to keep all that illegal shit buried. Damn, I don't know that even an entire police force could help you now."

I ran a hand over my face and cracked my knuckles, resisting the urge to lay hands on him. Whatever it was Celia had imagined happening between us, I was pretty damn sure this wasn't it. "Is that right? So, as long as the club was keepin' your illegal shit buried, it was fine, but you're not willing to return the favor?"

Mikey's eyes narrowed in defiance before he grabbed another liquor bottle, taunting me as he tipped it back with a grin. "I'm out, Grey. I've got no interest in covering up for you anymore."

He was my son.

I loved him.

I was gonna send him screaming to the Reaper.

I lowered myself into the chair and retrieved my cigar from the small table, popping it into the corner of my mouth like Kate had done with her pacifier as a baby. "You're done? No talkin' you into staying?"

He grinned down at me condescendingly. "Nope. Now, if you'll excuse me, there's a redhead waiting for me downstairs. And I'd really like it if you weren't here by the time we make it back upstairs."

I wanted to jump up from the chair again and throttle the shit out of him, but I wasn't my old man. I refused to lay a hand on my kid when I was angry.

Instead, I leaned back and pasted a fake smile onto my face. "Already found yourself another one. Well, it never takes long with you, does it? Imagine how good you could be if you didn't think with your dick all the time."

He preened in front of the mirror like a goddamn peacock before responding with a terse, "Fuck you, Grey."

I laughed despite myself. "Yeah, that's about what I expected. Just remember, I came here as a warning, and I'm not known for repeatin' myself."

The kid had some brass balls on him. I'd fucked with Wolverine occasionally, but never outright defied him, knowing it was a good way to end up on the wrong side of a bullet.

As if punctuating his complete disregard for the club and all that had been done for him, the motherfucker rolled his eyes and walked away. "Whatever you say, Grey. Whatever you say."

CHAPTER FORTY-NINE

Grey: May 2010 (Age: 46)

The sound of the door slamming shut behind him had me jumping up, ready to lay into him again.

Fuck the consequences.

I no longer gave a fuck how long it took. I was going to beat sense into his thick skull.

The elevator doors closed just as I got to them, and I punched the metal with a low growl. "Fuck."

"Sounds like that went well."

I turned to see Celia leaned against the wall, fighting to keep a straight face.

"I'm gonna fuckin' kill him," I snapped. "Don't try to talk me out of it!"

She patted my arm softly, no longer fighting the grin that was stretching across her face. "Welcome to parenthood—"

"No," I cut her off. "Don't give me that welcome to parenthood bullshit. Kid outright defied me, Celia. Did it with a fuckin' smile on his face, too. Little shit suddenly thinks he knows more than me, as if he's been runnin' the show this entire goddamn time!"

Biting the inside of her cheek, she led me into the elevator, dead-panning, "I can't imagine what that must have been like for you."

"Wait," I said, just as the doors closed. "This shit is normal? They all act like assholes?"

She nodded. "I'm afraid so—"

"Why the fuck are you smilin' at me like that?"

Celia tried and failed to move her mouth into a solemn line. "I'm not—"

"You are. You think this shit is funny? Because I gotta be honest with ya, princess. He rolls over on the club, and we're all in for a world of hurt."

"Jamie, you've never had to deal with a rebellious child. The closest I think you came was when Mikey was eleven, but even then, he went home, and it was no longer your problem. And that's not the reason I was smiling. Well, it was partly—"

"You gonna enlighten me or just keep pointing out how I wasn't a real parent?" I growled.

"I'm not telling you that you weren't a real parent!"

She crossed her arms over her chest, pulling my attention to the deep v of her dress. Momentarily distracted with thoughts of hiking up her skirt and fucking her up against the elevator wall, I was pulled back into the argument with a muttered, "Jesus Christ, Jamie. Focus."

"Oh, I am."

She swatted my arm. "I'm serious. I wasn't trying to make you feel bad. It's just that all children push back to see what they can get away with. They're impulsive—"

"He's twenty-seven," I noted dryly.

"Exactly." She began ticking points off on her fingers. "They're impulsive, prone to emotional outbursts, and just generally looking for a way to outsmart their parents."

Holy shit.

"You mean we have to deal with this for the rest of our lives?"

She pursed her lips. "Well, when they become adults, they typically begin cleaning up their own messes. Look at Kate."

"So, you're sayin' our twenty-year-old is an adult, but our twenty-seven-year-old ain't? I'm confused."

"I'm saying that one of them is constantly testing the limits, and the other is holding down a job while taking college classes and checking in on her little sister. Take from that what you will."

He hadn't had an easy childhood.

Hell, none of us had.

I'd seen things no kid should ever be forced to witness. Celia had been ripped away from her parents. Mikey hadn't lived in fear of the monster under the bed, but the one who walked through the front door every night.

For the longest time, it had eaten at me that I hadn't been able to give him the same life as the girls. Every time I'd tucked them in and read a bedtime story was just another reminder of what my son was going without.

I didn't see the damage I'd caused until later, though. My girls hadn't been given some unfair advantage. They'd been forced to grow up thinking their father was dead. Sure, Angel had stepped up and filled the role as best he could.

But he wasn't their daddy.

Kate had lost the first man she'd ever loved at seven. Instead of seeking that connection out in another man, she'd closed herself off. Maybe deep down, she knew that nothing good would ever last. Maybe she didn't want to go through the heartache of losing someone again.

It wasn't as if I'd ever be able to ask her the reason.

Dakota had gone the opposite direction, completely immersing herself in her comics, and setting the bar so damn high that no man would ever measure up unless he was Thor himself.

"Celia?" I asked as the doors opened into the lobby. "How do you handle the one who still acts like a kid?"

"Easy." The smile returned to her face. "You remind them of who the parent is."

Slim and Lou stood by the front doors, practically bouncing with excitement.

"Can you believe she said yes?" Slim asked, bumping me with his elbow.

"Who said yes?"

"I did." Celia grinned up at me, looking like a cat who'd just caught a canary.

"Said yes to what?" I frowned.

Something flashed in Slim's eyes, and he glanced around before wrapping an arm around my shoulders and lowering his voice. "What we were talkin' about upstairs. I told her she didn't seem like the type, but she said she'd wanted to try it for a while now but wasn't sure how you'd take it."

I jerked away, narrowing my eyes at Celia. "She did, did she?"

"Yeah," he stated proudly. "I told her it was your idea in the first place. Now, I thought it'd be better if we did it down by the beach. Away from all the strait-laced assholes. What do you say?"

I took in his shit-eating grin and the hopeful look in her eyes. My son of a bitch best friend had just talked my wife into an orgy.

After I finished with Mikey, I was coming for him next.

"Over my dead body," I said firmly, and Lou's eyes widened in surprise.

"You're really going to deny her this experience? Even John let me give it a go—how old was David then? Three? Four? It felt like we were teenagers again—sneaking around in the backyard, praying we didn't get caught."

I held up my hand. "What the fuck? You did it in the backyard while your son was sleeping inside? And now you wanna do it on the beach? You never considered doin' it in a bedroom?"

"I'm pretty sure that's a good way to get kicked out of the hotel," Louisa said with a frown. "Not to mention the smell it would leave behind. I bet you'd be on the hook for replacing all the furniture in the room as well."

"The smell?" I questioned, much louder than I'd meant to. "What the fuck are you guys doin'? I ain't replaced shit at the clubhouse, and people do it there all the fuckin' time. This is what you want to do, Celia?"

Slim fought to hold it together before leaning over with his hands on his knees. "Jesus fuck, your face," he said through a wheeze of laughter.

Celia looked between the two of us before asking, "Wait, what is it you two were talking about upstairs?"

"He thought—" Slim's hand went to his throat as he forced out,

"Thought we were gonna have an... orgy!" His chuckles turned to cackling, and he swiped at the tears on his cheeks.

Celia's eyebrows disappeared under her hair. "You what?" she hissed at me. "I'm not doing that!"

"Damn right you're not doin' that," I snapped back. "It's why I said over my dead body!"

Lou brought a hand up over her mouth, shoulders shaking with laughter. "John, really? You're too old to be acting like this!"

"Oh, too old?" he asked with a half shrug. "Not what you said to me this mornin', Louisa. If I'm rememberin' it right, you wanted to know how I had so much stamina. Ain't that right, darlin'?"

"Oh, for fuck's sake," I grumbled when a flush crept up her throat. "Anyone care to tell me what it is we're doin' down here?"

Celia pushed past me and through the front doors. "We're going down to the beach to get..." She glanced around before mouthing: *High*.

The tension left my body, and I followed her out with a relieved sigh. "Thank Christ, princess. Thought I was gonna have to take Slim out—"

"Fucker." Slim slung his arm around my shoulders as we crossed the highway. "You name one time when you've bested me. One."

Celia linked arms with Lou as they made their way down the seawall before looking back at me. "I can't believe you thought I wanted to do... that."

"I can't believe you thought I'd be pissed about you wantin' to smoke. Why the fuck would I care?"

Her gaze softened, and she let go of Lou to jog back to where I stood under the streetlight while they walked on ahead. "You just worked so hard to get clean. I didn't want to trigger something by asking."

Weed hadn't ever been a drug that left me fucked up, but when I got clean, I did it cold turkey and without a crutch to lessen the withdrawals.

"That explains your guilty smile in the elevator," I said with a grin. "Don't worry about me. Do what you want, and I'll be right here to make sure you're safe."

She moved as if to kiss me before freezing. "Why do you smell like a cigar?"

Fuck.

In a perfect world, Mikey would have listened to reason, and I would have had time to run back to the room and gargle with mouthwash.

"I, uh, I smoked one while I was waitin' in Mikey's room earlier," I admitted. "Didn't plan on runnin' into you so soon after or I would've freshened up. I'm sorry, darlin'."

Celia shook her head and leaned in until her mouth was within inches of mine, taking me by surprise. "It's not like you haven't smoked one in front of me before—"

"I know what it does to you. Believe me, I ain't tryin' to—"

She silenced me with a soft kiss before pulling away again. "Hey, Jamie?"

"Yeah?" I answered softly.

The outer corners of her eyes crinkled as she grinned, and it struck me how far we'd come in a decade. I was sober, and my girl was looking up at me like she had that day in the record store.

I'd do whatever it took to keep that smile on her face for the rest of our lives.

Celia took my lower lip between her teeth, nipping lightly, before letting her hands roam over my ass. "It's working," she said with a squeeze.

"What's workin'?"

She gave me another grin before skipping down toward the beach like a small child.

"Celia?" I called after her. "What's workin'?"

Her long, dark hair fell over her shoulder as she looked back at me. "When I smelled the cigar, I didn't think of him. I thought of you."

CHAPTER FIFTY

Mike: May 2010 (Age: 27)

I held up my empty shot glass. "I'll have another."

The bartender nodded and grabbed the bottle of tequila. I glanced down at my watch and scanned the bar for the tenth time in the last five minutes.

She was late.

And I was still pissed over Grey showing up in my hotel room with warnings.

Well, Charlotte—if that was her real name—was definitely going to get angry fucked first. If she wanted soft and sweet, then her ass should have been down here ten minutes ago.

What had she gone to her room to do? Shower and start from scratch? Fuck. I'd be sitting down here alone for the next hour and a half, if that was the case.

The bartender slid my shot across the bar to me and I downed it almost immediately.

You know—who the fuck did Grey think he was? He threatened a peace officer. If I wasn't such a nice guy, I'd come at him and his fucking club with the entire arm of the law on my side.

I didn't owe him shit.

Patrick's face immediately popped into my mind. "Ah, Christ." I held up the shot glass in my hand. "Another, please. Fuck it. Just bring me the entire bottle."

What happened with Patrick had been an accident. I wasn't some cold-blooded killer. I massaged my temple and stared down at the bar top. I'd just been a kid—a stupid kid who made a stupid decision to defend himself.

My mom had stitched up my leg as best she could, but I still had a wicked scar that was reminder enough of how immature I'd been back then. I didn't need Grey popping in to do the same.

"Is this seat taken?" a feminine voice whispered in my ear, and I turned, with a smile on my face.

"You're—not who I was expecting."

The blonde giggled and sat down on the stool next to mine. It was the same woman who'd accosted me at the wedding. What had Charlotte called her? Oh right, Sandra. *Sandra, the seven, who wanted to be fucked.*

"Sorry to disappoint, but she's not coming." The grin was still fixed on her face, even as mine faded.

She wasn't coming?

I tried to look like the news didn't bother me. "What happened? Beauty problems? She meet someone else in the elevator?"

She shook her head. "She's having a little trouble holding her beer." Just in case I had any misconceptions about what that meant, she then pantomimed vomiting all over the bar top.

Jesus.

"Do you think I should check on her? Get her some club soda or something?"

Who the fuck was this guy? I didn't go check on drunk chicks. I left that mess for someone else to clean up.

Sandra smiled, but it looked more like a sneer. "She's fine. I helped her into bed. She'll be right as rain in the morning."

I tried to think of how many beers she'd had. It couldn't have been more than two. Hell, maybe she'd loaded up at the reception and I didn't see it. "Okay then. Well, Sandra, lovely to see you again. I'm just gonna head back up to my room now."

Her hand landed on my thigh and slid up. "Wait. Just because she's indisposed doesn't mean you have to go to bed alone."

I let the liquor and her words sink in. If I went back to my room alone, then I was basically telling Grey he was right. She wasn't my first choice. Hell, she wasn't even my tenth choice, but it was late and the odds of finding someone else were slim.

I poured another shot from the bottle. "Fine. Let's go. Straight fucking and then I want you out of my room when we're done. Think you can handle that?"

Sandra leaned down and nipped my earlobe with her teeth. "I like it rough."

I gave one parting glance to the bar—hoping that Charlotte had miraculously recovered and shown up. But it was the same people as before.

The back table was a group of middle-aged golfers. Next to them was the sports fanatic and his long-suffering wife, who'd been glued to her phone the entire time I'd been down here. I bet she was on Pinterest. She seemed like the type.

There were a couple of tables that must have come from David and Elizabeth's reception, but I didn't recognize any of them. Plus, they'd paired off into couples and I wasn't looking for a fight tonight.

Looked like it was just me and Solid Seven Sandra for the evening.

Sometimes, luck was a bitch.

CHAPTER FIFTY-ONE

Mike: May 2010 (Age: 27)

The knocking sound grew louder. I groaned before tossing the pillow over my head. It was like they were using a fucking jack-hammer on the door.

"Room service," the voice called out cheerily, and I cursed.

I didn't order fucking room service. I knew no one else had either, because the minute the sex was done, Sandra's ass was back out in the hallway. Older women were all the same, expecting the man to cater to her desires. Well, fuck that.

I kicked the covers off and threw the door open. The woman's eyes widened as she quickly looked me up and down. "Room service," she squeaked out before thrusting the tray into my hands and bolting back down the hall.

"Yeah? Well, if you didn't want to see it, you shouldn't have shown up so goddamn early!" I called after her before kicking the door shut.

I climbed back into bed with the tray and lifted the lid. Someone had arranged the eggs and bacon into a smiley face—like something you'd see done for kids. Next to it was a note—

"Turn to Channel 2... or 11... or 13... or 26. Enjoy your meal!"

I grabbed the remote and switched on the television set. It looked like aerial footage from the beach. Nothing spectacular. Then I read the ticker along the bottom of the screen and my blood turned to ice.

Remains were discovered early this morning near Stewart Beach in Galveston. It's believed they could possibly be those of Patrick Roy, a young man who went missing back in 2001.

Holy fuck.

Oh, sweet Jesus.

That was what he'd meant by a warning.

The knocking began again at my door, followed by a terse, "Mike. Open the goddamn door."

I jumped up and threw it open, still completely nude. Still not giving a fuck.

David shut the door behind him and ran his hands down his face. "What the fuck is this, Mike? You swore we were in the clear on this."

I pointed helplessly at the television. "I—we were. I don't know what happened. It's going to be okay, David. Just calm down."

He grabbed me by the shoulders and shook me. "Calm down? Calm down? I'm supposed to leave for my fucking honeymoon in less than two hours. What part of this seems like it's going to be okay to you? And Jesus fucking Christ, put on some damn pants!"

I slipped on a pair of boxers that were lying near the bed and grabbed my cell. My father would side with Grey no matter what. I wasn't even sure the man in charge would even take my call after the way I acted last night.

Shit.

I thought I knew it all. I didn't have a fucking clue. You didn't walk away from Silent Phoenix. I thought I'd made it out—just like Beast temporarily had after his turn at Russian Roulette. Grey had simply handed me the revolver and let me put a bullet in my own head. I'd thought he was just seeing my side of things, but he knew all along I'd come around. Dangle a fucking body over the beach and suddenly Mike was compliant again.

Hadn't I seen enough from the club to know how they worked? Nobody left and went on to be successful. No, they left in pieces, to be disposed of somewhere in the desert.

I could have waited around and called their bluff, but these guys didn't seem like the type to give a deadline before dropping the hammer.

"Mike—earth to fucking Mike. What's your big plan, Detective? How are you gonna fix this? And if you don't have a plan, then let's walk your happy ass down to my room so you can tell my bride I'm going away to federal prison for the rest of my natural life!"

I wiped his spit from my cheek and nodded. "Yep, I got all that. If you'll just give me a motherfucking minute here, I'll have you all squared away to go off on your honeymoon. Okay, princess?"

David snarled, and then went for the minibar. "It's fucking empty!"

I shrugged and scrolled through my phone contacts. "I got a little thirsty last night."

Okay, I was going to have to swallow my pride and call Grey directly. I found his contact and waited for the call to connect while David kicked over the wastebasket and cursed. I covered the speaker. "Sweetie? Daddy's on an important call. So, I'm gonna need you to shut the fuck up. Mmkay?"

He frowned at me just as someone picked up. "Yes?"

I knew it wasn't safe to talk openly, so I slipped into the code I'd used with them over the past year. "Yeah, I-uh was calling to order a pizza."

Grey laughed softly. "Well, I'll be damned. See, last I heard, you were all done with pizza. Said it gave you indigestion and that you'd much rather stick with salad. Is that not right?"

Well, he wasn't going to make it easy.

"Yeah, the last twelve hours have really helped me understand how much I love pizza. I just don't think I'm ready to give it up. Pizza for life... or some shit like that."

I could hear him talking to someone in the background. "You believe this shit, C? After all your hard work laying the leftover dough out on the beach, this shithead decides he wants pizza now."

"Not a fuckin' chance," my father growled. "Once a traitor, always a traitor."

That was about what I'd expected.

David watched me expectantly, and I had to look away. I didn't have the heart to tell him there was a slight chance he might not make it on his honeymoon after all.

Grey clicked his tongue against his teeth. "You hear that, Mikey? C's feelings are hurt. I think he's afraid that if you come back, you'll just change your mind a few months down the line."

I shook my head, even though he couldn't see me. "No sir, absolutely not. Let's just say that I've seen the alternative to a life without pizza and it's a life I don't want. Just give me another chance. I'll get the fucking pizza any way you want it."

"So, you'll order it the way we say to order it and quit going off and doing things your own way?" His tone was the same as it had been the night before, but I didn't miss the threat in his words this time around.

"No, whatever you want. I'm in."

There was silence for a few seconds, and then he was back. "You've been granted a reprieve. We'll have that pizza over to you directly. One condition, though—the hard drinking ends today. Get it out of your system because the liquor clouds your judgment and makes you a liability. Are we clear?"

"Yep. It's done."

I hung up the phone and stared at the ticker on the screen, wondering how long it would be before the story changed. The club was powerful. I don't think I'd realized the extent until I was on their bad side.

"So?" David leaned into my face.

I nodded. "It's being taken care of—may have just sold my soul to Satan, but it looks like you'll get the honeymoon of your dreams after all, pumpkin."

CHAPTER FIFTY-TWO

Celia: September 2010 (Age: 38)

I slid the drawing across the counter. "This is what I want."

Ryan studied the image before shaking his head. "You know I'm gonna have to clear this with Grey."

He reached for the cordless phone, and I placed my hand on top of his. "Look, he's kind of in the middle of something and doesn't want to be disturbed, but trust me when I say that he knows about this."

"Remember that time I gave you a ride home from the library during a rainstorm? Because I do. I'd be happy to tattoo the fuckin' Statue of Liberty across your back, but only with his blessing."

With a sigh, I gestured for him to make the call.

So much for it being a surprise.

"Uh, Grey? Hey, it's Ryan over at *Inked on Broadway*, and I'm sorry to bother you, but uh, your Ol' Lady is here, and she's wanting a tattoo —what's that? Oh, it's like a bird or some shit—"

"Phoenix."

Ryan looked up at me with a furrowed brow before correcting himself. "Oh, it's, uh, actually a phoenix. What? No, I didn't ask." He covered the mouthpiece and looked up at me again. "He wants to know where you're putting it."

I briefly chewed on the inside of my cheek. "Tell him I want it over the thirteen."

He rubbed at his forehead. "She, um, she wants it over a thirteen? Does that mean some—oh, she's right here. Yes, sir. Whatever she wants. Got it." He pulled the phone from his ear. "He wants to talk to you."

"Hey," I answered. "I wanted it to be a surprise."

He laughed roughly. "Should have gone to another shop then, darlin'. I know everybody comin' and goin' out of *Inked*."

"You gonna waste any more of my time or let me get back to it?" I asked cheekily, enjoying the way the color seemed to drain from Ryan's face.

"You're takin' some big risks there, princess. Better watch it, or I just might have a surprise for that smart mouth of yours when you get home."

"I look forward to it, Pres." I ended the call and handed the phone to Ryan with a triumphant grin. "You heard the man."

He shook his head. "You're gonna get us all killed, Celia."

I shrugged and followed him into the booth. "Does he really know everybody who comes in here?"

"What do you mean?" he asked distractedly while arranging the various bottles of ink on the counter.

"I mean..." I settled into the chair. "He said he knew everybody who came by. Do you have to call him for every single customer?"

"Nope." Ryan studied the picture again before looking up at me. "He usually sees them on the cameras. Now, where do you want this?"

I pulled the skirt of my dress up over my hip. "Here."

He tucked his lip between his teeth as he studied it. "Looks like it scarred pretty aggressively. Where'd you have it done?"

"I didn't. It was done to me. Look, can you fix it or not?"

"Yeah, I think we can hide most of it with..." He snagged the photo and held it up to my leg. "The shading on the head. The wings might extend up onto your stomach and lower back some. What do you think?"

The wings could've extended up to my neck, and I wouldn't have cared if it meant I could look in the mirror and not be reminded of them.

Feeling as if a weight had been lifted from my shoulders, I happily agreed.

Ryan scanned the image onto his computer and began enlarging it. "Celia, this is fantastic artwork. Do you mind me asking who designed it? Maybe we could bring them on here."

I laughed softly, ignoring the bitter tang of regret on my tongue. "Well, she's only sixteen, but my daughter, Dakota, drew it for me."

In actuality, she'd drawn the phoenix for the city's local art contest, but hadn't won. There was no way for her to have known about the mythical bird or what it symbolized for her father and me. I knew that, but it hadn't stopped me from stealing it.

I was forced to sit back and watch helplessly as my mother enrolled Dakota in tap and ballet classes while ignoring her raw talent for art.

I wasn't the only one who appreciated the work she'd put into it. Jamie had studied it for hours, noting the similarities between Dakota's drawing and the comics. He'd promptly had it tattooed on one of the few blank spots left on his back.

"You know, it wouldn't matter if she was twenty-six. She's Grey's daughter," Ryan added knowingly. "And completely off-limits."

We might've been barred from seeing our children, but it hadn't stopped us from doing everything in our power to keep them safe.

Within reason, of course.

When he found out Dakota was being bullied in junior high, Jamie had pushed to take the kids out. It had taken quite a bit of convincing to talk him down.

After making a few adjustments, Ryan printed out a larger version of Dakota's drawing and applied it to my skin like a temporary tattoo.

My eyebrows pulled together as I stared down at my hip. "That's it?"

"No," he chuckled. "Haven't even started yet. Get comfortable because this is gonna take a while."

There was a sharp rap against the wooden door frame, and Ryan glanced up over my shoulder.

"Hey, man. I don't have time today, but one of the other—"

The man sighed. "You're kidding, right? I've had this booked for weeks."

Recognizing the voice, I slowly looked over my shoulder with a wince. "Hey, Mikey. I didn't mean to take your appointment."

He pulled his eyes away from where they were zeroed in on my ass and looked up toward my face. There was a sort of guilty pleasure in witnessing the moment he realized who I was.

"Celia?" He crossed the room and went in for a hug, only to pull back to study the design. "Holy fuck, that's cool. Is it your first?"

I nodded and was struck by how much he resembled his father. Not that I would ever tell Jamie that.

There'd been bad blood between the two of them since Galveston. I hadn't realized my biker would take my advice literally to get Mikey back in line; going as far as feeding the news outlets reports of skeletal remains being found on the beach.

Even months later, I still didn't know who'd been more upset with Jamie's form of discipline—Mikey or John. After Slim stormed into our hotel room, demanding to know how there was any evidence left behind, Jamie admitted that he probably should have waited until David was off on his honeymoon.

Despite the chaos, the plan worked.

While Mikey was still sleeping with any woman who made eye contact with him for longer than three seconds, he had sworn off the hard liquor.

In Jamie's mind, the damage was done, and there was nothing Mikey could do to get back in his good graces. Refusing to see the similarities between them, he kept his distance, only interacting with his son when absolutely necessary.

After checking with Ryan, Mikey pulled up a chair. "Are you getting this because of the club? Is that something the Ol' Ladies do now?"

"No," I admitted, hoping he didn't notice the circular scar. "I got it for me. You know the history behind a phoenix, right?"

He shrugged. "A little. My old man was always going on and on about it when I was a kid."

The buzzing from the tattoo gun temporarily ended our conversation. I'd grown up with a fear of needles and had never understood Jamie's obsession with ink.

Until now.

The needle scraped across my skin, evoking a strange sense of catharsis. I closed my eyes with a long exhale and leaned into the pain, releasing the things I'd held on to for far too long.

At the feel of someone squeezing my hand, I opened my eyes and found Mikey watching me with a solemn expression. "It stings like a motherfucker, so you've got to train your mind to focus on something else, so you don't feel it."

He might have misinterpreted how I was feeling, but there was more truth in his words than he'd ever know.

"Tell me about the tattoo I prevented you from getting. Again, I'm really sorry about that."

Mikey shrugged and held out his arms. "Not like I don't already have a few. And, if we're being honest here, I, uh, hadn't actually fully decided."

I studied the swirled script woven through barbed wire. Most were quotes related to war... to suffering. Our best efforts had never been enough when it came to him. The deck had been stacked against us, the same as it was when my mother took the girls.

Mikey may not have come from my body, but he'd always felt like mine. I mashed my lips together and blinked back the tears.

"'*Perfer et obdura, dolor hic tibi proderit olim,*'" I carefully recited the quote I'd come to know by heart. "Be patient and tough; someday this pain will be useful to you."

His eyes narrowed as he thought it over before repeating the words back to himself with a slow nod. "I like it. You write that?"

Ryan paused and looked up at Mikey with raised eyebrows, and I fought to hold back the bubble of laughter. "Me? No. That'd be the Roman poet, Ovid."

Mikey laughed, suddenly looking a little unsure of himself as he reached for my hand again. "I knew that. I was actually trying to pay you a compliment, darlin'. You know, what are the odds that I'd get to be here when you got your first tattoo?"

His palm was sweaty against mine, and I had a sneaking suspicion that his feelings toward me were more Oedipal than familial in nature.

I swallowed. "You know, I'm not sure it has anything to do with odds. Maybe coincidence or luck."

His thumb traced lightly across the back of my hand, making it easy to see how he'd been so successful with women. If the piercing blue eyes didn't get them, the feel of his fingers on their skin would.

That was the distinct difference between him and his father. Mikey knew there was a game and had learned to play it well. With Jamie, it had all been instinct.

"I have to admit, growing up, I had a pretty big crush on you," he said softly, eyes going dark with lust. "Never imagined I'd find you spread out like this, getting your body inked."

As much as he wanted to convince himself that he had feelings for me, this was just another ploy to get back at a particular biker. He might have only been nine years younger than me, but Mikey was like a piece of knockoff art—beautiful to look at, but he'd never measure up to the original.

"Hey, Ryan." The gun stopped buzzing, and he looked up at me warily, clearly aware of the entire exchange. "What do you think Grey would say if he were here right now?"

The lust that had been in his eyes only moments ago disappeared, and Mikey released my hand. "Celia, I don't think we need to—I was just fucking with you—"

"He'd kill him," Ryan stated simply, before going back to work.

I was prevented from saying more when one of the other guys walked in, holding his hand over the mouthpiece of the cordless phone. "Got a situation, boss."

He pulled the gun away from my thigh with a long sigh. "What is it, Stitch?"

"I got *Hub City* on the phone; says it's urgent."

"You see I'm in the middle of something, right?" Ryan snapped, and Mikey stood up with a wide grin.

"Stitch, sweetie, can't you see that—"

"Shut the fuck up, Sullivan," Stitch growled. "Wouldn't be interrupting if it wasn't important. *Hub City* says they've got a guy looking to cover up his club colors—"

"What guy?" I asked, struggling to turn enough to face him. "What does he look like?"

Stitch ignored my question and continued. "They aren't entirely sure it's the same one the club's looking for, but felt it was worth mentioning."

With a dry mouth and racing heart, I pushed past my fear and climbed down from the chair before facing them. "Give me the phone."

Stitch looked at Ryan. "Boss?"

"Give her the goddamn phone unless you want to be taking your meals through a straw from here on out." Ryan snapped, pinching the bridge of his nose.

"How stupid would the guy have to be to go to a place here?" Mikey questioned. "Even if the club doesn't own *Hub City*, they have eyes and ears everywhere."

"You knew the club was looking for these guys?" I stammered, wondering how much Jamie had revealed.

"Yeah." He nodded. "Apparently, they stole something pretty valuable from the club. Grey's made finding them priority numero uno, so I'm thinking it must've been a fuck ton of cash."

Or something.

Stitch handed the phone over and walked out with a muttered curse.

"Hello?"

"Who's this?" a male voice demanded. "I asked to speak with Ryan, not his bitch."

"Do you have enough men to hold him?"

"Bitch, did you not hear me? I talk to Ryan or—"

"Listen, asshole," I seethed. "I'm Grey's Ol' Lady and the only one who can tell you if you have the right guy in your shop. So, stop fucking cursing at me and listen."

The line went silent, and for a brief second, I thought he hung up. "I'm sorry—I didn't know it was you—if we could just keep this between us..."

Mikey... the prick at the other tattoo shop... they were all the same when I mentioned Jamie's name. I wanted to command that kind of respect, but not by using fear.

"If you have the right guy..." I paused to take a deep breath. "He'll have a four-leaf clover tattooed on his lower abdomen, right above his... you know."

The man chuckled. "Above his cock. Got it. Hold tight for me."

I'd seen it in my nightmares for so long, the image was permanently ingrained into my memory.

Ryan and Mikey watched me intently, and I brought my hand up to cover the phone. "You need to call it in to him, Mikey."

"Celia?" he asked gently. "How do you know about that?"

I didn't want to see sympathy in his eyes—didn't want his pity. "I know about a lot of things, Mikey. It comes with the territory."

"Alright, Grey's Ol' Lady..." The man came back on the line. "We got him. Does he want my guys to deliver, or is this a pick-up?"

"We'll be there in fifteen." I ended the call. "They've got him. Ryan, I'm so sorry, but I'm going to have to come back another day."

He nodded with a thoughtful look on his face, no doubt taking in the brand on my hip, along with the details of what I knew, to work them out in a way that made sense.

I would not waste a second worrying about what he thought he knew.

We'd found Hawk.

CHAPTER FIFTY-THREE

Celia: September 2010 (Age: 38)

Hawk spat out a mouthful of blood before grinning up at me with red-stained teeth. "You called out Cobra for refusin' to get his hands dirty, but look at you—sittin' back while your muscle does all the work. What's wrong, Celia? Afraid you'll chip a fingernail?"

I grinned back, all while grinding my teeth down into the gum tissue. "I thought maybe we could talk while Carnage here pays you back for kneeing him in the groin. You know, tit for tat."

"Tits, huh? Do you still feel my teeth on yours? God, your flesh was so soft, I could have ripped you apart usin' just my mouth."

Your enemy will try to bait you into doing somethin' stupid. It could be they want you distracted while they make their move or, if they know they've been beat, they'll use it hoping to get a quick death.

I drew strength from Jamie's words, refusing to let Hawk get under my skin.

Carnage drove a fist into Hawk's stomach, and he let out a sharp burst of air before chuckling again. "Carnage, is it? If you ever tire of babysittin' bitches instead of doin' actual work, you oughta get a go at her cunt. Fuckin' tight as hell. Well, at least she was before I got her good and wet. Ain't that right, Celia?"

I sucked in a quick breath just as Carnage roared, "I volunteered for this position, asshole! You don't fuckin' look at her... you don't fuckin' talk to her unless you're ready to give up Cobra."

After transporting Hawk to the storage facility and removing the club tattoo he'd wanted so badly to cover up, Jamie had turned him over to me.

"Where's Cobra?" I asked, retrieving the small rectangular contraption from a table.

"The fuck do you care where he is? He ain't the one in charge anymore. Carnage, my man, if you're not into fuckin' her cunt, go for the throat. None of that half-assed bullshit either, no sir. All the way down, until she's fightin' for air—"

Carnage reared back and head-butted Hawk's face with such force that even I winced. "Gave you a warning. You should have listened."

It was obvious the impact had broken his nose with the way he was violently struggling against the ropes, trying to catch his breath. Blood ran in streams over his lips, but it wasn't enough.

It would never be enough.

Killing Manny hadn't brought me anything other than an urge to kill again. In the beginning, I'd sought forgiveness and a way to piece myself back together. Now, I knew better. There was no magic button I could press to undo the trauma my body had endured; no way to wipe it from my memory.

It didn't mean I was going to stop, though.

I would not rest until every last one of them was in the ground.

"You know, in medieval Europe, they used these." I held up the device. "The thumbscrew. Apparently, they were highly effective in obtaining confessions."

Hawk stayed silent as I moved behind his back, slipping the fingers of his right hand between the metal plates. It was only fitting that the hand he'd used to batter me would be the first one I maimed.

"So, once the fingers are inside, you just alternate tightening the screws on either side. Like this." I demonstrated before stepping back. "Where's Cobra?"

He stared straight ahead as if I hadn't said a word. I twisted each screw another turn and tried again. "Tell me where he is, and this can all be over."

Carnage watched with rapt attention as I turned the screws, tightening until the bones of Hawk's fingers cracked audibly between the plates, and he cried out.

"Fuck! You want a confession?" he screamed. "Here's your fuckin' confession! Cobra don't mean shit. He answers to Saint... sooner or later, we all answer to Saint!"

"Who is Saint? Where can we find him?"

He laughed, and his lip split open again, sending a river of blood down the side of his mouth. "Find him? You don't find him... he finds you."

I calmly reached for my trench knife and held the tip of the blade to his throat. "Tell me where he is."

"This time, it ain't about Grey. Death is comin' for you." There was no time to react before he jerked his head forward, impaling himself on the sharp blade with a choked gurgle.

His feet kicked wildly at the air beneath him, but his eyes stayed on mine, and I was sure that if he weren't gasping like a fish out of water, his lips would've been curled up in a cocky smirk.

In one move, he'd taken away my power. Enraged, I forced the blade out through the back of his neck before punching it through the side, silencing him.

His head fell to his shoulder at an unnatural angle, and even Carnage stepped back with raised palms. "Holy shit, Celia! He said to let you handle it, but I didn't—fuck!"

I resisted the urge to sink the blade into his flesh again... to taunt his corpse with whispers of how soft he was and how easy it had been to rip him apart. I wanted to tell him his threats meant nothing—that Death had already come for me on a bathroom floor ten years ago.

It was over, but we were still no closer to finding Cobra. If what Hawk had said was true, there was now a mysterious Saint to add to our list.

The room suddenly plunged into darkness, and I stumbled back, no longer comfortable being anywhere near a corpse. Despite my strict Catholic upbringing, I was convinced that Hawk's spirit had already escaped hell and was back to torment me.

"Carnage?" I whispered.

"That wasn't me. Wait here, and I'll see if we tripped a breaker."

"Okay." I didn't want to be left alone but didn't know how to voice my paranormal concerns to a biker who'd just watched me nearly take a guy's head off without breaking a sweat.

I listened to him feeling his way back to the door before he let out a startled, "The fuck?" There was a brief struggle and then the sound of something heavy falling to the concrete.

"Carnage?" I whispered, with a growing sense of dread.

"No, Ma," a voice whispered back, and chills raced across my skin. It sounded just like Manny.

I pulled air into my lungs and lowered myself into a crouch, wondering again why I'd insisted Jamie let me do this on my own. I couldn't defend myself from something I couldn't see.

The back of my boot connected with a metal pipe, sending it rolling across the floor, clearly giving away my position. The attacker's body collided with mine before I had a chance to move, and we both went down hard on the concrete.

He wasn't heavy like I'd expected. Even when his arm went around my throat, I easily escaped. It soon became apparent that he'd had some martial arts training when he shifted and took my legs out from under me before trying again. Clearly, we were at a stalemate until one of us tired.

I was no longer afraid.

I was furious.

His pants of exertion became more pronounced the longer it went on, but neither one of us was giving up. My fingers brushed against the handle of my knife as I went down for what felt like the fiftieth time, and I grabbed it before driving the blade into his thigh with a roar.

"Fuck!" he cried out sharply. "You fuckin' stabbed me!"

I flipped onto his back and jerked his head toward me just as the lights came on again.

"Rick?"

"Nah, my ma calls me Little Ricky after Lucy's kid in *I Love Lucy*," he groaned in response as Carnage stumbled over, holding on to the side of his head.

"He hurt you, Celia?"

I shook my head and rolled back to the floor. "I'm okay."

"Celia?" Rick cried out. "Oh, fuck! You gonna tell my ma about this? I swear I didn't know it was you. They said there was no one here... said I just had to free the guy and get out—"

Carnage yanked him up. "Who sent you?"

"My—my boys."

Ignoring the pain in my hip, I got back to my feet and faced him. "Why would they send a nineteen-year-old kid in here? Have you thought about that? It's because you're expendable. How could you turn on the club that raised you?"

He shook his head. "Nah, my ma—" his breath cut off in another groan. "My ma raised me."

"And you're just going to ignore Bear, who's probably headed this way because Grey has eyes everywhere?"

His eyes widened. "Bear? Shit. Might as well kill me now."

Carnage tightened his hold on Rick's arms. "Maybe we save the killin' for your ma, you little shit. She's gonna be mad as hell when she finds out you attacked Grey's Ol' Lady."

Molly's mother had retired down in the Houston area not long after I lost the girls, and after battling several lengthy illnesses, had come to rely on her daughter more. Once, after too many drinks, Molly had admitted that Rick was spending too much time with a local gang, but I doubted even she knew just how bad his situation was. If so, she never would have left him alone.

The three of us jumped when the door burst open, flying into the wall with a resounding clang. Jamie was the first one through, the haunted look in his eyes a clear indicator that he'd been watching the cameras and had ridden like hell to get here.

He looked over to where Hawk's body hung limply from the ropes and then back over to Rick before his gaze came to rest on my face as if asking: *You good?*

I nodded with a sigh as Bear walked in. The minute he saw who it was, his gaze darkened, and he approached with clenched fists. "You went runnin' back to the fuckin' gangbangers after your mama begged you to stay, didn't you? Jesus fuckin' Christ, son, do you know the trouble you're in?"

"You aren't my real dad, so you can stop pretending for your friends."

Jamie stepped forward and jerked Rick's chin up toward him. "You show some goddamn respect when you're talkin' to your old man—"

"*¡Vete a la chingada!*" he snarled. "My old man was murdered, and I'm not stopping until I find out who it was."

I winced when Jamie grinned, knowing it would not end well for anybody.

"Well, guess what? You found him. I sent your father to the Reaper. Wanna know why?"

"My father's uncle said he was murdered in cold blood," Rick said quietly, sounding less like a vicious thug and more like a scared little boy.

"Cold blood? He found out your mama was knocked up with you and cut her belly open before leavin' her to bleed out on the floor. Did the world a favor when I put him down."

Rick's chin moved toward his chest, but Jamie forced his head back again with a low growl. "You ain't a man. Might have acted tough when you laid hands on my Ol' Lady, but look at you now—pissin' your pants like a baby. Way I see it, Silent Phoenix owns your ass now. Two options..."

He held up two fingers. "You can either give up your gangbanger *amigos* and work for me, or you can keep up the shitty teenager bullshit you got goin' on, and I'll send you back to your buddies in pieces."

As much as I wanted to intervene on Rick's behalf, I wouldn't disrespect Jamie. Every action had a consequence. I just hoped Rick made the right decision, so he lived long enough to regret his.

"Don't be stubborn, boy," Bear begged him. "For once in your fuckin' life, do the right thing."

Jamie added, "Before you answer, I got one little thing to add. That man behind me? He stepped the fuck up and raised you as his own. I might have ended your father, but that man's been your daddy. So, you choose option one, there ain't gonna be any more disrespect. Am I clear?"

Rick sniffed and nodded. "Yes, sir."

"That's what I like to hear." Jamie clapped him on the shoulder.

"Now, you gonna tell me what I want to know, or am I carvin' you up first?"

Sweat ran down the sides of Rick's face. "I'll tell you everything you wanna know. I'll pledge to do whatever you need, but could we take a second to fix my leg first?"

His eyes rolled back in his head, and he slumped forward with a soft sigh as Jamie looked down to where blood was pulsing steadily from the wound in his thigh.

When his eyes met mine in question, I shrugged. "May have forgotten to mention that I stabbed him."

"Jesus, Celia." He ran a hand over his face before waving Bear over. "Call Eli, get him put back together. If he gives us what we need, send in one of the club whores as a gift."

He pointed at me. "You. Outside. Now."

I watched him through narrowed eyes and waited for the other bikers to leave before marching toward the stairs, bracing myself for the lecture that was inevitably headed my way.

The day's events played at high-speed in my head, and I rubbed my forehead in frustration. Between arguing with Ryan, getting mouthy with Jamie, fighting off Mikey's advances, and cursing at the guy from *Hub City*, I'd also commited a murder and a stabbing just to round things out.

I'd be lucky if he ever let me leave the farmhouse again.

"Heard you visited with Cueball this afternoon."

I froze, halfway up the stairs, and slowly turned around. "Cueball?"

He took the stairs two at a time until we stood at the same level. "Owner at *Hub City*." His hands went around my waist, leading me up against the wall.

"Look, I know you're mad—"

Ignoring the fact that I was still covered in blood, he lowered his head and silenced my objections with his mouth before growling, "I ain't mad. Your actions caught Hawk, and then you just casually stabbed Molly's idiot son. Fuck, princess. You'll be runnin' the entire club before long."

His lips trailed down my neck, and I shuddered, gripping his vest in my fists. "That'd—"

He shredded the neckline of my t-shirt and looked up at me with a smirk before sucking one nipple into his mouth while rolling the other between his thumb and forefinger.

Pleasure flooded my body, making my thoughts hazy and hard to grasp, but I fought through the fog to moan, "That'd make me a queen... not a princess."

Jamie's lips moved off my breast with a soft pop, his eyebrows drawn together. "Is that right? And who the fuck is in control right now?"

I lifted my chin with a confident grin. "Your motherfucking queen is."

"That's my girl."

CHAPTER FIFTY-FOUR

Grey: January 2013 (Age: 49)

"You remember the last time we were up here?" Slim asked as he blew the dust off an old cassette player.

I looked around the old apartment, struck by how little had changed over the years. Sure, Phantom had met the Reaper and Bear had taken over. But mostly, the old body shop still looked exactly the same.

If Slim hadn't come to town with Lou for her mother's eightieth birthday party and to visit David, I doubted I would have had reason to ever come up here again.

"Shit, we had to have still been in high school." I walked over to where a heavy wool blanket still hung on the paneled wall and lifted the corner with a low whistle. It was like opening a time capsule. "I'll be damned."

Slim hurried over. "Our porn stash is still here? Hell, I figured Bear would have thrown all this shit out."

"Not just porn." I held up a stack of my old comics. "These have gotta be worth some money."

"Oh, I got somethin' even better." He went back over to the cassette player, and the soft strains from a synthesized guitar filled the room. Cranking it up, he dropped onto the worn-out beanbag chair with a contented sigh. And it was like we were kids again.

"Zeppelin? No shit. Don't tell me, uh—" I wracked my brain and nodded along to the beat, trying to place the song. "Fuck, what was this one called? Album was *Physical Graffiti*—'Custard Pie.' Right?"

Slim lit up a joint and leaned back, exhaling a stream of smoke. "You fuckin' cheated by waitin' til the chorus to answer. God, why'd we ever leave this place?"

"Life happened. You had to run off and get married and have a baby. Not only that, but you set the bar so fuckin' high that the rest of us could never compete." I pulled a cigar from my pocket and lit up just to keep my hands busy.

"The fuck you talkin' about?" he asked as the next track began playing. "What do I have that you don't?"

I puffed on the cigar and spun the skull ring on my finger before sinking down onto the chair next to his. "It's just—you always seemed to know how to do it right, Slim. You married Lou and kept her safe. You had David and from what I've seen, kid's fuckin' perfect—"

"Perfect? Is that what you think my life is?"

He stood up and took another drag. "I pushed my son to work hard for the things he wants, only to find out this weekend that he's a goddamn workaholic. Elizabeth looks like she's ready to throw in the towel, and I've been scratchin' my head, wonderin' where it was I went wrong. I've loved his mother from the moment I laid eyes on her, but maybe I didn't make her enough of a priority in his eyes."

"Shit, if you didn't make your Ol' Lady a priority, then I guess we're all fucked. So, David is tryin' to find the balance between bein' a husband and a business owner. Least he's not out fuckin' around."

Slim shook his head with a chuckle. "Mike still ain't got his shit together? I'm callin' it right now. There's gonna be a woman that does a fuckin' number on that kid and settles his ass down. When that day finally comes, you'll call me up to tell me I was right. No, wait... you'll ride your ass down south and take me out for a steak dinner."

"Fat chance of that, fucker. Kid's liable to end up in the ground with the way he goes after married women. Between him and the fact that my daughters think I'm dead—shit. You ever wish everything would just fall into place at the same time?"

"That's human nature, my friend. We set out with this perfect goal in mind, only to find out that the course to reach it is constantly changing." He took another drag and exhaled. "Best you can hope for in the end is that your kids grow up to be decent people."

I blew a smoke ring up toward the water stains on the ceiling tiles. "David will figure it out, trust me. You walked away from club shit when your family needed you. That part of you is in him."

"Always dividin' my time between my business and the club. Poor kid must've thought I worked all the fuckin' time," he mused. "What about you, Jamie? What parts of yourself do you see in your kids?"

I frowned. "You know I ain't high, right? This feels more like the conversation you have when you're fucked up—"

"I'm serious." He sat back down. "When you look at them, what do you see?"

"Mikey—well, Mikey is just like his old man—"

Slim held a finger up. "I'm gonna stop you right there. You ever looked at Mike and saw the part of yourself that believed he was invincible? That's what I always thought about you when we were kids. Seemed like nothin' could take you down."

"Yeah. Given how shit has gone, I think life took that as a challenge."

"I know you wanna believe the kid's a lost cause, but he ain't. He just needs a little guidance—"

"A little?" I interjected. "Had to call in a fake tip to the crime line in Galveston just to get him to stop drinkin'. I know for a fact that he's hit on my girl before, but can't tell you if it's because she's a fuckin' knockout or if he really just hates me that much."

"Maybe the apple don't fall far from the tree," Slim pondered, drumming his fingers across his lap to 'Kashmir.' "Maybe he sees the life you have, and he's jealous. Think about it, Jamie. Despite the mistakes you've made, you still have a better life than anything he ever saw growing up. Maybe you're his Slim."

"Never said I was jealous of you, asshole. Just said I felt like you've always had your shit together. Don't get it twisted."

He took another hit. "Yeah, to me, that sounds like jealousy. Now, you gonna let me make my point or not?"

"Wish you'd get it the fuck over with. I'm gettin' gray hair," I muttered.

Slim's eyes were half-open, the joint dangling from his lips while he nodded his head to the music. Clearly, he'd found the sweet spot and was fully relaxed without being impaired. "You gotta tell Mike the truth. I've been thinkin' about the shit with David. He might make bad choices, but he's always known that I'm a phone call away. In fact, I'm thinkin' I'll get through the rest of the weekend and give him a call when I'm back home, to see if I can help him get his priorities straight."

When he fell silent, lost to the faded Farrah poster on the wall, I waved a hand in front of his face. "You gonna finish that in a way that makes sense or—"

"Mike don't have someone to call when shit's spinnin' out of control, Jamie. You think Comedian is gonna offer any quality advice? If he can't snort it, shoot it, or fuck it, he ain't interested. You've gotta be that person for him, and when the time is right, you tell him who the fuck he really is."

I thought it over. "You really think he could ever settle down? That he and I could ever have a solid relationship?"

He mulled it over with a slow nod. "I saw the way he looked at you when he was a kid. He wanted you to be his dad—shit, I bet there were times he even let himself pretend you were. Right now, though? He's angry because his hero is forcin' him into a life he don't want."

I picked at the leather on the beanbag chair. "I didn't know what else to do. He was comin' after the club—"

"You're not hearin' me. Might not be the life he would have chosen for himself, but it's the one he needs. Even if he don't know it yet, kid's been searchin' for a family his whole life. You and I know that when shit goes down, there's no better support than your brothers." Slim ran a hand over his face before continuing.

"He may never wear a kutte, but he needs to see the good side of the club. If you're just gonna call him in when it goes south, then you're missin' out on a relationship. You gotta help him remember the man he grew up worshiping; not by tellin' him, but by showin' up when he needs you."

It made sense.

I'd thought tough love was the only way I'd get through to him, but it had pushed him away. Mikey didn't want to be indebted to some club. He wanted to belong.

"You want me to go ahead and tell you that you're right, or wait a few years to keep you humble?"

He scratched at his beard. "You know I think I'd like a plaque—somethin' I can hang on the wall in my office that commemorates the day Jamie Quinn listened to reason."

I flipped him off with a smirk. "Well, you'll be waitin' til hell freezes over for that one."

CHAPTER FIFTY-FIVE

Grey: March 2013 (Age: 49)

My phone vibrated across the nightstand, the buzzing intensifying with each pulse. I'd stayed up late again, searching the internet for anything related to Saint—churches, other MCs—I'd even looked into a Saint Anthony's preschool. We'd been chasing leads on Cobra for over three years, but no one seemed to know the elusive Saint.

All we had to go on was Hawk's word, but it wasn't as if we could bring him back to tell us more. The things he'd given up before falling on the sword were vague and cryptic at best.

I closed my eyes when it stopped and was close to drifting off when it started up again. With a groan, I rolled over and fumbled blindly for the phone before bringing it up to my ear. "This better be important—"

"Jamie?" The voice cut off in a sob, and I sat up, suddenly wide awake.

"Louisa? What's wrong?"

She hiccuped loudly. "It's John. He—he had a heart attack—"

"Which hospital is he at? I can be down there—" I threw my jeans on and jogged into the living room, searching for the keys to my bike.

It was a nine-hour ride under normal circumstances, but maybe I could cut it down to six if I pushed it.

"You can't!" she wailed. "Jamie—listen to me. They did everything they could, but—" Her voice cut off in another sob. "He's gone."

Tears stung my eyes, but I shook my head. "Slim ain't gone. I just talked to him on the phone last night. He's comin' to help me fix up a house—just tell the doctors to work harder because—"

"It was just too much for his body to take, and I—" she sobbed. "I don't know what the fuck I'm supposed to do right now!"

I pulled myself together long enough to quietly say, "You don't have to do a goddamn thing, darlin'. I'll be down there by tonight—help you get everything sorted."

"He was here... and then he wasn't! I just want to wake up from this nightmare," she moaned. "How am I supposed to tell David?"

I strode out onto the front porch, letting the screen door slam shut behind me before pacing from one end to the other, unable to sit down... unable to accept the truth.

My best friend was gone.

Grief barreled into my body, taking me down to my knees just as Celia ran out, eyes wide with panic. I thrust the phone into her hand and stumbled out into the orchard, unable to fight the heaviness settling against my chest like an anchor.

After my conversation with Slim, I'd gone out and bought Mikey an old farmhouse. I could have found him something in town, but if he was anything like his old man, I knew he'd need a place where he could get away from the constant noise.

I'd sold it to him through one of my dummy companies for next to nothing, knowing it'd be a project for us. Slim and David had offered to help, and between the four of us, we'd had plans to restore it. The bond between Mikey and me would've been strengthened, while Slim and I relived our glory days of doing manual labor for the club.

I stared down at my hands, seeing the evidence from years of hard living, but somehow remained convinced that we were too young for this.

The first rays of sunlight broke through on the horizon, bathing the orchard in light, but it didn't seem fair. I'd been courting death my entire life—had even come close on more than one occasion, only to be stopped at the last possible second by a man who'd refused to give up on me.

He'd saved my life, but I hadn't been able to save his.

With a roar, I struck the trunk of one of the pecan trees; pummeling the bark until it flaked off onto my bloody knuckles.

I wanted to scream; wanted to use my fists to tear through another person's flesh until they felt the depth of my pain in their bones. This time, there was no enemy I could go after. No blood that could be shed to make things right. The sniper who'd never missed a shot had been taken out suddenly by his own body. Where was the justice in that?

We still had our entire lives ahead of us. There were plans left to be made. Goals that hadn't been reached. Enemies to fight shoulder to shoulder.

I wandered the orchard, feeling more lost than I ever had in my entire life, finally realizing what Slim had always known. It didn't matter how far gone I thought I was, he'd always been there to pull me back. He was the first call I made when something went right and the first to call me when something went wrong.

He was my reset button.

Even now, I found myself searching for the phone I'd left with my wife, needing to call and hear him tell me that things were going to be okay.

It was almost surreal. I couldn't imagine living in a world where I wouldn't hear his voice again. There'd be no more pranks played at my expense or nights spent arguing over who would kick the other's ass in a fight.

I didn't know how many hours I spent walking in circles through the trees, trying to come to terms with the magnitude of what I'd just lost. When I finally looked up, I was standing not in the orchard, but in front of the Texas Redbud I'd planted. Even on autopilot, there was a part of me that knew exactly what I needed.

A place to grieve.

Celia had added a bench a couple of years ago, and I sank down onto it with a clenched jaw and a heavy sigh.

"I, uh, I ain't been out here to visit you in a while," I began, letting the tears fall onto my cheeks. "Didn't really know what to say after your sisters got taken away. Maybe I thought you'd be disappointed in your old man. You know—"

My voice cracked, and I exhaled the sob that had been resting in my throat since I got the phone call. "When you're young, you think you have all the time in the world. Me, I always thought the club was my measure of success, and I put everything into runnin' it like a fuckin' empire."

Realizing what I'd said, I hastily added, "Sorry, your mama hates it when I curse. Maybe we'll just keep that between the two of us. What I'm tryin' to say is that I put everything into the club, only to realize later that I'd never get that time back. And I think if I had it to do over again, I would've been more like Slim."

My shoulders shook as grief fought for a way out of my body, leaving behind a hoarse voice and a void that I'd never be able to fill.

"I told you about Slim before, remember? First time I met him, I was scared shi—to death. He was a lot bigger than I was, and some of those biker kids—they didn't take well to newcomers."

My vision blurred as I thought back to that afternoon. Donald had been drinking the hard stuff, and Ma and I had done everything we could to stay on his good side as he drove us down to the canyon. I thought I'd escaped a beating only to be dragged behind a building by an older boy just minutes after arriving.

I'd never been hit by another kid before that day, and I remembered touching the blood, almost in shock as it ran from my nose. That was when I learned it wasn't just my old man I had to watch out for; it was anyone bigger than me.

I continued. "Slim walked up as another kid was beatin' my a—butt, and I thought, 'Here we go. This is how I die.' I was convinced he was gettin' in line to go next. Only he didn't. He threw the kid off and helped me clean up my face—even gave me his shirt since mine got torn. Never mind that it was too big, and my ma knew almost immediately what had happened. That was just the kind of guy he was."

I pinched the bridge of my nose and ground down on my molars, struggling to hold it together. "He knew exactly what he wanted in life, but was never too busy to help someone who needed it. And, unlike me, he knew what to fight for and what to leave out to die."

My body jerked painfully as I forced myself to say the words aloud. "I'm telling you this because—because Slim met the Reaper today, and I don't know what happens after... but I like to think he's somewhere up there with you. So, don't you worry, you ain't gonna be alone anymore. Slim's gonna watch out for you and keep you safe until it's my time."

The ground vibrated beneath my feet, and for a second, I was sure that it was a sign from the other side.

I turned back to see a convoy of bikers coming down the road and swiped at my eyes, convinced I was imagining it. Clouds of dirt kicked up from underneath what had to be over a hundred bikes as they filed down the driveway, two by two.

Celia was standing on the front porch, with both hands covering her mouth and tears streaming down her face as I rounded the house.

I realized I was still barefoot and wearing only a pair of jeans as I jogged up the steps toward her.

"You did this?"

Her eyes squeezed shut, and she nodded, shoulders curling over her chest.

I cut the distance between us and pulled her into my arms. "You got no idea how much this means—" my voice cracked as I swiped my thumbs under her eyes, catching her tears.

"You needed your brothers," she whispered up at me. "Now, more than ever."

Wolverine was the first one off his bike, pulling his sunglasses off to reveal bloodshot and swollen eyes. His boots thudded heavily against the wood as he made his way up the porch steps. "Jamie—" he ground out.

I nodded. "Wolverine."

To anyone watching, it would have looked like nothing more than a casual greeting, but it ran so much deeper than that. Besides Slim, Wolverine was the only other man in my life that had given a damn. The only one to see me as anything other than a waste of space.

I couldn't speak, but with him, I didn't have to. With one word, he'd conveyed that he was beside me in the trenches. With one word, I'd let him know I needed him to take the reins.

His nostrils flared as he squeezed my shoulder with a jerk of his head before stepping up to the railing. Once every bike was in front of the house, his voice filled the yard.

"We lost a brother today. John "Slim" Greene wasn't just a Nomad. He was a father, a husband, and, most importantly, a brother to any man who needed him. He wore his colors with pride until the very end, and we will continue his legacy by living like he did—with honor."

He paused and mashed his lips together before looking at me. "Pres, I've reached out, and almost every chapter will be meetin' up at certain points to ride in a funeral formation down south. Think it'd be right for you to ride between. Slim would have wanted it that way."

My throat tightened, making it difficult to swallow. In funeral processions, one biker rode in the middle to represent the fallen biker. It was usually reserved for a close friend or family member.

I pinched my lower lip between my fingers and took a deep breath. "It don't seem right to move on—to live in a world that he ain't in. If he were here right now, there's not a doubt in my mind that he'd tell me to harden the fuck up and quit my bitchin'."

Several people chuckled, and I looked up toward the sky. "And I'll do it because I know that's what he would have wanted. But first, we're gonna stand as a club and honor his memory by ridin' down to be a support for his Ol' Lady and son."

Someone shouted, "Once a brother, always a brother!"

Celia came to stand at my side as another biker repeated it, slipping her hand into mine. It grew into a chant, and I wondered if Slim could hear us from wherever it was he'd gone.

Had he known the impact he had on people when he was alive?

Could he have even known the hole he was leaving behind with his death?

When I was a boy, I'd believed in heaven and hell. Times were simpler then—good people went to heaven, and bad people were taken to Hell. If you were pure, you lived a long time, but if your soul was tainted like mine, you'd be struck down with the wrath of an angry god.

Now, none of it made any sense.

Because if there were a god, he would've let Slim live forever and sent me to hell in a pine box decades ago.

To be continued...

Ready for Mike and Lauren? Keep reading for a sneak peek of *The Renegade*, book four of the SPMC series. Order today by tapping **HERE**!

Confused about the recommended reading order? Look no further!

The Deserter (Book 1 in the Silent Phoenix MC Series)
The Protector (Book 2 in the Silent Phoenix MC Series)
The Renegade (Book 3 in the Silent Phoenix MC Series)
The Traitor (Book 4 in the Silent Phoenix MC Series)
The Savior (Book 5 in the Silent Phoenix MC Series)

* Operation Fit-ish (Book 1 in the Operation Duet)
* Operation Annulment (Book 2 in the Operation Duet)

*Optional, but will definitely enhance your reading experience.

Worried that you'll miss my next release? Click here to receive an email notification the minute it goes live!

Want to be the first to know when my books go on sale?
Follow me on BookBub!

PREVIEW OF THE RENEGADE

ABOUT THE BOOK

I may wear a badge, but I haven't been on the right side of the law in years.

Silent Phoenix MC has had me in their cross-hairs since I was eighteen and it doesn't matter how hard I fight, I'll never outrun the sins of my youth.

A chance meeting on the beach changes the game. Suddenly, I'm consumed, not with tequila or women, but by a pint-sized redhead with a personality as big as the great state of Texas.

There's no coming back from the things that I've done. I'm cut from the same cloth as my old man and guys like us- we don't deserve second chances.

Something about her makes me feel like I'm worthy of just that though.

As an officer of the law, I'm sworn to serve and protect, but who am I kidding? With as deep as I'm in, I could very well be the one to destroy her.

The Renegade is available now for purchase. Simply tap on the title, or read on for a sneak peek at what's to come.

THE
RENEGADE
A SILENT PHOENIX MC NOVEL
SHANNON MYERS

THE RENEGADE

Mike: May 2014 (Age: 31)

"Hey, man. Glad you made it."

I surveyed the empty living room before turning to David. "Hey— Where's the talent for tonight? I didn't sign up for a sausage fest—"

His smile faded, and he rounded on me. "Look, tonight's not a date."

I pinched my gray button up between my fingers. "Then why the fuck am I dressed up? I'm not putting out for you now, asshole."

David sighed. "It's just, Lauren is Beth's friend—and her boss. She's off-limits for obvious reasons."

I nodded. "And... what about her other friends? You said, and I quote, 'Mike, come out for a surprise anniversary blah blah with Beth and our friends, blah blah.' Friends implies more than one. So, where are the other ladies? You know, ones who aren't off limits to me."

"It's just the four of us, man," he responded easily. "There isn't anyone else coming."

"See, to me, that sounds like a date. And last I checked, Elizabeth had another friend. Hmm..." I tapped my index finger against my lips with a smirk, enjoying the way the color drained from his face. "Now, who could I be thinking of?"

He glanced down the hallway before lowering his voice. "You know why Jess isn't here. Don't fucking bring it up again."

"Then don't fucking tell me who I can and can't hit on," I snarled in response.

God forbid I actually get to make any decisions regarding my own life.

He turned away from me and yelled down the hall, "Beth, c'mon! We have to leave no later than seven. You have five minutes."

"So, does this Lauren chick know we're not on a date? Because I would sure hate for any of us here to be under the illusion we're gonna have fun tonight."

David spoke through clenched teeth. "Doesn't matter. She's off-limits. End of story. And I will sure as hell knock that shit-eating grin off your face if you—"

The click of heels against the wood floor stopped him mid-tirade and saved me from embarrassing him on his special night, which was sounding like something I was going to bail out of the first chance I got. I turned, and for a split second, couldn't seem to find my breath.

It was her.

Charlotte.

Charlotte was Lauren, Elizabeth's boss. I didn't know whether to be relieved that she wasn't one of David's relatives after all, or furious that the asshole had put a woman with a body like hers on the no-touching list.

She was even wearing the same dress she had at the wedding, although it looked better than I remembered. And the red hair I'd wanted wrapped around my fists had grown longer in the last four years.

I watched with a smug sense of satisfaction when she stopped mid-stride, green eyes widening as they moved over my face in recognition.

David and Elizabeth were talking, but I couldn't hear a damn thing. Couldn't focus on anything but her.

Her pink lips curved into a soft smile as she extended her hand toward mine. "Hello. Lauren Santiago. Nice to meet you."

I gripped it tightly in mine, before croaking, "Mike—Mike Sullivan."

So, one of us had recovered from their shock more gracefully than the other.

David ushered the two of us out front while he and Elizabeth locked up the house. One of his 'big surprises' sat waiting at the curb, a stretch limo that felt like overkill, even to me.

Infidelity... limousines. Seriously, where did it end with this guy?

"So, how's that surfing career panning out?" Lauren asked, biting down on her lower lip, instantly taking me back to the moment I met her.

My heart pounded with lust, but I forced a grin, as if seeing her again was no big deal. "I gotta say, surfing's not so good here in the desert. You know you still owe me that drink."

A part of me wanted to ask why she'd never shown up to meet me, but Comedian hadn't raised a pussy.

Her smile faltered slightly, but she recovered enough to say, "I do still owe you a drink. Let me buy you a round tonight?"

I shook my head like a defiant toddler and muttered, "It doesn't count."

The garage door went up, revealing David and Elizabeth. Her eyes went round at the sight of the limo and she turned to David in shock.

"Happy Anniversary, baby," he said, grinning from ear to ear.

Lauren bounced up and down in excitement. "We pulled it off!"

Any irritation I may have felt vanished as the momentum made her tits jiggle beneath the dress, and I wondered how she'd react if I threw her over one shoulder and hauled ass back to my truck.

I let out a low growl at the thought of taking off with her like some deranged kidnapper, earning more than one confused glance from the others.

"You planned all this?" Elizabeth asked, bringing a hand to rest against her chest. "How in the heck did you keep it a secret?"

David slipped an arm around her waist and steered her over to where the driver stood waiting beside an open door. "I've got a few tricks up my sleeve. I can still keep some things from you."

His words triggered another surge of anger. Sure, it was all well and good for him to fuck his wife's best friend, but god forbid his single and ready to mingle buddy be given the same opportunity.

I grabbed the brown paper bags from the backseat of my truck and looked up just in time to see Lauren bend over to retrieve something from the backseat of her own car. The green dress rode up over her hips just enough for me to catch a peek of lace from the black boy shorts she was wearing.

"Knew it," I whispered to myself, while simultaneously wondering how in the hell I was going to keep my dick locked away for the evening.

Lauren reappeared with a large paper bag in hand and slammed the car door shut with her hip. I followed her into the limo like a stray dog, wracking my brain for something to say—preferably something that wouldn't end with me getting laid out by my best friend.

Between the two of us, it seemed we'd purchased enough alcohol for a frat party. The minute my ass hit the seat, I began doling out beers, needing a second to get my thoughts and emotions under control.

I planned on only having a couple—nothing that would put me on Grey's radar. As he'd specifically mentioned hard liquor, I figured a beer or two wasn't likely to earn me an ass beating from a club prospect.

I'd keep a clear head and honor David's request like the goddamn gentleman I was.

That plan went sailing out the window when Lauren wrapped her pretty pink lips around the bottle and tipped it back to take a swig.

I ran a hand over my face and took a long drink from my beer, not even tasting it. No, I was fighting a raging hard-on, imagining Lauren's lips around my cock—picturing the sounds she would make as she took me deep.

She laughed at something Elizabeth said. Like, really laughed, with her head back and eyes closed. Christ, the woman was even more beautiful than I remembered her being four years ago.

David caught my eye and ran the flat of his hand over his throat—a warning to keep my hands to myself.

Unfortunately, my brain hadn't quite latched onto the concept and was spinning fantasies that were wild, even by my standards.

I was well and truly fucked.

"Found any up-and-coming artists I need to know about?" I asked, alone with Lauren for the first time all night.

After buying a couple of rounds for everyone, she'd disappeared, leaving me to act as third wheel for two people who were missing a prime opportunity to make use of the bench seat inside the limo.

I finally extricated myself and found Lauren leaning against the patio railing, staring off into space.

She turned toward me with a distracted smile. "You know the art world, always changing..." Her voice trailed off, and she looked down to pick at her nail polish.

The playful banter we had in Galveston was noticeably absent here. Maybe I'd been ditched at a hotel bar because she'd known even then what I was just figuring out.

It had all just been a game of pretend.

I skimmed Lauren's bare arm with my fingertips, desperate to know if the jolt I felt the first time we touched was still there.

Instead of leaning into me, she pulled away as if my touch burned her skin.

"Hey," I said, keeping my voice low. "Did I say something to piss you off?"

Lauren lifted her head to face me, eyes overly bright, as if she was on the verge of tears.

Fuck.

I didn't know what to do with a crying chick. My hand itched to reach out and touch her again, but I wasn't sure my ego could handle being rejected a second time.

Her lower lip quivered. "I'm sorry. I've built up this image of you in my head, and it's still surreal to think that you're here right now. You've been here the whole time—I'm just trying to reconcile you with Jack."

Jack?

Right. The fake name I gave her that night.

I rested my forearms against the railing and looked straight ahead, trying to keep the edge out of my voice. "Do I... do I not measure up to who you imagined me to be?"

I held my breath as she struggled to find the right words. Maybe the girl four years ago had considered a romp on the beach with a stranger, but I worried the woman in front of me wanted much more than I would ever be capable of giving.

She started and stopped four different sentences before she got out what she needed to say. "It's not that simple. At David and Elizabeth's wedding, I wanted to meet you for that drink—I did. But I was worried about what you'd think about me after. The woman who came with me, Sandra, said I shouldn't do it. Said I'd hate myself in the morning."

Ah, fuck.

That explained a lot of things. Her 'friend' might have hit the nail on the head with her assessment of me and my motivations, but she'd only done it to help herself out.

Lauren pressed her lips together before admitting, "You know, I've often wondered what would've happened had I gone back to your room with you."

This time, when I reached out to touch her, she didn't pull away. She moved closer, bringing her palm up to rest against my chest. It was a cause for celebration and more drinks, but instead of letting her go, I kept my arm wrapped around her shoulder as I guided us back inside.

Shit-eating grin firmly restored, I decided to go for broke. "Let's grab another round and you tell me more about these thoughts you've had. And be honest, am I wearing clothes in them?"

Lauren patted my chest and shook her head. "Leave it to a man to turn it around and make it about sex."

"Darlin', looking at you, it's hard to imagine much else."

She tilted her chin up at me defiantly. "Is that right?"

Oh, I was so getting laid tonight.

I nodded dumbly and lowered my head. Lauren's eyes fluttered to a close, but just as our lips were about to touch, all hell broke loose in the bar.

"You wanna get your fucking hands off my wife, or do you need some help?"

ACKNOWLEDGMENTS

A writer is only as good as the people behind her. I'm lucky enough to have an entire city.

Rebecca Pau- Bex, thank you again for designing the perfect cover to complement this series, and for threatening to terminate our friendship contract during this book. I appreciate you loving these flawed characters as much as I do, and I can't wait to begin torturing you with Savior.

Beta Readers- Thank you for always dropping everything to read these chapters. You guys are the best. Your feedback continues to push me to improve this story. Give yourselves a big pat on the back because Grey and Celia would not be what they without you.

Jean- Thank you for shooting the most perfect cover for this story. Your ability to capture raw emotion and turn it into something almost ethereal is second to none.

Amanda Renee- Thank you for being yourself. While your looks made you a perfect Celia, it's your personality that sold me. You are such a positive and uplifting role model for women, and I look forward to working with you again. We will have our tequila and bonfire night someday soon!

Emily- Thank you for dealing with my Shannonigans. You keep me sane when I'm losing my mind, and are always quick to remind me when it's a full moon, so that I can become one with the earth again.

Ellie- Even though I'm the princess and you're the rebel, we just make it work. Thank you for not blocking me on social media and for taking this on eleven days before release. I'd tell you that you're the real MVP, but you'd probably let it go to your head.

Readers- Thank you for you messages of impatience. Seriously.

Deserter is a lot darker than Renegade and Traitor, and putting it out there took a big leap of faith. I worried that maybe I wouldn't be able to meet your expectations, but the demand for Protector silenced those fears. I know I made you wait a little longer, but I hope you can forgive me.

Laura- Bunny, thank you for loving Grey. I knew that if he'd captivated you, then he must've been pretty special because you don't waste time with peasants. You've pushed me to delve deeper into my writing and capture the characters' emotions. Some day, I will have your tears, and you will forget all about Cap. Oh, and thanks for being friends with a little psycho like me.

Lily- Thank you for demanding to know where Protector was headed the minute you finished Deserter. Your excitement and honesty have me raising the bar with every book. #GreedyforGrey

Wendi- Thank you for standing in the bar area at P.F. Chang's, letting me dump out the entire series plot while we waited for a table. Thank you for still showing up for our friendship, even when you know I have a tendency to become a recluse. I love every second we spend together, and look forward to more book discussions in our future.

Denise- Thank you for messaging me and offering your critique partner services for Protector. Even though I didn't give myself enough time to write and critique, I am very much looking forward to reading more from you.

Ashley- Thank you for being my critique partner and my roommate at Inkers Con. I made sure everyone knew that I was with the photographer, leaving them all impressed and a little jealous.

Jodi- Thank you for being my platonic life partner and my daily writing buddy. I feel like outsiders may be frightened by our texts, but you and I know that only people in true love discuss murder and torture. *Investigation Discovery* has nothing on us.

Zach- Thank you for always being available to drop everything and read chapters because I'm freaking out, convinced I no longer know how to string sentences together. You push me to dig deep when I need it, and I love you for it. You're my toughest critic, and my biggest champion. I know you like to give me the credit, but I wouldn't be where I am without your love and support.

ABOUT THE AUTHOR

Shannon is a born and raised Texan. She grew up inventing clever stories, usually to get herself out of trouble. Her mother was not amused. In junior high, she began writing fractured fairy tales from the villain's point of view and that was the moment she knew that she was going to use her powers for evil instead of good.

After an unplanned surgery in 2014 and a long pity party, she decided to pen a novel about the worst thing that could happen to a person in order to cheer herself up. She's twisted like that. Thus, *From This Day Forward* was born and the rest, as they say, is history.

She resides in the Texas desert with a posse of men (nothing like she'd imagined in fantasies) and plethora of fur babies.

Find her online at: http://shannonshaemyers.com
Or in her reader group: https://www.facebook.com/groups/630229377127363/

ALSO BY SHANNON MYERS

From This Day Forward Duet

(David & Elizabeth's Story)

From This Day Forward

Forsaking All Others

Standalone Novels

(Travis & Katya's Story)

You Save Me

Operation Series

(Dakota & Zane's Story)

Operation Fit-ish

(Kate and Nate's Story)

Operation Annulment

Silent Phoenix MC Series

(Grey & Celia's Story)

The Deserter (Book One)

The Protector (Book Two)

The Renegade (Book Three)

The Traitor (Book Four)

The Savior (Book Five)

The Mercenary (Book Six) *Coming 2022*

Fairest Series

(Charm & Neve's Story)

Through The Woods

(Killian & Ariana's Story)

Wait For It

Fictioned Series

(Hayden & Jake's Story)

Protagonized

www.ingramcontent.com/pod-product-compliance
Lightning Source LLC
Chambersburg PA
CBHW050918030726
47503CB00007BB/2360
* 9 7 8 1 7 3 3 2 7 4 8 1 4 *